A FORGERY OF FATE

LEGENDS OF LOR'YAN

THE BLOOD OF STARS
Spin the Dawn
Unravel the Dusk

SIX CRIMSON CRANES
Six Crimson Cranes
The Dragon's Promise

Her Radiant Curse

A Forgery of Fate

A FORGERY OF FATE

ELIZABETH LIM

Alfred A. Knopf
New York

A Borzoi Book published by Alfred A. Knopf
An imprint of Random House Children's Books
A division of Penguin Random House LLC
1745 Broadway, New York, NY 10019
penguinrandomhouse.com
rhcbooks.com

Text copyright © 2025 by Elizabeth Lim
Jacket art copyright © 2025 by Tran Nguyen
Map copyright © 2025 by Virginia Allyn

Penguin Random House values and supports copyright. Copyright fuels creativity, encourages diverse voices, promotes free speech and creates a vibrant culture. Thank you for buying an authorized edition of this book and for complying with copyright laws by not reproducing, scanning, or distributing any part of it in any form without permission. You are supporting writers and allowing Penguin Random House to continue to publish books for every reader. Please note that no part of this book may be used or reproduced in any manner for the purpose of training artificial intelligence technologies or systems.

Knopf, Borzoi Books, and the colophon are registered trademarks
of Penguin Random House LLC.

Editor: Katherine Harrison
Jacket Designer: Ray Shappell
Interior Designer: Michelle Canoni
Production Editor: Melinda Ackell
Managing Editor: Jake Eldred
Production Manager: Tracy Heydweiller

Library of Congress Cataloging-in-Publication Data is available upon request.
ISBN 978-0-593-65061-5 (hardcover) — ISBN 978-0-593-65062-2 (lib. bdg.) —
ISBN 978-0-593-65063-9 (ebook) — ISBN 979-8-217-11682-9 (int'l ed.)

The text of this book is set in 11.25-point Sabon MT Pro.
Paintbrush ornaments by b.illustrations/stock.adobe.com
Stingray ornaments by nereia/Shutterstock.com
Wave illustration by marukopum/Shutterstock.com

Manufactured in China
10 9 8 7 6 5 4 3 2 1

The authorized representative in the EU for product safety and compliance is
Penguin Random House Ireland, Morrison Chambers, 32 Nassau Street,
Dublin D02 YH68, Ireland, https://eu-contact.penguin.ie.

Random House Children's Books supports the First Amendment
and celebrates the right to read.

To my favorite girls, a book about three sisters for three sisters: Charlotte, Olivia, and Penelope

A FORGERY OF FATE

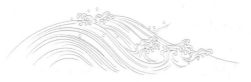

CHAPTER ONE

Mama used to fancy herself the best fortune teller in Gangsun—that is, until Baba disappeared at sea.

Her talent was in reading faces. She could divine someone's lifespan from the texture of their hair, whether they'd be faithful lovers from the way their mouth slanted. Too often she'd go up to strangers and pinch their earlobes, for that was her way of gauging how prosperous they'd become. Mama loved nothing more than money.

With such a gift, you'd think that Mama would've married the richest merchant she could find. Certainly not Baba—a middling trader with blue hair, grand dreams, and nine coppers to his name. But no matter how my sisters and I begged, neither would ever tell the story. All Mama would say, with a sniff, was "Foreign faces are harder to read. Had I known your father would chase adventure over riches—"

"She'd still have picked me," Baba finished for her one autumn morning. His eyes twinkled. "Your mother knew from the start what I was."

"A pirate," Mama muttered. "A thief."

"An *adventurer*," I said at the same time as Baba. With a

grin, he lowered his voice to a conspiratorial whisper. "And once, in another life, your mama was one too."

I stared at him, convinced that he was telling tales. I couldn't imagine my prim mama with her hair down, let alone chasing after bandits or swilling rice wine with sailors.

She saw my skepticism and waved it away. "Those were desperate times. Before I had my three girls."

I longed to know more, but Baba and Mama exchanged a look that drew the shutters over their past.

Mama picked me up and set me on her lap, her voice softening. "Thankfully, your fate will be different, Tru." She touched the mole by the right corner of my mouth. "This means you'll never go hungry, and you'll have a gift for making coin."

"Will she have a gift for saving it too?" Baba teased. He eyed the silk shawl draped around Mama's shoulders and the new bangles at her wrists. "Because her mother certainly doesn't."

Mama glared, but her mouth betrayed the smallest of smiles. "Being married to a Balardan makes it harder to earn people's trust," she retorted. Her gaze raked over Baba's hair, which shimmered dark blue under the summer sun. "I need to look presentable in case you scare away all my customers."

"Your daughter isn't a customer. She didn't ask for her fortune to be read."

"I don't mind," I said quickly. "I like it when Mama reads me."

Back then, it was the truth. I was young and gullible, and no one believed in Mama's abilities more than I did.

Baba clicked his tongue. When Mama was out of earshot,

he leaned down until we were eye to eye and said, "No one can see the future, Tru. Not even your mother."

"But she says—"

"Mama likes to . . . pretend," said Baba in his lowest voice.

I frowned. "I don't understand."

"You remember that old story about the fish and the dragon?" he asked, instead of explaining. "Fortune finds those who leap, my Tru. Whatever yours is—riches or love or adventure—you make it yourself. Nothing is predetermined. Not by the gods, not by the lines on your palm or the creases on your brow." He counted my worry lines with his fingers. "Or else these lines mean you'll have seventeen children."

That made me giggle.

"See? It's nonsense." Baba tousled my hair. Then—as if by magic—he drew out a wooden ship from behind my collar.

"Oh," I breathed as Baba dropped the ship onto my palm. It was as small as a teacup and still in a rough state, but the smoothly sanded sails and the outline of a magnificent phoenix along the bow gave me glimpses of its potential. "It's going to be your finest yet."

"I think so too," Baba agreed.

Art and the sea, those were what my father loved most, after his family. When he was away, he carved us trinkets of marvels he'd encountered on his travels: monkeys and tigers, shadow puppeteers, bridges cast like crescent moons—my younger sisters and I had an entire collection under our bed. This was the first time he'd shown me something that he was still working on.

"When it's finished, I want you to paint it for me."

My eyes went wide. "Me?"

"Yes. Falina says you steal into my cupboard when I'm not here. The one with all my paints and brushes."

Demon turds, of course she'd given me away. I grumbled to myself, wishing my younger sister had never been born.

I wanted to deny the stealing, but we had a rule in our household, and that was never to lie to family. "I only did it once," I admitted. "Maybe twice."

"Why?"

"I was curious. I saw a painting of the Twin River Mountains inside Aunt Lili's bakery, and they looked like two pears next to each other. She said she bought it for thirty jens." I waved my arms. "Thirty jens! I wanted to tell her I could draw them better, for twenty."

"Could you?"

The corners of my mouth twitched into a smile. My pride would be the end of me. "Yes."

A hearty laugh rumbled out of Baba's throat. "That's just what I wanted to hear. Balardans have art in their souls, Tru. I was hoping one of my girls might paint." He unrolled the leather case he kept on his belt, and his fingers danced across a set of carving knives before they landed on a slender paintbrush. "Here, to get you started."

I held the brush between two fingers, surprised by its lightness. It was white and pointed, like the tip of a horse's tail, and the handle was made out of bamboo. I'd seen a dozen like it in the marketplace, but that Baba had bought it for me made it the most special in the world.

"The hair's made out of weasel," Baba said, looking a little sheepish. "Not very elegant, still it makes for the sharpest lines. You'll need that in a magic paintbrush."

"A magic paintbrush?"

"A game I played when I was a boy. I'd paint anything I could dream up: flying sailboats, birds that could tell stories, and lanterns that never went out." He leaned forward to whisper conspiratorially, "Then I'd say, 'Magic paintbrush,' and they'd all come to life."

"Truly?" I breathed.

"Well, not truly," Baba confessed. "It's a game of imagination. A game where the only rules and limits come from here." He tapped my forehead.

I exhaled with wonder. "Then how do you know who wins?"

"The best games have no winners or losers."

I pictured playing with my sisters. All Fal would wish for were dresses and jewels, and Nomi—my thoughts turned tender—she'd want a mountain of books. My youngest sister was a genius; at four years old, she could already read better than Fal and me.

"Use the brush to paint what's real, or paint what isn't," said Baba. "So long as painting it makes you happy, that is the best practice."

My heart swelled. "Thank you, Baba."

"My paints are yours now." He brought the wooden ship forward. "Think about which colors you'll use on it. One day, if fortune permits, it'll be a real ship that we'll sail together."

"If fortune permits?" I said, raising an eyebrow. "We make our own fortune, remember?"

He laughed. "Indeed, Tru. So we will."

In the weeks that followed, "magic paintbrush" quickly became my favorite game. Every afternoon, my sisters and

I played while Mama read foreheads and destinies in the kitchen.

Nomi adored our games. Fal did too, though she'd never admit it. She'd hover over my shoulder as I brought to life the talking fish and singing trees from Nomi's stories, casting a critical eye on every stroke. Then at night, we'd squabble over the ship I'd paint for Baba. Fal wanted it to be pink, Nomi purple. In my dreams, it was always blue—like the endless sky over the sea—with phoenix wings that were powered by starlight. As soon as I grew up, I'd sail it with Baba and take on the world.

Little did I know, fortune had other ideas for me.

It started with my hair. Soon after my tenth birthday, it changed color overnight. "Bandit blue," my mother hissed when she saw. A damning sight anywhere in the city—I might as well have been born with three heads and an extra pair of arms.

Mama was devastated. She sought potions to turn my hair black again, but magic was expensive and hard to come by, so instead she'd make all manner of concoctions for me to drink.

Nothing worked. No tonic, no dye, not even a hat could fully hide the electrifying blue of my hair, and cutting it only made it grow back faster. Secretly, I loved it. Unlike Falina, who'd inherited both Mama's and Baba's best features, I wasn't worth looking at twice except for my hair. The whispers it got aggrieved Fal, who wished she didn't have anything to do with me. Naturally, that only made me love it more.

By the time I was thirteen, its color was so bold Baba joked that if he could make it into a dye, we'd be rich enough to buy a house on Oyang Street, where only the wealthiest merchants owned manors.

"How can you jest about a thing like this?" lamented Mama. "Her marriage prospects are ruined."

"Wonderful," said Baba. "She can come sailing with me."

Mama stared at him, aghast. "Maybe in Balar, you barbarians would make an adventurer out of a girl, but here—"

"Here in Gangsun, a woman can't run a business without her husband's permission," Baba cut in. "She can't even own her home. Things will be different for my girls."

"Yes, they will marry rich," said Mama, who always had to have the last word.

They didn't talk about my hair again because, a few days later, Baba announced that he was going away. He had accepted an urgent voyage that would take him halfway across the world. More than that, he couldn't tell us. But we were used to his secret assignments.

"Will you sail across the Taijin Sea?" Nomi asked while Baba folded his warmest coats into his traveling chest. She had half a fried cruller—left over from breakfast—in one hand and chomped on it while she spoke. "I hear there's dragons there. If you see one, will you make friends with it? Promise, Baba. I'd love nothing more than to know a dragon in my lifetime."

Baba chuckled. "I've sailed the Taijin thirteen times, Nomi, and never once have I come across a dragon. But if I do, I'll certainly send it your tidings."

"Send it this too." Nomi reached into Mama's pan for the last cruller. She inhaled the smell of it with her eyes closed, then presented it to Baba as if it were her greatest prize. "The best friendships are made over food."

Baba hugged her then, and I joined in too. Even if I had a hundred sisters, Nomi would always be my favorite.

"Where are you going, Baba?" Falina pressed. "Must it always be secret?"

"It's only a secret because I haven't yet received the details of the assignment," replied Baba. "All I know is a treasure's been found in the North, and I'm to transport it to the capital."

"How long will you be away?" I asked.

"I should hope to return no later than winter."

"Winter!" Falina was sullen, and for once I couldn't blame her. "That's months from now."

"Just in time for the snow," replied Baba. "And don't we love snow—my pine, my plum, my bamboo?"

At Baba's calling, my sisters and I bit back further protests. The names were inspired by his favorite painting of three trees covered in snow: Nomi was bamboo, Falina was plum, and I was pine. In spite of the cold, these trees didn't just survive; they thrived. A way of reminding us to be strong.

"No more long faces," Baba said. "Only your mother is smiling."

Mama was *elated,* which anyone could have guessed from breakfast. Usually our morning fare was watery vegetable broth and burnt rice, but today a feast awaited us. There was fish congee with all the toppings—chives and dried shrimp and salted eggs—and an enormous pan of fried crullers, her specialty. Mama only made crullers when she foresaw good tidings in our future.

"This is the trip that's going to change everything," she'd said, dropping a cruller into Nomi's bowl of congee. "I can feel it." After we ate, she gathered us around Baba. "Come, ask your father what presents you'd like him to bring back."

"Pearls and opals," Falina blurted, always having to go first. "A new silk dress and matching jacket for every day of the week, and slippers! Embroidered slippers with upturned toe caps." She paused and glanced at me. "Are you painting this, Tru? I don't want Baba to forget."

Fal's favorite pastime was getting on my nerves. Trying not to roll my eyes, I hovered my brush over the precious sheet of linen parchment I'd saved for today. "Is that all?" I asked, starting a portrait of Falina with opal earrings and a pearled headdress. I was tempted to paint all the dresses tattered and stained but resisted. Least favorite sister or not, it was bad luck to draw unhappy things with my magic paintbrush.

"Add a bronze mirror too," she said, "like the princesses in Jappor have."

"How do you know what the princesses in Jappor have?" asked Baba.

"Mama told me."

"Naturally she did." Baba exchanged a smile with our mother. "Mirrors are expensive, Falina, but I'll see what I can do."

"Thank you, Baba." Fal kissed him on the cheek. Next came Nomi, whose request was the same each time.

"I should like a sack full of books," she said in as low and serious a voice as her eight years could manage. "And if you can't find a dragon, I will settle for a mermaid."

"One with waves of green hair and a violet tail painted of twilight?" I already knew.

"And pearls underneath her eyes," added Nomi excitedly. "I read that mermaids cry pearls. The purest pearls in the sea."

"That sounds painful," remarked Falina.

"Not if you're a mermaid," Nomi said. "It's as natural as bees making honey."

While Fal clucked her tongue at our sister's romantic notions, I humored Nomi and added a dragon and a mermaid to my painting. The paper was getting crowded, thanks to all of Fal's dresses, but I was rather proud of my dragon. I didn't know what dragon scales and noses were supposed to look like, so I'd drawn a series of uneven ovals that ended up looking more like teardrops, and a straight and proud nose—the sort Mama said resembled a waterfall of money—and a tail that fanned out like a flame.

"I don't think dragons have legs like that," observed Fal with a wrinkled nose. "He looks like he's walking, not swimming."

"I like him," said Nomi, taking my side. "He looks regal. Almost real."

He did look real, except I hadn't given him pupils yet. Baba said that a dragon's eyes were its spirit, and to always add them last when drawing a creature as unpredictable as a dragon—lest it leap off the page and whisk me away.

"Don't forget to leave space for your wish, Tru," Baba reminded me. "What would you like?"

I didn't have to think long. "I'd like you to finish carving this," I replied, passing him the small wooden ship he'd made for me years ago. "I'm ready to paint it."

Baba smiled, but his eyes turned wistful as he took the piece from my hands.

"Did I say something wrong?" I asked worriedly.

"No. No." He slipped the wooden ship into his bag. "I'm just thinking how much taller my girls will be the next time I see them."

With that, he scooped Nomi into his arms, mussed my blue hair, and patted Falina's braid, then slid his arm around Mama's waist. She made a face, but when she thought we weren't looking, she scooted closer to him.

My painting was done. I'd drawn the five of us in front of Baba's ship, with Fal's dresses dancing in the air and Nomi's dragon watching skeptically, and an extra-large pan of fried crullers in the middle for good luck. Together, we blew it dry. Then in unison, as if we were priestesses blessing a charm, my sisters and I chanted, "Magic paintbrush."

One by one, Baba embraced each of us. When it came my turn, I wouldn't let go.

"Never mind the wooden ship," I said into his ear softly. "Or Fal's dresses and Nomi's mermaids. Only promise that next time we can all come with you."

Baba cocked his head to the side, his eyes twinkling. "Are you sure Fal would want that?"

"Nomi and me, then." I smiled, tucking the ends of his green scarf over his shoulder. "She can look out for dragons while I count our treasure."

"You are my treasure," Baba said, kissing my forehead. "You and your sisters and your mother." He touched my hair tenderly. "And this will be the last time I leave my treasures behind."

Then he left for the port, his traveling chest under one arm and leather satchel swung over the other, a corner of my painting peeking out of the half-open flap. Nomi and I ran to the window, watching him braid through the crowds on the road. I was grateful that his Balardan blood made him tall, so I could track him until he turned the corner.

When he did, I closed the window shutters and started on the dishes. Baba had left us dozens of times before. There was no reason to think this time would be any different.

How wrong I was.

Four months later, on the gray and wintry morning before New Year's, a pot shattered in the kitchen.

Nomi heard it first. She was the lightest sleeper of us three, and she jolted up, kicking me awake. "What was that?"

I stilled, listening to the aftermath of the sound. Silence.

"I don't know," I whispered back. "Maybe it was a rat."

Nomi let out a silent shriek. "A rat?"

"They're out to celebrate New Year's Eve," I teased, sitting up to peer out the window. There were lanterns hanging off the larches, and overnight, blue waterbells had bloomed. Star shaped with yellow bells, they were the first envoys of spring—and my favorite flowers. "Come see, all the shophouses put up rat banners. Tomorrow it'll be their year."

Nomi rubbed her eyes. "I hate the year of the rat."

"Don't say that. It's the first of a new cycle."

"In Balar there's no rat year. Only numbered years. Makes more sense for keeping track, don't you think?"

Nomi, so young and already so regrettably practical.

She jerked her head, suddenly sitting up in the bed. "I hear Mama."

So did I. "You stay here where it's warm," I told her as I started climbing over Falina—who wore cotton buds in her ears and could sleep through a monsoon. "I'll go see."

Inside the kitchen, I found Mama sobbing. At first I thought it was over the broken pot of waterbells, the mangled flowers and orange clay pieces scattered across the tiled floor.

Then I saw the letter in her hand.

My heart sank and sank until I could hardly breathe. All I could croak out was one word: "Baba."

I'd never forget how the air leaked out of Mama as she spun to look at me. How the muscle in her jaw jumped and her lips pinched together tight, as if she wished, for my sake, that I were still asleep. She sagged against the wall, and the letter dropped from her hand. I caught it before it fell into the puddle of dirt.

The paper was wet at the creases, the bright red ink smeared from old rain. The characters in Baba's name were missing a few strokes—bureaucrats never knew how to translate his name to A'landan—but even so it was clear enough: TO THE FAMILY OF ARBAN SAIGAS.

The rims of my eyes were burning, and the ink blurred as I read. Baba's ship had been caught in a storm. Most of the crew had survived, thanks to him. But Baba was lost.

Lost. The word exploded in my head, and suddenly I felt like I was swimming in the pages of Nomi's dictionary, trying to find a meaning of the word that wasn't *missing, vanished, gone.*

Dead.

No, no, it couldn't be.

"Is Baba . . ." I couldn't say it. My knees buckled, and a strangled cry tore out of my throat instead. Mama covered my mouth with her hand.

"Don't wake your sisters. Let them sleep a little while longer."

It was too late for that. Nomi was behind the door, her jacket half-buttoned as she slipped out of the shadows. She had heard everything. Falina too.

Falina scooped Nomi up in her arms. My youngest sister's lips had turned bluish, and she clutched at her chest as she coughed, her lungs convulsing with shock.

Tears welled in Fal's eyes as she patted our sister's back. "Stop it, Nomi."

Not knowing what else to do, I reached for Nomi's hand, wiped her nose with my sleeve. *It'll be all right*, I wanted to tell her. *Fal and I will take care of you.*

But the words wouldn't come. Only tears.

I held my sisters, desperately rewriting the morning in my head. A morning where Baba came back like he always did. With presents, with little carved animals and sweet treats wrapped in banana leaves, and new stories. Any moment, he'd stride through the door.

But as the seconds passed, it became clear that each scene I envisioned was an illusion. A fanciful dream and nothing more. Nothing could undo the stinging reality of Mama slumped against the wall, Baba's name in red smearing the crescents of her fingernails. Baba, dead.

That was when Mama blurted, "Your father isn't dead."

Nomi gasped for air. "What?"

"He isn't dead," Mama repeated.

Fal looked up, unsure. "But that letter . . . Baba . . . Baba's lost at sea."

"*Lost* only means he hasn't been found yet," said Mama. "I'm the best fortune teller in Gangsun. That means I'm practically the best in the world."

"Can you find him?" Nomi dared ask.

"Yes," she said. "But I'll need money first." Her jaw tightened. "Your father didn't leave us much of that."

Her tone was thick, not with resentment but with worry. This was a side of Mama I'd never seen before. She put on her gloves, picked up her basket. "Sweep the floor. I'll be back in an hour."

"Where are you going?"

Mama hesitated. "To buy more rice."

I knew the rice was just a cover. She was going to confront Baba's business partners for answers—and for money. Now that he wasn't coming back . . .

Using my sleeve, I blotted Nomi's tears. "Cry all you need," I said, holding her close.

While Nomi sobbed in my arms, Mama disappeared out the door without another word.

Fal touched Nomi's shoulder. Nomi was her favorite too, and the only time we came together was for her. "Didn't you hear what Mama said?" she asked. "She's going to find him."

The conviction in Fal's voice made Nomi look up.

"You . . . you really think he's . . . he's a-alive?" she asked us shakily. She sucked in a breath. "You think . . . you think Mama can find him?"

Fal looked at me, her bloodshot eyes reflecting the same desperate hope as Nomi's.

The letter had gone limp on my lap, the coarse paper stained with tears. Red ink smudged my fingertips, the sight forever seared into my memory even after I wiped my hands clean.

No, I should have said. *I don't think she can.*

That would have been the truth. But for the first time, I'd seen the cracks in Mama's stony veneer. I knew she was pretending. She *had* to. For our sake.

And, seeing as our fortunes had turned to ash, I put on a brave face too.

"Yes," I lied to my sisters. "I think she can."

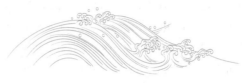

CHAPTER TWO

Five Years Later

I was not in the mood to deal with thieves.

Any other day, I might have been flattered that they were after me. Not today.

I'd spent a month forging the painting rolled under my arm—mostly on an empty stomach—and I just wanted to sell the damned thing and stuff my face with something other than boiled cabbage and dumplings. *Cabbage-stuffed dumplings* no less. So help me, I was bringing four chickens home tonight. A bucket of fried noodles too.

If I sold the painting, it would be my biggest deal yet. The goal was to net at least three thousand jens. The auction house would get a third, and Gaari and I would split what was left. The agreement rankled me, but that had been our deal since we'd met, and much as I hated to admit it, he deserved the cut. It wasn't easy to find a dealer who kept his word. Or whom I could trust . . . mostly.

Hunger panged my gut, and I tucked the scroll tighter under my arm while I swerved left, trying hard not to look back. Twenty paces behind trailed a trio of Gangsun's most despicable art thieves.

To anyone else, they bore a passable resemblance to scholars. They wore the typical button-down jackets in joyless blue, with matching boat-shaped hats and yolk-yellow fans. But scholars didn't usually stalk about the marketplace with veins bulging out of their necks and knives poking out of their sleeves. Needed more acting lessons, these thieves.

And Gangsun needs civil prefects who actually enforce the law, I grumbled in my head. I glared at the two ivory-collared prefects I passed, but they were too busy watching a cricket race to notice me, a pretend noblewoman trying not to trip over her menace of a dress.

In fairness, that was probably a good thing. Though the thieves behind me could have used a thrashing from Governor Renhai's cane, I wasn't exactly the most law-abiding citizen either. Come to think of it, my crimes would likely earn me *more* time in prison.

Trying to hurry, I hiked up my skirt and cursed Gaari's advice to playact as a noblewoman today.

Your art'll fetch a higher price if you look rich, he'd said.

He'd better be right.

Summers in Gangsun were usually cool, but not today. Sweat beaded along my hairline, and gods, my wig itched. But I didn't dare scratch it. My own blue tresses were tucked under a high pile of black knots and braids that Fal had spent all morning wrestling together, pinned in place with peacock feathers and silk chrysanthemums.

"Are you sure this makes me look rich?" I'd asked my sister. *"It's piled like a tower of buns on my head. Weighs as much too."* I tried turning my neck, but I could hardly move without the wig threatening to slip off.

"Stop that!" cried Fal. "I haven't finished pinning you down."

As Fal inserted two more pins at my hairline, securing the wig, I got to work too. I sucked in my cheeks, painting generous contours so they'd look fuller and less hungry, thinned my thick brows with flesh-colored cream, and gave my nose a daintier bridge. Within minutes, I did look different. Well-fed and rich, hardly a peasant off the street. But my hair . . .

"Still think it looks like a pile of buns," I muttered.

"Lumpy buns. Don't you think, Nomi?"

"For Saino's sake, you're a portrait artist," huffed Fal before Nomi could reply. "Don't you pay attention to anything? All the ladies of the first rank wear their hair like this."

"Why would I want to look like a lady of the first rank?" I said, smearing away my mole with my brush. I painted a new one by my eye instead. "I'd be eighth rank at best."

Fal stabbed a feather into my wig. Hard. As I winced, she replied, "Still rich. Everyone rich tries to look like they're of the first rank."

"Everyone rich also doesn't wear shoes like that," said Nomi, glancing up from her book to nod at my feet. "Should've kept to being a monk."

My eyes flew down. Demon turds, she was right. Noblewomen didn't wear flat straw shoes that could pass for a horse's breakfast. They wore silk slippers with embroidered peonies, and little upturned toe caps whose purpose I had yet to understand.

"Can you let out the hem on my dress, Fal?" I asked.

"It's not *your* dress," she replied. "It's the tailor shop's, and I'm going to get fired if I'm late again—"

"I can't go out like this. Unless you want to spend the rest of this year's wages getting me out of prison."

With a grumble, my sister set to work. "Just don't get the dress dirty," she warned when she'd finished. "Mrs. Su's already suspicious about the tear I stitched up for you last time."

"I'll do what I can."

"And, Tru?" Fal crossed her arms, but the worry in her eyes was genuine. "Try not to get robbed—or killed."

Oh, I was trying.

Sometimes I wished Fal were the one who had to do all this playacting. If there was one good thing about my younger sister, it was that she could charm a sparrow into a snake's nest. I'd bet she could get the scoundrels behind me to *escort* her to the auction house—and pay for her palanquin ride home too. But deals were dangerous, and I wouldn't put my sisters in danger. Mama did enough of that already these days.

I cut diagonally across the south market, shouldering my way through crowds of shoppers. Thank Amana, the auction house was just ahead.

A tremble shivered down my spine, and I threw a last glance back at the thieves, letting my eyes linger an extra beat on the one with long ears. This wasn't the first time I'd seen him.

Then I burst through the auction house gates. Inside was a long and serene courtyard with a large bronze tank in the center, the water within mirroring the heavens. As I passed my reflection, the effect of Fal's wig and my makeup made me beam. I was practically unrecognizable. A proper lady of the eighth or ninth rank, so long as you didn't look at my shoes.

I scanned the length of the courtyard for a hunched man with white hair. Gaari was always easy to see but even easier to hear. My ears picked out his deep and gravelly voice to my left, where he chatted garrulously with two art appraisers.

I tapped his shoulder, interrupting what sounded like an intense quarrel about where to get the best noodles in Gangsun. "I'm here."

"Lady Vee?" said Gaari, squinting his one eye. He took a moment to recognize me. "Praise the Sages! I was worried you might have lost your way."

He bowed, but under his breath, so I alone could hear, he muttered, "You're late."

"There were thieves," I muttered back, pairing my response with a glare. *Told you I should've been a monk.*

Gaari didn't waste a second. "Thieves?" he repeated, loud enough for all to hear. "*Thieves*, you say? No wonder you look so harried, Lady Vee." He made a show of gesturing at the open doors. "Guards, be on the lookout for riffraff trying to infiltrate this fine establishment. Come, Lady Vee, let us find Mr. Jisan. He's been waiting."

Never one for subtlety, my friend Gaari. But it worked for him. The guards immediately straightened, and their attention flew to the street rather than lingering over my straw shoes and lack of identification papers. Swiftly—and Gaari's legs were so long I almost had to skip to catch up—he led me down the corridor into the office where the art authenticator waited.

Like all government officials, Mr. Jisan was dressed in

blue so dark it was nearly black. His face was long like that of a mantis, and he stooped over his desk, commanding a neat tower of pamphlets and scrolls, a myriad of glass disks for examining art at a close angle, and a hefty red seal for authentication.

I'd met him twice before, but he didn't recognize me. Ironic, since his life's work was to tell whether something was true or false. But to a man like him, it'd never occur that a woman might be clever enough to cheat him. That was the beauty of the scam Gaari and I had cooked up, and gods, it was satisfying.

"There, there," Gaari said, patting the air above my shoulder as we entered the office. "You mean to say, they attacked your palanquin? The brazenness of those rascals!"

The act was on, and I bit down hard on my cheek to summon a nice, rosy flush. "The thieves followed me all the way from Hansun Park," I said, lifting my voice an aggrieved octave. "I had to cut through the market to get here! And my poor maid . . . she was so terrified. She tried to lead them astray, but—"

"They still trailed you," Gaari finished for me. "How terrifying. Were there many?"

I glanced at Mr. Jisan. His head was still bent over his work, but his hands weren't moving anymore. He was listening. Considering.

Thieves meant there was interest in my scroll. Interest meant there was profit to be had, and who didn't love profit?

"At least five," I finally replied, voice shaking. "Maybe more. They're still outside—dressed as scholars."

"Ban Nu's reprobates, I'd say." With a harrumph, Gaari

turned to Mr. Jisan. "Your Honor, will you send your guards to take a look? We cannot have thieves loitering about Gangsun's oldest and most reputable auction house—"

Mr. Jisan set down his magnifying disk, the clatter of the glass swiftly cutting Gaari off. "No thief will dare enter an *estate* under the protection of Governor Renhai," he said narrowly. "Your scroll, if it is indeed worth anything, will be quite safe here."

"Oh, that is a relief, Your Honor." I took out my fan and batted it. "Thank you for setting my mind at ease."

"My graciousness has its limits." Mr. Jisan cast me a sideways glance through thick spectacles, and I could tell that he'd judged me to be a lady of low rank. Hardly someone who'd bring in the prize of the day.

"You were due an hour ago," he chided me, "and I am a busy man."

"You'll be glad you didn't miss this one," said Gaari, waving the scroll. "Lady Vee is an avid collector of portraits. She has one of the finest collections in West Gangsun."

Mr. Jisan sniffed. "That wouldn't be difficult to do. There's scarcely any interest in portraits these days. *Faces age, empires fall, but land is eternal.*"

It was a quote from my least favorite Sage, who was responsible for the A'landan obsession with landscape painting. Mountains and rivers and forests and villages—*that* was what sold for thousands of jens these days. Unfortunately, that wasn't what I specialized in forging.

"I'm fascinated by faces," I replied, pretending not to hear, "and what they reveal about character."

"Any street artist can paint a portrait," Mr. Jisan said.

"Few masters waste their time on the form. It is amateur work. Rarely sells for more than a few hundred—"

"Few masters indeed," Gaari interrupted. "But those would include Master Lei Wing. Wouldn't you like to see it before you dismiss it? It's one of his originals. Dated the year he went missing."

At that, Mr. Jisan perked up. Interest buzzed in his dark eyes, and he motioned for the scroll. "Show me."

While Gaari carried forth the scroll, I backed into a corner and folded my skirt over my shoes. My wig itched again, and thanks to the sun flooding in from the windows, sweat was accumulating on my nose and under my arms. What a nuisance! Once this was done I was never playing a lady again.

I just hoped no one would hear how my heart hammered. This was the part of the transaction I hated the most. Either I'd end the day with a fat sack of coins in my pocket, or Mr. Jisan would ring that tiny bronze bell hanging at his side, and his guards would gleefully rumble in, hack off my right hand so I'd never paint again, and gouge out Gaari's remaining eye. *Then* they'd take us to prison.

Enough, Tru, I chided myself. *The authenticator hasn't even begun the inspection yet!*

Mr. Jisan unwrapped the scroll. First, he'd inspect the artist seal on the right corner of the paper. That was Gaari's handiwork, and the real reason he earned half my cut. Gaari had a highly criminal talent for carving identification stamps, which explained the first rule he'd given me when we'd started working together: *Only pick artists who are dead.*

The dead couldn't contest the unlawful use of their seals. Even then, I typically chose artists who'd died young, who'd been famous but not *too* famous. The profits were lower, but safer. Besides, I had no illusions about my skill as a painter—I was better than average, but nowhere near a master.

If you ever get caught, it's both our necks at stake, Gaari never failed to remind me. *And thick as it is, I'm rather fond of my neck.*

I was fond of mine too, even the painful throb of its veins as yet another second passed without Mr. Jisan uttering a sound. Sometimes, a vivid imagination was a curse.

The second rule:

Don't copy an artist's work. Paint a new one in the same style.

That was common sense. I didn't exactly have a personal library of classic art pieces, so I couldn't have copied them stroke for stroke anyway.

And the third rule—

Mr. Jisan pushed his spectacles up his nose, disrupting my thoughts. "Hmm."

My pulse spiked. "Hmm?" I echoed.

Gaari darted a warning glance in my direction. *I'll do the talking.*

"Tell me about this work," said Mr. Jisan.

"It's a Lei Wing original," Gaari replied. He folded the brocade cuffs of his sleeves while he spoke, then he leaned over the authenticator to give a more detailed introduction. "An early work, but he's already begun to master the meticulous style and come into his own. Notice the signature clouds, the rolling hills in the distance? They embrace his hometown, which he missed dearly during his service to the emperor."

Gaari said nothing about the actual subject of the portrait:

a fisherman in the middle of netting a catfish. I'd modeled the face on an elderly basket weaver who'd taken daily residence on a corner of Dattu Street, deep in concentration as he worked. Someone I doubted Mr. Jisan would ever notice, even if he walked past him every day.

"What about the river?" queried the authenticator. "Lei Wing didn't paint rivers like this. The motion, the composition—it's all wrong."

My eyes dipped to the water winding between the fisherman's legs. Two catfish swam in the foreground, one light and one dark. Their eyes and tails were so lifelike they could have swum out of the parchment. But that wasn't what made my breath catch. It was the serpentine shape of the river. If you stepped back, concentrated hard enough, it looked like a dragon, and the fish its two eyes.

My fingertips tingled, and I held them still by bunching up my skirt. "I see nothing amiss," I lied. "I've seen plenty a Lei Wing piece with rivers like this before."

"I haven't," said Mr. Jisan flatly.

"Which makes this piece all the more special," said Gaari, wielding his silkiest tone. "Just look at the energy in the fisherman's fingers. Those knuckles and knobs. Who else could paint hands like Lei Wing? And that expression on his face! Doesn't he look like he might talk back at any moment? The piece will fetch a handsome price."

I stared wretchedly at the river while Gaari covered up for me. Honestly, I barely remembered painting it. Then again, that always happened when I worked late and on an empty stomach. Such a simple mistake, but it could be the end of me.

I'd have to be more careful.

"The detail is there," Mr. Jisan allowed. "The pose is similar to the *Rice Farmer*."

"So it is," Gaari said, twisting his lips. A token move that I knew all too well. With a sense of perfect timing, he started to roll up the scroll.

"What are you doing?" Mr. Jisan demanded. "I wasn't finished inspecting—"

"I'm an honest man, sir," said Gaari. "It's occurred to me that you are less than enthusiastic about portraits, and I'm not here to waste anyone's time. If you'd like to pass, simply say the word. I've an appointment with Lady Vee to speak with Mr. Wan, and we are running quite behind on time—"

"Mr. Wan?"

"Yes. He's expressed interest in Lei Wing's works many times. But we thought to approach you first, since you were so kind with the Chuli landscape that my associate sold you last time."

"That was through you, Mr. Gaari?"

"Indeed." Gaari bowed.

I held my breath as Mr. Jisan beckoned Gaari for my painting, and as he unrolled it onto his desk once more. I could feel my chest constricting, my lungs pinching and demanding new air, when at last Mr. Jisan gave a nod. "I'll take it."

"Wonderful news!" Gaari exclaimed. "You'll not regret it—"

"But first," said Mr. Jisan, waving Gaari away. "Enlighten me, Lady Vee. Just how did you acquire Master Lei Wing's art?"

I closed my fan and lowered it to my side. The best lies

were spun with threads of truth, and the reason Lei Wing was my favorite painter to forge was because . . .

"He went missing at sea," I replied calmly. *Like Baba.* "My father dabbles in trade and encountered a merchant who'd smuggled Lei Wing's last works out of Kiata. When I heard about this piece, I wanted it."

"It is a rare find," Mr. Jisan agreed, but his look was still hard. "Why are you selling it now?"

Were I Tru, I would have told him to go piss in a dragon's beard. I needed money, obviously. My family had been surviving off boiled cabbage dumplings and I would have kissed a rat to sink my teeth into something that had actual spice and crunch. But I wasn't Tru; I was Lady Vee.

And as Lady Vee, I raised my sleeve and wiped an imaginary tear from the corner of my eye. "My father is often at sea, and my mother is superstitious. She believes Lei Wing's work will bring ill fortune to our family."

It was the first time I'd liked Mr. Jisan, the way he rolled his eyes at my fictional mother. "Then rest assured, we will find the piece a proper home," he said.

At last, Sages be praised, he signed the verification papers and stamped them with his seal.

"It is genuine," Mr. Jisan told his subordinates. "Add it to the list for the next auction today."

I was so relieved that I forgot not to scratch at my wig. Before anyone saw, I quickly blew away the stray piece of blue hair that fell over my eyes.

Gaari nearly had to push me out into the courtyard. I knew the routine; he wouldn't leave with me. He would see the transaction through, then find me afterward.

"Well done," he whispered. "Lunch is on me."

Thank Amana, I was starving. "At Luk's?" I asked hopefully.

"You fancy noodles?"

"I always fancy noodles."

"Good. So do I." Gaari grinned, his gray eye shining. "See you there."

CHAPTER THREE

One good thing about Gaari, he was never late. Precisely an hour past noon, I spied him sauntering down the street, his white icicle of a beard and the bandage over his eye making him an easy mark. Next to me with my blue hair, we stuck out like spiders in a sugar jar.

"You look well rested," he greeted me. "Where'd you stash your costume?"

I patted the knapsack over my shoulder. "Fal will have my head if I spill soup all over her dress," I said dryly. "Shrimps secured?"

Shrimps. Our code word for money.

"Fattest ones yet."

My chest swelled. "Good. That's very good. No trouble with the thieves?"

Gaari blinked, as if he'd forgotten about my entire ordeal. Then he caught himself. "Ah, them. No, not a rascal in sight." He chuckled. "Maybe they beat us here for noodles. Look at this line!"

There were at least twenty-odd people still ahead of us. I

let out a woeful sigh. "I've been waiting since I left the auction house. Should we try somewhere else?"

"Not a chance," Gaari said, towing me away from the line. "Leave it to me."

"We'll lose our place—"

"Have faith, Saigas. Come with me." From his pocket, Gaari swept out a wooden fan and used it to poke and prod other patrons aside. I lost count of the glares we got as we shuffled inside Luk's and made for the stairs in the corner. By some miracle, no one stopped us. Not one of the staff batted an eye.

Gaari parted the beaded curtains and motioned at the corner table. A waiter was already setting down a pot of fresh tea and two cups for us. When he saw Gaari, he bowed deeply.

Interesting.

"How much did you bribe him?" I whispered when the waiter slipped away.

Gaari landed on his stool. He looked tired and snapped his fan shut. "I wouldn't waste your hard-earned coin like that."

"Then?"

A pause. "You could say he's a former associate. He owes me."

"A former associate?" I raised a curious eyebrow. Gaari was famously private, and I'd never met anyone else who worked with him. "Shall we invite him to eat with us?"

"Don't get ideas," warned my friend. "He lives by the third rule too."

The third rule: No questions outside the job.

I scowled. "You run quite the operation, all these people

keeping secrets for you. You always know where and how to find me, whereas I . . . I don't even know if your beard is real."

"Of course it's real!" Gaari looked offended that I thought otherwise. He made a show of stroking his chin. "My life is not interesting. I'm just an old man who enjoys his noodles and happens to run a successful scam every now and then."

"Scam indeed," I muttered. "Watch your tells, *old* man. Every time you lie, you find a way to bring up noodles."

"You see, Saigas? You know me better than anyone." He raised his tea to me before sipping more. "I'll dry my cup to your powers of observation. They're paying for lunch today."

I rolled my eyes, but I drank too. The waiter was returning to take our orders, and from behind the sheath of my curtain-long bangs, I stole a better look at his face. A bell-shaped nose, cheeks as round as eggs, long ears, and black hair swept neatly under a hat. I'd seen him before, but where? I *never* forgot a face.

Ah. The answer pecked at the back of my mind, and I set my teacup on the table.

"You know, it's funny," I said slowly, regarding Gaari, "those thieves today came out of nowhere. There were plenty of other rich women they could've followed. And yet, they homed in on me."

Gaari was washing our spoons in an extra cup of tea. "What are you getting at?"

"Were they yours?" I pressed. "Did you hire those thieves to follow me?"

He swept the end of his beard over his shoulder. "We're here to celebrate. Must we talk about such unpleasantries?"

"That waiter was there. Your *associate*."

Gaari's cheek twitched. It was the barest flinch, almost imperceptible, but I knew to look out for it. "His name's Tangyor," he mumbled. He pointed a spoon at me. "It's to my detriment that I forget how observant you are."

"The truth, Gaari. Now."

"I do hire ruffians on occasion." Gaari crossed his legs. "The more traffic a piece gins up, the higher price it fetches. Sometimes, that traffic needs a bit of a push."

"And you didn't think to tell me?"

"Ignorance makes your playacting more sincere." He shrugged. "Just something I've noticed."

If I hadn't finished my tea already, I would have thrown it at him. "I could wring your neck if it weren't so thick. Don't go behind my back again."

"Now, now, Saigas." Gaari wiped the corner of his mouth. "I got you an extra thousand jens, didn't I?"

I resented the gasp that escaped me. "An extra thousand?"

He gave a smug nod. "Told you the shrimps were fat today."

I didn't want to be so easily won over, but what a boon! An extra thousand would put me weeks closer to my goal. It was a struggle keeping my voice even. "At least tell me who won the auction."

"The less you know, the better. You're the talent, I'm everything else."

"Third rule," I muttered, still hating it. I sank back into my chair, inwardly grousing at my employer. Three years working with Gaari, and I knew close to nothing about him. Didn't know how he'd lost his eye or how old he was. I didn't even know if Gaari was his real name.

I doubted it was. A man like him, who valued the act as much as the art, would obviously shroud himself in a few layers of mystery. I respected that. What bothered me were the little chips in his facade I caught from time to time, the fault of my own perceptiveness. Maybe the beard and the white hair were questionable—but once, early in our acquaintance, I'd observed that the skin on his neck was smooth, unlike his face. At times his eye, too, seemed bright, almost youthful. Cunning.

"I don't know why I trust you," I said aloud, both for myself and him to hear.

"Because you'll never get a table at Luk's without me," replied Gaari cheerily. "Now that I've introduced you to this place, you know that every other noodle shop is second-rate."

I wiped my freshly rinsed spoon with a cloth. Only Gaari would fish out a compliment when none had been given. It was true, though. The man did have good taste in noodles.

"I swear, this place must be run by kitchen demons." He inclined his chin at how busy it was downstairs. "Speaking of which, our lunch is here."

As soon as he said it, a potpourri of spices seduced my nostrils. Cinnamon and white cardamom, clove and star anise and mountain ginger. My nose was in heaven. A steaming bowl of freshly hand-rolled noodles landed in front of me, chunks of sinewy beef and spinach floating inside the brown-red broth.

I salivated. Of all the foods in the world, noodles made my belly happiest. Gaari and I had our differences—he favored landscapes over portraits, medicinal over black tea, and garlic over chilis—but there was one thing he and I agreed on, had practically staked our friendship on in fact. Noodles were king.

And the ones at Luk's—divine.

So divine that I momentarily forgot my anger at Gaari. I dipped a wooden spoon into the noodles, scooping up a splendorous dollop of oil and inhaling the steam it let off. But first, before I could feast, I twisted open the small jar on the side of the table and shuttled a heap of chopped chili peppers into my soup. My bowl turned a dazzling red.

Then I dug in.

With each bite, my tongue burned with glorious heat. I didn't stop to drink, to speak to Gaari, or even to breathe. Good food was consumed in silence; any extra air would interfere with my taste buds. And so I stooped over my bowl, beads of sweat sliding down the precipice of my cheeks as I devoured my noodles.

Gaari observed my little ritual, looking amused.

"What?" I said.

"I've always wondered who taught you to eat with so much spice. It's not a southernly thing to do."

I sat up and patted the perspiration from my face. In my head, I answered silently. *Baba.* It was cold in Balar, he'd said, and the spice helped clear the nose and warm the belly. I used to hate it, used to cry at the slightest smear of pepper in my rice. But I developed a resistance over time. After five long winters of going hungry in the cold, I'd graduated to the hottest chili peppers I could find. And now I could eat them raw.

Of course, that story I kept to myself. "My father" was all I said.

"Your father," repeated Gaari. "Who gave you your blue hair? You never talk about him."

"He's dead. That's all there is to know." I shoveled another spoonful of noodles into my mouth, punctuating the end of the topic. "Third rule."

Gaari chuckled. "Well played. You know, Saigas, sometimes I think you have as many secrets as I do." He wiped his mouth, a tell that he was about to change the topic. "I've told you the one behind Luk's broth, haven't I? They boil the base with kelp. Just a knot of it, but it adds an oystery flavor. Precious flavor that you're *ruining* with those peppers."

"Then be glad that it's my bowl, not yours."

"Indeed." Gaari chewed on his noodles, looking thoughtful. "I think I'll tell Tangyor not to let you in at Luk's anymore."

I nearly choked on my soup. "What? Because of the peppers?"

"Because you were careless today," Gaari said, leveling his gaze with mine. "Did you think I'd let that pass simply because the piece fetched a good price?"

"I thought we were celebrating," I said with a wince. "Must we talk about such unpleasantries?"

Not a smile cracked his grave composure. "You cannot afford to make mistakes in this business," he said. "You're a good forger, Saigas. It isn't like you to deviate from your assignment. The extra bends along the river, the two catfish in the pond. The *dragon*."

My eyes flew up.

"Yes, I saw it," said Gaari. "You'd best pray that Jisan doesn't before the piece goes to its buyer. Lei Wing would never have painted such a thing." He frowned. "Explain yourself."

I parted my lips, but what could I say? No story I made up would be satisfactory for Gaari. I knew him. He'd relentlessly ask question after question, until I was forced to tell the truth. And the truth was my secret.

"It won't happen again" was all I said.

"It won't," Gaari agreed. "Because you're not going to forge any more paintings."

"What?"

"Your talents are wasted imitating the dead. Give it up. Do your own work."

I stared at him. "Have you gone senile, old man? I'm no visionary. My skill's in copying what others have done. That's why you hired me."

"So I did." Gaari looked tired again, the white in his beard suddenly losing luster. "But that dragon had a spark, Saigas. A spark of something special. Where did it come from?"

A muscle in my hand spasmed, and I dropped my spoon as my mind reeled with excuses. "Nowhere," I said quickly. "Nomi used to make me paint them. I must have done it without thinking."

"Perhaps you should *try* thinking." Gaari leaned forward. "*Try* painting your own art. You know what they say about the luck of the dragons. You could make a name for yourself."

I folded my hands together over my lap, holding them still. "You're a swindler, Mr. Gaari, and you made good coin today swindling. Should you be questioning me?"

"No one chooses to be a thief," he said. "If you made your own art—"

"I can't afford to take a chance with my own art. My

mother—" I caught myself before I shared something personal. "I need to take care of my family."

"Then do it for your family." Gaari touched his bandaged eye. "Otherwise, sooner or later, you'll get caught."

A shiver raced down my spine. Not for the first time, I wondered whether someone had double-crossed him in the past. Whether that explained his third rule.

Gaari's cheek twitched again. He rose. "Enjoy your noodles."

"You aren't finishing yours?"

"I have another appointment."

I crossed my arms. "Gardening?"

It was what he always said he had to do when he left. A corner of his mouth quirked. "You see, you really do know me better than anyone."

He dropped a heavy pouch of coins onto the table. My payment. As I lunged for it, Gaari held on to the other end of the drawstring.

"Think on what I said," he spoke, before letting go.

No, I replied in my head. *My answer is no. It will always be no.*

Ever since Baba had disappeared, strange things happened when I painted my own work. Things I'd never told anyone—not Mama, not Falina. Not even Nomi.

I didn't wish Gaari farewell, but it was as if he'd cursed me. After he left, I kept imagining dragon tails in the curve of my noodles. Even my vegetables seemed to form the shape of a face, silently haunting me.

I scowled at my bowl and devoured every last noodle with a vengeance. Every drop of soup too.

My belly full and my mouth smarting with spice, I peeled open the money pouch to count the coins. But that scoundrel Gaari! "Demon turds," I exclaimed, "this is only half of what I was supposed to get."

A shadow fell upon me, and when I looked up, the waiter with the long ears was at my side. Tangyor, I remembered. He was carrying a tray, which he placed before me.

"Courtesy of Mr. Gaari," he said, head bowed.

On the tray was a scholar's hat, like the ones the thieves had worn this morning. I glared, but Tangyor's expression was inscrutable.

Slowly, I lifted the hat. Underneath, in an identical pouch to the one I had, was the extra thousand jens.

"Mr. Gaari never breaks a promise," said Tangyor. He finally acknowledged my glare, and the barest smile appeared on his face. "There's no need for concern. My colleagues and I won't be following you." He paused. "Unless orders change."

"Just what do you do for him?" I demanded.

"I serve noodles." Tangyor bowed, then he reached for my bowl and my chilis, taking them both away. "Customers are waiting, ma'am. I am glad you enjoyed your meal, but kindly be considerate of others."

With that, he turned and disappeared behind the beaded curtain.

"The audacity of that old man," I muttered. First, hiring his henchmen to chase after me. Then getting them to kick me out of Luk's!

I slung my knapsack over my shoulder, ready to storm out into the streets. In my haste, the scholar's hat toppled onto Gaari's stool. There it sat, looking forlorn and forgotten.

The sight appeared like a dream, and one I'd seen before. My mood instantly brightening, I picked the hat up and dusted its black folds clean. Nomi had always wanted a hat like this.

I tucked it under my arm, then out onto the road I returned, whistling to the glares of the Luk's customers still waiting in line. Everything had gone better than I'd foreseen, and nothing—absolutely nothing—could ruin my mood.

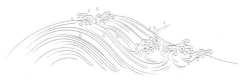

CHAPTER FOUR

Money sang in my pocket, coins clinking together like the sweetest music. Turned out I was my mother's daughter after all, because gods, I *loved* money. The sound of it, the smell, the weight, even the grime around the coin edges.

I counted my earnings with my fingers, tapping a mental abacus as I worked out how long the money would last, how much I could save. Whether I finally had enough to get my family out of Gangsun.

We were close, I concluded. Just one more sale, and we'd have enough to leave the city and start afresh. Maybe we could move to Port Kamalan, Niyan, or even Bisandi.

Or Port Onsun. My heart gave a twinge. That was the port where Baba had last been seen, before he'd taken off for the Taijin Sea.

Deep down, I knew I should cross it off my list. That after five years, it was a certainty Baba was gone, and we shouldn't waste precious coin and time trying to find him. That it was an obsession that would ruin us all. But still I yearned for answers. I knew my sisters did too.

The central marketplace buzzed, so crowded I had to suck in my stomach to squeeze through. Tomorrow was the Ghost Festival, which honored the dead. It was the day the gates of Heaven and Hell opened, when all spirits were permitted to visit earth. My least favorite festival.

"Peanuts, tangerines!" cried the merchants selling ritual food and wine. "Roast pork, very fresh!"

"Thunderbolts of Saino," others shouted, holding up firecrackers and grotesque masks for warding off evil. "Strike down all evil spirits and protect Gangsun eternally!"

The firecrackers tempted me. Nomi delighted in watching them explode, and Fal liked burning them too—but my budget was fifty jens, and as much of it as possible was going to food.

Everywhere I went, my blue hair drew mistrustful stares, and people clutched more tightly at their purses. A silly instinct, if you thought about it. If I *were* a thief, I'd know exactly where their valuables were. But it was like sorcery, being able to make the crowds disperse with my presence. It made shopping almost . . . fun.

From the festival tents, I purchased a stack of spirit money—joss paper with silver strips—a prayer lantern to honor Baba, and a bag of sweet pancakes for Fal. The rest of my coin I spent at the wet market: a slab of raw pork ribs, a half dozen duck eggs, three black chickens, a bag of slightly bruised pears, and one fresh crab. I probably overdid it, for when I returned home, Mama immediately rose from her chair.

It was never a good sign when she was there, waiting for me with a cup of twice-brewed tea.

I dropped my bags on the ground, and out of respect, I took the tea and drank. Its bitterness left my mouth dry.

As soon as I set the cup down, she began the interrogation. "How much did you sell?"

"Enough to feed us for the next week," I replied. I passed her the lantern. "This is for tonight."

She ignored it. "You spent everything on spirit food?"

"On food for us."

"Tru! I told you—"

"It's not your business how much I spent," I said over her. My tone was even, and I took pains not to raise it. "Falina and I pay the rent. We are responsible for this household."

Mama stepped back, stricken as though I'd slapped her. I'd been raised the A'landan way, to obey my parents and never argue or question them. But the past few years had taught me a hard lesson: that if I relied on Mama, my sisters and I would be short a roof over our heads.

"How much?" Mama said again.

I waited a beat too long. "Three hundred."

She knew I was lying. Her face darkened, and she grabbed my sleeve, reaching for my knapsack.

"Mama!" As we twisted about each other, I blocked her arm with my own. "Stop."

"Give it here," Mama cried. "Let me see!"

When I wouldn't give in, her hand came swinging.

The slap was harder than either of us expected, and it knocked the air out of me. My hand jumped up to my cheek, and Mama jerked back. She'd aimed for my shoulder, for me to let go of the bag. I knew that much from the shock that filled her eyes.

Mama's strength went out. She crumpled to the floor, tears streaking down her cheeks.

Setting down my knapsack, I knelt beside her. A mouse scurried toward the groceries, but neither of us moved. I spoke first: "Why do you need the money?"

I touched her arm. "Mama, tell me."

"You should take Fal and Nomi," she replied. "Leave me. I'm not worthy of being your mother."

Sometimes she said this to be dramatic. But I could tell that wasn't the case today. Something had happened. Something terrible.

I turned my mother by her shoulders. She'd become small and frail, and her wrists were nearly half the size of mine. But that wasn't what saddened me most. It was her eyes. There used to be such fire in her gaze. Such strength.

What happened to you, Mama? I wanted to ask, but I didn't dare.

In the months after Baba disappeared, Mama had been a barrel of strength. Every morning when the first light tinged the sky, she'd wake us to search for Baba. "We'll scour the entire continent to find him," she'd say. "We won't stop until we do."

We hounded every sailor in every port for news, we rapped on gates and wrote messages on strips of bamboo, passed them out across the city to spread word about Baba. But all we learned was that his ship had sunk and the cargo could not be salvaged.

It became clear that we'd have to leave Gangsun if we wanted answers. "In the spring," Mama decided. "Until then, we'll focus on raising the money."

But oh, how that first winter tested us. Our rooftop

buckled under the snow and our windows were rimed with frost. Then Nomi got sick, with a cough that seeped deep into her lungs and a fever that wouldn't go away. I'd never forget how Mama spent every last coin of our savings on medicine and doctors—and how the three of us cried when Nomi's fever finally broke.

Things will look up from here, I'd thought. *They have to get better.*

I was wrong.

Come spring, Mama couldn't find work. Losing a husband was not good for business, especially if your business was seeing the future.

Dejected, she found her way into Gangsun's gambling dens, certain that her Sight would give her an advantage. "One more try," she'd say every time she lost. "The sprites of fortune are with me still. They'll carry me through another day."

One unlucky round of tiles was all it took. Just like that, Mama lost our house, and my sisters and I lost the world we'd known. Our clothes, our toys, the paints in the cupboard, and Nomi's prized collection of books, the coppers in a jar Fal had been saving to buy her silk slippers. We didn't even have enough warning to take Baba's box of wooden trinkets.

I snuck inside a few days later, but everything had already been sold off. All I could salvage were some old blankets, Nomi's dictionary—torn and missing pages—and one of Fal's dolls. The box of trinkets was gone, along with anything else we'd had of Baba's.

Fal wouldn't speak to Mama for over a month.

"That was the last time," Mama pled to us. "No more. I've learned my lesson."

But there was a reason A'landans called bad habits "the

touch of demons." They were like curses, hard to break. Mama would keep her word for a little while, but before long she'd be back to her old ways again.

"It's up to you and me now," Fal had said to me after we lost the house. "Promise me, Tru. No matter what happens between us, no matter how much we fight, we stay together. For Nomi. For Mama."

She'd taken the words from my own heart. "No matter what it takes," I added slowly, "we get out of Gangsun." I raised my chin. "We start again."

And after five years, we were close. So close.

I helped Mama up, pulled out a stool for her from behind our table, really a wooden board that sat on the bucket we used for storing rice. This was our home now, a ramshackle room behind the fish market, which Fal and I had rented because it was cheap and had no roaches. The landlord hadn't lied about the roaches, but instead there were mice, and a rotting stench that wouldn't go away no matter how much incense Mama burned. I couldn't complain. We had a window, which Nomi—who was getting tall—stuck her feet out of some nights so she had enough space on the bed, and we had a narrow closet that I'd converted into a tiny place to paint. Most importantly, it was warm in winter.

Mama leaned against the table. There was a bowl of rice beside my empty cup of tea, a small well in the center. I imagined Mama picking at it for hours, eating one grain at a time.

I'm lost, Tru, her eyes spoke. *Like your baba.*

I took Mama's hands in mine. "How much do you owe?"

Shame flushed her cheeks. She looked away.

"How much?" I asked again, as gently as I could. "Tell me. I won't be upset."

Then I saw the bruises on her wrist. Four fingerprints, and the arched indents of fingernails.

Anger rose to my throat. "Who did this?"

From the way Mama's body folded, she didn't have to say anything. I already knew.

"Mama, why?" I cried softly. "You know better than to gamble in one of Madam Yargui's dens."

Mama flinched. "It's not what you think. I was trying to find answers."

I'd heard this story before. Mama was convinced that Yargui had something to do with Baba's disappearance. It was an obsession that drove her, an excuse she made to justify her habit.

Did you get those answers? I wanted to ask. *Was it worth risking everything? Our house, our future?*

"What does she want?" I said instead.

"She said if we can't pay . . ." Hopelessness pooled in Mama's eyes. "She'll take Falina."

The air punched out of my lungs. The world swayed, and my mouth tasted like ash. My sister was a pretty girl; Yargui had had her sights on her for a while. If I couldn't pay off Mama's debt, she'd sell Falina in the forbidden markets to become a servant, a courtesan, a concubine. I didn't want to imagine the possibilities. The only certainty was that my sister would be taken far from Gangsun, and we'd never see her again.

A fate I would never allow.

"When are they coming back?" I said.

"Tomorrow night." Mama's voice cracked. "They have guards watching the house to make sure we don't run."

Of course they did. I glanced out the window, but there

were dozens of people milling about. I'd never be able to pinpoint the spy.

In my head, I let out a string of curses. Aloud, I was already plotting. "I made two thousand. I spent fifty already, but I can borrow more if I need to—"

"It won't be enough."

Mama was clenching the bowl of rice, her knuckles pale against the filter of sunset.

I frowned. "How much do you need?"

When she told me the sum, my eyes rounded in disbelief.

Mama hung her head. She didn't bother to explain. "I'm sorry, Tru."

What hurt most about her apology was that I knew she meant it. I knew she'd gladly go to prison if it would pay off her debts. But that wasn't an option. Not with Madam Yargui.

"I'll get the money," I said grimly.

I left Mama with the groceries, my mind numb as I climbed out the back window. I slipped out into the alley, where a narrow trail ran along the canals, and where the fishmongers tossed the innards and bones. The smell here was unbearable, which meant it was always empty.

Well, mostly.

I said into the shadows, "You heard everything."

Slipping out from behind a boat, Falina hopped over the canal to join my side. "Eavesdropping is a family tradition."

So it was, back when Mama read fortunes and we three girls listened in behind the kitchen and made secret commentary about her clients. What I'd have given for those days again.

"I've got two hundred, Tru," said Fal. "Two hundred and nine, if you include my coppers. It's not much, but . . ."

The courage in my sister's voice nearly broke me. "All these weeks we've been eating cabbage dumplings, and you've been hoarding two hundred jens?"

It was a weak attempt at a joke, but it got Fal to smile. A little. "I still want silk slippers."

"With those ridiculous upturned toe caps?" I laughed quietly. "You're the vainest girl I've ever met."

"Joy on the feet rises to the heart. Happiness is expensive."

It was a rare moment that Fal and I didn't fight. Even rarer that I had the urge to hug her. I wrapped my arm around her, drawing her close. Here we were, our family on the verge of catastrophe, and we were joking about embroidered slippers. That was how you knew our situation was truly hopeless.

"I forgot to tell you," I said, breaking the silence, "your dress is inside the house. The hem got dirty, but it isn't too bad."

"Oh, damn the stupid dress." Falina looked up at me. "You won't let them take me, will you?"

Her jaw trembled, the only betrayal of her fear.

"Pack, just in case," I said. "If you don't hear from me by noon, take this alley into the fish market. Bribe whoever you have to. Get out of Gangsun."

Falina pressed her lips tight. "I don't want to leave."

"Would you rather Madam Yargui take you?"

"I could cut my hair. Scar my face."

"Then Madam Yargui would take Nomi too. Not just you. Don't say such things without thinking them through."

Fal knew I was right. Her arms fell to her sides, defeated.

"I'm scared," she whispered.

I took her hand. In spite of the summer heat, her fingers were cold. I warmed them with mine. "I won't let anything happen to you. I promise."

"Let what happen?" wobbled a small voice from behind us.

"Nomi!" I whirled to face my youngest sister, who had arrived with a festoon of bamboo firecrackers. As usual, her pigtails were braided unevenly, and her collar was loose a button that I itched to fix. "I thought you were at the shop."

"I left work early. Thought I'd come back and read until the festival starts." Nomi lowered the firecrackers. "But Mama's crying by the stove. She wouldn't say why."

Fal and I exchanged a look. I cleared my throat. "That's because Mama's—"

"Don't you lie to me," Nomi warned, raising her voice. "Or you, Fal. We don't lie to family."

A rule I'd broken too many times.

My shoulders sank. "She owes Madam Yargui twenty thousand jens," I said truthfully. "By tomorrow night, or else they're taking Fal."

The color drained from Nomi's face. She hooked Fal's arm protectively. "So we're coming up with a plan."

I loved how she'd included herself in the *we* without a moment's hesitation. "Tomorrow's the Ghost Festival," I replied. "Maybe I'll pick some pockets—or rob a temple. Everyone will be out praying."

"All you'll get is paper boats and spirit money," retorted Falina. "Plus a thousand years of reincarnation as a centipede. You can't steal from someone observing the Ghost Festival. It's bad luck."

"You could rob the governor," suggested Nomi. "Or any of the manors on Oyang Street. They've got to have scrolls signed by the emperor or boxes of gold ingots lying about."

"Then get our throats slit?" Fal said. "We have a night to plan, not a week. Besides, you forget what an awful thief Tru is. She got caught half the time just picking pockets."

"That's how I met Gaari," I protested, "and how I got a job."

Fal ignored me. "We'd have better luck praying to the money frog. Or knocking on Governor Renhai's door and *asking* him to help us catch Yargui."

Nomi huffed a laugh. Everyone knew the governor was in Yargui's pocket.

"I could light these firecrackers," said Nomi. "I made them with charcoal and sulfur from the shop. They'll explode bigger than usual ones to—"

"Frighten away Yargui's men?" I finished for her, shaking my head. "They're not evil spirits, Nomi."

"Firecrackers can be dangerous," insisted my sister. "They can be weapons so long as we're clever about it."

"I'll paint something," I said firmly. "I'll get Gaari to sell it in the morning."

"What can you paint that'll sell for twenty thousand?" asked Nomi.

Eighteen thousand, I corrected silently. At this point, every jen mattered. "You know how Mama used to say she was the best fortune teller in Gangsun?"

My sisters nodded, uncertain where I was going with this.

"She was wrong," I said. "*I'm* the best. And I'm going to get that money."

Fal gave me a flummoxed look. "It's not funny to pretend. This is serious."

"Do I look like I'm pretending? Trust me."

I reached into my knapsack for the scholar's hat I'd retrieved and settled it on Nomi's head. "Gifts, from today."

Nomi's eyes grew misty. More than anything, she wanted to test into the National Academy, become an imperial official, and ensure our family never had to worry about money again. But the Academy rarely accepted women, not to mention a girl with Balardan blood. Besides, she was still young. It'd be years before she could earn her own scholar's hat.

"Your fisherman painting sold?"

"For two whole thousand jens," I replied. "I was planning for a celebration tonight. I even bought chickens."

Nomi touched her hat, saying nothing. My gift felt empty, a moment's distraction from the possibility that our family might soon be torn apart. But my sisters and I had learned to cherish even the smallest joys. We knew they brought us strength in hard times.

"And, Fal," I said, "no fancy shoes for you, but I bought pancakes. Your favorite—with lotus-seed paste. They might be cold by now . . ."

Fal snatched the bag. She tore it open and passed one to Nomi, then me. I shook my head. "I don't like sweets."

"Liar." Fal bit into her pancake and let out a blissful sigh. "I won't feel bad eating your share, though. I can smell the garlic and chili on your breath. Only you'd pick noodles over cakes."

I laughed. The cakes were a family favorite. Cheap and delicious, and probably what had kept us alive that first winter after Mama lost our house.

As my sisters ate, completely unbothered by the stench of rotting fish and sewer water, my chest tightened. If not for them, I'd have left Gangsun years ago. Would have snuck aboard the first merchant ship leaving for Port Onsun, maybe disguised myself as a boy and tried to pass as a sailor. I would have traveled the world twice over by now, searching for Baba.

But in no world could I ever have abandoned my sisters. No matter what it took, I'd make the best future I could for them. I wouldn't let them down.

"It's the eve of the Ghost Festival," I told Fal as I turned back for our room. "Ask Mama to come out here with the prayer lantern. You three should light it for Baba and send it down the canal."

"What about you?" Nomi asked.

I glanced up at the sky, at the whirlpool of stars whispering with possibility.

No one can see the future, Baba told me once. *Not even your mother.*

Mama couldn't see the future. But I could.

I'd been ignoring the tickle in my fingers for too long. "I'm going to paint a miracle."

CHAPTER FIVE

I sat on an overturned pot and whittled away at an ink stick, its edges rubbing off on my palms like tar. It was better than confronting the blank scroll in front of me. What could I possibly paint in one night that would pay off Mama's debts?

Forging a new piece was out of the question. The Lei Wing painting had been my best work yet, and that had only netted two thousand jens.

I'd have to paint something new. But what?

A landscape? The view outside our window offered little inspiration. Across every rooftop, clotheslines hung from eave to eave, old laundry fluttering like banners. Along the canals, festival lanterns bobbed up and down, leaving a glowing kiss of light upon the water.

Almost beautiful, if you overlooked the mounds of trash and the rising stench of fish bones. But not a miracle.

Nomi followed me inside and lit my candles with a flame stick. She glanced into the closet, her pity for me clear on her face. "Will you be in here all night?"

The space was cramped, barely wide enough for me to

stretch my arms, and if I stood on my toes, my head hit the ceiling. But it was a place to work. That was all I needed.

"All night," I confirmed.

"You sure I can't help you? I can stay up too."

"I paint best when I'm alone." I tossed her braid affectionately. "Don't look so worried. You go on with Mama and Fal, then get some sleep. When you wake up, I'll have a masterpiece ready to sell."

Much as I tried to hide it, we both heard the tremor behind my bravado.

"I'll pray for you," Nomi mumbled.

After she left, I cleaned my hands and shut myself in the closet. I swept my fingers down the wall, feeling for a thin stack of joss paper I'd hidden between the bricks. Using my nails, I pried the pages out, then blew dust from the cover.

This was my sketchbook, bound tightly with twine. Inside were simple drawings: mostly faces and a smattering of objects like hats and linen shoes and broken cart wheels. Nothing special to the ordinary eye.

But to me, a compendium of secrets.

It'd started with a game of magic paintbrush. My sisters and I had stopped playing after Baba disappeared, but the winter when Nomi got sick, I picked up my brush to cheer her. "I don't believe in magic anymore," Nomi'd said, bringing a pang in my heart. So instead of mermaids and dragons, I painted cookies and books—simple pleasures we could no longer afford. My fingers tingled with every stroke, as if they were dancing with sparks, but I shrugged it off as excitement from revisiting an old pastime. "Magic paintbrush," I'd sometimes murmur after finishing a painting.

A few days after our game, I spied a volume of Nomi's favorite ghost stories buried under a thin coat of snow on the street, along with a small bag of fresh almond cookies that must have fallen from someone's purse.

A coincidence, I told myself. But the tingle in my hand came back, and it wouldn't go away. Every day I ignored it, it grew heavier, until my fingers dragged like iron. So I painted again. I painted faces I had never seen before—a girl with freckled cheeks, an old woman carrying buckets of water over her frail shoulders, a prosperous tailor cutting silk in his shop window. I painted water jugs, copper bracelets, rusted boats in the canal. . . . It didn't matter what I conjured from my brush. Every single sketch became real.

Then I painted Gaari.

I had never seen the old man before and had no reason to know of him. But his likeness leaked out of my brush hairs as if they were possessed—his squinting gray eye, his pipe-shaped nose, the high forehead and icicle of a beard.

By the time I spotted him in the flesh, buying grilled chestnuts on Dattu Street, I had enough experience with my visions to know our fates would touch.

So what did I do? I tried to rob him.

"*A bit tall for a thief, aren't you?*" Gaari had mused, his first words to me. *He'd caught me by the wrist.* "*And with that blue hair . . .*" *He clucked.* "*A memorable thief is one who gets caught.*"

I squirmed, but his grip was tight. He was stronger than he looked.

"*You were picking my pocket, so it's only fair that I pick yours,*" *he said, lifting the scrap of paper that peeked out of my sleeve.* He viewed the sketch I'd made of him. "Now, what's this?"

I jumped, trying to reach for it. "Give that back!"

"Sons of the Wind," Gaari whistled, admiring my portrait of him. "You've a gift for faces, my friend."

"I'm not your friend."

"Not yet." He folded the sketch with one hand. I twisted and jerked, but he still wouldn't release my arm. "See those three prefects over there?"

I didn't look. "Let me go."

"Either I tell them you're a thief and you start running—with that blue hair of yours, I really don't think you'll get far—or you listen to my proposition."

I hated him already. "What do you want?"

"Look at the prefect in the middle. The one with the pimples and the unshaven beard. Really look at him." Gaari gave me a second, then he spun me the other direction and handed me a pad of paper. "Sketch him. If your drawing's good enough, then it's your lucky day—I'll not only let you off, but I'll give you a job."

I was both weary and wary of this old man. "A job?"

"Painting. I've been searching for someone specializing in portraits. It's not a popular market, but there's profit to be made."

I had no idea what he was talking about. "And if it's not my lucky day?"

"Then you'll be spending the evening in jail. Well, what say you?"

It wasn't much of a choice, but I was intrigued. I took the paper.

Mama had raised me to read faces. I'd never considered it a talent before—this ability to memorize someone's features and commit their likeness to paper. After all, I forgot plenty of more important things: festival dates, street names, how many oranges Nomi asked me to buy at the market. But once I saw someone—really got a good look at them—I could easily recall their face, from the shape of their nostrils to the creases on their lips.

And so it was easy enough drawing the prefect; I even captured the mole on his nose, down to its three sprouting hairs. I had a soft spot for moles. They made faces look happier.

"Good enough?" I asked the old man.

As Gaari studied the sketch, his mouth slowly slid into a smile. "I told you we'd be friends," he said. "Now, do you like noodles?"

The next months changed my life. Gaari introduced me to his operation. He invested in me, gave me books to read and assignments to practice; he even sold my early reproductions. They only made a handful of jens, but it was enough to put food on the table.

I worked hard. Over and over, I copied the works of the greats, mimicking the pressure of their strokes, the precision of their lines, until Gaari deemed I was ready for the auction houses. I found that forging paintings stifled that mysterious tingle in my fingers. Only when my attention drifted, or when I painted solely from my imagination, did the magic overcome me again. Over time I came to learn that what came out of my brush was no coincidence.

They were glimpses of the future. *My* future.

"Let's pray that my future has eighteen thousand jens in it," I muttered.

I flipped to the end of my sketchbook, past a sketch I'd made last week of a man with long ears and a scholar's hat. He was leaning forward, captured midstride, his eyes intent on whatever or whoever was before him.

Tangyor, it turned out. Gaari's associate.

I'd been worried about that one. Thank Amana he ended up being harmless.

The last drawing in my book was the only one that hadn't yet come true. A vision that had baffled me for days but now gave me a grain of hope.

It was of a ring on someone's hand. Even on paper, the center stone was effulgent, glittering brightly while bordered by nine dark pearls. It looked expensive. Potentially twenty-thousand-jens'-worth expensive.

I tipped my sketch to the light and studied it. There was a smudge on the jewel, but I didn't think much of it. What was more important was finding out when the ring would come into my possession. In the background, I'd drawn larches, but those were planted all over Gangsun. And the hand? It wasn't mine or one of my sisters'.

"Do I steal it from someone?" I wondered aloud. "Or is it payment for a painting?"

It was silly to ask. The vision couldn't talk back, and the throbbing weight of prescience in my hand answered no questions. I'd tried before. Tried asking for cheats to help Mama win at tiles, tried asking how I might make enough money to get my family out of Gangsun.

Tried asking where Baba was.

Swallowing hard, I set the sketch aside. I'd find out soon enough about this ring. I knew little about my visions except that they always came true.

Right now a new one was on its way. The nerves in my fingers were electric, buzzing stronger than ever before. The feeling had tortured me for days, but I'd held it back so I could finish the Lei Wing piece. Clearly that'd been a mistake. That dragon I'd painted in the river had almost cost me everything.

Or perhaps it was the key.

That dragon had a spark, Saigas, Gaari had said. *A spark of something special. Where did it come from?*

I dipped the tip of my brush in ink, then hovered it over the scroll.

All it took was letting go.

When I forged paintings, I focused so intently I counted my every stroke. To summon a vision, it was the opposite. My eyes half closed, pupils rolling back. I'd enter a dance, the music a song only I could hear. In swift, bold strokes, my brush birthed mist, clouds, and sea. The waves came howling, the clouds low and thick. Everything about them was unnatural, but my fingers were far from done. They leapt to the center of the scroll.

There, a curious shape emerged.

He arrived in a series of lines and strokes, his form falling from my fingers with such ease it was as if I'd painted him a thousand times. His scales unfolded from the tip of my thinnest brush, each endowed with the detail of a crane's feathers, with every crypt and furrow in place. His horns mirrored the curve of the tiled eaves outside my window, and his claws pierced out of the sea's tumultuous waves, each nail arched like a sickle moon.

I opened my box of paints and fluttered my fingers over the colors. I rarely painted with color. It was expensive, hard to mix and set properly. Besides, I'd learned over years how to be expressive enough with black, white, and the immeasurable worlds of gray in between.

But this dragon demanded more, so I reached for my pot of azurite and bestowed a hint of pale blue upon his silvery scales. His horns I imbued with the color of old gold, and the nails on his claws I shaped after shards of onyx. I hesitated at his eyes.

Only one was visible in the painting. Traditionally, an artist would keep it pupil-less—lest the dragon acquire a spirit and come to life—but the tingle in my hands wouldn't permit me to leave the eye blank.

Squeezing out the excess water from my brush, I wavered among my paints. Should the eye be black, like twilight during an eclipse? Or should it dazzle with brilliance, like an osmanthus flower in bloom? Both answers seemed right, though I couldn't explain why.

Without another thought, I dabbed into my yellowest paint and dotted the eye. It was a knife of sunlight piercing out from a storm. It glowed.

That was when my trance ended. It was like being pulled out of a dream, and I dropped my brush, trembling. My temples throbbed as the world turned clear once again and the tingle left my fingers. Then, sucking in a lungful of air, I tilted a candle to the parchment and viewed what I had done.

"Hello, dragon," I whispered.

I stared. I'd never painted anything like this before.

In the past, my visions had manifested as simple drawings, clearly the works of an amateur. But tonight, I'd painted what some masters would never achieve in a lifetime.

I blew at the ink, and I could have sworn his whiskers

flickered. This dragon was a thousand tiny brushstrokes, the scales so delicate and fine they shimmered, even though I'd only used coarse liquid ink.

He looked different from any other dragon I'd seen. His full form was obscured by turbulent waves, and his gaze was to the moon, so I could only see his profile, but that was enough. I'd never seen anguish on a dragon's brow before.

I moved him closer to the window to let the ink dry. The beginnings of dawn seeped over the horizon, and outside my door I could hear Mama snoring and Nomi mumbling in her sleep.

Usually I asked Nomi to help me write the inscriptions for my paintings, but tonight I already had one in mind. In the corner of the scroll, I wrote:

> *Should you chance upon a dragon, be on your guard.*
> *Keep your distance, and his luck will be with you for*
>   *ninety-nine years,*
> *But venture too close, and he will whisk you away into*
>   *his watery kingdom,*
> *Where all your fortunes will be his.*

Cramps shot up my wrist, but the tingle in my fingers was gone. Finally my hands were at peace.

What had I painted? There were no dragons in A'landi anymore. How was this a vision of the future? How would this help me save Falina?

I blew out the last of my candles. Like it or not, I would soon find out.

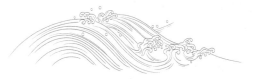

CHAPTER SIX

The next morning, I found Gaari at Luk's taking breakfast, slurping noodles so long he'd choke if he didn't bite into them. Shimmering globs of oil skimmed the soup, bobbing like dragon eyes. I blinked the sight away, trying to hide my desperation as I settled onto the stool across from him.

"Straight to the noodles," I said by way of greeting. "I didn't even know that this place opened so early."

Gaari looked up. "How did you know I'd be here?"

"I can see the future."

He laughed, as he always did when I said that.

"Tangyor let me up the stairs," I confessed. "I hounded him first thing in the morning for your address, and he said you were here. Must be my lucky day." I poured myself a cup of tea. "How are the noodles?"

"Springy. You want some?"

Tempting, but I'd already eaten, wolfing down an entire chicken and three pears first thing when I'd awoken.

"I'm not here to eat," I replied. "I'm here on business."

"Business?" Gaari said with his mouth full. He picked a

tiny round of onion off his beard. "Shouldn't the haul from yesterday have tided you over?"

It should have, I thought bitterly. "My mother has debts to pay."

"Still gambling, I see."

"One of the four vices," I quipped. "Thinking she can see the future runs in the family."

Gaari's cheek twitched. He wasn't in his usually snappy mood. "What do you have to sell?"

Ever so carefully, I lifted the scroll from my knapsack. The ink was barely dry; Nomi and Fal had spent almost an hour fanning it this morning while I'd obsessed over the last details. I held the scroll up, tugging at the ribbon bit by bit. I'd watched plenty of art auctions. I knew how important it was to tantalize the buyer. To pique his interest.

"I've heard that the emperor's birthday is coming up," I started, "and that all the lords in the Fengming Hills are vying to outdo each other with their gifts. I might have something that can help one of them."

Gaari raised a white eyebrow. "What is it?"

I waited an extra beat for showmanship. Then, dropping my voice to a whisper, I spoke, "A dragon."

"A dragon." Gaari puffed up with surprise. "Why, Saigas. You actually listened to me."

"Only for the money. How much can you get?"

"I'll need to see it first."

I held the scroll back. "I need this sold today. It's urgent. Tell me you have the time, the means, the contacts. Otherwise, I'll have to find someone else."

Gaari's brow furrowed. "What's the matter? Who is threatening you?"

I shook my head. "Third rule."

"Blast the third rule. If you're in trouble, then—" He drew a deep breath. "Give me a few hours. I can get help."

How much help? I wanted to ask, touched by the offer. Over the years, Gaari had proved to be as much a friend as a business associate. But I held back. Madam Yargui was the city's most feared crime lord. Her men slit throats for sport, while Gaari . . . Gaari's hired hands were actors. Better at rolling noodles than throwing punches.

"Can you sell today or not?" I said.

Gaari looked pensive. "It's the Ghost Festival. Might be hard to find a buyer while everyone's at the temples praying to the dead."

My shoulders fell as I started to rise. "Then I'll have to try someone else—"

"Sit," said Gaari, pulling me back into the chair. "How much money do you need?"

"Eighteen thousand. By sundown."

Gaari gave a low whistle. He set aside his noodles. "That is a considerable ask indeed. Some would say impossible." He stroked his beard. "But . . ."

"But?"

"But I have an idea." Gaari's voice dropped, and he leaned forward. "There's a young lord who comes and goes from Gangsun. You've heard of the Demon Prince?"

"No." Unlike Gaari, who hobnobbed with everyone he saw, I had no patience for gossip.

"He occupies the fourth mansion on Oyang Street, right next to Governor Renhai, but he's a recluse. Richer than a king with the manners of a beast. Anyone who so much as steps into the shadow of his property either lands in jail or goes missing. I hear he put two magistrates in his dungeon for trying to pay him a visit."

"What a ridiculous title," I said. "Why do they call him the Demon Prince?"

"Because everywhere he goes, he wears a demon mask."

"A demon mask?" Now, that was interesting. "What for?"

"Because he's ugly." Gaari laughed. "Well, that's my theory. Some say he's a monster. Or an actual demon."

"He can look like a goose for all I care, so long as he's rich. Could I sell the painting to him?"

"Not to him, but to Renhai."

"The governor?"

Gaari gave a sly nod. "Renhai despises him for snubbing an invitation to his daughter's wedding," he confided. "If he learns that the Demon Prince is interested in your work, he *may* just want to buy it."

"You mean he'd buy it out of spite."

"One of life's greatest motivations."

I bit down on my lip, considering. "I don't know. . . . We've always tried to stay away from government boars before. Are you sure you want to get close to the king pig?"

"Trust me, it'll work," said Gaari. "I'll go myself to make an introduction. I'll knock on every house on Oyang Street if I have to."

I thought about the ring with the nine pearls. Such a jewel *would* belong to someone who lived on Oyang Street. Especially someone like Renhai. "You can really do it?"

"Depends on your dragon."

"See for yourself." I set down the scroll and untied the ribbon. "It still needs a seal, but I trust that you can help me . . ."

My voice trailed off. Footsteps thumped up the stairs,

and in a moment of chilling prescience, the hairs prickled on the back of my neck.

"What's wrong?" asked Gaari.

Thump thump. Thump thump.

I squeezed my scroll into my knapsack. "Get out of here, Gaari. Go!"

No sooner did I speak than the beaded curtain swept open with a tinkle, revealing five men in white sashes. I recognized the one with sideburns and cursed.

"There she is!" he shouted. "Get the old man too."

"Nine Hells of Tamra," Gaari muttered. "This is your third rule?"

I didn't get to respond. Gaari grabbed my hand, and together we barreled toward the back stairs. The entire restaurant shook as we scrambled down. Madam Yargui's men were smashing the chairs and tables, and customers were screaming as they fled. It was pandemonium.

Just my luck, more of Yargui's men awaited me downstairs.

"Go!" Gaari hissed as the men advanced. "There's an exit in the kitchen. Take it."

Tangyor had joined Gaari's side, along with two more waiters.

Any other time, I would've stayed to fight. But Fal needed me.

I ducked between the waiters and dashed into the kitchen. It was abandoned, pots still boiling and knives still out. As I scanned for the exit, I heard the chilling beats of a slow clap.

Dread unfolded in the pit of my stomach. It was Puhkan, Madam Yargui's second-in-command.

He was leaning against the only exit, wide green sleeves

neatly folded back, and not a hair out of place. Madam Yargui's gentle assassin, he was called. A more deceptive name had never been given.

"You've grown up, Truyan," he remarked. His tone was courteous, a mask for what I knew to be his true nature. "Remember me?"

How could I forget the man who'd torn my sisters and me from our home? I could still taste the persimmon I'd been eating when he'd smashed down our door in the middle of the day, how its sweetness had soured in my mouth when he'd grabbed Mama and held her at knifepoint, declaring that our house now belonged to Madam Yargui.

Yes, I remembered.

He was older now, his skin not quite as tight about his eyes. But his black hair was slicked into a familiar tail down his back, and I remembered the disk of jade swinging around his neck. He'd threatened to strangle Nomi with the cord if she didn't stop screaming.

"I thought I had until sundown," I said. Behind my back, I reached for a cleaver. I gripped it tightly. "Why are you here?"

"I hear you're an artist," Puhkan said, skimming by the question. "Imagine my surprise to learn you were doing honest work, Truyan. Apprenticing with a painter, perhaps even applying to a school. But wait. That's not the path you chose, is it?" He snickered. "Like mother, like daughter, it seems. Both cheats."

I shuddered. "What are you talking about?"

"I saw that lovely sister of yours—Falina, is it? She was trying to run away, against my mistress's explicit instructions. Madam is displeased with this breach."

Oh gods. "If you hurt her . . ."

"You aren't in the position to make threats. Your sister is unharmed, so long as you do as I say. Now, drop the knife."

I dropped the knife.

"That's a good girl." Puhkan kicked the cleaver away. We both knew he didn't need it to best me in a fight. He advanced toward me, his jade necklace swinging. "Madam Yargui asked me to send a message: The price for your sister's freedom has gone up. Now she requires fifty thousand jens."

I balked. "My sister's not worth fifty thousand jens."

"She is to you," Puhkan said cruelly, and the truth of it cut deep. No matter how much Fal and I fought, I'd scrounge a *million* jens to save her if I had to. "But since you say so, Madam Yargui will take both your sisters." He cocked his head. "I hear the little one likes to read."

If only I hadn't given up my cleaver, I would have taken a good swing at Puhkan's face. I bit down on my lip, so hard I tasted blood. "I'll need more time."

"She's in a generous mood," allowed Puhkan. "You have until midnight."

"Midnight?" I cried. "That's impossible!"

"Greater things have been done in less time," said Puhkan, dipping a wooden ladle into the vat of boiling soup next to me. He drank, then let out a breath. "What's the matter, Truyan? Don't think you can get the money?"

My mind was spinning. "Take *me* instead."

"You?" Puhkan threw his head back as he laughed. "No one will buy a girl with barbarian hair."

"That's not what I meant." I was desperate, and my pleas were spilling from my lips faster than I could think them through. "Take me into Madam Yargui's den. I can paint—"

"Paint what?" Puhkan sneered. "Portraits?"

"The future," I cried. "I can paint the future."

As soon as the words came out, I wished I could take them back. My visions were a secret that no one—not Mama, not my sisters, not even Gaari—knew. And I'd just shared it with my enemy.

Puhkan wasn't laughing anymore. He looked thoughtful, his dark eyes swirling with keen interest. "Tell me, Truyan, if you can see the future, why aren't you running?"

I didn't understand—until he opened the door.

Outside, mere steps away from the restaurant, was a force of prefects. At first I assumed they were here to arrest Puhkan, but the way he was gloating . . .

My stomach sank.

"It seems Mr. Jisan reported you to the authorities this morning, after a very helpful and very *anonymous* tip." Puhkan smiled, revealing a set of square white teeth. "You're welcome."

In my imagination, I sent knives and cleavers flying at his head. Reality, unfortunately, wasn't quite so promising.

I was cornered.

Still smiling, Puhkan kicked the door wide. In his loudest voice, he shouted to the prefects: "The girl's in here. In the kitchen."

Damn it. I stumbled back, my hands at the counter. Spoons, napkins, small bowls, uncooked noodles—nothing I could use. I reached farther back, until I grasped a glass jar. *There*.

The moment Puhkan turned his back to me, I leapt. Closing the space between us, I hooked my arm around his neck.

For good measure, I dipped my fingers into my jar of bright red chili oil and stabbed a generous glob into his eyes.

A howl erupted from his lungs, the most beautiful I'd ever heard in my life. That alone made it worth it—something I tried to keep in mind as Puhkan found a knife on the counter.

Nine Hells, I cursed. I scrambled away, narrowly missing a thrust to my ribs. If not for the chili blinding his eyes, it could have been a fatal blow. As he swung, screaming all sorts of foul names at me, I ran back into the restaurant.

"There she is!" Yargui's men shouted when they spotted my return.

Daggers flew in my direction, as did soupspoons and bowls. I ducked behind a table, joining a crowd of Luk's men.

If not for the knives and the screaming, it would have felt like a delirious food fight. Teacups, bowls, even jars of vinegar—I flung whatever I could find at Yargui's men, letting out a gleeful cheer whenever something shattered against their heads.

I was doing quite well for someone who didn't know how to fight—until a bold arm hooked me from behind by the waist.

It was a good thing I saw who it was before I smashed the remains of my chili jar into Gaari's face. Never had I been so glad to see my friend. For the first time since I'd known him, his robes were spattered with dirt, and what appeared to be dark blood.

The restaurant was in shambles, men crumpled in every corner under piles of wood. The floor was wet with soup and noodles.

As the prefects scrambled after me, I ran back up the stairs with Gaari. "You've still got your scroll," he rasped, sounding relieved. "I've sent a messenger to find you in the hills."

"Don't you see the prefects downstairs?" I exclaimed. "They're after me. I can't sell it to Renhai anymore."

"Do you need the money or not? Trust me."

There wasn't time to explain that I needed over double the original amount. "What about you?"

"Don't worry about me." Gaari's nostrils were flared, and his cheek twitched more violently than I'd ever seen it. But my focus was on his eye, ever bright and burning. "Go now, my friend, and—may you have the luck of the dragons."

That was all the warning I had as I reached the top of the stairs, where Tangyor—ever-helpful Tangyor—pushed me out the window.

CHAPTER SEVEN

I fell onto the roof, clay tiles digging into my back as I slid toward the ground. Too late I noticed the rip in my knapsack. Before I could catch it, my scroll tumbled out, rolling down the slope of the roof in the opposite direction.

Panic ratcheted in my chest. But thank Amana, my scroll caught against an eave. It lay ten paces from me, completely unraveled, edges flapping.

"Sons of the Wind," I cursed. Inch by inch, suddenly mindful of every breeze and draft, I crawled toward my dragon. Its inky eyes watched me, silently judging. I glared back. "You'd better be worth all this trouble. Now, don't move. Don't even think about it."

I was on my knees, not daring to even breathe as I stretched my arm out, reaching with my fingers before the parchment blew away. There! I pinched the corner. I nearly rocked back with relief. But as I raked my dragon toward me, a powerful gust of wind knocked me off balance—and carried my scroll into the sky.

"No!" I shouted as it flew away. "Damn it!"

And that was how the prefects found me.

"Truyan Saigas," they shouted from below. "You are hereby charged with the criminal offense of reproducing sacred imperial art. Come down at once."

I wasn't listening. My eyes were on the scroll. It had shot up high above the trees and was cruising over the festival like a kite. I had to get it back.

"Get down right now!" the head prefect cried. "Or else we shall use forc—"

He didn't get to finish his threat. I leapt down, tackling him to the ground and cutting him off midsentence. Before his colleagues could grab me, I shot up and ran.

The streets were packed, and I wove through the parades of people beating pots and hand-strung drums. I needed to get lost in the commotion. Needed to blend in.

I fumbled at my sash, quickly draped it over my blue hair. From one of the merchant tents, I lifted a fan and flicked it open, pressing it against my face.

At every corner, children were setting off firecrackers. "Thunderbolts of Saino," they chanted. "Protect us from evil!"

I whispered a quiet thanks to all the boisterous festivalgoers. Soon I couldn't even hear the prefects shouting for me. But I knew better than to get smug.

Don't look back, I told myself. *Keep moving.*

Nine Hells of Tamra, what godforsaken spirit had possessed my scroll?

At least it was making for the hills, the opposite direction as the prefects. I scrambled after it, almost getting run over by a carriage in my haste. Maybe there *was* such a thing as the luck of the dragons. At the last moment, I vaulted onto the back step of the carriage, clinging to the gilded ledge as it trundled up.

By now I'd lost my pursuers. Then again, what fool would ride straight toward the Fengming Hills, where the governor himself lived? Here, every house was walled off, each a private compound marked by towering willows, with patrols circling every corner.

Anyone would tell me I was doomed. But I happened to be an optimist.

The carriage trotted up the peak, only a turn away from Oyang Street. The winds were still here, and bless the Sages, my scroll was finally making its descent.

It wended down with the grace of a swan, skimming the tops of the willow trees toward one of the manors.

Fall in a tree, I prayed through clenched teeth. *Don't pass the walls.*

As though it heard me, the scroll landed on a thick bough with a gentle sigh.

Yes! I thought, hopping off the carriage onto the road.

I ran as fast as I could, my hair whisking my back as I cut toward the tree. I'd climbed the first branch when the spirits of misfortune decided to possess the scroll one last time. To my horror, it tumbled off the bough and dove past the wall. Straight onto the manor's property.

I wanted to scream. Honestly, this day couldn't get any worse.

I ducked under the leaves, darting a quick glance behind me—but the manor was quiet, not a guard in sight. Every Oyang property had patrols. So why, today, in the middle of the afternoon, was this one deserted?

Apprehension knotted in my gut. "Just hurry up, Tru," I mumbled to myself.

I climbed higher, advancing up the tree until I could see into the garden on the other side of the wall.

If someone had told me the grounds below belonged to the emperor himself, I would've believed it. The garden was resplendent, an oasis from Gangsun's jumble of sweat and spices. Each shrub was meticulously cared for without a single dry patch, the flowers—azaleas and magnolias and others I couldn't name—bloomed bright and healthy, and a cerulean pond was framed by sloping pathways and multiple arched footbridges.

Among all this natural beauty lay my scroll, nestled in a thorny bed of the ugliest roses I'd ever seen.

The only thing separating us was this damned wall. It wouldn't be a pretty fall, with all those prickly vines, but I didn't hesitate. *Fortune finds those who leap,* I thought, bracing myself. Then I jumped.

My elbows scraped against the wall, and sharp thorns grazed my ankles and back. But by some miracle, I landed on my feet.

I swept a leaf off my trousers and waded through a thicket of black roses poking at my skin. The flowers were like inkblots, dark and shapeless, their stems covered in big, fat thorns.

Thorns, it turned out, that had cut into my scroll.

I couldn't believe it. After everything—fighting off Puhkan, running across half of Gangsun, and eluding the prefects—my scroll was ripped, torn right through the center of my dragon. So much for selling it.

I plucked up my scroll and angrily snapped off an offending

flower. Now how was I going to get forty-eight thousand jens? How was I going to save Fal?

As soon as I looked up, I had my answer. Across the garden was a compound of blue-tiled houses overlooking yet another long and limpid pond. Sunlight gilded their curved roofs, and my desperate imagination pinioned precious rubies and emeralds onto the geometric lattices of each window. My morale was instantly boosted.

Get inside and steal something, I instructed myself. *Jewels, silks, gold, and jade. That ring with the nine pearls.*

The ring was in my future. Was I meant to steal it here—in this manor? *Yes,* I thought, as I wound my damaged scroll to a close. I picked up my feet and started treading out of the flower beds.

First I'd have to get out of this garden. The fastest way was across a gallery of winding footpaths, but obviously I couldn't take that. Thankfully, there was the pond. Framed by a forest of tall reeds, it led all the way to the main mansion.

I ducked into the reeds and made my move. Every now and then, I darted a glance at the wooden pavilion overlooking the water, but I saw no one inside. Still, I steered clear of it by keeping close to the banks. Halfway to the mansion, a turtle emerged by my side, skimming the surface of the pond.

At first I ignored it. Then, when it craned its neck out of the water to peer at me, I nearly fell back in astonishment. The creature was enormous—the sort that swam with whales and lived for centuries. And it didn't look pleased to see me.

"My turtle doesn't like trespassers," growled a thick voice from behind. "That makes two of us."

My heart lurched in my chest. I started to run, but a flash

of lacquered wood shot out from behind me, hooking me by the arm. I tottered along the edge of the pond, and for a fleeting second, I considered diving into the water.

"I would reconsider that escape plan if I were you," the stranger warned. "My turtle has orders to drown anyone she deems . . . unfriendly."

The cuff around my arm turned out to be the handle of a dark red umbrella. I wrenched at it, but the stranger's hold was firm.

"I won't warn you again."

"You must not get very many guests," I muttered.

"None," he confirmed. His shadow eclipsed me. "Turn around."

With a grimace, I obeyed. In my periphery, I glimpsed a figure shrouded entirely in black, from the hem of his cloak to his sleeves, obsidian threads so finely woven they glittered under the light of the sun. I raised my gaze—to a man in a demon mask.

Wonderful, absolutely wonderful. Of all the manors to infiltrate, I'd picked *this* one.

I found my voice. "Now, that is the most impressive-looking festival mask I've ever seen."

I could hear his bewildered exhale, equal parts disdain and disbelief. A tiny triumph, catching him off guard. But his distraction didn't last long.

He speared the end of his umbrella into the ground with such force that I jumped back.

"Why are you here?" he snarled. "Speak the truth, or it'll be the dust of your bones that nourishes this garden tonight. Starting with the roses you so dishonorably tried to steal."

"I wasn't stealing a rose," I countered. "I fell onto them."

"While trespassing."

"I wasn't trespassing. The spirits of the Ghost Festival possessed my scroll." I brandished it with a quick wave. "That's why it landed in your garden."

"The spirits of the Ghost Festival possessed your scroll," he repeated. He leaned on his umbrella with a sneer. "Does that explain why you were sneaking off into the mansion as well?"

My cheeks grew hot. "I was looking for the exit."

Even *I* didn't believe me.

"You trampled my rosebushes," he thundered. "You dragged your filthy shoes across my shrubs and befouled the air with your presence. If you think you can trespass onto my property, destroy my roses, and simply walk free"—he drew tall, blocking me from the path—"you are mistaken, krill."

"Krill?" I echoed.

"That's what you'll soon be, for stealing."

First fertilizer, now food for his turtle. This Demon Prince was delusional.

I shouldered past him, intent on leaving. A mistake.

He sprang in front of me and emitted a beastly roar that boomed across the garden. The earth shuddered, the pond went still. Any other day, I might have had the sense to feel afraid, but not today. Not today.

"If you're going to kill me," I said, "just do it already. I'm in a bit of a hurry."

His eyes pierced through the mask, startling me. How hadn't I noticed them? They were mismatched, unlike any I'd seen before. One as black as the rose in my hand—so liquid and dark I couldn't make out his pupil. The other yellow like the sulfur powder I'd ground to paint fire once.

The Demon Prince, he was called. But his eyes weren't those of a demon. Not quite human either.

"You really have a death wish, don't you?"

"No, I simply don't understand why you care so much about a single rose. You have so many. And, to settle the matter, it was your flower that tore into my painting." I raised my ruined scroll to view. "If anything, you should be paying *me*."

"I assure you, that flower is worth far more than anything you might possess."

"Are you out of your mind? It's a flower." I shook my scroll. "This is an original masterpiece."

"We shall see," he said. Too swiftly he plucked it from me, undoing the cord with ease. My dragon scroll came unbound, his tail winding to the ground.

"You say my flower tore into your scroll?" said the Demon Prince. "I see no disrepair."

"Then you must be . . ." The words died on my lips. He was right; the rip was no more. Vanished, as if it'd never been.

He lifted the painting so it was level with his gaze. Then, suddenly, his yellow eye glowed with vehemence. "From where did you steal this?"

"I didn't steal it." I stood on my toes, reaching for the edges of my parchment. "It's mine."

"Your life depends on the truth, krill." The Demon Prince held the scroll higher. "How did you come about this painting?"

"I drew it."

"*You* drew this."

Again that mixture of disdain and disbelief.

"With ink and a brush," I snapped. "Is that so hard to believe?"

His attention didn't waver from my painting. "Countless artists have tried to paint dragons in their lifetimes, but it is impossible to capture their spirit without having seen one."

"*No one's* seen a dragon."

"Then either you have a very powerful imagination, or you have Sight." He tipped his head down, studying me. "Perhaps both."

There was something unnerving about being stared at through a mask. It was his eyes, I decided. Bright and dark at once and utterly unfeeling. For the life of me, I couldn't place where I had seen them before.

"I will keep this," he said, rolling up the scroll. "And in return, I will permit you to leave this property."

The nerve of this man. I was tired, apparently smelly, and running out of hope. But for Fal's sake, I mustered some entrepreneurial spirit. "If you like it, I'd be willing to part with it. Say, for fifty thousand jens."

Was that a laugh I heard behind the mask? Or a rude snort? I couldn't tell.

"Don't press your luck, thief. Begone before I change my mind about letting you live."

I wouldn't budge. "Fifty thousand jens."

"The scratches on this page aren't worth fifty let alone fifty thousand."

"Then I'll paint you another one. As many as you want. Right now."

He leaned forward, smelling my desperation. "Pray tell, what does an urchin like *you* need with such an inordinate sum?"

I considered lying, but there was no point. "My mother owes a debt. I have to pay before midnight."

"Thus you thought to steal from me."

"Technically, I thought to steal from Governor Renhai."

He canted his head. "Then you'd have been caught, and short two hands by the morning. For naught, since Renhai has nothing worth stealing in his mansion."

"So I made the better choice coming here?"

"That remains to be seen."

I scowled, filled with loathing for this ogre of a man. What did he want me to do? Beg? My dignity could hardly stomach the thought. But for Fal and Nomi . . . I fell to my knees, bowing as low as I could. "My mother's debt is owed to Madam Yargui," I said. "If I can't pay, she will take my sisters. Please, if you have any jens to spare . . . it'll save my family."

I heard a sniff. "Your personal matters are of no concern to me."

He spun to leave.

"Wait!" I cried. "I'll do anything."

Too late, I regretted my big mouth. The Demon Prince halted in his step, his dark cloak billowing.

Up to this point, his every word had been a thorn in my side. But now, when he made no growl, no snarl or thunderous roar, it was his silence that was torture, an agonizing counterpoint to the unrest raging inside me.

At last he spoke, "Take this. It should be enough to pay off your mother's lenders."

He tossed a ring, the throw so crisp I caught it without realizing. I held it out on my palm, my knees buckling as I recognized what had come into my possession.

It was the ring from my vision, exactly as I'd drawn it:

nine black pearls in a circlet around a giant white opal. Even the smudge on the opal was there—a cloudy reddish spot in one corner. At first I thought it was from the light, but it didn't go away no matter how I angled the ring.

Strange, I thought. With a frown, I looked back at the garden.

Whenever a vision manifested into reality, an uncontrollable tremble came over me, making my teeth chatter. But in this moment, I felt nothing.

There were no larches here, I realized, and the hand I'd foreseen wearing the ring had been human. It couldn't be the Demon Prince's. So whose was it?

I tucked away my unease. "This is worth fifty thousand jens? You are sure?"

"There is only one like it in the world. I assure you, it will cover your debts."

His self-assurance annoyed me, but I didn't argue. I knew this ring was the key to saving Falina. I slipped it over my thumb, the only finger it fit.

A moon gate had appeared in the middle of the garden—leading to a carriage parked along the road. I could have sworn that neither had been there a moment ago.

"Shanizhun," the Demon Prince said, "escort our guest to the carriage and take her home. See to it she doesn't step on the moss."

Shanizhun? Who was he talking to? I saw no one else with us in the garden.

But my heels suddenly went up, for an invisible something—or *someone*—carried me not quite gently through the moon gate, into the carriage.

The door shut me inside.

For a moment, I was stunned. I was no stranger to magic, thanks to my visions, but I'd never seen anything like this: gates and carriages materializing out of thin air, invisible spirits flying me off my feet.

And the Demon Prince! He couldn't be human. With the mask he wore, his fixation with those strange black flowers, even his hair! During the course of our encounter, it had grown longer until it was past his shoulders. His posture, too, had changed. Earlier he had leaned heavily on his umbrella. Now he no longer seemed to need it.

While I wondered about all this, one of the shutters inside the carriage lifted. The Demon Prince stood outside, the wind still beating against his cloak.

"When my business in Gangsun is finished, I will call on you to fulfill your end of the bargain."

"What will I owe you?" I asked warily.

"That, we shall discuss next we meet." He gave an imperceptible nod. "Until then, Truyan Saigas."

The window shuttered once more, and the wheels started to turn. As I leaned my head back against the carriage's firm cushions, a chill coursed through my blood.

I never gave him my name.

It was nightfall when the carriage dropped me off a street away from home. Never had I run as fast as when I bolted out into the fish market, taking two stairs at a time past the washroom we shared with three other families, the kitchen that always smelled like burnt rice, then home.

Lantern light flickered from underneath our door. I wrapped my hand around the knob, my heart accelerating with every inch I pushed forward.

Inside, the room was dark. Shadows chased the walls, and I could barely make out Mama's huddled form, sitting on the bed.

I rushed to her. "Mama," I said softly.

"Tru!" she said, grabbing my hand once I appeared. She held it so tight it hurt. "Thank Amana, I was worried."

"Where are Fal and Nomi?"

"Here," replied Falina, coming out of the closet. Nomi was there too, hands clenched behind her back. I didn't like how my sisters glanced at each other, their faces pale.

Then I saw him. Seated at our wobbly kitchen table, eating peanuts and tossing the shells out the window into the alleyway.

Puhkan.

"You're early," he said. "I take it you're here to beg for more time?"

He wasn't alone. I marked two of his men standing in the corners, knives unsheathed.

My pulse doubled in my chest. I twisted the ring from my thumb and held it out. "Here."

At the sight, Puhkan stood. He'd expected me to return empty-handed. "Impressive," he said, admiring the ring. Even in the dark, it glittered. "Who'd you steal this from?"

I didn't owe him an explanation. "It's worth what Madam Yargui asked for. Fifty thousand jens. Now leave us alone."

Puhkan closed his fist over the ring. "I happen to have a present for you too."

He reached into his pocket and pinched forth a triangular piece of maroon-colored cloth. I didn't know what it was, but as he tossed it my way, I felt a wave of premonitory dread.

The cloth landed on my arm with a moist splat. It was damp, and its dye smeared the pale fabric of my sleeve.

No, not dye.

Blood.

"I believe it belonged to a friend of yours," said Puhkan. He dipped his head in mock sympathy. "My condolences."

All of me went cold. This cloth . . . was Gaari's eye patch! Bile surged up to my throat, and I choked on my own breath. "You . . . you—"

"Sank a knife into his back," Puhkan finished for me. "Threw him into the canal. A bunch of his friends too."

I wanted to murder this man. First for what he'd done to my mother, and now for killing my friend. Fal gripped my arm before I did something rash.

It hurt to speak. "Gaari had nothing to do with this."

"He was hardly innocent." Puhkan shrugged. "A petty criminal, unworthy of the space he took up. A good lesson to you Saigas girls to learn some respect."

My sisters gathered next to me, Nomi hiding behind Fal. "Get out," I said. "We're done."

Puhkan fitted the ring over his finger. "I don't think so."

His men lurched forward, and that was when I smelled the sulfur.

Nomi had shot up, and she hurled a string of burning red firecrackers over her head at Puhkan. "May Saino strike you down!" she shouted.

Smoke exploded, and the firecrackers popped and

thundered wildly across the room. "Go!" Fal cried. I grabbed Mama's hand, and the four of us raced outside.

We didn't get far.

Fal screamed first. Then Nomi.

A beat later, a sack fell over my head, and all went dark.

CHAPTER EIGHT

"Slowly," murmured a woman's voice. A blur of light gradually became my mother. "Slowly. Don't sit up so fast."

The back of my head ached, and my eyes were sticky with grime. I felt like I'd been unconscious for a week. "What happened?"

Fal stated the obvious: "Yargui took us."

I let out a groan as I sat up. The floor was cold, and ropes chafed at my wrists and ankles.

I blinked. "Did they hurt you?"

"We haven't been awake long enough for that," replied Nomi.

Ever practical, my youngest sister. Though now that I thought about it, I *had* smelled winksweed on those sacks over our heads. Probably enough to knock us out through the afternoon.

"Where are we?"

No one answered, and I wished I hadn't asked. Once my vision came back into focus, I knew exactly where we were.

Our old house.

It was falling apart, the wood on the walls stripped bare, the ceiling weeping dust. Still, as clear as yesterday, I could picture the way it had been. In my mind, I resurrected the wooden screen that my sisters and I had hidden behind while eavesdropping on Mama reading fortunes. The hall my sisters and I scampered down, chasing each other while wearing Baba's sailing clothes, tripping over his long sleeves and landing hard on the smooth walnut floor.

I shook away the memories.

Right now we were trapped in the kitchen. Insects skittered from unseen hollows, their activity making the shadows dance. All four of us huddled together. We hated roaches.

Nomi blew at her bangs. "I wish I'd poisoned them," she muttered, and it took me a moment to realize she was talking about Puhkan and his men. "Stupid firecrackers didn't do anything."

I inched closer to her. "It was brave of you," I said, "and very clever. Did you make them yourself?"

Nomi nodded. "They were supposed to explode more, not just give off smoke."

"Maybe it's good they didn't," I reasoned. "We were still in the room."

Nomi sighed. Her stomach growled loudly. "Do you think they'll feed us? Or will they just kill us?"

"Hush," hissed Mama. "I'm trying to pray." Her hands were locked together, and she looked up, silently imploring the gods to save us.

I gazed up too, but for a different reason. Looking down meant I'd see the bloodstains from Gaari's eye patch, still on my sleeve.

Heat pricked the corners of my eyes, tears on the verge of falling. *I'm sorry, my friend*, I thought. *When I make it out of here, I'll avenge you. I swear it.*

"Tru," Nomi whispered. "You all right?"

No, I wasn't all right. But this wasn't the time for me to mourn.

"Are there shards on the ground?" I asked, getting to business. I used my feet to shuffle through the debris. There were pieces of porcelain, dead roaches, and remains of other pests I wished I didn't have to look at.

"Don't bother," said Fal. "The big pieces have all been swept clean."

"So they have," came a familiar silky voice.

Puhkan joined us in the kitchen. "My men and I took pains to smoke out the rats; we wanted the house to be in proper order for your arrival." He sniffed. "I can still smell the fire, can you?"

Now that he said it, I *did*. Shadows leapt from a brazier behind us, flames crackling.

"It's just kindling for now," said Puhkan. "But if you start taking too long . . ." He tapped Nomi's nose with the end of a burnt matchstick. "Little alchemist, I, too, enjoy playing with fire."

"Don't you touch her," I hissed.

"Or what?" Puhkan laughed. "You should be proud of your daughters, Weina. The youngest has a scholar's mind; your second daughter, an exquisite beauty. And the oldest . . ."

He gave me a look I didn't like.

"What are we doing here?" said Mama. A spark of her old strength ticked in her jaw. "I know Madam Yargui to be a fair woman. My daughter paid—"

"Which is much appreciated," said Puhkan, fluttering his fingers to show off the ring. It shone spectacularly, but something else caught my eye. That cloudy red spot on the opal was back. And it was moving.

"Let us go," I said. "A deal is a deal."

"Don't look so cross, Truyan. Your stay here has nothing to do with the sparklers your sister set off last night. If anything, any other day, we might have even offered her a job. You too, for your thievery. But . . ."

"But what?"

"But you said something interesting at the noodle house," Puhkan said. "At first I thought it was the rambling of a foolish girl, but I haven't been able to forget it. Remind me again."

I bit down on my cheek. My big, stupid mouth.

"I said I could read fortunes," I lied stoutly. "Like my mother."

"No, no." Puhkan rubbed his eyes, still bloodshot from the chili. "You said, specifically, 'I can paint the future.'"

"I lied."

He clucked. Next I knew, his fist came flying at my face.

Nomi screamed as I flew back. I landed on my stomach, my chin scraping the rusted ground. Yet it was my cheek that stung most, the outline of the opal ring imprinted onto my skin. As I screwed up my face, I tasted the coat of blood on my teeth and spat, "Still upset about the peppers, I see."

"Oh, I've been seeing red all day. I don't expect it's about to stop." Puhkan picked up his knife and pressed the flat of his blade into my neck. He spoke into my ear, "Now, the truth."

"Leave her alone," pled Mama. "If you or Madam want your fortune told, you've only to ask. I still have Sight that—"

"Do you recall the game you played when you lost this house, Weina?" Puhkan interrupted.

Mama went rapidly pale.

"It was fortune's toss," he answered for her. " 'One more throw,' you said, before you gambled away your house. 'Fortune is with me still. I can see it.' " He leaned forward. "Your Sight has come back, I take it. How about another toss?" He dug the knife into the swell of my throat. "This time for your daughters' lives."

Mama was stricken. She shook her head vehemently. "No."

"How can you refuse? If you win, I will let all of you go. If you lose"—Puhkan inclined his chin, and his men grabbed both Nomi and Fal by the necks—"you can stay in your old house forever—as ghosts."

"Leave her alone," I rasped. "I'll play."

"You?" Puhkan pinched me by my chin.

"I'm the real fortune teller. What, are you afraid I'll win?"

He let out a low laugh. "Simple rules: I throw five tiles in the air. You paint which ones will land facing up. If you're right, your family can go. If not"—Puhkan drew a line across his throat—"that clever little sister of yours will get a bloody necklace."

My jaw throbbed with pain. *Damn it,* what was I doing? I couldn't control what I saw.

It was too late to back out. One of Puhkan's men set a piece of parchment on the ground, cut the ropes binding my wrists, and gave me a brush soaked in cinnabar ink.

Puhkan bounced a sack of tiles on his palm. The cloudy spot on his ring was still moving, but no one else seemed to notice. "Falina, you'll toss. Little alchemist will call out the tiles. That way all the sisters can be involved."

"Draw bamboo," Nomi urged me. "There are more bamboo tiles than any other in the game. Your odds are highest."

Nomi didn't believe I had Sight, and I wished she were right. A game of odds could be influenced. There were 164 tiles to choose from: flowers, the four directions of the wind, bamboo, and circles. Bamboo was indeed the sensible choice.

The problem was, I did have Sight. A faint tingle shivered down my fingers, pulling me toward the brush.

The parchment was wet, a layer of water glimmering as red ink from my brush dripped onto the page. While Puhkan taunted my sisters about our game, I stared at the opal ring on his finger.

It was clear now that the hand in my vision had been Puhkan's. And the trees? Outside the kitchen window, larches rustled, swaying like upright feathers. I'd grown up with them, hung lanterns on them at every festival. How could I have forgotten?

But that smudge on the opal was still a mystery. I tilted my head, squinting at it. Reddish light yawned from the jewel, its shape almost like . . . like a wing.

A *wing*.

Suddenly my teeth chattered, and a violent tremble coursed through my body, as it did whenever a vision at last came true. I clasped my shaking hands together so Puhkan wouldn't see.

"Are you ready, Truyan?" he was saying as his men cut Falina's wrists free and shoved the bag of tiles into her arms. "We're starting."

As the tremor passed, my eyes were already starting to roll back. I couldn't fight off the premonition that was about to seize me. This had happened before, always when I'd been in a desperate situation, my heart pounding in my ears the way it did now.

Holding my brush at a slant, I dragged it to the paper, and before Falina made her toss, I began to paint.

The ink was wetter than I liked, so I carefully made downward strokes to minimize smearing. Slowly the lines of a bird formed. Her neck was long and curved like a crescent moon, her wings majestic as a crane's. Peacock feathers extended off her grand tail, which nearly trailed off the page. Last, lifting my brush upright, I drew her eyes, a gleaming crimson.

A phoenix. If I were playing for odds, it was the worst choice, because there was only one. But I had a feeling.

"Magic paintbrush," I murmured as I came out of my trance.

At the words, puffs of steam hissed from the phoenix's outline. Her wings bubbled up from the damp parchment, her crimson eyes blinking alive.

If you want to live, she uttered in my mind, *stop gawking and get the ring back.*

I nearly dropped my brush. "What in the—" Icy mist clogged my throat, closing it off so I couldn't speak.

"Time's up," said Puhkan. "Alchemist, announce the tiles."

Nomi's voice trembled. She could see what I'd painted, and from her expression, I knew it didn't match the tiles Falina had thrown.

"Only one piece has landed face up," Nomi whispered, the color leaching from her face. She held up the tile. "Three bamboos."

"And what did your sister paint?" Puhkan leered, though he already knew the answer.

"Don't—" Falina cried, but the men pushed her to the side.

Puhkan stalked toward me, a dagger at hand. "A pity," he said. "Ghosts it is."

A shock of water burst out of my painting, throwing Puhkan against the wall before he swiped at my throat. Mama and Nomi rammed him from the side, and Fal dropped the nearest brazier onto his head.

Get the ring! the watery spirit shouted in my head. It sliced through the ropes binding my ankles. *Now!*

Shooting to my feet, I seized the ring from Puhkan's hand, slid it onto my thumb. Immediately, the opal in the center started glowing, iridescent colors swirling into a mist that soon flooded out.

"What's that?" Nomi cried.

"I don't know," I said, ushering my family out of the kitchen. "Let's get out of here."

A phoenix, made entirely of water, peeled off my tile painting. Her every feather rippled with the intensity of a cascading waterfall, and her wings were crystalline, each ridge like a shard of ice. Her red eyes blazed. *There's a carriage outside,* she rasped. *Get inside. You owe Elang'anmi a debt.*

With that, she flew over Puhkan's men, swiping at them with her enormous talons.

"It's a spirit," the men gasped.

"Petty sorcery," snarled Puhkan. "Cut it down. Burn it."

His men kicked over the brazier and charged at the bird, slashing through her feathers with their daggers. But no steel or iron could penetrate her, and she hissed at them.

"Run!" I shouted, grabbing Mama and my sisters.

We made for the window in the back of the kitchen, the

same one I'd stared out of when Baba left home for the last time. Countless times I had laid my head against the wooden sills, waiting for him to come home. Now I kicked through the milky paper panes and helped my family escape onto the road.

At the last minute, I glanced back at the phoenix. Puhkan and his men were waving torches at her. The fiery heat made her feathers melt and flicker, and the phoenix's red eyes darkened dangerously. Rushing forward, she spread her wings wide, flying through Puhkan and his men and dousing the torches until they were but wisps of smoke.

The air turned cold, and the men grew afraid. "Please, divine spirit. We mean you no harm."

The phoenix rose high above them, her magnificent wings still spread. A few of her feathers had melted from the fire, and in a dramatic display, she revived them one by one—only this time, each feather was icicle sharp at the tip.

The men tried to run, but the phoenix whipped her tail around them in a loop. Using her wing, she smothered Puhkan's face, digging into his temples with her feathers. His skin went translucent like the jade disk hanging over his chest.

I climbed out of the window right before he screamed.

As promised, a carriage was waiting on the road. I recognized its gilded wheels and the carved dragons along the roof. My family was already inside, and once I joined them, the horses took off, making for the hills.

Behind, our old house went up in flames. Puhkan's men fled through the door, yelling and shrieking. While Mama and my sisters stared, embracing each other in relief, my gaze went to the sky. I was looking for the phoenix, but she was gone. All that was left was a cloud of silvery mist floating toward the carriage.

It sneaked inside through the window slats and gathered over my hand. In a blink, it vanished, and I looked down at the opal ring, which had turned suddenly cold on my finger.

I swore I heard a laugh tinkling within its hollows.

CHAPTER NINE

"You've got a cut on your face," Mama said, her first words since we'd escaped. "On your cheek."

I touched the gash and looked at Mama tiredly. Of all the things I expected her to talk about—Puhkan capturing us and burning down our old house, the watery phoenix that had burst out of my ring to rescue us, this lavish carriage that was taking us who-knew-where—of course she'd fixate upon a scratch on my face.

"It'll heal," I said.

"Be more careful next time. Scars are not good for fortune. They're not pleasant to look at either. Don't smile until it heals, or it'll stretch out—"

"Mama!"

Mama pursed her lips, but she let it go. All this fuss was just to hide what was really on her mind. "Is it true?" she asked me then, very softly. "You can paint the future?"

The same question perched on my sisters' brows. They looked at me with identical expressions—parted lips, sucked-in cheeks, and oval-wide eyes. But I knew my sisters well enough to tell what they were thinking: Fal didn't believe me; Nomi wanted to.

"Sometimes," I answered.

I expected a slew of questions to follow, but Mama merely folded her hands over her lap. Without another word, she leaned back and closed her eyes, pretending to fall asleep.

That was when Nomi crept forward in her seat. "Did you see Puhkan's face at the end, all blank and empty? Like a dead fish. What do you think that bird demon did to him?"

Fal frowned. "What makes you think that was a demon?"

"Its eyes. They were red." Nomi snorted. "Nothing like a phoenix."

I was quiet, but my fingers instinctively brushed across the ring.

Nomi rested her chin on my shoulder. "All this time I thought you were a boring art forger. Turns out you can see the future, and you've been consorting with demons." My sister's eyes sparkled.

Fal clenched the edge of her cushion. "Enough, Nomi. Tru hasn't been consorting with demons." A hesitant pause. "Have you?"

Thank Saino for his timing. A gate rumbled open, loud as thunder, cutting off any reply.

We had wheeled into a courtyard, long enough that it stretched out of sight. Then the mansion sprawled into view: a two-story building with sloping, capped roofs; celadon-glazed windows; and sweeping magnolia trees at every door. In the center, a hooded figure was descending the stairs to meet us.

"Is that the Demon Prince?" Fal gasped. She spun to face

me. "Demon turds, Tru! What's he doing here—what are *we* doing here, at his house?"

Honestly, I didn't know. "I met him yesterday," I said. "He bought a painting. Said he'd call for me again."

"You made a deal with a demon?!"

"Stop panicking, he's not a demon," retorted Nomi. "Demons have red eyes. His are yellow, and"—she paused, squinting—"black, I think. He's a sorcerer."

I said nothing, but I was staring too. He looked different than yesterday. Taller, fuller—if that was the right word. His hair was knotted and secured by a tidy gold headdress. The umbrella was absent. Gone, too, were his obsidian robes, his cloak now a shell-white mantle that trailed long behind him, like a band of cloud.

Elang'anmi, the phoenix had called him. *'Anmi* was an honorific, which meant his name was Elang. A soft, musical name. It didn't fit him. He looked more like a Zhagar or a Yangonin—Balardan for "reaper of misfortune."

He was also wearing a different mask. A plain black one that concealed only the left side of his face, so I could make out the angles of an unyielding jaw, imperious cheekbones, and a stern mouth that I doubted had ever uttered a single kindness.

Mama must have had a different reading of his face, for she instantly perked. With a quick hop she disembarked the carriage, dusted her skirt, and tucked her hair behind her ears, beaming as he approached.

"You must be the lord of this estate," she said, smiling widely. "Our most gracious thanks, Your Highness, for coming to the rescue of my humble little family."

Mama yanked on Fal's and Nomi's arms, bringing them

down with her into a bow. She tugged on my arm too, but my muscles had fossilized into stone. I wouldn't budge.

"Thank you," my sisters spoke.

"Truyan!" Mama elbowed me. "Where are your manners—"

"You are welcome," Elang said, his voice skipping over Mama before I could respond. I expected him to growl and bark and yell the way he had when we'd first met, but he was acting vaguely courteous. Which only put me more on edge.

"It is late, and I gather that you and your daughters have been without a proper meal." He gestured at four turtles waiting beside the courtyard entrance. "Allow my servants to show you to supper in your lodgings."

Mama hardly blinked, as if turtle servants were perfectly ordinary. "Rooms?" she exclaimed. "You're offering us a place to stay?"

"For tonight," said Elang. "Rest now. Enjoy the hospitality that my estate has to offer."

The turtles came forward, one of them offering a bowl of what smelled like medicinal soup. Nomi sniffed it, then was starting to sip when I drew the bowl away from her.

"You shouldn't accept drinks from strangers," I said tightly.

"It is medicine," Elang spoke up. "And *we* aren't strangers."

I could feel his gaze on me, magnified by the burning weight of my mother and sisters' curiosity.

"You and your family have nothing to fear," he continued. "You are safer here than anywhere else."

Needing no further reassurance, Mama plopped down on a turtle. "You heard him, Truyan. Drink up and come along. It's been a day."

I stole a sidelong glance at my sisters. Fal, for all her earlier condemnations of the Demon Prince, was already making cooing sounds at one of his turtles, and Nomi was curiously studying how they waddled. I held in a sigh. My sisters were exhausted, hungry, and still coming out of the shock of our ordeal. I couldn't blame them for accepting Elang's hospitality.

As for myself? I curled my lip, refusing to give in. "You go on," I told my family. "Rest first. I want to speak with the *prince,* alone."

"Don't be long," Mama said sweetly. She steered her turtle to my side, still smiling while she hissed in my ear, "And don't be rude, Truyan. I know you. Whatever you have up your sleeve, don't spoil this opportunity. We have nowhere else to go."

Mama pulled away and waved brightly. "I'll see you later, dear daughter."

As my family proceeded into the manor, I turned to Elang.

"Who are you?" I demanded. "How did you know to have a carriage waiting where Puhkan had taken us?"

"Most people would simply be grateful for such help." Now that we were alone, Elang's tone had become frosty and clipped, every word on the cusp of a snarl. "You were nearly killed. Go on with your family."

I wasn't going anywhere until I had answers. "That ring you gave me," I insisted. "There was a spirit inside it. Why did it save us—what do you want from me?"

"If you want to know, then you will go without supper."

The way he said it, as if that were the ultimate punishment, both comforted and distressed me. To think, Mama thought *I* was the ill-mannered one.

"I want to know," I said.

"Then follow me." In a dark whirl, he pivoted out of the courtyard for the main mansion. He moved like a storm cloud, his walk so fast and fluid I couldn't tell one step from the next. I panted to keep up, certain he was trying to lose me with such a pace, though once we entered the house, he abruptly came to a halt midstride.

"If you insist on coming this way," he said, his back still to me, "it would be courteous of you to remove your shoes. They're leaving mud stains upon my floors."

I lowered my eyes to the rich rosewood floors, upon which I had indeed left tracks of mud. My attempt to wipe at them with my shoe earned me a vociferous grunt.

Fine.

With a grunt myself, I took off my shoes and carried them in my hand.

"Don't touch anything," Elang growled before pacing down the hall.

As if he'd heard me breathing hard, he slowed his pace so I could keep up. Anywhere else I might have been grateful. But here I sensed that every act of hospitality was being tallied into a debt that I'd soon owe.

Art slathered every wall, porcelain vases and brightly woven carpets animating the long and unlit corridors. Deeper into the house were tapestries of Mount Jansu—the island of the immortals—life-sized sculptures of the Great Sages, and painstakingly detailed scrolls of Amana's children: the sun, moon, and stars. Most were pieces I'd never seen before. Could they be originals? I wished I could linger to find out.

How long had the Demon Prince resided in Gangsun? It couldn't have been more than three or four years. With all this art, surely I would have heard his name among the city's prominent collectors. Then again, I'd always left the auctions to Gaari.

At the memory of Gaari, my steps grew heavy. He'd been more than my business partner; he'd been my mentor, my confidant, my friend. And because of me, he was dead. Biting my cheek to keep from crying, I looked away from the art and directed my gaze straight ahead.

Our destination was a small library that smelled of paper and dried ink. Two sculptures of whales framed the doorway, but my eyes jumped straight to the desk, which bore stacks of books—many of which were about painting. Beside a reading lamp was a pair of brass-rimmed spectacles and an open box filled with writing brushes.

So I was dealing with a learned monster. Nomi would say that was the most dangerous kind.

The air was warm, and a sweet and herbal smell came from a pot on a corner table. "Tea?" offered Elang. "It's chamomile, fresh from the Spice Road."

My imagination yanked me forward in time, past a sip of poisoned tea to Elang standing over my corpse, steeping my soul in a kettle before he drank.

"I'm not here to have tea with you."

"Suit yourself."

I sat, gravitating naturally to the green cushion across from his desk. I sank, muscles sighing as the silk soothed my bruised side. I hadn't realized how exhausted I was; I could have fallen asleep right then and there. If not for Elang.

Here in this house, surrounded by books and teacups, he seemed less a monster and more a man. But I knew better than to lower my guard.

"Who are you?" I demanded once again. "You consort with demons, you have turtles who do your bidding, and you wield . . . magic." I paused. "*What* are you?"

"Many would like to know, but few are privileged with the truth." He sipped. "You have the Sight. You tell me what I am."

I would have gritted my teeth if not for the pain in my jaw. He was really starting to get under my skin.

"You're not a demon," I said aloud.

"Because of my eyes?" He made a point of blinking. "Your sister knows her lore."

Of course he'd heard that. His ears were sharp, literally.

"Demons do not keep manors on the most expensive street in Gangsun," I said, "or parade about in masks, or idle themselves with corrupt government officials."

His eyes narrowed. "I don't idle myself with anyone."

"Renhai's your neighbor. You said there was nothing in his house worth stealing. That implies you've visited before."

Elang set down his teacup. "Humans give off a foul stench. His is one of the foulest."

Strong sense of smell, I added to my mental list. And what had he called me in his garden? *Krill.* Food for his turtle, no doubt, but a strange insult all the same.

"You aren't a demon," I said again. "You aren't a sorcerer either. Sorcerers are charming and . . . and don't go about extorting innocent painters."

"Innocent?" Elang made some noise that sounded like a snort.

"Nor are you a god or a spirit or a ghost. You're . . ."

I honestly didn't know.

He was waiting, those yellow-black eyes boring into mine. Why were they so familiar? Where had I seen them before?

"Scourge of Saino, take off the mask," I grumbled. "The festival is over. Are you as ugly as they say, or do you truly have something to hide?"

Half of his mouth smiled. "You had only to ask."

Ever so slowly, as if he knew every second tormented my curiosity, he lifted his mask.

I didn't mean to recoil, but I'd had no warning. His face was unlike anything I expected. It was two faces, really, as though a line were drawn straight down the center, dividing the two sides in half. One was human, with a smooth, tanned cheek and sculpted black brow; half a nose; and half a hard, square jaw. Features belonging to a man who'd clearly received an extra moment of the gods' attention.

Strikingly handsome, Fal would say. Even with the yellow eye. It was a shade I'd never encountered before: paler than amber, deeper than gold. The exact color seemed to change with every flicker of the light—making it impossible to pin down.

Then, as if the gods had decided to play a cruel and twisted joke, there was the not-so-handsome half.

Reptilian was the first word that came to my mind. From forehead to neck, argent-blue scales stippled his skin, each like a flat teardrop shining mirror sharp. And this other eye . . . it wasn't actually black but the darkest gray, larger and rounder than his human one, and wreathed by a feathery brow. He kept his mouth closed, for which I was glad. I didn't want to see his teeth.

What could he be? Both his hands, which he had kept balled at his sides, revealed sharp clawlike nails. And he had horns! Gold horns piercing up from his temples that I swore hadn't been there a minute ago.

The answer came in a scalding wave of revelation.

"You're . . . you're a dragon!" I whispered.

"Well done," he said, his voice equally soft. "I am Elangui Ta'ginan Yuwong, lord of the Westerly Seas, prince of the Third Supreme Kingdom."

So not a demon prince but a *dragon* prince. What in the Hells of Tamra was a dragon prince doing in the middle of Gangsun?

I gathered myself and raised my chin. "I am Truyan Saigas." I didn't have any titles, but I was self-conscious of how insignificant my introduction sounded, so I added, "Of West Gangsun, daughter of Arban and Weina. Master art forger of the Dor'lin District."

The "master" part was a bit of an exaggeration, but I didn't care.

"I know who you are," he said.

"And I know you," I said, lifting my chin to meet his mismatched eyes. Now I knew why I'd found them familiar. "You're the dragon I painted."

"Half dragon," Elangui corrected. His voice was tight. He was watching my reaction—for what, I couldn't fathom. "Your powers of observation serve you well."

"That's how you knew I have . . . visions," I went on, "and why you wanted the scroll."

He tilted his head, as if it entertained him to watch me flail for answers.

"And," I realized, "it's why you had your demon save me from Madam Yargui's men."

"Corpses can't pay off their debts," Elang said dryly. "And

speaking of debts, I have decided how you'll repay mine. With a painting."

I could have jumped up and danced with relief. In my desperation, I'd offered *anything*, and all he wanted was a painting? Praise Amana.

"A promise is a promise," I allowed. "You provide the brushes and the paper, and I'll paint the most magnificent piece you've ever seen. Might take a while, but it seems you've got plenty of extra apartments in your estate—"

"The painting I require cannot be done in Gangsun. Or in A'landi, for that matter."

I looked up, confused. "Then where?"

A corner of Elang's mouth ticked upward, minimally. "Ai'long."

I made a loud gasping sound. "Ai'long!"

"You are familiar with it?"

Of course I was. Every child on the continent grew up on tales about the dragon realm. Me more than most, thanks to Baba. He'd had a trove of sailors' stories. He'd told me a touch of a dragon's scales could heal any ailment, their voices were thunder incarnate, and their home, Ai'long, was a realm of merfolk and talking fish, so beautiful that no mortal could visit without being changed forever.

"I have a proposition for you," said Elang.

From the moment I'd entered this room, the conversation had veered in directions I'd never imagined possible. I had a feeling things were only about to get more interesting. "I'm listening."

"As you may know," he said, "the enchanted waters of Ai'long are ruled by the God of the Seas."

"The Dragon King," I murmured.

"King Nazayun is my grandfather. I displeased him, and consequently, I am prohibited from returning."

"You mean you've been banished." I leaned forward with interest. "Are you a criminal there?"

He glared. "During my absence, my domain has fallen into disrepair. I must return as soon as possible. But to do so, I need the assistance of a human."

"Me," I said. That much was obvious. "The answer is no. I promised you a painting, not a reunion with your grandfather."

He gave me an incredulous look. "Is that what you think I want?"

Then he laughed—a deep and rumbling sound that made the walls judder. I crossed my arms. "What's so funny?"

"You really do have quite the imagination," he said. With one last chuckle, his humor drained away, and the half dragon turned solemn once more. "I haven't finished yet. You are a wanted criminal, are you not? Sought after for art forgery, theft, violence—"

"*I* was attacked," I protested. "I'm not a violent person."

"Perhaps, but the moment you leave my property, you will be pursued, caught, and put in jail for the remainder of your life."

"That seems rather harsh," I griped. "I think the sentence for art forgery is really only a decade."

"Most prisoners don't survive the full term of their sentence," Elang reminded me. "Madam Yargui will certainly see to it that you do not."

He was right. And in that instant, the rest of my protest died on my lips.

"I have the means to ensure your safety," he said, "and

your family's. In exchange, I ask that you help me break my exile so I may return to Ai'long."

I looked up at him. Those strange eyes of his—one light, one dark—were unexpectedly intense, but I didn't trust them. *Never make a deal with a dragon*, the old tales said. *They are cunning, mercurial creatures. You will never win.*

But what about a deal with a half dragon?

I finally reached for my tea. It was still hot. *Impossible.*

"Explain to me how a human would help you return home," I said carefully. "I know your lore. No mortals are permitted in the dragon realm unless they are specifically invited by the Dragon King himself."

"Or unless they are wed to a dragon."

I swore I had hallucinated his reply. "What did you say?"

Not a muscle in Elang's jaw twitched. He was calm, too calm. "It so happens that the Dragon King's stipulation for my return is that I fall in love with a human—and bring my bride with me to Ai'long."

His gaze fell on me. "That will be you, Tru Saigas."

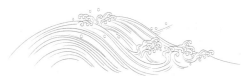

CHAPTER TEN

"Me?" I spluttered, almost springing out of my chair. "Are you out of your mind? I don't even know you. How can you be in love with—"

"Don't be dense, krill." Elang looked cross. A red flush dusted his human cheek. "Don't imagine I would *choose* to take someone like you as a bride. It would be for appearances only. Until our business is complete."

Business? Yesterday he wanted to kill me, today he wanted to marry me. I was starting to think that the mishmash of bloods going up to his head had warped his senses.

"I'm not going anywhere with you," I said. "I know the stories. Dragons disguising themselves as humans and seducing innocent men and women, luring them from their homes, then turning them into concubines and never letting them leave Ai'long."

"Where *do* you get your stories?" Elang balked. "First, you'd be my equal, my wife—not a concubine. And second, it'd be temporary." He muttered something incomprehensible before expelling an exasperated breath. "It is an elegant solution. One that permits me to return to Ai'long and allows you to accompany me."

The man had gall. "What makes you think I'd *want* to accompany you?"

"You are entitled to refuse," he replied. "Only understand that, in that case, you and your family will leave my property in the morning. The governor's prefects will arrest you, and Madam Yargui will take your mother and sisters away."

"That's blackmail."

"Call it what you will." He poured himself more tea. "Your troubles outside this estate are not my concern. For me to be involved, it is more than fair that I should have a price."

"You call an arranged marriage a price?"

"As I said, it'd be temporary."

"*How* temporary?"

"That depends on how quickly you can deliver my painting," said Elang, sipping calmly. "Once it is finished, there will be no need for further deception. You will be free to resume your lawless activities in peace."

I glared. "What about my mother, my sisters?"

"Your family will not be joining," he replied. "It is difficult enough to contrive a way for you to come."

"I won't leave them."

"You will, if you wish them to live," said Elang. "Ai'long's protocols are strict, and my grandfather and I are not on cordial terms." He reclined into his chair. "But do as you like—they are your family, not mine. I care not what happens to them, and I did promise you'd be my equal."

Insufferable dragon. I downed my tea in one gulp and hated that it really was quite comforting. I almost forgot about my swollen cheek and the pain in my jaw. "Where will they go, then? Madam Yargui will be looking for them."

"While you are in Ai'long, your mother and sisters will reside here on my estate. You have my word that they will be protected and want for nothing."

I noticed his pause. "But?"

"They will not be permitted to leave or receive visitors, for their own safety. Until you have kept your end of the bargain." Elang preempted my objections by lifting a small wooden chest onto his desk. "Should you succeed, your family may have this as payment for their troubles."

Inside the chest shone a mound of sparkling jewels. Rubies, emeralds, diamonds—some as large as chestnuts—an emperor's bounty! Not to mention, they sat atop a generous bed of plump and lustrous pearls.

I hated that I was tempted. Just a handful of these jewels would be enough for Mama and my sisters to live comfortably for years. No more scrambling to find work, no more worrying about having enough coin to buy Nomi medicine in the winter. We could finally leave Gangsun and find out what happened to Baba.

"Say I come with you to Ai'long," I began. "What would I need to do? What are the parameters of this . . . arrangement?"

"You would need to convince my grandfather that our marriage is genuine."

"You mean, make him think we're in love?" I had to restrain myself from cackling. "I'm not that good an actress."

"Dragons measure love in many ways. Some fondness for me will suffice." Elang inclined his head, an eyebrow ticking upward. "That is, unless you prefer to—"

"No!" I didn't even want to hear what he had to say. Just imagining having to embrace this monster, to *kiss* him . . . I shook away the thought. "Fondness is fine."

"Agreed." He sipped again. "Now, once my grandfather is convinced, then we may progress to the next part of our deal."

"The part where you need me to paint the future," I remembered. "Let me guess, a cousin has been trying to take your throne, and you want me to reveal who. Or maybe you—"

"Your imagination is most amusing," Elang said, not sounding amused at all. "But spare yourself from guessing. You won't have it right."

Insufferable and arrogant *dragon,* I adjusted in my head. "What do you need me to paint?"

"If I tell you now, you will have to accept our deal." His yellow eye glowed. "Or I will have to kill you."

Normally I'd roll my eyes at such an ultimatum. The problem was, I believed him. "I can keep a secret."

"Not this one."

"You don't trust me?"

He gave me a look that said, *Obviously not.* "I suggest that you be patient and take the evening to read over the contract with your family. We will revisit this discussion."

"What you're saying," I concluded, "is that my mission will be dangerous."

"Everything about Ai'long is dangerous."

I closed the chest of jewels. "Then this isn't enough."

Years of dealing with Gaari had taught me to negotiate. I wasn't settling for this deal.

"I want *three* chests of jewels," I asserted, "which my family will keep *regardless* of whether I succeed. I want tutors for my sisters while I'm away—for whatever they wish to study. I want Nomi to have an education rivaling the National Academy's, and I want Fal to have the wardrobe she's always dreamed of: silk dresses and slippers and jade hairpins. Everything a lady might wear."

Elang leaned back, his expression inscrutable. "Is that all?"

"No." I leaned forward, picking the prince's dark eye to focus on. "There's one more thing. I had a friend in Gangsun—an old man." The muscles in my throat strained. "He died yesterday, defending me from Yargui's men."

Elang was unmoved. "If he was old, then it was likely his time."

"He died because of me," I said sharply.

"What is your request?"

Heat swelled to my throat. I struggled to keep my voice steady. "His name was Gaari. I don't know his surname, or even where he lived. But will you find him, and will you see to it that he's buried and given a shrine?"

A shadow passed over Elang's face, and his nostrils flared. He probably thought me a sentimental fool, but I didn't care. "It will be done," he said. "Your requests, I will honor them."

"Do you need me to write it down for you? The restaurant, Gaari—"

"I'll remember."

Without another word, Elang opened a drawer to his left and presented me with a lacquered box. Inside was a book bound by a single red twine.

"This is a contract outlining the details of my proposal."

The paper was thick and fine, every word perfectly printed in minuscule calligraphy. I flipped through, startled to see my name on nearly every page. Impossible. How had he written this all in one day?

I pushed the contract back toward him. "I'll read it after you've included my additional terms."

"Everything you asked for is there."

"The lessons for my sisters, the—"

"It's there."

His tone dared me not to believe him.

Grudgingly I took the box. "Are we finished?"

Elang leaned forward in his chair, and goose bumps prickled my skin as he slowly pressed his mask back to his face. I could understand why he wore it. To the left, he was a dragon with glossy blue scales, a plumed white eyebrow, and a snout rather than a nose. To the right, he was a man with a boyishly smooth cheek, a sharp and implacable jaw, and an ever-furrowed brow softened by flyaway strands of black hair.

Either half would have been striking on its own. Beautiful, even. But together, the stark difference between the two made for a chilling effect. Especially with that yellow eye, burning like a ruthless torch.

I could hardly look at him without shuddering.

"For tonight, yes," he finally answered.

With the subtlest lift of his fingers, the doors opened. "My servant will attend you and answer any questions you may have." Elang rose, his claw outstretched in a gesture for me to leave. "I await your decision in the morning."

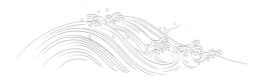

CHAPTER ELEVEN

Demon, spirit, fairy—whatever lived in my opal ring—did not like me. That much was clear as she guided me across Elang's courtyard, making me cut through brambles and plots of dirt instead of keeping to the illuminated paths.

I wondered if she had heard my entire conversation with Elang. Maybe she thought it as preposterous as I did. Or maybe it'd been her idea.

Hurry up, she hissed in my head when I dawdled to admire a view. Her mist folded around my bare ankles, icy cold stinging my bones. But I couldn't help taking my time. Elang's home was beautiful in the night. Lanterns hung from every tree and eave; against the blue-tiled roofs they were a sea of stars, mirroring the constellations above us.

I followed her into a wide house with red-painted doors. Milky-white paper paneled the windows, and under the light of the half-moon, each sheet shone like a pearl. Inside, Mama and my sisters were finishing up dinner. A feast, it appeared, from the empty bowls that cluttered the round table.

At the sight of me, Mama instantly rose. "What's the matter, Tru? What did His Highness say to you?"

The words I'd rehearsed fled my tongue. What could I say, that he was a half dragon who needed to marry me so I could accompany him into Ai'long?

"Where did all this food come from?" I asked instead, setting down the box that was under my arm. It'd been a day, as Mama liked to say, and gods, I was hungry.

"It's wonderful, isn't it?" Mama beamed. "All we have to do is put our hands together, and whatever we wish for appears on this cloth."

Fal demonstrated with a dramatic clap, and on the table materialized a tray packed with my favorite dishes: strips of cold bean curd in chili oil, red braised pork, steamed custard with chunks of salted egg, and a simmering bowl of glass noodles with prawns bobbing up and down in the broth.

I couldn't resist. I picked up two spoons at once and sampled everything I could.

Fal surveyed me with a cheeky smile. "I thought you'd be concerned about poison."

"An hour ago, maybe," I mumbled with a full mouth. "But now, if it's poison, at least it tastes good."

"It's *magic,*" said Nomi. "Like Baba's old games."

I gave her a tender look.

"What's this?" Mama had opened the lacquered box without asking. "The prince gave you a book?"

Before I could stop her, Nomi swooped it up and skimmed the pages. "It's a marriage contract," she said, brow furrowing. "To the Demon Prince?"

I wished I'd gotten one more bite of noodles into my mouth before this debacle began. I swallowed without chewing. "He's a dragon, not a—"

"An actual prince wants to marry my Tru!" Mama breathed. "And not just any prince, a *dragon* prince!"

"A half dragon, Mama," I said, unnerved by her interest. "Don't get excited, please. It's an arrangement: I help him return to Ai'long, and he'll give us money to pay off your debts and erase my record with Renhai. It would only be an act."

"Even so, this is what girls dream of!" She squeezed my shoulder. I hadn't seen her this animated in years. "Think, Tru! If you marry a dragon, they'll have to make you an immortal. You'll be like the gods themselves, invited to weddings in the high heavens, to luncheons with the flower fairies of Mount Jansu." Mama clapped. "What an opportunity for my daughter. My head is spinning just from the idea!"

My head was spinning. I'd thought Mama and my sisters might have a good laugh over the contract and convince me it was a terrible idea. Then we'd spend the night plotting how to evade Renhai's and Yargui's forces and take the first ship out of Gangsun tomorrow.

But no.

"The marriage would be temporary," I reminded Mama. "I'm not becoming an immortal."

"Then make him love you," she replied. "You're a beautiful girl, Truyan"—words she had never uttered since my hair turned blue—"and dragons are known to have their . . . temptations."

My cheeks flamed. "Mama!"

Mama's attention had already turned. She peered over Nomi's shoulder, her eyes moving like abacus beads as she scanned the contract's neat print. "You say you're helping him return to the dragon realm? There should be a reward for such a favor, and bridal gifts if he is the one who's pursuing your hand. . . ."

I stopped listening. My mother, who had always wanted her daughters to marry rich, was living her dream. She didn't care that there were gaping questions to be answered. That this Lord Elang was all but a stranger to me, and not even fully human!

"Where are the turtles?" I asked suddenly, looking about the chamber.

"Gone," replied Fal. "They left after they brought us here. Why?"

"You haven't seen any guards, any servants?" I pressed.

Fal and Nomi shook their heads.

"Then who taught you how to summon dinner?"

"That phoenix demon in your ring," supplied Nomi. "Shani."

I recognized the name from my first encounter with Elang in the garden. So *that* was Shanizhun.

I rubbed the opal with my thumb. "Shani!"

In a gush of wind and mist, two watery wings spun out of my ring and took upon the shape of a familiar, unsmiling phoenix. "There's no need to shout," she grumbled. "I can hear you."

Like a real bird, she hovered in the air, wings tucked to her sides. But unlike a real bird, she was made entirely of water and was transparent except for the edges of her form, which shimmered like ice.

"Elang said he'd send someone to answer my questions," I said. "I take that to be you?"

"All the other servants have been dismissed," replied Shani tartly. "And all the other servants happen to have guppy brains, so yes. That's me." She turned to Nomi, her feathers rippling as she spoke: "You ought to know, there's no such thing as a phoenix demon."

"But you're a phoenix," Nomi pointed out.

"I only look like one because it's what your sister asked for. I can be anything I want." To demonstrate, Shani took on Nomi's shape, except again, she was transparent—and her eyes were red.

"Are you a river spirit, then?" said Nomi, who enjoyed guessing games. "I've read they like sleeping in stones."

"A river spirit?" Shani huffed. "You were closer before. I sleep in the opal because it's brittle and cold. The perfect home for a water demon."

"A water demon," echoed Nomi. "I've never heard of that before."

"That's because I'm the only one," Shani said crisply. She shifted into a shapeless haze, her eyes stabbing out like two red thorns. "I don't have all night. What questions do you have about my lord?"

A dozen queries sprang on my tongue. I started with the first: "Elang gave me the ring knowing you were inside. What do you do for him?"

"What demons do best," Shani replied with a purr. "I brew chaos, I pry out secrets, and I spread sweet, sweet catastrophe." Then she sniffed, slinking back toward the wall. "And sometimes, when I'm forced to waste my talent, I look after hapless young humans such as yourself."

"He asked you to look after me?" I said. "I don't need a bodyguard."

"Says the girl who was nearly killed by ruffians this afternoon," replied Shani. "You're lucky Elang'anmi sent me to follow you. Otherwise you'd be a pile of ash and bone by now—and I'd have to find him another true love."

I knew sarcasm when I heard it. Unfortunately, Mama did not.

She leaned forward, eyes bright. "Is the dragon prince really in love with my daughter?"

"He hasn't complained about her stench the way he does with every other human," said Shani, flashing her icicle-sharp teeth in a smile. "I'd call that love."

"Why can't she just pretend to be married," said Fal, "and not actually go through the ceremony?"

"Because the Dragon King's patrols would sense that your sister was a trespasser," the demon replied. "They'd seize her and bring her to the palace, where she'd be executed in the most excruciating way possible."

Nomi couldn't hide her morbid fascination. "What do you mean, excruciating?"

With a whoosh, Shani adopted the form of a human boy. She looked keen to tell the story: "Years ago there was a trespasser who had a fear of frogs. When Nazayun found out, he cursed him so whenever he made a sound, a frog jumped out of his mouth." Shani demonstrated, spitting out a toad. "Eventually, a big one ripped out of his throat and broke him apart. Quite a messy death. One of my favorites."

She pivoted back to her shapeless haze and floated atop a divan. "What would be most excruciating for the tuna-haired thief, I do wonder. I'm sure the Dragon King will have something special planned for his favorite grandson's wife."

"You're not doing a very good job of selling your lord's proposal," I said thinly.

"Demons aren't merchants," replied Shani. "We don't

flatter and lie when there are more delicious ways to get what we want." She made a smacking sound. "My instruction was only to answer your questions, not win you over."

"How considerate," I muttered. "Then tell me this: Why does Elang need to take a bride in order to return home? Why must he fall in love?"

"Because he can't."

"Can't what?"

"Fall in love. He's cursed."

I frowned. "He never mentioned a curse."

"He doesn't like when I call it that." Shani let out a grainy laugh. "But that's what it is, his lack of a pearl."

"I thought every dragon had a pearl." Nomi's frown mirrored mine. "It's their heart, isn't it? Their source of magic and power—"

"And feeling," the demon interrupted. "Lord Elang's was taken from him when he was a child because his father, the late lord Ta'ginan, wed a human without the Dragon King's blessing. Until he reclaims his pearl, he cannot become a full dragon, nor command the respect he needs as a prince of Ai'long." Shani paused. "Nor can he have a heart. Unless . . ."

"Unless what?" Mama said anxiously.

"Unless, against all odds, he finds his Heavenly Match. The one who will break his curse." Shani bestowed me with a smirk. "A role he's asked your daughter to play."

"Of course she'll agree." Mama tsked. "It's a divine honor."

I ignored my mother's enthusiasm. "How does his curse get broken?"

"Only Elang'anmi knows the answer to that. And he can't tell you. He can't tell anyone."

"Of course he can't," Mama echoed.

How inconvenient, I thought as my brow knotted with revelation. Elang had only taken interest in me after finding out about my visions. Could it be, he hoped that my Sight would help him get his dragon pearl back, bypassing the need for a pesky true love?

"No matter," Mama was saying. "You've found the right girl. Tru is a master of deception!" She scooted closer to the demon, wearing a sly smile. "But it's no small undertaking, you know, asking her to jeopardize her life by going to Ai'long. She will be rewarded for her bravery, won't she?"

"Looks like Mama's on her favorite topic again," Fal murmured to Nomi and me.

Money, we all mouthed at the same time.

"Nomi!" Mama called. "I think we should revisit the contract. How about a clause regarding the valuation of the jewels?"

While poor Nomi went to work, I drew Fal to the dining table. "He's a tyrant," I grumbled. "An arrogant, callous, self-centered fiend with no regard for anyone but himself. Look at him, keeping us prisoners here!"

Fal knew me. She waited.

My shoulders sagged in defeat. "What do you think?" I asked her quietly. "Would *you* go?"

"Would I marry the dragon prince?" My sister sat beside me. "I used to think I'd marry any sort of prince, even a frog, so long as it was rich. But this is Ai'long. No one comes back from Ai'long." She bit down on her lip, trying to keep a brave face. "And if I lose you . . ."

"You won't."

"How do you know? That Lord Elang, everyone calls

him the Demon Prince. You can't trust him, he's a . . . a monster."

"He might be," I allowed, "but he did save us from Madam Yargui." I heaped a spoonful of steamed egg custard into my mouth. It was devilishly smooth and delicious to a fault. "And he has good taste in food."

Falina shook her head at me. "Always leading with your stomach." She gave me a wan smile as I ate. "Have you at least seen his face?"

I didn't know how to describe Elang's face. A dozen different words teetered on the tip of my tongue—*terrifying, handsome, cold, melancholy*. None of them felt right.

Lost, came my answer, but I didn't say it aloud. "It doesn't matter. I've made up my mind."

"Let me go in your stead," persisted Fal. "I'm sixteen, that's of age to be married." She picked up a knife and spun it between two fingers. "If he turns out to be a monster, I could stake him in the heart."

"I don't think a knife is enough to kill a dragon." I thought of Elang's iron-thick scales. "You heard Shani—he doesn't have a heart."

"Poison, then? Nomi could help."

I shook my head. Much as I appreciated Fal's offer, this was my problem to solve. Besides, it wasn't a wife Elang was after; he needed my visions.

"It has to be me," I said. "Me, in exchange for three chests of jewels and anything you and Nomi can wish for."

"Tru—"

"When I come back, we'll have enough money to build a new life anywhere we want to go. We'll get Mama out of Gangsun. We'll look for Baba."

It was rare that I brought up our old promise to find Baba, and Fal's shoulders went soft. "It isn't fair. You nearly died saving us from Yargui, and now this?"

I touched her cheek. "Don't worry too much. I can see the future, remember? I'll be fine."

"Still. I've got a bad feeling."

"What are you girls chattering about in that corner?" called Mama.

"We're talking about what bad business this all is," Fal responded promptly, exchanging a glare with Shani. "Tru can see the future. Why should she work alongside a disgraced and exiled prince? She could go to the Dragon King himself."

Shani's red eyes glowed with displeasure. "Go ahead. Round up the turtles and shout into the streets while you're at it. Tell everyone about her visions. Your big mouths will get your sister turned into sea foam."

"Calm down," I told the demon. "Fal was only joking."

"I hope so," said Shani. "Because I warn you, if any detail of our little proposal leaks . . ." She made a fearsome hiss. "Ask your friend Puhkan how he's faring. I promise he barely remembers his name."

At my sisters' stricken expressions, Shani cackled and spiraled back into the opal ring.

"No wonder everyone hates demons," I muttered, twisting the band off my finger. I sealed it inside the lacquered contract box. "At this rate, I might despise Shani more than Elang."

"There's no need for such vitriol," chided Mama. "The demon's only doing his bidding. And didn't you hear what she said about Puhkan? We ought to be grateful to her."

"Grateful?" Fal exclaimed. "Did you not hear her threats to kill us?"

"A good servant looks after their lord's safety."

"More like their best interests," my sister mumbled.

"Speaking of which," said Mama, turning to me, "I don't see what there is to dither about. Arranged marriages happen all the time; usually the bride and groom don't even see each other's faces! You're lucky, Truyan, dragons are known to be devastatingly handsome. You might even find you want to stay married—"

"Not a chance," I cut her off. "He's a monster, inside and out."

"He's a *prince*—who's generously offering you a fortune—in exchange for a brief trip to Ai'long."

I was too tired to argue with her. "I'm going to bed."

"You're not going to paint? A vision might help to—"

"Maybe in the morning," I interrupted again. The truth was, I didn't need to paint. I'd already made my decision. I'd known since the moment Elang had promised to keep my family safe.

I found my room and lay down on an unfamiliar bed. The silk was cold against my skin. I missed the smell of fish in the air and the windowsill at my feet where I could perch my ankles.

In the darkness, I let myself cry. At first in relief that my family and I were alive. We'd come so terrifyingly close to losing everything, but at least for now, we were safe. Gaari hadn't been so lucky. As I thought of him my emotions thickened into sorrow, and I whispered a prayer for my old friend.

It was a long time before the sleep spirits claimed me.

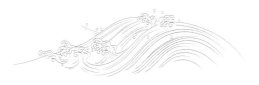

CHAPTER TWELVE

The next morning, I found Elang in the garden, tending to those hideous inkblot flowers.

He kept working even as I drew near, nicking off dead blooms with his bare hands and tossing them into the pond.

"What are they called?" I asked in lieu of a morning greeting.

The scales along Elang's ear raised like hackles, the only acknowledgment he made of my presence. He kept working. He was dressed in a swath of cloud-white silk, hardly appropriate gardening attire. Meanwhile, I wore the same ragged outfit as yesterday, swapping in a new tunic but only because the old one was stained with Gaari's blood.

I tossed my hair behind my shoulders as I straightened. "I've made my decision."

Finally I had Elang's attention. He wiped his hands—his *claws*—of dirt. "I'm listening."

His black mask was as jarring as ever. Paired with his cloud-white robes, he reminded me of Tamra, the god of death. Except for the clashing yellow and gray eyes, eternally at odds.

"A month," I said, getting straight to the point. "I won't be away from my family for longer."

"I wouldn't have asked for more," intoned Elang, "for that is the time I require as well. By happenstance, the end of the month coincides with the Resonant Tide in Ai'long."

"The Resonant Tide?"

"When the waters are darkest in my realm. It oft occurs when you humans are celebrating the end of a dragon year."

It was currently the middle of the dragon year. I clasped my hands together, ignoring the sudden pressure in my fingertips. "Wait. It's *six months* until the new year."

"Six months on land is equivalent to one month in Ai'long." He leaned ever so slightly forward. "That is what you asked for, is it not?"

It was then that I remembered the stories, that time flowed differently in Ai'long than in the mortal realm. "You tricked me!"

"That is what you asked for, and it is what I granted. In any case, a month in the mortal realm would be mere days in Ai'long. You couldn't possibly complete my task in time."

He was already starting to grate on me. How would I endure a whole month with this monster?

Three chests of jewels, Tru, I reminded myself. *Three chests of sparkling, chestnut-big jewels. My family will never have to worry about money again.*

"Fine, but there's one more thing," I said. "I want to know what the painting is."

At that, Elang's lips parted against the edge of his mask, and he rose to his full height. "Walk with me."

He didn't stride ahead this time, deliberately keeping

a pace that I could match. I followed him deeper into the garden, across the paved promenades and a grove of longan trees. The drooping clusters of brown berries were the only fruits I'd seen so far. Beyond, up a short ascent of stone steps, was a wooden pavilion. Its roofs were blue, like the pond and sky.

"What is this place?" I asked as we entered.

Rather than answer, Elang sat on one of the benches. The air inside the pavilion shone with crests of color, like the sides of a bubble, and a coat of silvery magic lined every beam and rafter. "Sit," he said. "You wanted to know about the painting, did you not?"

"That depends. Are you still going to kill me if I change my mind?"

Elang's yellow eye burned. "You won't change your mind."

"That's presumptuous."

"We'll see."

I ground my teeth. Now that I knew he was cursed, so much made sense. His hard-hearted arrogance toward everything and everyone around him. Even his mask.

I plopped myself down on the other end of Elang's bench. "I think I know what you want me to paint for you."

He lifted his chin expectantly.

"Your pearl," I revealed. "Without it, you're trapped between two worlds, never fully dragon nor human." I bit down on my lip. "I know a little of what that's like. But at least no one questions that I'm human."

He still said nothing.

"The pearl is your heart," I went on. "Getting it back is the only way you'll become a full dragon and find your place in Ai'long. There could be nothing you want more than to find it."

"So you heard about the curse," said Elang flatly.

"You need my help," I stated. "You should know, I can't control what I see in my visions. But I'm willing to try and help you find your pearl."

His gaze narrowed. "You offer this because you pity me."

I leaned back against the pavilion wall. "I wouldn't go that far. There's the three chests of jewels too. But you're not what I thought, Lord Elang. You may have no heart, but you aren't without feeling."

For the second time, he laughed.

"What's so funny?" I asked.

"I thank you for devoting so much thought to my . . . affliction," he said, finally taking off his mask. "But you are mistaken."

His eyes met mine, and I couldn't stop myself from recoiling. I'd seen his face before. The horns, the iron-thick scales, the ringed and hooded eye—all in stark disharmony with the human side. Yet here, under the brunt of daylight, the line splitting the two sides of his face was sharper. More visceral.

Seeing my reaction, he turned, fixing his gaze resolutely on the pond. "My pearl is what I want *others* to think you're here for. I know precisely where it is, and you need not concern yourself on the matter. Do you think I would involve a human like you, and *marry* you, simply for the sake of an irksome curse? No. Your mission is far more important than that."

I didn't understand. "What could be more important to you than breaking your curse?"

"The future of Ai'long," he replied. He lifted a claw to my face, and I held my breath as he traced his talon-sharp nails along my jawline, leaving only the narrowest strait of air between us. His voice fell lethally soft. "You see, Truyan Saigas, you are going to help me overthrow the Dragon King."

All at once, my world tilted, and everything came into staggering focus.

The Dragon King. The God of the Four Supreme Seas. The ruler of the sea dragons, who controlled the monsoons and storms that devastated A'landi's coasts.

I shot up to my feet. "Are you out of your mind? You want to overthrow the Dragon King?"

"Say it louder," Elang urged. "His spies are everywhere. Maybe even among those fruit flies hovering above the longans."

I tensed. Longans were called dragon eyes. But so what if the Dragon King heard me? "I didn't agree to murder," I whispered in a hiss. "I read through the contract three times. Nowhere did it mention killing—"

"Your conscience may rest easy," said Elang. "No one is going to die."

"But you just—"

"I said *overthrow*. Your imagination leapt to *assassinate*."

I put my hands on my hips. "That's how it's done in A'landi."

"Well, gods don't perish as easily as mortals do," Elang replied. "And you needn't whisper. My grandfather's power is weakened on land, and my estate is outside of his reach. He'll only hear you if you decide to bellow like a whale."

I scowled, certain Elang had enjoyed putting me on edge. "Why are you doing this?"

"A good question." Elang rose to my side, his arms locked behind his back. "In your stories, King Nazayun is rarely kind. Imagine that cruelty multiplied a hundredfold."

"You mean, you hold a grudge?"

"You have a gift for understatement, Truyan."

I sighed. "What exactly would my role be?"

"You'll need to study my grandfather's likeness. For a portrait."

My brows pinched. "A portrait requires a sitting, or at least a meeting. I'm guessing the Dragon King is not amenable to this."

"He is not. Under ideal circumstances, I would take you to his palace to meet him in person, but our situation is . . . delicate. Regardless, I'm sure he will come to you in some form or another. My grandfather despises me, and he'll be displeased that I've returned. But he'll also be curious about you. My wife."

My wife. Even the sun couldn't keep me from feeling cold.

"Why the look of distress?" Elang asked. "You've painted dragons before."

The scoundrel. He knew exactly why.

"It takes time to re-create someone's likeness," I replied. It wasn't a lie. "How am I supposed to study your grandfather if I can't even meet him?"

"You *will* meet him, eventually. That much is inevitable if you are to succeed at your task. Until then, I have engaged the most qualified aide to counsel you. And you'll have your Sight."

"I'm not understanding," I said. "What does a portrait have to do with vanquishing the God of the Seas? It's just a painting."

Elang turned to face me fully, his yellow eye netting the

light of the sun, turning almost gold. The sight unsettled me, but I didn't look away.

"It will be anything but *just* a painting," he said. "It must be precise, every hair in place, every muscle and ridge and scale. No detail can be missed."

My whole body tensed. Even without the specifics, I was starting to register the enormity of what Elang was orchestrating, and the consequences it might have for all involved.

"There are plenty of better painters in the world," I said. "Sorcerers, even. Ask one of them."

"I cannot. Any candidate with sorcery would raise my grandfather's suspicions. Whereas Sight, quite ironically, is imperceptible."

No one had ever looked at me so intently before. I flinched and averted my gaze. "Then you're out of luck," I said. "Do what you must to me. Have Shani erase my memory, lock me up in your dungeon. I don't care. But if I harm a god, there will be a price to pay—what good will jewels do my family if Nazayun smites us dead? At least Yargui and Renhai are human. My family can escape them. They won't be able to escape the Dragon King."

I turned on my heel and had gotten as far as the edge of the pavilion when Elang said, in his lowest voice:

"What if I told you that the Dragon King was responsible for sinking your father's ship?"

I staggered, the wind suddenly punched out of me. "What?"

"Your father," Elang said, "was last seen in Ai'long."

I went numb. That was impossible. No one had seen a dragon in centuries. Even if they had . . . Baba had been on a ship with a crew of forty men. I'd talked to the sailors who'd been with him, who'd seen him last. None had uttered a word about Ai'long. Truth be told, they hadn't said much of anything.

Five years of searching, and I'd found nothing. It seemed too lucky, too serendipitous that here Elang appeared, promising to have all the answers. Yet what if he was telling the truth—could Baba be in Ai'long?

Could he be alive?

"There are thousands of sailors who go missing at sea," I said, finally finding my voice. "How would you even know who my father is?"

Elang reached into his jacket and pulled out a folded piece of paper. It was wrinkled and yellowed by time, but I would have known it anywhere.

It was the drawing I'd given Baba before he'd left. On the last day I'd seen him alive.

My hands shook as I unfolded this relic of my past. Three girls, their parents, a dragon, and a flock of flying silk dresses. The lines were clumsy and the colors unblended and smudged, yet after all these years, the image was still dear to me. Still funny, too, though I couldn't bring myself to laugh.

I pressed it close, my chest aching from a wound that had never healed. *Baba.*

"One of my spies found it in the Dragon King's palace," Elang was saying. "I believe your father was a captive there."

I spun on him angrily. "This is how you knew I'd agree to help you. All this time, you were waiting to play *this*"—I waved the painting at him—"against me."

"Humans are predictable," he replied. "Yes, I knew you'd agree once you saw it. But it's not a game, Truyan. Nothing is being played."

"You're planning to play *me* against your grandfather,"

I said hotly. "I'm not a pawn, *Lord* Elang, and my past isn't something you can manipulate for leverage."

Not a flicker crossed Elang's face. He started to rise, completely unmoved by my outburst. "Shani will bring you a revised contract. This one, I advise you don't share with anyone."

I refused to let him have the last word. "You're despicable," I spat.

His shoulders tensed into a line. "Call me what you will. But you should know—I didn't want to tell you about your father unless I had to."

"Then why did you?"

"Because I know what it's like to want something impossible. How it keeps you up at night when everyone else is sleeping, and it ticks in your mind and haunts your every thought." His gaze met mine, and I wondered what a half dragon like him could possibly want. "You wish to know the truth about your father? You'll find it in Ai'long."

"When I meet the Dragon King," I finished for him, still fuming. "How convenient for you that our missions should align so neatly."

"The fates are not known for being kind. But they do have a sense of humor." Elang plucked the drawing out of my hand, and it vanished at his touch.

"Hey!" I cried.

"For safekeeping. It will be returned to you at the end of our arrangement."

He was maddening, but for all that I fantasized about smashing a lantern over his head, I couldn't deny the inkling of hope slithering into my heart. I grabbed his sleeve. "You said my art was found in Nazayun's palace. You really think my father is his prisoner?"

Elang eyed his sleeve, glaring until I dropped it. Then he replied, "It is likely that he was."

"*Was?*"

"I've inquired as to whether he's still alive. Thus far, I've found nothing. I can search more, if I am able to return to Ai'long."

Something about the raw look in his eyes told me he wasn't lying. Moreover, he needed me as much as I needed him.

Then I had no choice. My hands fell to my sides. "I'll need to know my family will be safe."

"Nothing will happen to your mother and sisters. You have my word as a dragon."

"As a dragon?" I echoed.

"Immortals are bound to their promises," he explained. "They cannot break them without suffering divine consequence. Something useful for you to know."

That did seem useful. I wet my lips, remembering a point that Mama had brought up yesterday. "*I'm* not going to become an immortal by marrying you . . . am I?"

"You'll only become an immortal if you take the Oath of Ai'long," Elang replied. "You'd have to swear fealty to the Dragon King, and I'd give you a piece of my pearl. That can't happen if I don't have a pearl."

That *was* a relief, though Mama would be disappointed. I had one last question, but I hesitated. "Will *I* be safe?" I asked. "You say your grandfather is cruel. I'm . . . I'm mortal."

"So you are." Elang loomed near. "My grandfather and I have an accord. He's sworn an oath not to harm my Heavenly

Match. As long as he believes you are the one to break my curse, he cannot have you killed."

I raised an eyebrow. "Why would he swear not to hurt me?"

"Dragons have some honor" was all Elang would say, rather tightly. "Even my grandfather."

That wasn't particularly reassuring. "What if he doesn't believe I'm the one?"

"You're a swindler, aren't you? *Make* him believe."

It was a struggle, holding back my glare. "I'll try."

"You will." His tone matched mine then, quiet and firm. "I've seen the lengths you'll go to, to protect your family. You should know, I would not have selected you if I didn't believe you up to the task."

Was he threatening me or offering a compliment? Whatever it was, his gaze was resolute, both eyes—light and dark—unwavering. He meant it.

"Then I have no more questions," I said. "I'll come with you."

An invisible string lifted Elang's chin. "I have your word?"

The way he said it, almost a whisper, made me look up. Had I heard the faintest trace of hope in his voice?

"Yes, you have my word . . . but only as a human."

A half laugh. "That's all I can ask for."

"Does this mean we're betrothed?"

"Almost, but now *I* have a question." He spoke slowly, "Is it Tru or Truyan?"

I blinked. "What?"

"Your sisters call you Tru, your mother calls you Truyan. Which is correct?"

It was the last thing I expected him to ask. "Call me Tru,"

I replied. "Just Tru. Truyan is what my mother calls me when she's putting on a show for strangers. Or when she's upset."

"Tru," Elang repeated. The wind lifted a lock of black hair over his eyes. "I'll remember."

"What do I call *you*?" I asked.

His lips twisted. He put his mask on again. "Just Elang. Not lord, not Elangui."

It was a start, knowing what to call each other. I wanted to laugh at the absurdity of it, but knew I'd end up laughing alone.

What have I gotten myself into? I thought as I saw the outline of a claw beneath his silken sleeve.

"Come with me to tell my family," I said. "My mother will never forgive me if she hears the news from someone else first."

CHAPTER THIRTEEN

"The dragon and phoenix approach!" Mama trilled loudly when she spied us emerging out of the garden.

I barely recognized her. It was as if she'd scoured the closet and handpicked every item vaguely associated with Ai'long. Golden fish ornaments gleamed in her hair, and round white pearls tinkled upon her wrists. For her robes, she'd chosen a brocade woven with emerald turtles; the final touch, embroidered on the bottom of her skirt, was a silver-stitched dragon.

Mama batted her fan against her chest as she took in the sight of Elang and me side by side, the rhythm of our strides reluctantly matching. She didn't bother with a greeting. "When is the wedding?"

"Tomorrow," I replied.

"Tomorrow!" Nomi exchanged a worried look with Fal. "That's so soon."

Mama was the only one who clapped. "How wonderful!" she exclaimed. "A daughter, betrothed. But one day isn't much time at all to prepare. I'll need to go to the Central Market, and the temple to pray—"

"My servants will take care of the preparations," said

Elang. "The wedding will be small, and private. There will be no guests from outside the household."

"No guests?" Mama's mouth twitched back and forth with displeasure. "This is my daughter's wedding. Surely I can invite a few friends. My neighbors, our local butcher, Mr. Tanpi and his wife—"

"They may come to the procession on Oyang Street," Elang replied, striving to stay polite. "But no one outside will attend the rites. There will be no banquet."

Mama knew when to pick her battles, and she let out a resigned sigh. "Very well, then. If you've made up your mind." She leaned forward, venturing so close to Elang I feared she would pinch his earlobes. "Family only."

"Indeed." Elang neatly stepped to the side. "Now, excuse me. I have my own preparations to make. My servants will return shortly and assist you in whatever manner you require."

"You aren't staying?" Mama asked.

"It's tradition for the groom to pick up the bride from her home," Fal added. "You will be coming to escort Tru, won't you, Lord Elang?"

His eyes flicked from me to my sister, then he replied, "Were she staying in her own home, I would consider the request. But this is my estate, and hence, I am unable to accommodate such a custom." He bowed, ignoring Falina's icy glower. "Until tomorrow."

Fal didn't wait until Elang was out of earshot. She seethed, "The nerve! Did you hear that, Tru?"

"I don't mind," I replied honestly. "It means I get more time with the three of you."

"The dragon's not wrong," said Mama. She hooked me by

the arm and tapped the mole by my mouth. "Forget about these silly games. It will be a happy marriage. I've read his face."

"Both sides?" I pried. "Or with the mask on?"

"He has thin ears, that Lord Elang," Mama went on, ignoring me. "A good thing. It means he will listen to his wife, and your marriage will be a harmonious one."

Any retort I could have come up with died on my lips. *Find yourself someone with thin ears,* Mama used to tell my sisters and me when we were young and Baba didn't listen to her. *Your baba's thick ones will be the end of us someday.*

"What's the matter, Tru?" asked Fal, who saw how my expression had gone grave.

A lump was swelling in my throat. I couldn't tell them what I'd learned about Baba—that he was possibly alive, the Dragon King's captive. It'd be cruel to give false hope.

"Nothing," I said, waving them off. I turned to my mother. "Thank you, Mama. I am grateful for your blessing."

Mama's mood was bright. "Let's get you changed. I can't believe you went to Lord Elang looking like *that*. At least brush your hair next time. I swear you'd go to your wedding in trousers if not for your sisters and me."

"Dragon's luck, phoenix's fortitude," Fal murmured in my ear as Mama prattled on. She didn't believe in superstitions any more than I did, but worry knit into her brow. She squeezed my hand. "I hope you know what you're doing."

As Elang had promised, the servants soon returned to the estate grounds. My sisters and I went to the garden to greet them. First were the turtles; they crawled out of the pond, then stood on their hind legs like humans and began to work on decorating the garden. Then came something that made Nomi's eyes bulge.

She pointed excitedly at the water. "Are those—"

"The pack arrives," Shani muttered. She tossed one of Elang's gardening trowels into her mouth, crunching loudly. "I loathe merfolk."

Nomi had stopped listening. She rushed toward the pond for a better view.

They were beautiful creatures, even from afar. They swam with the elegance of eagles flying, their tails shimmering behind them. One by one, they hoisted themselves onto land, drinking from the gourd-like vials around their necks. A turtle waited on them, passing out clothes while the merfolk's tails transformed into human legs.

Nomi's face glowed with wonder. "I didn't know that merfolk could become human."

"They usually can't," replied Shani. "Elang'anmi makes a potion so they can mingle among humans and find work in the city. Only lasts a few hours, then the lot of them come stampeding back to the pond. It's a daily disorder."

"They work in Gangsun?" Nomi mused. "I wonder if I've ever met one."

I wondered too. From every angle, their upper halves *did* look human. Long black hair, bony shoulders, and mushroom noses. But if you looked closely, their ears were long and pointed, and their pupils were edged like diamonds.

"Did you know merfolk have twice as many nerves in their hair as we do in our fingers?" Nomi was babbling. "That's where they store all their magic—and secrets. They never cut it."

"Never?" said Falina, twisting to look.

"We can ask. Oh, should we? Fal, why don't you go talk to them."

"Me? Have Tru ask. She's the one they're staring at."

It was true. While my sisters and I were whispering about the merfolk, they were murmuring and pointing—at me.

"You must excuse them," spoke a mellow voice from my left. "They're curious about the new lady of the Westerly Seas."

I whirled but saw no one . . . except a giant turtle with yellow-brown spots on her cheeks and the brightest green eyes I'd ever seen.

"Did you . . ." I hesitated, feeling more shy than foolish. "Did you speak to me?"

The turtle's lips stretched into the warm semblance of a smile. "Most creatures from Ai'long are different from what you know," she replied. "My name is Mailoh. I am in charge of Lord Elang's household, and it will be my deepest honor to prepare you for the rites tomorrow. Please, come with me."

I hesitated. My sisters were preoccupied with the merfolk: Nomi was interrogating a boy her age about whether his kind really cried pearls instead of tears, and Fal was helping a pair of mermaids arrange flowers. They wouldn't miss me.

"All right." I followed Mailoh. The turtle padded circumspectly into my chambers, dipping her head beneath the door frame. Behind her were two smaller turtles, each carrying a trunk on their back.

"Your robes and headdress," explained Mailoh, though I hadn't asked. "Shall we begin?"

"But the wedding's tomorrow," I said.

Shani had come too, and she perched on my arm, talons biting into my skin. "Turtles are slow on land," she said with a sniff. "It's going to take them all day and night to wash and wax your hair, scrub your skin, and slough off all the dirt—"

"We turtles are slow but thorough," Mailoh said hoarsely. "Now, back into your abode, demon. If you get any of the silk wet, I will personally hang you above a brazier."

Shani bared her teeth at the turtle, but she obeyed and flooded back into the ring.

"The foul creature loathes heat," Mailoh informed me. Her tone softened, belying a touch of affection. "It'll be better for her inside the ring anyway. All this time on land has been taxing for her, same as Lord Elang."

I lifted my head. "What's wrong with Elang?"

"Nothing, nothing. He simply travels too much while he's on land, searching for his Heavenly Match. But now that he's found you at last . . ." There was a twinkle in her round, hooded eyes. "Don't you worry, your wedding will be magnificent. Even the sand crabs will have heard of it by the time we are finished."

I wasn't worried at all; in fact, Mailoh was clearly more excited about this wedding than I was. "There's no need for all this fuss," I said. "Hardly anyone will see me."

"You think I'm dressing you to impress the humans?" Mailoh huffed a laugh. "No, dear girl. Lord Elang couldn't care less what the humans in Gangsun think of you. Whereas in Ai'long, a dragon's impression can often make the difference between life . . . and death."

I suppressed a shiver. If I thought Elang intolerable, I could only imagine the rest of his dragon kind. A bunch of godly immortals who acted more monstrous than divine. A king who conjured storms on a whim, who sank ships and broke families apart with not a care.

My fists clenched at my sides. "Then make me magnificent," I told Mailoh. "Help me create an impression when I enter Ai'long. Show them I am not . . ." I searched for the word Elang loved to use. "Krill."

The turtle's mouth bent into a wrinkled grin. "Just you wait."

Mailoh hadn't been lying about her thoroughness. The rest of the day, I didn't leave my chambers. Every speck of dirt was sloughed off my skin, and my hair was lathered and rinsed until it shone. The merfolk varnished my nails with vermillion lacquer, smothered my face with orange-scented cream, and even gave me rose petals to chew so my breath would be sweet. I spat them out when no one was looking.

When at last the ordeal was over, it was nearly midnight. I'd never been happier to be left alone and greet my bed. I collapsed immediately, sinking into a bank of cushions.

Only for my head to hit something hard-edged: the contract box.

It hadn't been there a moment ago, and nor had the red-eyed butterfly perched on the lid. She fluttered her wings, letting out a familiar cackle as I rubbed the back of my head.

I glared. "Elang sent you—as *that*?"

"Butterflies are symbols of undying love," Shani said. "I thought I'd be one for your wedding tomorrow. Congratulations, by the way."

"You should come as a mosquito," I muttered. "That'd suit you more."

"Such resentment is music to my ears." Shani glowed, her

antennae buzzing. "We're going to have so much fun together these next few months, you and me at the bottom of the sea."

"Is there a point to your visit?"

"Elang'anmi sent me with his tidings. And to fetch the contract, signed."

Always straight to business, that dragon prince. If he'd wanted me to look at the contract so badly, he shouldn't have conscripted Mailoh and her preening squad to fuss over me all day.

With a sigh, I pored through the contract's pages one last time. As expected, Elang was meticulous. Everything I'd requested had been added.

"I see he told you about our little plot against Nazayun," Shani observed, reading over my shoulder. She tutted. "You are aware what will happen if the Dragon King finds out, aren't you?"

"I'm aware." I flipped to the last page. "Frogs exploding out of my throat would be considered a mercy."

"And you're still signing?"

In the beginning, I'd agreed to do this for the money. Money to secure my sisters' futures and pay off Mama's debts so no one would ever bother our family again. Yes, I'd had doubts. I was no fool—when I'd discovered Elang was orchestrating a coup against the Dragon King, I'd wanted nothing to do with it. Until I found out about Baba.

I scribbled my name.

"Maybe you're not as spineless as I thought." Shani scooped up the contract. "Or maybe you're going to regret all this."

"I already do."

With a laugh, the demon gave me a good splash in the

face. It was cold and unexpected, and I let out a startled gasp. "Nine Hells, Shani!" I breathed. "What was that for?"

But Shani had disappeared, and in her place came Mama, carrying a basket and a wooden comb. There were oil stains on her sleeve, and the smell of salt and fried dough tickled my nostrils.

"How many times have I told you not to sleep with your hair wet, Truyan?" Mama said, looking scandalized. "You ought to know better. And on the night before your wedding! You'll wash away your luck and get a headache."

"I didn't—"

"Come, let me dry it for you."

Before I could protest, Mama sat on my bed, patting my hair dry with a towel. When she was finished, she picked up the wooden comb and set it on her lap.

"What's that for?" I asked.

Mama took a sudden interest in her hands; she looked nervous. "It's a Balardan tradition for a mother to comb her daughter's hair the night before her wedding."

There came a hiccup in my heart. Over the years, my sisters and I had been desperate for anything to do with Baba's heritage, and while Mama didn't speak or read Balardan, she did her best to teach us what she knew. Tonight she had brought a piece of him with her—for me.

"Thank you," I whispered.

Gently Mama threaded the comb through my hair and brushed it down my back, as if whisking through custard. "Mailoh did a good job with your hair," she said. "You look . . ."

"Tolerable?"

"Beautiful." Mama let the word hang between us before

she set down the comb and reached into her basket. "This is for you."

It was a fried cruller. I hadn't had one in years.

"Don't show your sisters—this is the only one that didn't burn. Eat it while it's hot."

I broke the cruller in two and offered her the bigger half. Together we bit down at the same time. The familiar crunch made my heart pinch with nostalgia.

"They're not as good as they used to be," Mama admitted. "It's been too long since I've made them."

"They're your best yet."

Mama swept her hand over my face, her fingers landing on the mole by my mouth. "You remember when I used to tell fortunes? I told you this mole was lucky, and it'd earn you coin. Wasn't I right?"

I humored her with a smile. "You were right."

"I used to think I knew everything about my daughters, but how you've all grown."

"Mama . . ."

"I wish the visions hadn't come to you, Tru, but the gods never give us more than we can handle. You must have questions. Tell me."

I hesitated. "Do you . . . ?"

"No," she said quickly. "Not me. Your grandmother."

"Grandmother?"

Mama pulled some blanket over her legs. "I wish you could have met her. She could see someone's face and know their future. Almost like you."

I thought of the tingle that crept down my fingers, how it turned into a burning itch and made my arm feel as heavy as lead. I thought of how every time my attention drifted from my work, I'd fall into a vision I never meant to foresee. "Did she learn to control it?"

"It depends on what you mean. She told me she learned to see years ahead of her. Sometimes she could even see the future's multiple possibilities, like tangled threads yet to be unspun. But two things never changed: She could never predict when her visions would come true. And she could never stop one from happening."

My shoulders fell. I could hear pain in Mama's voice, and I reached for her hand. "What did she say to you?"

"That I'd choose poorly. She never approved of your baba, said he'd break my heart one day. I married him anyway to prove her wrong." Mama forced a smile. "I was stubborn and rash, like you." She paused. "A jumper, like you."

It took me a moment to register her meaning. "Fortune finds those who leap."

"Something your father liked to say, even when we were young." She tucked my bangs behind my ear. "I used to be jealous of all the time you'd spend with him, did you know? Now I wish you'd spent more."

"Did you love him?" I whispered.

Mama pursed her lips tight. I didn't think she'd answer.

"He broke my heart in the worst way possible," she said finally. Her voice wobbled, on the verge of breaking. She whispered, "But if I could do it again, I'd still pick him. Pirate and adventurer and all."

I found I couldn't speak.

She blew out my candle. "Good night, my Tru."

My chest tightened as she left. Ever since I'd found out Baba could be in Ai'long, the hope I'd been secretly nursing these past years became all-consuming. I'd never imagined there was anything I could dread and want so much at the same time.

What I feared more than anything—more than the dragons, the mysterious realm every legend warned against, even King Nazayun—was the answers I might find about Baba.

Alive or dead. There were only two possible outcomes.

I'll find him, I thought as I drifted to sleep. *Even if I have to tear apart the entire sea, I'll find him.*

CHAPTER FOURTEEN

The next morning, Elang and I were married.

It was midsummer in the year of the dragon, an auspicious time to be wed, but the sky gods seemed to disagree. Plump, glutinous clouds eclipsed the sun, and not too far away, Saino beat his thunder drums, stirring up a storm.

As promised, the ceremony was small and private. It took place under a crooked magnolia tree in the garden, where a priest—who I suspected was actually a merman—spoke the words of rite and ritual to bless our union.

I listened with half an ear. The entire time, I knelt on a silk cushion, trying to balance the unwieldy crown on my head and sit up straight under the heaviness of my robes.

"I feel like a walking palanquin," I had joked to my sisters when they'd helped Mailoh dress me. *"I need a mule to help me go forward, these robes are so heavy! And no pockets?"*

"You're the bride, what do you need pockets for?" teased Nomi. *"A paintbrush?"*

Yes, a paintbrush. Ever since my visions had started, I

always carried one. "Why not?" I pulled up my veil and blew at its silk. "You'd bring a book if you were in my place."

"Will you stop fiddling with your veil?" Falina clucked her tongue at me and erased the powder from over my mole. "Keep it on. You'll be glad for it later."

She'd been right. Thanks to that suffocating sheet of silk, I didn't have to smile or pretend to be happy. I could scowl and stare off at the ceiling, even make faces at Elang if I wanted.

But I didn't. The ceremony was brief and efficient, and all too soon I was called to rise. Elang and I went through the rites, bowing before each direction of the wind and reciting old chants to thank the gods. Finally a long red ribbon was to be wrapped around our wrists—the "red string of fate" to bind us before the Heavens.

Tying the string was a custom in all weddings, meant to symbolically connect the fates of two people, forever. The stronger their love, the stronger their bond.

It'd be easy to cut since we had no bond. I glanced at Elang, wondering if he was thinking the same.

A mistake. He was wearing that intent, piercing gaze I had come to know, except today it was fixed on me as if nothing else in the universe existed, only us. And the way the gold flecks from my headdress spoked his eyes, it was almost . . . almost . . . I shook away the thought with a hitch in my breath. It was a good thing he couldn't see me. He was a better actor than I'd expected.

He folded back his sleeves to begin the ritual, and I saw his hands up close. His fingers were long and human, with hard, round knuckles. His nails, however, were black, curved almost like talons. I avoided touching them as I laid my palms atop his.

A quiet laugh escaped his nose. Elang closed his fingers around my hand, taking care that his sharp nails only skimmed my skin. I wasn't moved. Outwardly our pose might have looked tender, but I alone could feel the taut persistence of his hold—like a reminder that there was no turning back.

"I bind you to me, Tru Saigas," he spoke, wrapping the string around our wrists. "Until the end of our days upon this earth, under this heaven, and across the seas, our fates are one, our destinies entangled." He paused then to lift my veil, removing the silken red cloth over my head. When the candlelight bathed my face, he actually smiled. "Whatever course you may wend, I will follow."

Now it was my turn. I looked up at Elang, mustering a mimicry of his smile. For half a year, this would be the face of the man I'd call my husband. Mask or no mask, I could hardly look at him without recoiling.

"I bind you to me," I began, repeating his words. The vow tasted like paper, but I forced a measure of feeling into it, as if I were cherishing every word. "Whatever course you may wend, I will follow."

I, too, wrapped the string around our wrists, and the priest made a knot. A symbolic gesture, but I couldn't help thinking how it literally did shackle Elang and me together. Then the priest gave his final blessings, and the string shimmered with magic—until Elang and I were left with only two matching red bracelets.

Simple as that, it was over. By the laws of Heaven and Earth, I was now bound to the man beside me. I felt no different. Felt no sudden affection or loyalty to him. Only the invisible weight of knowing we were two people coerced to be together.

Rain descended in a soft drizzle, and an umbrella opened over my head.

It was Elang's. He'd already rolled down his sleeves, covering the red string so it was nowhere in sight.

"This is your chance to say your farewells," he murmured. "We won't return to the house after the procession."

He pressed the umbrella into my hand. It was the same one he'd carried when we first met, with a dragon carved onto the handle. When I looked up to thank him, he was already striding off toward his garden, watching the showers descend upon the flowers.

Mama approached me. "They say it rains when a dragon weds," she began, "and the sea sheds tears of joy." She touched my cheek. "Don't hold back your visions. Let them bring you home faster."

I caught her hand in mine. "Yes, Mama."

I bowed to her, then my sisters came under my umbrella. Fal's arms had been crossed all day, and she hadn't smiled once. "It's tradition for the groom to pick you up from your home," she grumbled. "For your sisters to interrogate him at the door and forbid him from bringing you to the ceremony unless he passes all our tests."

"You're going to hold this grudge over him for the rest of your life, aren't you?" I said.

"I'm a Saigas girl," replied Fal. "Grudges are my specialty."

I laughed. "What were the tests?"

"We were going to ask questions," said Nomi. "Starting

easy, like your favorite food, favorite color, favorite flower." She raised an imaginary bowl. "We were going to make him drink a numbingly spicy soup to prove that he could endure pain and hardship to be with you."

"He would have failed them all," I muttered. "Probably would have guessed dumplings and blue and . . . peonies." I stole a glance at Elang, who was out of a human's earshot but not a dragon's. "Everyone always says their favorite flowers are peonies."

"If he failed, we wouldn't have to let you go," said Fal softly. The way her eyes twinkled so reminded me of Baba.

"Oh, Fal," I said thickly. I took my sisters' hands. "I wish I didn't have to leave you."

"Don't waste your imagination worrying about us," said Nomi. "I'll be luxuriating in a dragon's mansion, reading six books a day. While Fal flirts with the merfolk."

Fal gave Nomi a playful punch in the shoulder, then reached into her sleeve. "We didn't have time to get you a wedding gift, but we bought this for you a while ago. For your birthday."

The box was red, pertly tied with a cloth ribbon. Inside was a jar of—

"Snake-eye peppers!" I cried.

They were green chilis, some of the hottest and most fragrant sold on the Spice Road. My favorite.

"We figured there won't be much in the way of spices in Ai'long," explained Nomi.

I didn't care about propriety or about the powder clumping under my eyes because I was crying. I drew Fal and Nomi into my arms and hugged them fiercely.

"Don't you dare get yourself killed," Fal said in my ear.

"Or every Ghost Festival day, I'll send you bland noodles with no spice. That'll be all you get to eat in the afterlife."

"The worst fate," I said, choking on a laugh and sob at once.

Drums and gongs resounded from the other side of the gates, and the carriage stopped behind me. It was time.

My youngest sister was easily two heads shorter than Elang, but she strode up to him, chin raised and eyes steely as though she were the dragon, not he.

"I might not have magic or be friends with merfolk or have a demon at my side," she declared. "But I have a brain. Bring my sister back to us, Lord Elang. Or in the name of all that we mortals are capable of, I will find a way to make you regret it."

They were big words for such a small girl, but Nomi's vow thundered above the rain pattering over our umbrella.

As expected, Elang said nothing, and his mask revealed nothing. Yet as my sisters stalked away, he grasped the hook of my umbrella and bore it with me against the rain.

The rain grew harder. I felt badly for Elang's attendants, who walked alongside our palanquin without hat or umbrella—until I remembered they were merfolk. They probably loved to soak in the rain the way I loved to bask in the sun.

Oyang Street was a residential road, accessible only to those who lived there. But this morning, it had transformed. Red lanterns hung from every branch, garlands of gold-painted ingots too. Along the cobblestoned walls were intricate paper cutouts of dragons and phoenixes.

Around us, the crowd was growing. Most had come to

glimpse the infamously reclusive Demon Prince, but I recognized several faces from the fishing district.

"Congratulations, Truyan!" they shouted. "May you have a hundred years of happiness, and may you have twice as many children as your mother!"

I was grateful when the attendants lit a spate of firecrackers. As they thundered loudly, the carriage sped ahead, leaving the crowds behind. I glanced at Elang, whose nostrils were most definitely flared—I couldn't tell whether from the smoke or the blessings. Probably both.

"Word's certainly gotten out about the wedding," I said, trying to sound cheery. "It's a good thing we're not having a banquet. Mama's friends must have a thousand questions."

Elang didn't reply. "Take my arm," he said instead. "We need to at least look like we enjoy each other's company."

Once I obliged, Elang angled us toward the window and waved to the crowds, nodded to the onlookers, even tilted his head close to mine. It was convincing enough that, for a few minutes, I forgot the forbidding chill that lingered between us.

It also helped that I was looking for someone.

"Keep your head inside," Elang said when we were halfway down the street. His voice was thin, sieving through his smile. "You're letting rain into the carriage."

My veil was damp, and I tucked it over my shoulder. "I want to look outside. It's not every day a girl marries a dragon prince."

"If you're looking for Madam Yargui, she isn't here."

I bit my lip—my tell that I was agitated. "How did you—"

"I have no patience for bandits," interrupted Elang. "She

and her men won't be a problem for you anymore. They won't even *remember* to be a problem."

Suddenly I wondered where Shani had gone this morning. "What about the governor's prefects? They know I'm a forger."

"See for yourself," said Elang.

His timing was impeccable. The moment he spoke, we passed Governor Renhai's house, and a cordon of prefects approached the carriage. Among them was the governor himself.

Immediately I jerked away from the window, while Elang tipped his head back against the cushioned seat as if we were stopping for a herd of goats to cross the road and not because I was about to be arrested.

I started to put my veil back on, but Elang caught my hand. "There's no need."

"That's the governor," I hissed. "He's going to . . ."

My voice trailed. Just outside, standing respectfully, were six prefects. As soon as they saw me, they bowed deeply, their eyes passing over my blue hair with little recognition. "His Honor, Governor Renhai, extends to you his warmest wishes." They presented a box of gold jewelry. "Congratulations, Your Highnesses."

I was flabbergasted, barely able to manage a nod. Elang, on the other hand, responded coolly, "The gods have been generous in this lifetime, to bless me with such a clever and beautiful bride." He was still holding—no, *incarcerating*—my hand. "Thank you, Your Excellency, for honoring us with your presence and your generosity."

The second the carriage rolled out of earshot, I yanked my hand back. I turned to Elang, demanding, "Shani's work?"

"She's enjoyed her time on land more than she lets on." That was all he would divulge.

I crossed my arms. "Must be nice for you, being able to throw magic at any trouble that arises."

"If that were so," said Elang darkly, "then you wouldn't be here."

He had a point. Chastened, I leaned back too, closing the curtains as the carriage trundled to the end of Oyang Street. The crowds didn't follow, most well-wishers staying back to receive the red envelopes Elang's attendants were passing out.

When the music had receded into a distant buzz, Elang took off his mask. He had freckles, I noticed for the first time. They were faint, peppered across the human side of his nose and fading onto the sharp cleft of his chin.

"Do you always wear that?" I asked, unable to help myself. "That . . . mask."

"You've seen my face. Wouldn't you agree it's necessary?"

I meant to disagree, but then he faced me, his yellow eye glinting even in the absence of direct light. The way it turned gold was unnerving, and despite my intention, I still flinched.

Proving his point.

"Can't you take a potion like you give the merfolk?" I pressed.

"Potions have limited effect against my curse. Why do you ask?"

Why? I supposed because I'd worn masks of my own. Not literal ones—but wigs for my blue hair and powders to shade my complexion and eyes so I'd look more A'landan. It did wonders for changing how people saw me, and I hated it.

"No reason," I lied. "Will you wear the mask in Ai'long?"

"Everyone in Ai'long knows what I look like," said Elang.

"Listen," he spoke again, changing the subject. "This will be the only time we have alone before we depart. Our entrance into the dragon realm is important. My subjects will be there to greet us, a few emissaries that the Dragon King has sent as well. They will be watching us."

I nodded, understanding. "You want us to look fond of each other."

"That'd be helpful." He hesitated. "I warn you, my grandfather's emissaries will be unfriendly."

"More unfriendly than you?"

He glared. "If you value your life, say nothing about being a painter, and nothing about your visions."

"Noted." I crossed my arms. "I've been warned."

He made a grunt. "One last thing. From this point forward, if I show you kindness or favor, it means nothing. If I give you a gift, or bestow upon you praise, it means nothing. Everything is for appearances only, and should you occupy a place in my thoughts, it is only to facilitate the mission we have agreed upon. I shall expect this to be the same from you."

I thought of the way he'd smiled at me during our wedding, how his eyes had gone unaccountably soft and he'd held my arm during the procession afterward. I'd be delusional to think it'd been anything more than an act, but somehow it stung just the same. I tossed my veil behind my back. "Don't worry, I'll be counting down the days until this is over."

"One month, in Ai'long's time."

"One month," I echoed.

It occurred to me then that the success of our arrangement

was just as vital to him as it was to me. Elang had plenty at stake: servants who relied on him, the future of his kingdom, and—obviously—his own life.

Realizing this didn't make me like him more or feel better about what we had to do, but at least we had an understanding. We were two people forced together. By fate, by ill luck, by choice, it didn't matter.

The procession was over, and the carriage rounded back toward Elang's manor.

We didn't say a word to each other the rest of the ride.

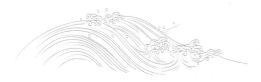

CHAPTER FIFTEEN

It was still raining when the carriage trundled onto an unmarked path, past a copse of pine trees into a mossy part of Elang's garden I'd never seen before. We stopped before a quay of tall reeds, where a pale yellow boat awaited. It was a narrow vessel, barely big enough for two, and it tilted under my weight as I boarded.

"Take this," said Elang, giving me the umbrella again.

I didn't argue. I'd been anxious all day for what was soon to come. The moment I'd leave everyone and everything I'd ever known behind—for the realm of dragons.

Some part of me had hoped that my family might be here for one last farewell, but the garden was empty. No merfolk, no turtles, no fish in the pond. Only Shani had come, keeping a vigilant distance from the boat.

I dipped under the umbrella as Elang rowed. Rain drummed the pond, making the water glitter. A splendorous sight, but I was more focused on what lay beneath.

It was impossible to gauge how deep the pond was, yet there *couldn't* be an entire kingdom under Elang's garden. Could there?

Then I saw it. A speck of violet light at the center of the pond, glowing with a burning intensity. I breathed, unable to contain my excitement. "Elang, is that . . . is that Ai'long?"

Elang set aside his oars. "It's close," he replied. "The light represents the edge of the mortal realm. Beyond is Ai'long."

The boat rocked in its place, and I gripped my umbrella with both hands. "So this is it? We jump?"

"Not yet." He bent, retrieving a lidded teacup he'd stowed inside the boat. Holding it with both hands, he offered it to me.

I quailed. "What is this?"

"A potion—so you can breathe underwater."

Oh. Right. I'd been wondering about that.

I peered into the cup. The potion looked like an herbal soup, darker and thicker than the ones Mama used to make for me when I was little, and those had been vile. *Deer intestines with black fungus*, she'd say, deadpan. I'd never known whether she'd been joking.

"I caution you," said Elang before I raised the cup, "the taste is foul. The experience after, unpleasant."

More curious than brave, I brought the teacup to my nose. A mistake. The most revolting smell greeted my nostrils, and Elang grabbed my hand before I dropped everything.

The boat rocked as I coughed. "What is this?" I fanned away the potion's fumes. "It smells like—"

"Rotted rat liver?"

My entire face puckered. That was very specific.

"It's not." Elang's lips twisted. "You recall the flowers

you trampled? They are known as sanheia roses, and this is a special tea brewed from their petals. It's called sangi."

He took my umbrella. "Now, drink before it gets cold. It will burn more when it cools."

Burn? Hells of Tamra, I should've asked for more money.

I lifted the cup once more. A thread of sunlight shone upon its porcelain lip. The last stripe of day I'd see in who knew how long.

This was it.

For Fal's and Nomi's futures, I reminded myself. *For Baba.*

I pinched my nose with my fingers, then poured the potion down my throat.

The taste was bitter, though not utterly repulsive. That was as far as I got, thought-wise, before the teacup fell from my hands and clattered onto the bow of the boat.

Elang took my arm, steadying me as I began to shudder. "Mailoh!" he shouted. "Mailoh, it's time."

"What's . . . what's . . . happening?" I asked.

Elang tilted my chin up. "Look at me. Tru, focus on my eyes."

My fingers curled into his arm. The world was slipping beneath me, everything blurring into a haze, even Elang's eyes. They were two disconsonant blobs of gold and gray, like an egg yolk and a stone, deliriously coming together into a dark eclipse.

"That's it," he said. "Focus on me. Your body is reacting to the sangi. There will be pain, and you'll feel like you can't breathe . . ."

As soon as he said it, a wave of heat scalded my throat,

like I'd swallowed a raging fire. I felt my jaw crack open, muscles stretching into a scream. Except no sound came out. I was drowning—on air!

Mailoh arrived, floating alongside the boat. "We have to get her into the sea," she urged.

"It's too soon." Elang gripped my arm more tightly. "Focus, Tru! Just a little longer."

The air had turned thicker than sand, and my lungs pinched with panic. All my life, I'd breathed without thinking. Now, suddenly, this most natural act was killing me, and the instincts I'd been born with fled in favor of something entirely new and unimaginable.

Water, I choked in my thoughts. I tried to inhale the rain. *Water!*

Shani dissolved into a splash over my face, giving me the breath I desperately needed.

"She's ready," said Elang, tilting my chin to assess the side of my neck. "Let's go."

He lifted me onto Mailoh's back. Then, stepping off the boat, Elang spread open his arms.

In a great dizzying tower, water rushed up from the pond. The force of it knocked me flat against Mailoh's shell. As I sat up, breathing in the icy spray, Elang began to part the waters.

Mist swirled above the pond, and thunder ripped the sky, silvery rain falling down in sheets.

A sharp tingle vibrated across my skin. This was the moment I'd foreseen in my painting.

Shrouded in storm and sea, Elang began to change. His hair turned a lustrous white, and his scales multiplied across his skin, stippling the bare flesh on his arms and most of his neck. His horns branched and doubled in length, and most dramatically, a tail swelled out from under his robes.

Only his face didn't change. Half of it was dragon, and half was human, his golden eye a glimmering coin against the dark.

"Water brings out the dragon in Lord Elang," Mailoh was murmuring. "Impressive, isn't he?"

He looked more monstrous than impressive, to be honest. But he could have grown four heads or shrunk into the size of a cockroach for all I cared. I just wanted to get in the water.

As if she sensed my impatience, Mailoh ferried me to the center of the pond, where Elang was waiting.

"Is she ready?" he asked the turtle.

My throat still burned, but I could answer for myself. I lifted my chin. *I'm ready.*

With a nod, Elang closed his arms. The tower of water roared, collapsing down in a rushing cascade. At the heart of the pond, the speck of violet light I'd seen swelled into a glimmering crown. I braced myself, grasping the rim of Mailoh's shell.

"It might be better if you rode on Lord Elang's back," spoke the turtle. "The journey can be rough, I wouldn't want you sliding off my shell."

I balked. Married or not, he was still a stranger to me. I wasn't about to climb onto his back and fold my arms around his neck. I definitely wasn't going to cling to his horns.

In the end, I didn't have a choice. Thinking she was being helpful, Mailoh tossed me to Elang. He caught me by the waist, muscles cording as he set me firmly upon his back.

"I'll see you in Ai'long," Mailoh cried before diving into the pond. Shani vanished after her.

"Now it is our turn," said Elang as I scrambled up his scales for something to grasp. He took my arms, folded them around his neck. "I would hold on tight if I were you."

That was all the warning he gave. There came a rhythmic rushing that I mistook for wind, then we plunged.

And before I could even think to say goodbye, I left behind the only world I'd ever known.

CHAPTER SIXTEEN

According to legend, the gateway to Ai'long was a magnificent waterfall, composed of the Three Great Rivers cascading side by side—and any fish that could leap across would become a dragon.

In reality, if there *was* such a waterfall, I missed it entirely. Because after Elang dove into the pond, he didn't stop. He accelerated down a never-ending chute of water, so fast I could barely keep my head up, let alone take in the scenery. All I saw was the parchment white of his hair as I buried my face between his horns, desperately holding on for my life.

I wanted to scream, but I couldn't even breathe. My heart had flown up to my throat, and my stomach was somersaulting so violently that I couldn't tell it apart from my lungs.

At last, when I thought I might actually swoon, came a wash of violet light. Then, with a jolt, we arrived.

I was still clinging to Elang's neck, my legs straddling the long chain of ridges that protruded from his spine. I tried to let go, but the world was spinning, and my muscles had gone stiff as ice.

"You humans are easily disoriented," Elang said, twisting

to face me. "The feeling will pass shortly. The first time taking sangi is the worst."

I choked on my breath. I'd have to take that foul potion again?

"Every morning," he said, reading my dismay, "or you'll drown."

I groaned inwardly. At least my head had stopped swaying, and the tightness in my throat was subsiding. As I reached up to rub my neck, my fingers came across soft, vibrating gills.

I drew a stunned breath. "I've become part fish." Another gasp. "And I can talk underwater!"

Mailoh laughed. She sounded less hoarse here; her voice was smooth like melted sugar. "We may be underwater, but Ai'long is one of the immortal realms, Lady Saigas. Its waters are enchanted, and you'll find you'll be able to talk and sing and eat and drink just like you do above. The sangi helps too. You won't even notice the change after a while. I take it you're already feeling better?"

I was, though part of me wished I'd grown fins along with gills. Every time I tried to let go of Elang, I started floating away. I windmilled my arms, but it didn't do much good. Feeling utterly ridiculous, I gave up and latched on to Elang's neck again. Hoping he hadn't noticed.

Of course he had. Unlike me, with my hulking movements, Elang swam with ease and grace. Thankfully, he didn't show his annoyance in front of Mailoh, but it still startled me when he circled his arm around my waist, guiding me forward without a word.

"I'm feeling much better," I told Mailoh hastily.

"How are your garments?" the turtle inquired. "We have

a moment before we're expected at the castle. I want to make sure you're comfortable."

My clothes did feel different, now that she mentioned it. On land, I'd felt like I was dragging a sack of rice. Underwater, my red sleeves floated about me in whorls of silk, and my cocoon of jackets and skirts was lighter than a fan. Still no pockets, but at least I could move. Except for that contraption of a headdress! I fidgeted with it.

"Is that bothering you?" said Mailoh, craning her neck to see.

"It's all right, I'll—"

"May I?" Elang's voice skipped over mine.

May I what? I was more curious than anything, so I nodded.

He lifted me so I faced him. The water had changed him, but not as much as I'd previously thought. His white hair fell over his eyes the same way as before, his shoulders were broad and straight, and his nails were sharp black crescents. His scales had become bluer, though, almost the same shade as the water.

I darted my gaze to the side while he touched my headdress. In a shimmer of magic, it became a simple golden circlet, with slender strands of rubies and pearls dangling down my hair.

My eyes flew up. I'd seen banquets materialize on cotton blankets, I'd been dressed by mermaids and talking turtles, and I'd just taken a potion that gave me gills. Yet this enchantment, borne from Elang's touch, was the first to make me gasp. It felt oddly intimate, in a way that made my stomach buzz.

"Thanks," I mumbled.

"Will you let go of me now?" said Elang. "I'd like to show some dignity when Grandfather's patrols arrive."

He knew just how to nettle me. Suddenly finding my strength, I pushed myself away from him. Mailoh took my hand, ushering me past the rocks ahead until we floated above a wide gray plain.

"Welcome to Ai'long, Lady Saigas," she said. "Behold your new home—Yonsar of the Westerly Seas."

In my mind, I'd uprooted my life on land to stay in Ai'long, the most beautiful place in all the realms. I'd imagined a kaleidoscope of coral forests sprawling across the ocean ground, fish that glowed like lanterns and spanned fins that put butterflies to shame. I'd expected palaces wrought of crystal and jade, cities built of marbled shells and stone, and water that was bluer than a peacock's feathers.

Not this.

Never had I seen such a desolate stretch of sea. The water was ashen and cast a wintry pall upon everything it touched, even my wedding robes. Every inhale smelled of ink, slightly spoiled and burnt.

Surrounding us, canyons gave way to chasms so deep they had no end. In the distance, I saw ruins. Toppled arches and broken moon gates. The ghostly remains of a city, leveled by a divine and ruthless force.

This . . . was the realm of dragons?

"It used to be magnificent," said Mailoh, reading my reaction. "There are still pockets of beauty, if you look hard enough. You'll learn to love it."

Honestly, I doubted I'd be here long enough for that. "What happened?"

"Nazayun." The name passed the turtle's lips like faraway thunder.

I went cold. In the distance appeared a blurred silhouette, the specter of a dragon. As he gathered his form, pale blue eyes pierced out of his watery projection. He met my gaze, then disintegrated into the sea.

I was shaken. "Did you see that? Was that—"

"The patrols are here," interrupted Elang. "Mailoh, get to the castle. We'll join you shortly."

From behind one of the cliffs emerged a shiver of sharks. At least a dozen, I counted. They were gray, blending in with the neighboring canyons. Their very presence stung, sending thorny vibrations across the water.

"They're here for me, not you," said Elang through his teeth. "Clear your mind, and whatever you do, don't fight the jellyfish."

Jellyfish?

Then I saw them, their glowing heads bobbing across the misty sea. Their numbers were few, only five or six, and they seemed to be merely observing us from afar. Why did Elang sound more worried about jellyfish than sharks?

"Elangui Ta'ginan Yuwong," spoke the sharks as one. Their voices were gratingly shrill, their eyes glassy and flat. "His Eternal Majesty, King Nazayun, has exiled you from these waters. You will be given only this one warning. Leave at once."

Elang raised himself tall, his tail sweeping out from under his robes. "I have met my grandfather's conditions for my return," he said. "Behold, the one whose heart I value more than my own, whose light shines without equal. My beloved bride, Lady Saigas."

The sharks regarded me, and I could have sworn they bared their teeth, just a little.

Make me magnificent, I had told Mailoh. I didn't feel magnificent at all; I felt like shark food.

"She will have to be your match for you two to proceed," they said.

Elang's hand found the small of my back, and he brought me close. Holding me, shielding me, it didn't matter which. This once, I was glad to have him at my side. I just hoped the jellyfish registered the sentiment as love, not terror.

Elang bowed his head. "You may administer the trial."

Two jellyfish came forth. I'd seen drawings of such creatures before in Nomi's books, even eaten one with Gaari, marinated in vinegar and sesame. But alive, they bloomed with soft smears of light and moved like flowers caught in the wind. It was mesmerizing, until I remembered they weren't friendly.

They descended upon us, their tentacles ribboning down with the effortless grace of silk.

Clear your mind, Elang had said, *and whatever you do, don't fight.*

For once, I listened to him. I went still, not daring to move as one of the smaller jellyfish swept a tentacle across my forehead. A second tentacle encircled my neck.

Who are you? it asked, in a voice that echoed eerily through my head.

"Truyan Saigas," I replied. "A human from Gangsun."

What is your business in Ai'long?

"I am newly wed to my love, the lord of the Westerly Seas. I return with him now to end his exile and begin our life in Yonsar."

The jellyfish leaned closer, its bulbous eyes mirroring my reflection. *You will have to be the Heavenly Match for his exile to end.*

I cringed as the pressure around my neck grew and the jellyfish wrapped its tentacles about my head, pressing firmly against my temples. Sharp pangs pulsed into my mind, like knives peeling layer after layer into my memories, my secrets.

My jaw went tight.

I fed the jellyfish memories of my wedding to Elang, of us exchanging indulgent stares and holding hands as we tied our red ribbon around each other's wrists. But its tentacles probed deeper; it became harder to focus. I had to concentrate on something so I wouldn't give away Elang's plot to overthrow Nazayun—or my visions. That something became Baba.

Your baba? The jellyfish latched on to this new direction in my thoughts. *Who is your baba?*

He's dead, I replied quickly. *I was only wishing he could have come to my wedding.*

The jellyfish tilted its head. Its skin flickered, and on its translucent surface, I saw the blurred contours of my father's face. Gradually he came into focus, unearthing the last memory of us together.

"You are my treasure," he said, kissing my forehead. "You and your sisters and your mother." He touched my hair tenderly. "And this will be the last time I leave my treasures behind."

Then Baba rose for the door. Here the jellyfish had dug into my deepest fears, for my memory became a nightmare. I saw my younger self run after him, trying to stop him, but the door closed and I couldn't open it no matter how I tried.

I would never see him again.

"Stop," I whispered, twisting, trying to get free. I wrestled the jellyfish's tentacles away from my face, but I couldn't get free. "Get away from me!"

Out of nowhere came a furious downward swipe of sharp black claws. That was all I saw before the jellyfish let out a high shriek and a clump of its tentacles floated into the abyss, separated from its body. The creature released me immediately.

You will regret that, Lord Elang, it spoke.

The sharks advanced, but Elang didn't lower his claws. A crystalline sword materialized in his grasp. "And you will regret harming my bride."

"Don't," I said, touching his arm. Still catching my breath, I turned to the remaining jellyfish. "I apologize on behalf of Lord Elang. I have nothing to hide. If there is more you need to see, then examine me further."

"Let her alone," Elang growled. "Her mind won't answer your questions." He lowered his sword. "Look into mine."

To my astonishment, the jellyfish brushed past me. Just like that, I was forgotten. Even the sharks backed away and left me alone.

The jellyfish approached Elang, their tentacles swaying forward. They beset him, burying my view of everything but his face. That was all I needed to see, really. In unison, barbs pierced out of their suckers—and their heads pulsed a bright white light.

Elang's brow folded, his fangs bared. He made no sound, not even a growl or a grunt, yet I knew he had to be in pain.

Again, the jellyfish pulsed. This time, Elang's body jerked. The crease on his brow deepened, and his scales paled a shade.

"Stop it," I cried, trying to weave through the jellyfish. "You're hurting him."

The sharks held me at bay, until there came one last pulse. This time Elang curled up in pain, and that was when the jellyfish decided it was enough.

The creatures retreated, retracting their arms as though they were ribbons.

"We have seen enough," they said. "The marriage is genuine. The terms for Lord Elang's homecoming have been met."

I swam up to him, grabbing him by the arm. *What did you say to them?* I wanted to ask. But instead, I said, "Are you all right?"

To my relief, there were no puncture wounds on his skin or on his scales. His eyes were half-open, his brow still pinched, and his scales were turning blue again.

"Are you all right?" I repeated.

Elang's claws closed at his sides, tight as flytraps. His eyes opened fully, and I could see the liquid yellow on his human half swirling back to its usual smolder, the dragon half's cinder black. In a burst, he straightened.

"We're finished here," he told the jellyfish. "You may tell His Majesty that the test is met, I am returned home."

You can tell him yourself.

An invisible current sent me reeling back, and as I regained my balance, the water churned, conjuring a colossal projection of a dragon.

King Nazayun.

"Welcome home, Elangui," he rumbled. "And welcome to Ai'long, Truyan Saigas."

At my side, Elang went tense. He bowed, and I had the sense to do the same.

"Your Eternal Majesty," he said, "we are honored by your visit."

"And you, Bride of the Westerly Seas?" the Dragon King asked. Even as a projection, his gaze was petrifying. "Have you come here of your own will?"

Collect yourself, Tru, I thought. *Chin up, shoulders squared. Spine against an imaginary stalk of bamboo.*

The act was on. I could pretend to be a dragon princess. I could pretend to be in love with Elang.

I reached for his hand, surprised I found it right away.

"Yes, I have." I shook my sleeve aside so Nazayun could see the red string around my wrist. "Before the gods, our fates have been tied. It is I who will break his curse."

It felt rather melodramatic to make such a declaration, so I punctuated my words by leaning on Elang's shoulder.

I could feel his muscles tensing with discomfort, so I only leaned harder.

Public displays of affection were distasteful among A'landi's upper classes, but if his grandfather was so obsessive about proof, I'd play my part. Besides, I never promised I'd be a lady.

"May you have luck of the dragons, Bride of the Westerly Seas," replied the Dragon King, dissolving into the water as he spoke. "Enjoy this wedding gift in celebration of your homecoming."

In a puff, he disappeared. And as our "gift," every shark and jellyfish in our vicinity was turned into stone.

The change happened suddenly, brutally, as though someone had slashed a knife through the water. My entire body jerked in alarm, and numbly I watched the sharks and jellyfish sink, the hollowed rounds of their eyes turned cold and lifeless.

At my side, Elang barely flinched. He let go of my hand. "Are you hurt?"

My head hurt, but not the rest of me. "No. Why . . . why did he destroy his own patrols?"

"Because he can," replied Elang grimly. "Because he's the god of dragons, and the entire sea is at his whim. Because he knew it would upset you."

Upset me was an understatement. Twenty living creatures turned into stone—all to make some lurid demonstration of power. It sickened me.

I bit the insides of my cheeks, my nostrils flaring. Gods help me, if I found Baba this way . . . I turned to Elang. "I'm not upset," I said, giving him a hard look. "I'm inspired."

The barest flicker of surprise crossed his face. He gave me a nod. "Good."

Then he shook his sword, and it transformed into the umbrella he always carried.

I watched, transfixed. "You did the same thing with my headdress." I wheeled my hands, unsure how to describe such magic. "After you touched it."

"I have a talent for transformation. I can change objects, so long as they're not alive."

"Could you do it on land too?"

"The water amplifies my powers," he responded. "Particularly, these waters." His arms fell to his sides, a slip of the red string around his wrist peeking past his sleeve. "The Westerly Seas listen to me, and now, as their lady, they will listen to you."

"You mean, I can turn umbrellas into swords?" I asked. More cheekily: "What about pebbles into diamonds?"

"You'll see in time." He didn't explain. Two turtles were approaching to escort us to the castle.

Before he needed to ask, I took Elang's arm and put on my brightest, most adoring smile. I was getting the hang of this. As regally as I could, I lifted my chin and adjusted my skirt to show off the embroidered phoenixes. Then I beamed at the turtles, ready for my entrance.

This was going to be my greatest role. I wouldn't mess it up.

CHAPTER SEVENTEEN

The entrance to Elang's home was carved between two cliffs, camouflaged by rock and shadow. I would never have seen it, if not for one detail. Under the foggy mist, round stones studded the mountainsides, each splotchy and dull. Not stones at all, I soon realized, but turtle carapaces!

"The Gate of a Thousand Shells," said Elang, preempting my question. "One of the great marvels of Ai'long. It has long been the stronghold of Yonsar, impenetrable since the First Era."

"It's impressive," I allowed, for there was no other word to describe it. What I'd taken to be a wall was actually rows of turtle shells stacked atop one another, so precisely that not a glimmer of light shone through their shells.

Before I could express more admiration, a low horn blew from within.

An orderly line of turtles rolled out to greet us. They stood to attention, necks craning in uniform stature, their heads bent respectfully low. I tried to smile at them as I passed, but not one smiled back. I doubted they even saw me.

Elang could have brought back a toad for a wife and no one would have noticed, I thought dryly.

"My lieutenants," said Elang, the only introduction he made. I nodded politely.

It felt more like a military procession than a marriage celebration. As we proceeded past the turtles, they raised their spears—crystal-forged weapons thrice my height, with forked tips that looked sharp enough to pierce through stone.

By this point, I'd amended my expectations of Yonsar. Originally I'd imagined a grand marble castle, with whales, dolphins, merfolk, and all manner of fish swimming to and fro across jade and marble tunnels and archways. But now I wouldn't be surprised if I'd be sleeping in a trench the next few weeks. Ahead, I spied no castle, not even a gate. Instead we advanced to the mountain itself, where Elang pressed his palm to the pewter-veined wall. He motioned for me to do the same, and when I laid my hand upon the rock, a door shimmered into existence.

"Welcome to your new home," Elang said, gesturing forward.

The moment I entered, floating sconces lit the cavernous hall. So Elang *did* have a castle. More a fortress, really, for it was scarcely less dull and desolate than the seascape outside. Someone—I guessed Mailoh—had taken the effort to hang a dragon-and-phoenix wedding scroll by the entrance, but the rest of the walls were bare, save for the veins of pale green moss limning the stone's many fissures.

"I'm relieved to see that no walls fell while we were on land," said Mailoh, turning sideways to squeeze past the narrow door. "You see, Lord Elang? Everything is in order as promised."

Elang merely doffed his jacket. His attention was on a bleak and barren field outside the window; it looked like nothing special to me, yet made him grimace.

For someone who's been exiled, I thought, *he certainly doesn't look thrilled to be home.*

"Where is General Caisan?" he asked. "He wasn't at the welcoming reception."

"My brother is in the War Pavilion," Mailoh replied. "He's been preparing reports on the storms for your perusal. I can fetch him if you—"

"There's no need." Elang put on a familiar frown, and I almost pitied whoever this Caisan was. "I'll seek him out myself."

"Not now, I hope." Mailoh smiled pleasantly. "You mustn't forget you have a very special dinner."

"Dinner?" It was the most hopeful word I'd heard since I'd left land.

"Didn't His Highness tell you?" Mailoh said. "A wedding banquet awaits."

I blinked. "I thought there wasn't going to be a banquet."

"It's only for the two of you," she explained. "Kunkoi's been in the kitchen all day preparing your favorite dishes."

My favorite dishes? All I'd told Elang was that I liked noodles. This was bound to be interesting.

"There's no need for a feast when one or two dishes will suffice," Elang said. His hair had turned black again, and he'd shed some of his dragon features, most noticeably the tail and whiskers. His horns still gleamed, as did the yellow eye. "Mailoh, will you check on it?"

"But, Your Highness, I thought you—"

That yellow eye burned.

"My mistake." Mailoh bowed hastily. "As you wish. I'll let Kunkoi know."

I was sad to see the turtle swim off, and especially to be left alone with Elang. I windmilled my arms, kicking deeper into the castle to explore, but he followed.

"Don't wheel your arms about like that. You'll tire yourself without getting anywhere." He caught me by my wrists.

"Relax," he said, guiding me forward before he let go of one wrist. With his free hand, he straightened my shoulders and adjusted my posture. "Start off on the ground. Imagine you're an anchor and let yourself sink, then move forward as though you're walking."

The instructions worked, and for the first time in Ai'long, I landed on solid ground, my toes curling into a rug of velvety green algae. I swooshed my arms, trying to steady my balance. "The water's heavy," I said. "It's hard to move one foot in front of the other."

"Don't think about it," said Elang. "It goes against logic, but once you let go of your resistance, you'll glide." He demonstrated at my side, kicking forward slowly. "All you need is a gentle push in the direction you want to go with your arms or your legs. It should feel like flying once you're used to it."

I copied his movements. With some practice, I could glide forward, even float and sink when I wanted. It *did* feel like flying. The water seemed to track my thoughts and follow me. The only thing I had trouble with was staying in one place. Whenever I wasn't moving, I'd start drifting up off to the ceiling.

Elang caught my arm, steadying me. "It'll get easier with practice."

His grip was firm, yet careful. "Thank you," I said, caught

off guard. What could I say back? "Your home, it's . . ." I searched for a word that wasn't *gray* or *desolate*. "It's sturdy."

Our exchange felt conciliatory, an attempt at goodwill on our wedding day. But all it showed me was the vast difference between us. His cold and lonely world to the warmth and radiance I had left behind.

He let me go. "Come this way. I'll show you to your room."

In the last five years, I'd spent my nights in plenty of odd places. Huddled up against the trees in the public gardens, in the attic of a shophouse, even in an abandoned carriage.

But never had I slept in a cave.

I entered my new room, surprised to find myself charmed. It was a spacious, surprisingly well-lit cave, far less grand than the apartment I'd been given in Elang's manor, but I liked its simplicity. The walls were a speckled granite, gently rounded along the corners, and a bed hung from the ceiling, suspended by pale green swaths of silk. There was even a window.

"This is where you'll be staying," said Elang. "I realize the space is not fitting of the lady of the Westerly Seas, but it's all the castle has to offer at the moment."

"You're talking to a girl who's been sharing a toilet *and* a kitchen with three other families for years," I replied. Then it occurred to me: "*We* won't be sharing this room, will we? The turtles won't expect us to . . ." I couldn't bring myself to finish the sentence.

"What?" said Elang, his brow raised a provocative fraction. "It *is* our wedding night."

An unwelcome heat crept to my cheeks. Gods, I could kill him. "That's not funny."

"Rest assured, my curse precludes any such expectations." His mouth set into a thin, dispassionate line. "And, to answer your other question, I reside on the other side of the castle—near the barracks. It is an area you'd do well to avoid."

My relief gave way to curiosity. "Why is that?"

He ignored me and went to the window, and drew my attention to a cloud of silvery haze high above. "Ai'long's days do not align with the mortal calendar," he said. "We measure time by the tides. As they fall, the upper seas will glow silver, meaning it is evening. As they rise, the light turns red."

"Meaning it is day." I understood.

"That's correct," said Elang. He gestured outside. "There isn't much of a view, but when the water is clear, you might make out the Floating Mountains. They surround Jinsang, the capital of Ai'long."

"Where your grandfather lives." *And where Baba might be.* "When will we go?"

A shadow fell over Elang's face. "Not anytime soon. Right now it isn't safe to leave Yonsar Castle. The Dragon King has eyes and ears everywhere in Ai'long, in the stones, in the crevices behind the rocks that you cannot see."

"But—"

"I will help you find your father," he interrupted. "This I assure you. But you must help me first, with Nazayun."

When I said nothing, he passed me his umbrella. It'd been refitted with a strap along the length of the canopy, permitting me to swing it over my shoulder. "I advise you to keep this."

I cocked my head. "Don't tell me it rains in Ai'long."

"Your kind is known for being slow and clumsy underwater," said Elang, ignoring the remark. "This will help you navigate your way until you can swim properly."

He had a way of being insulting and helpful at the same time.

Remembering how I'd nearly floated away upon arriving in Ai'long, I took the umbrella. I turned it in my hands, noting its lacquered handle—still a carved and unsmiling dragon. "You've stopped calling me krill."

"I think it best to save such indignities for humans I'm *not* married to." He paused. "Further, you didn't seem to like it."

"You're observant," I said dryly.

"If there's a term of endearment you prefer, you're welcome to share it."

My jaw dropped, ever so slightly. "Just Tru." I didn't ask him if he had one. The idea seemed absurd.

"Just Tru, then."

I let out a breath. "Just how often are we supposed to see each other?"

"Dinner is the only time I request your company. Usually I take it alone, but it would arouse suspicion if we didn't eat together. Will that be tolerable?"

That wasn't so bad. I nodded. "Does that begin with our private banquet?"

He gestured at the door. Blundering swimmer and all, I beat him outside.

CHAPTER EIGHTEEN

I'd arrived in heaven.

A feast awaited, a dozen platters lining a round banquet table. No noodle soups, but each dish looked tantalizing. I edged along the marble surface, breathing in the aroma as I narrowed my choices to the plate of rice noodles smothered in glistening gravy, the nest of translucent bean thread noodles bathed in a scramble of crab and egg, and the bowl of wheat noodles still sizzling atop an evergreen bed of watercress. I was so preoccupied with my decision that I didn't see the merman descending from the ceiling, holding a gourd of wine.

"If I may," he said, "I'd recommend the fried noodles with the perch and black vinegar sauce. It's a specialty of the castle."

I looked up, discovering a young man with a brassy-orange fish tail and purple-black hair that ballooned and deflated as if breathing.

"Thank you," I said, taking his advice. "You must be—"

"Kunkoi." He somersaulted down to greet me and swept

the smoothest bow I'd ever seen. "The moment I heard that our new lady had an appetite for noodles, I knew we'd be friends. But I must admit, I thought Lord Elang was exaggerating about just how ravishing you are. Never have I been gladder to be wrong."

"*Ravishing?*" I raised a brow. "He really said that?"

"No," said Elang crisply, through locked teeth. "What I *did* say, Kunkoi, was that we wished to dine alone—"

"Yes, yes, I remember." Kunkoi raised his wine gourd. "But I wasn't at the welcoming reception. It'd be rude if I missed the chance to greet the Lady Saigas."

"Now you've met," said Elang. "You may take your leave."

Kunkoi rolled up his sleeves. "Five mortal years in exile, and you really haven't changed at all, my friend." He uncapped the gourd. "I'm afraid you've married a killjoy, Lady Saigas. Your husband didn't even want a party to hail his return, let alone celebrate your wedding."

Elang's lips thinned with displeasure. "Parties are a waste of Yonsar's scarce resources. Same as wine."

"It's an endless gourd," Kunkoi protested. When Elang changed the nearest goblet into a teacup, he grumbled, "And they say dragons are mercurial. How is it I work for the one who never changes?"

In response, Elang calmly folded back his sleeve. He was knotting ours together, both for our act and so I wouldn't keep floating off my seat.

"You're newly married," Kunkoi went on. "No one will begrudge you some fun. It's not like you have a court or actual subjects. A lord of your standing ought to have every fish and mollusk still in these wasted waters invited to feast, but instead you and Lady Saigas are in this grit-ridden hall, eating by your lonesome selves." He kicked his fins at the sand banks below. "No sprawling vines of water poppies and simmer-lilies, no boisterous music, no ribbon dancers. Even that pet demon of yours isn't here."

Elang moved closer to me by what felt an enormous inch. "The only person I desire to eat with is my wife. Starting today and going forward."

A flush came over my cheeks, and I had to stare into my noodles to keep from giving myself away. Bolts of Saino, he was good. Even I almost believed him.

Kunkoi certainly did, from the grin that spread across his face. "Interesting," he mused, pouring wine into a single silver cup. "I thought all your heartless heart cared about was tea and Yonsar, but it seems I was wrong. Lady Saigas must be special indeed."

He handed me the cup, then capped the wine gourd with a flourish. "Lady Saigas, you must tell me how you two met. Don't spare any details."

I expected Elang to cut in and steer the topic away. After all, he'd said he wanted to eat alone. But he was quiet. Listening.

Demon turds, I thought. "I . . . I was trying to sell a painting to the governor and went to the wrong house," I said, semi-truthfully. "I fell onto his roses."

"You fell onto his prized sanheia bushes, and he didn't turn you into a worm?" Kunkoi took the chair opposite me. "It truly must have been love at first sight."

I had to hold in a snort. "Something like that."

"Elang never does anything unpremeditated. He probably

hates you for catching him off guard. How did he sweep you off your feet?"

"With money," I replied. "Lots of it."

Kunkoi laughed, thinking I was joking. "Very unromantic. Very *Elang*."

Elang looked like he wanted to strangle Kunkoi—and me. With some restraint, he straightened, fists uncurling at his sides. "Are you finished? You ought to be inspecting the guard and not prattling on with my wife."

Every time Elang said *my wife,* I took a massive bite of noodles.

Kunkoi groaned. "What did Caisan tell you? That croaker, I told him not to accost you on your wedding day. He's been in a sour mood since the last storm, when Nazayun practically pummeled us into the—"

"Kunkoi." With one word, Elang extinguished the merman's good humor.

"Ah, right." Kunkoi cleared his throat and cast me a bright smile. "How about more watercress, Lady Saigas? It's good for the gills."

"What are the storms?" I asked.

"Something Lord Elang was going to tell you about tomorrow, rather than on this happy day." Kunkoi served me another heap of noodles. "But since you're asking, they're tokens of King Nazayun's . . . affection. He sent quite a few to Yonsar while Lord Elang was away."

"Which is why the realm is so empty," I murmured.

"Most of the merfolk left. The storms are harder on my kind than on the turtles, you see." Kunkoi gestured at his fins. "No shells."

I had witnessed the Dragon King turn his own forces into stone. I would flee too, if I were in Ai'long. "Kunkoi, are your friends and family—"

"They are safe," said Elang. "They've left. Kunkoi ought to as well."

"If I leave, who will cook for you? A good chef is a physician of sorts, and the turtles have deplorable taste in food, all bland and slimy. Don't even get me started on your demon."

Elang was unmoved. "If you stay, you might die."

"Might, or might not. At least the wine here is good." Merrily, Kunkoi raised the entire gourd. "A toast to living. Now that Lady Saigas is here, we'll have a better shot at it." He bowed. "I'll leave you two to enjoy your first meal together as the lord and lady of Yonsar. Don't bite into the noodles. I rolled them extra-long, for your life together."

Kunkoi made his departure, and I was left alone with Elang, who still hadn't touched his dinner. Instead he sipped his tea, using it as an excuse not to talk to me. I knew that game. Usually I played it well, but not tonight.

"It's comforting to know you have a friend," I said, breaking the silence. "*We* should at least try to get to know each other, for the sake of appearances. Dinner is a good time for that. Nomi used to say that the best friendships are made over food. She wanted to meet a dragon and charm him with crullers."

He took another sip of tea. Even had the gall to refill *my* cup. "More likely she'd have gotten herself turned into a cruller."

I twirled my noodles, silently grousing. "You're the one who wanted us to eat alone. If every dinner is going to be this stimulating, I'd like to know so I can bring a book next time."

He set down his tea. "I'll have a selection curated for your studies."

He really was going to make this difficult, wasn't he? "Are you even going to touch your noodles?" I asked then. "As your wife, I should at least be aware of whether you eat as humans do. Or will you be hunting whales and sharks with your claws, and picking at their bones while the rest of us sleep at night?"

"I eat as you do," he responded after a glacial beat. "And sleep. Is there anything else you wish to know?"

Finally, an actual answer. "Are you a thousand years old?" I pressed. I was curious, to be honest. "You don't look a day over three hundred."

He gave me a narrow look. "The tides of time in Ai'long are different than in Lor'yan," he responded. "But I age wherever I am. I am twenty-one suns."

He was only three years older than I was. Surprising. "You act older."

"I've been wanted dead since I was born. Such a life does wonders for one's maturity."

I almost laughed. "So I didn't marry an ancient elder. Just a heartless young man-dragon. That's reassuring."

"Is the interrogation finished?"

I tilted my head sideways. It was impossible reading someone with two faces, I decided. What I knew was he was stronger than a typical man. Much stronger, given how ready he'd been to take on the sharks earlier. He was fast too. And his scales were thick like armor. Not to mention, he had magic. "Can you get sick? Can you get hurt?"

"Yes. To both." He didn't like this topic. "I heal faster than full-blooded humans, but I bleed like you, and I hurt like you. Does that answer your questions?"

It did. I scraped the side of my bowl for the last of my noodles, while Elang had yet to begin eating his. "That was quite a welcome your grandfather gave us."

"It'll be the first of many," said Elang tightly. "But you may rest easy for now. Since he has acknowledged our marriage, no harm will come to you today."

"But tomorrow?"

"Tomorrow is a new day."

How cheering. I leaned back in my chair, taking a moment to let my food digest. "On the bright side, at least I met him."

Elang eyed me, sidelong. "What is your meaning?"

"I know it was all just water, and that wasn't his *physical* body, but still." I was thoughtful. "I saw his face. I never forget a face. When will we get to meet him in person?"

"In all the seven immortal ages, that question has never been asked with such alacrity."

"What can I say?" I shrugged. "I want my three chests of jewels."

And answers about Baba.

"If we're unlucky, he will come to us," said Elang. "You recall the patrols. He has his eye on Yonsar."

He reached for his soup and drank straight from the bowl, finishing it in one long sip. He still hadn't touched his noodles.

"Worry about meeting my grandfather later. For now, you have work to do." Elang pushed aside his bowl. "Study all you can about dragons and learn to take control of your visions. Shani will help you."

"Shani?" I scoffed. I hadn't seen the demon in hours. "Some bodyguard, she didn't even help when we were attacked today."

"We didn't need her help. If she had shown herself, she would only have aggravated the patrols."

"No surprise. She's a demon."

He gave me a hard look. "In your world, demons are feared and reviled. But they are not always deserving of such scorn. You ought to know better than most, what that feels like."

A tingle passed over my skin. Not once had I spoken to Elang about being half-Balardan. How it'd been impossible for me to get a job because the shopkeepers assumed I'd steal from their tills. When we went to the temple, I told Falina and Nomi—who passed easily as A'landans—to pretend they didn't know me, so they could pray in the front instead of having to wait in the back.

Shame scorched the back of my throat. Yes, I knew what it was like. I had a feeling Elang did too.

"Shanizhun was one of the first demons to be born," said Elang. "She's nearly as old as the gods, and few have known my grandfather as long as she. I'd advise you to respect her guidance."

I gave a numb nod.

"Good." Elang dipped into his noodles. "Mailoh will bring you sangi in the morning, and afterward she'll give you a tour of the castle."

"A tour?" I perked up.

"You're the lady of the Westerly Seas. You ought to know your own home."

"Does that mean I get to see the treasury?" I asked coyly. "Or do you use those powers of yours to turn ordinary rocks into rubies?"

Deeming my questions unworthy of reply, he reached for his silver cup. "A toast to us," he said, raising his drink. "May our time together be short, and may we part as unfamiliar to one another as we began."

It was the oddest wedding toast, yet I wouldn't have asked for anything different. I raised my cup and drank.

The rest of dinner, Elang ate his noodles in silence. At least when I was looking, he didn't bite into a single strand.

CHAPTER NINETEEN

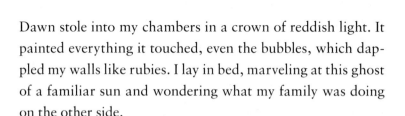

Dawn stole into my chambers in a crown of reddish light. It painted everything it touched, even the bubbles, which dappled my walls like rubies. I lay in bed, marveling at this ghost of a familiar sun and wondering what my family was doing on the other side.

It'd been a long time since I'd had a morning to myself. Nomi was the scholar in the family, but I loved to read too. As promised, Elang had sent a stack of books to my door. No adventure or romance novels, sadly, but I delved into the thickest tome I could find, the *Registry of Ai'long's High Courts*. It was far more riveting than I expected, leaving out no scandal or crime. I was so engrossed that I didn't hear Mailoh arrive with my sangi.

She peered over my shoulder. "Reading about our lore, I see. You are the twenty-third human wife of a dragon. You would've been the twenty-fourth, had the Dragon King's heir married that Kiatan princess, but—"

"Don't tell me." I raised a halting hand. "I haven't gotten that far yet. I'm still only in the Second Era, when General Lusi's son swiped the Emerald Dragon's whisker."

"Ah," said Mailoh. "Still a thousand years before Lord Elang was born. A fair warning, you'll not find anything about him in that book."

"I'm not surprised," I said wryly. "I've gotten a sense that he's not very popular around here."

"In a way, that's to your advantage. A half dragon's bride need not go through the traditional rites of Ai'long. Trust me, they can be quite awful."

"Sangi is bad enough," I said, spying the bottle on her tray. "Can't I skip a dose? I promise I won't drown."

"The drowning isn't what will kill you. Don't forget you're at the bottom of the sea. Miss a dose of sangi, and the weight of these waters will come crushing down until you're naught but bubbles and foam."

Goose bumps bristled across my skin, and not just from the cold. "On second thought, I appreciate your punctuality, Mailoh."

Mailoh huffed a laugh. "You're funny, Lady Saigas. No wonder Lord Elang loves you so."

"If he loved me, he'd find a way to make sangi taste better."

"Cheer up, I brought cake. You might find it goes down easier with something sweet."

I instantly perked as she lifted the lid of a bamboo steamer. "Thousand-layer cake," said Mailoh. "It's one of Kunkoi's specialties. He doesn't get to make it often since Lord Elang doesn't like sweets, and, well, we don't get many human visitors."

"You don't eat cake?"

"Our diet is mostly fish and algae," said Mailoh. She gave a small smile. "Sometimes jellyfish, when we're lucky. You'd better drink, you only have a few minutes left."

I'd been skeptical that anything could wash away the foul taste of sangi, but this cake proved me wrong. The salted egg custard was sweet yet savory and coated my tongue in a sumptuous cream. I let out a happy sigh. "I might actually look forward to these morning rituals. Is Kunkoi looking to take on an apprentice?"

Mailoh looked scandalized. "You're the lady of the castle—you're not to cook."

"It seems everyone in the castle has multiple roles. I can paint murals on the empty walls and make cakes. Noodles too. I've always wanted to be better at making noodles." I winked at her. "I could make jellyfish noodles for you."

"We'll see," said Mailoh, amusement brightening her round eyes. She sent my tray sailing away, and I set down my book, letting myself float off the mattress. "Now, for your tour. Where would you like to see first? Don't say the kitchen. I will not abide the lady of the castle toiling away, especially on her very first day."

I tucked a brush into my sleeve, in case I needed to take notes. "Show me all the secret passageways. I want to see the dungeons, the treasury, and especially where Elang hides all his expensive art."

Mailoh chuckled. "You've been reading about Jinsang Palace. Our little castle is not quite so grand. There are no hidden passageways that I'm aware of, though Lord Elang does store his tea collection behind the most unsightly tapestry of the Floating Mountains. That's the closest that I can think of to a secret room. And a treasury."

I wrinkled my nose. "A treasury of dried leaves and tin cans?"

"Yes, mostly. It's where Lord Elang keeps the valuables he

acquires from his trips to land. Tea is his main conquest. Last I checked there were also a few old maps."

"What about art?" I suggested. "There must be a gallery somewhere."

"Lord Elang doesn't collect art."

"But in Gangsun, he had so many . . ."

Was it my imagination, or did Mailoh suddenly tense? "The only paintings he loves are yours, Lady Saigas," she assured me. She wrapped a shawl around my shoulders. "You'll have to fill our barren halls with your works."

I frowned, but I let it go. She probably knew about my background as a forger. "Let's start off with the barracks, then. Elang mentioned that side of the castle was off-limits."

"As it should be! The entire wing is still damaged from the last storm. Don't look so disappointed—you look as though you *want* Lord Elang to be keeping secrets from you." With a laugh, Mailoh glanced up at the crimson stripes staining the afternoon. "Perhaps we can squeeze in a visit to the garden before the seas turn too rough. An old turtle like me is always worrying about the weather."

"There's a garden?" I couldn't imagine anything growing in this wasteland.

"Yes, many! They used to be Yonsar's great pride. But now . . . well, the courtyard is still lovely, and it has walls that are inlaid with gold. Perhaps Shani will know of other treasures."

"Shani's coming?"

"She's always with you," said Mailoh, reminding me of my ring.

I glanced down at the opal. Elang wanted me to trust the demon, but I barely trusted him.

When Mailoh wasn't looking, I rotated the ring so the opal faced my palm.

I closed my fist and followed the turtle out.

From outside, the castle had appeared a hidden fortress, a warren of mysterious secrets and treasures. Inside, it reminded me more of a forlorn chest of drawers.

The space was larger than I had expected, with the majority of the grounds spanning behind the two cliffs that camouflaged the castle. There were indoor ponds with stone fountainheads modeled after Elang's dragon ancestors, galleries with domed ceilings so high I felt like I was standing at the bottom of a vase. But the walls were always bald, save for the perfunctory tapestry or scroll, and each chamber was empty. No lanterns, no furnishings, no people.

"The storms have driven away most who live in the Westerly Seas," explained Mailoh. "Even my youngest daughter was sent away—Lord Elang bade all the children to leave for their safety, and many of the merfolk have sought refuge ashore."

I could hear the ache in her voice. "Why have the turtles stayed?"

"Yonsar is our home," she replied. "We will stay until the end."

She moved on. In the bowels of the castle, we came across a mantle of ferns and hanging roots. Mailoh swept it aside, and beyond was an open inner courtyard.

"This is my favorite place," she said. "The Court of Celestial Harmony."

I could see why. In the center was a floating pavilion with

a crystal roof, the pattern of its ridges bringing to mind an iridescent carapace. The water here was warmer, alit by the faintest golden glow. I sifted the sand through my fingers, marveling. Each grain was star shaped.

"A remnant of the beauty that once was Yonsar," Mailoh murmured wistfully. "It's believed that the Luminous Hour originated here."

"The Luminous Hour?"

"It's a gift from the merfolk, honoring the sacred peace between them and dragons. Thousands of glowing pearls float across the realm, and the waters of Ai'long are at their brightest. It's very beautiful, and there's always a joyous celebration—even here in Yonsar."

Will I see it? I wanted to ask, but Mailoh didn't know that my stay here was temporary.

"When is it?" I asked instead.

"It comes a few days before the Resonant Tide."

"When the waters are at their darkest," I mused. "How poetic."

"Lord Elang's only seen it once. Did you know, he tried to capture some of the pearls and bury them here? He'd bury crabs in the sand banks too; he trained them to scare anyone passing by. He was quite a rascal when he first came to Ai'long."

I found that difficult to imagine. "What happened?"

"His mother found out. She made him return the pearls—and the crabs."

His mother, who I'd gathered was human. Mailoh didn't elaborate, and I sensed the topic was off-limits, even for her.

I spilled the sand back onto its bed. "I like it here too. It's warm."

"It wasn't always cold in Yonsar. When Lord Elang breaks his curse, the waters will be warm once more."

The plaintive hope in her voice caused my chest to tighten. Even Mailoh thought I was here to find his pearl. I wasn't looking forward to letting her down.

Just beyond the court, I noticed a barren field, along with a row of short walls trellised in green buds. "Is that the garden?" I asked.

"Part of it. Lord Elang's been attempting to revive some of the flowers, but they never survive the storms. So he's begun transplanting a few closer to the Court of Celestial Harmony as an experiment."

Elang, gardening *here*? I could hardly imagine anything surviving, let alone thriving, in this bleak seascape. "What flowers?" I asked.

"Thorny ones," said Elang himself, approaching us from behind, "with poisonous barbs that shoot out to deter intruders."

"My favorite kind," I replied tartly. My hackles rose as I whirled to face him. I knew he was alluding to our first encounter.

Mailoh, however, did not. She beamed to see Elang here. "Your Highness, we weren't expecting you."

"I ended my meeting with the general early." Elang planted himself at my side, beholding me in his gaze. "I missed my wife."

His eyes met mine, both darkly intense. Even though I knew he was acting, my heart quickened a notch. His hair was black today, just like the roses he'd been planting when we first met. It made him look less devilish, more human.

"Have you gone up to the rooftop?" he asked, gesturing

at the pavilion. "It boasts the best view of the garden, perhaps even the whole of the castle grounds."

I put on my coyest smile. "Why don't you take me?"

Not the bat of an eyelash ruffled Elang's poise. Without taking his eyes off me, he said, "You are relieved of your afternoon duties, Mailoh. I'll show Lady Saigas the rest of the castle personally."

The turtle was practically bubbling. I could read what she was thinking—*Look how joyful Lord Elang is now that he's found his Heavenly Match.* I struggled to maintain my smile as she bounced into a bow, then swam away.

The instant she was gone, Elang's demeanor changed. He put distance between us, and his countenance became about as affectionate as an urn. "Follow me."

"Where are we going?"

"I requested dinner with you daily. It is nearly time."

Was it? Usually my stomach was an infallible tracker of mealtimes. "I thought you were going to show me the rest of the castle."

"You've seen enough. I'd rather suffer through our evening ritual sooner, before the smell of you repels my appetite."

He really was a demon turd. "If you find me so repulsive, you can eat alone."

"That isn't what we've agreed to."

Without another word, he spun back toward the castle. Just as on land, he liked tormenting me with his speed. By the time we reached the moon-shaped doors, I was breathless, and they shuddered to a thunderous close barely a beat after I made it inside. Meanwhile, Elang continued down the endless hallway, his shoulders leaning slightly forward as he swam. I couldn't help admiring his grace, the way he moved through the water without a ripple. If only he didn't have the personality of a bludgeon.

When I finally caught up, he was already seated at the banquet table, drinking tea. A simpler meal than yesterday awaited, only two dishes. A morass of noodles in golden gravy and a whole steamed fish wreathed in plump leafy greens. I sank into the seat beside Elang, observing the otherwise-empty hall. Yesterday I hadn't appreciated how immense it was; it could have easily entertained hundreds, with its many round marble tables, the high crystal ceiling—stained an exquisite pea green that would have cost a fortune in the human world, the floating lanterns alit by luminescent lotus buds. Yet I doubted it'd seen such a crowd in years. There was a whiff of decayed grandeur about the entire castle, but especially here. The walls were enameled with mother-of-pearl, but the finish was cracked and dented, many areas patched with stone; the pillars were veined with a gray and dire-looking coat of algae. Even the cushions on my seat were tattered.

"No Kunkoi tonight?" I asked.

"The staff has been instructed not to interrupt."

By *instructed*, I suspected he meant *warned*. It was so still in here, not even the lanterns dared flicker. With a sigh, I helped myself to a mass of noodles. Swimming was tiring work, and I was hungrier than I'd realized.

I ate quickly, using my full mouth as an excuse to ignore Elang. After all, he'd made it clear he wanted nothing to do with me. He didn't touch his noodles. All he did was drink his tea, to the point I wondered whether it was enchanted like Kunkoi's endless gourd.

"Do I really smell that bad?" I asked. "Or do you simply hate noodles?"

No answer, but Elang set down his drink. "Have you had a vision?"

So *that* was what was on his mind. I scraped a heap of noodles into my mouth. "I only arrived yesterday. I haven't even had time to pick up a brush."

"Then why is there ink on your arm?"

Sure enough, there was a black smudge peeking out from under my cuff. "It's just a map of your castle. I drew it during the tour."

"On your arm?"

"I forgot paper." I shrugged. "It was convenient."

"But you didn't forget a brush," he noted crisply.

"I've always got a brush with me."

"In case you have a vision?"

Demons of Tamra, he was obsessed. "Nomi says books are pocket gardens," I replied. "To me, a brush is pocket magic."

He lifted an inquisitive eyebrow.

"For taking notes and recording secrets," I replied, "and drawing maps of new places in case I need to make an escape. I've got a good memory, but even I can't remember every turn and corner, especially in a labyrinth like this. A brush can capture those details, and more."

"You are a strange girl, Tru Saigas," said Elang, looking unamused. "At least keep it in your pocket."

"I don't have a—"

He reached for the end of my sleeve, sparks of magic rushing from his fingertips. When I glanced down at my jacket, a new pocket had appeared, with a button to keep my brush and ink safe.

I looked up at him. *Thank you*, I meant to say, but the words caught in my throat. He was still holding my sleeve, his human side facing me. This close, I could feel the vibrations of water thrumming from his skin, could see my reflection in the glow of his yellow eye. It was beautiful, that eye, in a feral and unearthly way. But it belonged on the dragon half of his face, not the human one. The way it was, I couldn't tell which side was more beastly. Which side might bite.

"Someone's coming," Elang said, drawing me back with a claw. "I know it's difficult for you, but try to keep quiet."

No sooner did he finish speaking than a giant turtle came storming through the doors. "Where is that treacherous ingrate?" he demanded, waving his spear.

"General Caisan." Elang's voice sharpened. "I thought I made it clear we were not to be disturbed."

So this was the general. He had bright green eyes like Mailoh, though that was where their similarities ended. His neck was spindly, head jutting out like a flower on the end of a stalk, and his dark shell resembled a beetle's carapace more than a turtle's. Long slash marks mutilated the plates, such that some were cracked and even overlapping. He didn't have the look of someone who'd bring me cake in the morning.

"Do you know what she's done?" cried Caisan. "I speak of the demon Shanizhun." Another wave of his spear. "Come out, you ingrate!"

In a dramatic plume of mist, Shani burst out of the ring. It was the first time I'd seen her since leaving Gangsun. She wasn't a phoenix anymore and instead had taken on what I suspected was her natural form: a stingray-like fish with a downturned mouth and a lengthy spiked tail. It suited her better.

She flapped a fin over Elang's shoulder. "It was only a snack," she said. "After so long on land, you can't blame me for missing a taste of home."

"You see how brazen she is?" Caisan spluttered. "Have sense, Lord Elang. First she abandons you to Nazayun's patrols, then this morning my third lieutenant is found with his memories tampered with. She is clearly up to something."

"Enough, both of you." A low growl rumbled out of Elang's throat. "General, if you wish to disrupt my dinner, the least you could do is properly greet Lady Saigas."

I didn't know how humans appeared to turtles—perhaps we were as insignificant and gormless as stalks of kelp—but it seemed that only then did General Caisan finally notice me.

His round eyes swiftly took in my blue hair, then the opal ring on my finger. "Welcome, human. I see that you have already made your allegiances known."

"She's smarter than she looks," quipped Shani, "marginally. Which is still more than I can say about you."

Elang sent the demon a silencing look. "It was *I* who requested that the lady wear Shanizhun's ring," he said, turning to the general. "And she has a name."

"Yes, I am aware." Caisan glowered. "Truyan Saigas of West Gangsun, daughter of Arban and Weina. Master art *forger* of the Dor'lin District."

I flinched. Those were the exact words I'd used to introduce myself to Elang.

"You will address her as Her Highness, Lady Saigas, the High Lady of the Westerly Seas."

Caisan viewed me with clear disdain. "Is the above world so wretched that there was no other creature to ally yourself with than this . . . this—"

"Visionary painter?" I suggested wryly.

Caisan glared. "Scoundrel."

"Careful where you tread, Caisan," said Elang. "This *scoundrel* is now my wife."

Did I imagine it, or was there a touch of menace in Elang's voice, and a firm emphasis on the word *wife*?

Caisan landed into the sand banks with a thud, bowing his head low. "I beg you allow me to find you a proper partner, Lord Elang. The fate of Yonsar rests upon His Eternal Majesty believing you've found your Heavenly Match. This creature is neither believable nor suitable."

"I found it hard to believe as well," said Shani, "but he did marry the krill."

"Enough!"

Elang took my hand in his. "The strongest bridge is made of truth," he said, bringing my fingers to his mouth. "Deception will crumble, given enough time."

I thought he was going to bite me. It wasn't an unreasonable conclusion, given how the sharp tips of his teeth were skimming the water above my fingertips. But no, instead he placed the gentlest kiss on my knuckles, the heat of his breath warming the chill from my skin.

Against my will, I felt my pulse quicken. It wasn't lost on

me that the red strings on our wrists were touching. What on earth was he doing?

Finally Elang set down my hand. "General, I remind you that you swore to me an oath. You would do well to abide by it and extend such loyalty to Lady Saigas. She commands the Westerly Seas, same as I. Am I understood?"

Not once had Elang raised his voice, but as he spoke, the water vibrated, and a rush of susurrations hummed against my skin.

Caisan felt it too. "Yes, Your Highness." He bowed stiffly. "Forgive my insolence, Lady Saigas. I welcome you to Yonsar."

The turtle backed away, leaving us to resume our meal. Elang had taken no more than a bite of his noodles when suddenly, underneath the table, he wrapped his tail around my ankle.

I startled. "What are you—"

The tips of his claws were protracted, and his hair was turning dragon white, golden horns lengthening. Our bowls flew off the table as he grabbed me.

"The storm approaches," he shouted. "Into position!"

The walls shuddered, and an alarm resonated across the castle in a blaring chorus.

"General," Elang called to Caisan, "order your vanguard to the Spine. I want the south court bolstered by as many shells as possible."

The south court? That was where my room was.

Outside, the turtles moved into position. In a wave, they rushed for the castle walls, latching themselves to every bare surface. Their heads shrank back into their shells as they lined up across the castle, bracing for the incoming storm.

Hundreds of turtles, all in place within a minute. It was an astonishing feat, but I didn't get to watch long.

Elang seized me by the waist and hurled me away from the window—a moment before a cataclysmic wave fell upon Yonsar.

CHAPTER TWENTY

The entire sea shook, underwater waves the size of mountains lashing out at the castle. Debris spilled from the ceilings, and the crystal walls swayed, whistling like paper against wind. My every instinct screamed to find cover. Now I understood why so many had left Yonsar.

I climbed onto Elang's back, my arms wrapped around his neck as he barreled through the castle halls. His hair had become white, and his yellow eye glowed as his scales turned warm under my fingertips—signs that the dragon in him had taken over. It made him dizzyingly fast.

"Watch out!" I shouted in his ear. Outside, rocks winged against the walls, gales of sand leaking through the cracks. I lost count of how many times we narrowly escaped the toppling pillars, how many times Elang swerved before a door exploded.

At last we came to a halt.

"Your room," he said. There was a break between his words, the only sign that he was out of breath. "The south court is the safest place to be during a storm. It's against the

Spine; you'll be safeguarded by the mountain—and my best soldiers."

He ushered me through the round door. "Stay here. Shanizhun will protect you."

I whirled. He hadn't come inside. "*You* aren't staying?"

"I'm needed at the front." He unhooked his cloak. "Wear this. The silk is stronger than any armor, and the lining will heal minor wounds."

I wanted to insist that I go too, but I knew it'd be foolish. What good could I do outside against a storm? I pushed the cloak back his way. "You keep it. You'll need it more than I will."

His jaw clenched, as if he wanted to argue. Instead, he gave a curt nod. "Shanizhun, see that she does not leave this room. I'll be back when it's time for her sangi."

Without another word, he was gone, and Shani iced the door shut.

I swam to the window. Hundreds of turtles were forming a wall around the castle, using their hard shells to barricade us from the storm. I picked Mailoh out by the yellow spots on her shell, right before a fold of dark sea swept her out of sight. No matter how hard I looked, I couldn't find Elang.

I wiped my fingers on my sleeve. They still burned where his lips had touched, something I wanted to forget as quickly as possible.

"Can the turtles survive the storm?" I asked Shani.

"I doubt *everyone* will survive." Shani lounged on my bed, entirely too nonchalant about the whole affair. "How many casualties we get will depend on Nazayun's mood."

I closed my eyes, suddenly grateful that Elang had sent

away the children of Yonsar. At least Mailoh wouldn't have to worry about her daughter.

"You should go and help them," I said.

"My orders are to stay with you."

"I'll be fine on my own. Nazayun can't harm me, remember?"

"Don't be stupid. The curse might prevent him from killing you, but never for an instant think you're safe here. That's how you'll lose a limb—or two."

Shani, ever the font of reassurance.

The blasts were fainter in my room, short staccato bursts rather than a continuous stab. But I could still feel the storm intensifying, drawing nearer. Outside, the wall of turtles blocked my view. All I could see were the ribbons of debris that leaked between their shells.

"Why does he hate Elang so much?" I asked, pulling away as another blast struck the castle. "I read that dragons often marry merfolk and humans. Elang can't be the only one of his kind."

"But he is," replied Shani. "Children born of such unions are either dragon . . . or not. There are no halflings. And in the rare case that one is born, they're executed at birth."

"Elang survived," I pointed out. "Was he spared because his father is Nazayun's son?"

"He wasn't spared—he was cursed. His *mother* had the sense to pretend he was dead and keep him away from Ai'long. She raised him in the desert, as far away from the sea as she could. Still, they were always on the run."

I tried picturing Elang as a boy, his two faces covered by a black mask. Friendless and alone, with no one but his mother to trust—because anybody could be one of his grandfather's assassins. It couldn't have been easy for him, a half dragon growing up in a harsh and arid land—when water was the source of his strength.

"Why won't he just break his curse?" I asked. "He knows where his pearl is. Why make Yonsar suffer?"

"Because Nazayun's cruelty isn't limited to the Westerly Seas. It isn't even limited to the dragons." Shani's red eyes glittered. "You're just a human, you're too stupid to understand."

"Now you sound like Caisan."

Shani threw me a withering look.

I scooted closer. "Stupid or not, it helps for me to at least try. I'm stuck in Ai'long until I finish Nazayun's portrait. And I've got a feeling there's some trick to it. Not exactly something he'll be clamoring to flaunt on his palace walls."

The demon was silent, and I sensed I'd struck a chord.

"Show me how to paint him," I said. "Elang said you know him better than anyone."

"I more than know him," she hissed. "I've spent lifetimes emblazoning his wretched form into my memory." Her pitch rose with fervor. "In my dreams, I nick off his scales with my talons one by one, and I score the skin from his eyeballs slowly, painfully. Then I smother the light of his sacred pearl and drink his soul."

What did he do to you? I wondered, but I knew better than to ask.

"Perhaps you'll have your chance," I said instead.

"Fate never favors demons," said Shani through her teeth. "If it did, the Eight Immortals might've chosen *me* to vanquish Nazayun, not some foolish mortal."

"The Eight Immortals are involved?" My eyes widened.

According to legend, they were a secret council of deities that oversaw peace among the realms.

Shani merely sniffed. "Even a squall sprite has more promise than you. I saw the dragon you painted. It was so ordinary, so boring, so *human*. The least they could've done was chosen a master painter, not some tuna-haired swindler." She shivered into a puff of mist, sliding back into the opal ring. "You're just a waste of my time...."

Her words were a jab to my pride, yet I wasn't stung. What she said was true; I wasn't a master painter. I'd never formally trained, and only by forging the works of less popular artists had I barely been able to make a living.

But I'd capture the Dragon King's likeness. I *knew* I could.

"His scales overlap from neck to tail like a fish," I said aloud quietly, "but not in the head. He's a snake, in that way."

The mist swirled within the opal, the only sign that Shani was listening.

"He has roughly ten thousand scales," I went on. "Nine whiskers—four on the right and five on the left—and his pearl is lodged left of his chest, where it glows like a hazy moon."

The demon crawled out of my ring, still misty. "What of his eyes?" she asked.

What I remembered was that they were wintry, the palest blue before gray. I hadn't caught anything more.

"An artist always paints a dragon's eyes last," I said evasively. "They carry his spirit."

Shani saw through my ruse and made a harrumphing sound. But she did return to my desk.

"This is going to take a lot of work," muttered the demon.

In one languid motion, she shifted into a smaller imitation of Nazayun, shuddering when her transformation was complete.

She opened Nazayun's eyes, two wan and glittering ovals whose cold made me shudder. In the Dragon King's own merciless tone, she spoke, "Let us begin."

Confined to my room, I chased the hours by studying with Shani. "We're doomed," she'd say of my progress. "Nazayun is a dragon, not a lizard. Do it again."

The demon made for an exacting mentor. She sat on my shoulder, hurling insults into my ear when I made one mistake, tearing the parchment in half when I made two. Not once did I complain. The work took my mind off the storm, and off Baba.

All night I painted. Even when my fingers cramped and pruned, and new calluses formed where I held my brush, I pressed on. But I *was* only human. At some point, my eyelids grew heavy, as if weighed down by sand, and my brushstrokes started to drag.

The last thing I remembered was mixing a new well of gray paint.

I slept, but not deeply. Every time there came a lull in the storm, some part of the castle would subsequently explode. And toward the end of the night, when the sea was so dark not even the dawn lights could pierce its murk, the ring on my thumb grew cold.

"She fell asleep at her desk."

It was Shani speaking. My eyes were closed, but I could

tell from the ripples in the water that we weren't alone. Someone else had come.

I heard a rustling of pages. "Her progress has been pitiful," the demon went on. "There's no chance she'll be able to paint him—she can't even summon a vision."

There came a low murmur, but I couldn't hear what was said.

"Yes, she still despises you, though I suspect she is growing less fearful of you. Are you certain you don't want me to erase her—"

There came a brisk slice in the water, cutting off her reply.

It had to be Elang, I thought. No one else could silence the demon so effectively.

I could feel his presence grow nearer. He swam gracefully, his movements barely conjuring a ripple. In three quiet strides, he was at my side, his shadow eclipsing my bed.

The glass lip of a vial prodded open my mouth. I tried to peel open a sliver of eye, but Elang touched my forehead, and a wave of sleep overcame me.

Sangi washed down my throat, and I floated back into the sweet oblivion of my dreams.

In the morning, my fingers tingled.

Shani stepped on my hand, pressing harder when I winced. "You've been biting your lip and twitching your fingers for the last hour," she said. "Your mother's a gambler, you should know better than to have a tell."

"It's just a tingle," I explained groggily. "I get them because of my—"

"Visions. Finally you show a hint of progress." The demon waved a fin at the parchment. "Paint it out."

No. "After the storm ends."

"Now," insisted the demon. Shani sneered. "What, are you afraid you might make the castle collapse onto us?"

Yes. I bit my lip. *Or worse.*

The sneer was helpful, though. I ambled toward my chair, not remembering ever leaving it for bed. I picked up my brush.

When I first began to understand my Sight, I'd *thought* I could change the future. I used to tell myself, *If I can paint Baba alive, it will be so. I'll make it so.*

But every time I tried, pain shot up to my chest, immobilizing me. I would get as far as his silhouette before my hand would convulse, and I'd make an involuntary sweep with my brush, blotting out Baba's face with ink.

Leaving me as I'd been before, with only the ghost of his memory imprinted upon my heart.

My Sight could only give me glimpses of what was to come. Rarely had it done any good. Hadn't warned me about Gaari's death, hadn't given me answers about Baba, hadn't saved my family from losing our house.

But I had to try.

Muttering under my breath, I let my pupils roll back. I inhaled, blanking my thoughts and cutting away each string that tethered me to consciousness.

Once I let go, the glittering sensation in my fingertips rushed up to the backs of my eyes, sweeping them with a warm, hypnotic wash. The edges of the world blurred, and the rattling blasts from the storm became rinses of sound.

It was like painting in a dream. The Dragon King's head—

his hair, his eyes, and his whiskers—flew out of my brush. I painted jagged cliffs and a dense fog that curled around his beard. It was a place that I didn't recognize, and if I'd been fully awake, I might have asked Shani about it. But I was trapped in a dream, my lips pressed so tight that I couldn't part them.

Then the tingle behind my eyes flushed away, and slowly I came out of the trance.

There was a lull in the room, an odd silence from the demon that I wasn't used to.

"Was it real?" I asked. "Did I paint . . . Nazayun?"

"Come look for yourself."

It was always a jolt, seeing my vision manifest on physical paper. But there he was, the Dragon King in all his glory, looming before a frosty ridge. Lightning darted from his eyes, and his talons curled into the pallid sand. And his scales! They were like plates of sapphire, crisp and blue.

"He's beautiful," I whispered.

"He *is* a god," said Shani, landing on my shoulder. She pinched my bone. "Don't be too giddy. Good things rarely come from a visit with His Eternal Majesty."

I wasn't listening. "Look at the texture of his scales," I murmured, tracing my fingers over the sketch. "They're smooth. Translucent."

"And so?"

"He'll be an apparition when we meet," I explained. "Elang said my portrait has to be as accurate as life itself. If I'm going to do that, I'll need to see him in the flesh."

"What do you think I've been doing?" huffed the demon. "I know Nazayun better than anyone."

"Do you know how the shadows of his whiskers fall on his scales? Do you know whether light travels into the gaps between his teeth or how his muscles crease when he moves?"

Shani glowered.

"Most portrait artists wouldn't either," I allowed. "But I'm a forger, not an artist. I make my living on noticing things. It's my job."

"And my job is to keep you alive. You want to parade over to Jinsang to meet the Dragon King? Be my guest. But don't blame me when you foresee yourself as a puddle of sea foam."

"You're being dramatic."

"*You're* being naïve. Like I said, I know Nazayun better than anyone."

I would have rolled my eyes, except that was precisely when I saw the blood.

It was a shallow red pool I'd painted on the ground, obscured by the swirls of ice and debris surrounding King Nazayun. But once I made it out, it was unmistakable.

"Shani," I whispered, lifting the edge of the painting so she could see too. "Whose blood is that?"

"Yours, I'd guess," she replied tartly. "Demons don't bleed red."

"That isn't funny. Will you take another look?"

She sizzled with displeasure, but she studied what I'd painted more closely. "Never mind the blood," she said at last. "The frost is the real clue. There aren't many places in Ai'long *that* cold. Only the Northerly Seas, or maybe the bottom of the Western Fold."

"What's the Western Fold?"

"A chasm along the Spine. It's not far from the castle."

"That has to be where we meet Nazayun," I replied. "Will you take me when the storms are over?"

"Why bother? I thought everything you see is inevitable."

"It is, but a push can't hurt."

"Elang'anmi won't like you going behind his back."

Honestly, I didn't care what Elang thought.

I folded my sketch, pocketing it in my skirt. Soon I'd meet the Dragon King. I would make every second count.

CHAPTER TWENTY-ONE

When the walls stopped whispering and the water tasted like ash, I knew the storm was over. By the next morning, the turtles had dislodged themselves from the castle. They floated amid the wreckage, hanging like a constellation of sorrows. Quietly they crooned a low song and beat their shells to mourn the fallen.

Elang was in a grim mood. He didn't even acknowledge me when I found him, clearing rubble alone in the garden. He looked like he'd been there for hours; dust and sediment muddied his tunic, and his hair, usually swept into a tidy knot, was matted against his back, clinging to the silvery-blue ridges of his spine.

I tried not to shiver as I trudged toward him. Outside my room, the water was as frigid as snow. It was still thick, too, and I opened my umbrella to shield myself from falling debris.

"Dumplings?" I offered, slightly breathless as I crouched beside Elang. "Kunkoi brought them last night, but they're still chewy."

Elang didn't look at me. "You shouldn't be out here."

He sounded tired. I returned the dumplings to my pocket

and shuffled closer to him. "I'm sorry about the turtles," I said softly. "Can I help?"

"You aren't needed here." His yellow eye was cloudier than I'd seen before. "Go back inside."

He turned to a pile of fallen boulders and placed his palm upon the largest one, his face contorting in concentration. I watched the rock shrink, becoming grains of sand. When it was done, he let out a shaky exhale and gripped his left shoulder, as if he was in pain. Then he swept aside the rubble until he found the next boulder, and he repeated the enchantment.

"Is your shoulder all right?" I asked. "I've seen it bother you before."

A grunt. "It's nothing. An old wound."

"From the jellyfish? I could look at it for you—"

"That won't be necessary." He started to motion a turtle over to escort me inside, but I moved closer to him, undaunted.

"I had a vision yesterday."

Finally he spared me a glance. "What was it?"

My hands were half-frozen. I breathed to warm them before unrolling my painting. "Look here, Shani thinks this might be the Western—"

"The Fold," he finished for me. His jaw locked when he saw the blood. "You ought to return inside. There are rocks falling, and the currents are unpredictable."

"Is that all you have to say?"

He put his hand over mine. Anyone looking on would think we were being affectionate; they wouldn't see Elang firmly nudging me toward the castle. "It's a vision of *your* future. If you stay put, it won't come true."

Simmering with frustration, I folded the vision back into my pocket. Meanwhile, Elang was still turning rocks into sand. It took me a moment to realize he wasn't just clearing rubble.

"What are you searching for?" I asked.

It'd been only days since we'd met, but I was starting to learn the clockwork of his two faces, to read the narrowing of his mismatched eyes and the brackets that formed around his mouth when he left words unsaid. The dragon side was less good at hiding its emotions, I found. The vibrance of his scales was muted, his pupil constricted. Something was on his mind.

"Elang?"

"Mailoh is missing," he said at length. "We haven't seen her since last night."

I felt like I'd been punched. My voice crawled out of my throat: "I've got to help."

"There is already a search party," Elang replied. "Caisan's brought his best scouts."

"Let me—"

"There's nothing you can do. You can barely swim, and your human flesh is prey to the cold. It would be better if you went back inside."

Whatever I was going to say shriveled up in my throat. Behind him, a group of turtles appeared in the near distance, circling the castle perimeter. Seeing them made my chest tighten. Mailoh had a daughter, I remembered. A young daughter who had been sent away from Yonsar. I had been in her place once. I hadn't even known that Baba was missing—until it was too late.

"Have you tried looking beyond the canyons?" I asked Elang.

"Yes. Now go in—"

"What about the Western Fold?"

Elang could tell what I was thinking. "*No one* is permitted there, and that includes you."

"But Mailoh could be—"

"It isn't safe," he said, cutting me off. His shoulders squared; this wasn't easy for him either. "We'll find her once the sea has settled. I'll not risk any more lives."

It was the hardest thing, dragging my eyes away from the dark cliffs beyond the castle and making myself nod mutely. But a plan was already bubbling in my mind, and I couldn't give it away. "I'll leave."

His jaw relaxed. He'd been prepared for a longer argument. "I'll call for you when it's safe."

I pretended to head back inside the castle, but as soon as I was out of Elang's sight, I dipped into a thicket of coral and rubbed at my ring. "Shani, I need your help."

In a glittering cloud, the demon misted out of the opal. "Lying to your husband so early in your marriage?" she jabbed. "Doesn't bode well for your future together."

I wasn't in the mood for her quips today. I pulled her by the tail, bringing her close. "Hush and listen. Mailoh's missing. I need you to help me find her."

"Why should I care about that stodgy old rubberhead? Besides, you heard Elang'anmi's orders. We're not to leave."

"If you don't come," I said, twisting off my ring, "I'm going to grill your opal over the fire. See how you like sleeping on coals."

"Manipulative and extortionate." Shani's mouth quirked. "I respect it."

She thrust out her triangular fins, each lengthening until they resembled her old wings. She became just large enough for me to ride on her back. "Hop on quickly. If we get caught, I'm blaming everything on you."

Together, we blasted out of the castle. I lay on my stomach, pressing myself flat against Shani's back as I scrabbled for some part of the demon to grasp. As a stingray, Shani had no ridges or small fins, and her skin was smooth and slippery. Riding on her back was as unwieldy as flying on a blanket. I couldn't say for sure that she'd rescue me if I fell off.

I hoped I wouldn't have to find out.

Around the canyons, the sea was thick, grit from the storm swirling in ominous patterns. "Mailoh," I shouted. "Mailoh, where are you?"

There was only silence.

"The scouts have already searched this area," said Shani as we traced the gorges and valleys. "She's not here."

"What about the Fold?" I said, pointing to where the canyons tapered off. The water there was darker, as if doused with ink. My stomach curdled with dread. What if it was Mailoh's blood that I'd painted in the vision? "In there, you see how dark the waters are? Mailoh could be inside."

"We're not going down there." She pulled away. "The currents are getting stronger. All the scouts have gone back already. If they haven't found her, then—"

"Don't say it."

My head rang with memories from the past: *We've done our best to look for him. If they haven't found his ship by now . . .*

After all these years, I still remembered how Mama's eyes had welled with tears, and how she'd turned away to wipe at her face. For months there'd been a damp spot on her collar.

"Mailoh's out there," I said firmly. "I know she is. We can't give up."

Shani flapped her fins, straining against the undertow. It was clear she wanted to go back.

"Come on," I persisted. "You're the fiercest, strongest demon in Ai'long. What are a few bad tides to you? Show the Eight Immortals what a mistake they made, overlooking you."

"Just shut up," Shani said. "We'll go back when I say so."

That was as much as I could ask for.

We dipped into a canyon, skimming the turbulent waters below. Tiny rocks pelted my eyes, but I didn't dare blink lest I miss a clue. I trained my attention to every crack and crevice, trying to find Mailoh's dark green shell, the yolky spots along its rim.

But there was nothing. The storm had washed the canyons clean, sweeping even the barnacles away. Plains of gravelly sediment lapped the seafloor, seemingly without end.

It grew colder the farther we drifted from Yonsar. Goose bumps prickled my skin, and as I buttoned my collar to keep warm, I looked down the sides of Shani's fins, searching for signs of frost. But I saw nothing.

Look harder, Tru, I told myself. *What happened to those infamous powers of observation? There's got to be something.*

"What about that?" I pointed at a series of black cliffs jutting out of the sand, like teeth engraved into the earth. "Those cliffs were in my vision. Can we get closer to look?"

"It's too dangerous," said Shani sharply. "Look how fast the currents are moving. It's a trap."

"I'm not afraid," I said. "If *you* are, then you can stay here. I'll take a look—"

Shani grabbed me by the ankle. "I'm not afraid of anything," she hissed. "It's your pathetic spine I'm looking after. You swim slower than a seahorse, and you want to dive down alone?"

She let out an exasperated grunt, the only signal she gave before she swooped, plunging into the dark expanse below.

It *was* a trap. The moment we dove between the cliffs, we were caught, sucked into a rush of eddying streams. Shani struggled and batted her fins, furiously trying to regain control, but the water was moving too fast. We sped forward, careening in every direction. Faster and faster, with no end in sight.

Then the seafloor began to quake, and I heard a terrible crashing sound, seemingly without end.

Just ahead was a dark and fearsome slat, a narrow gorge between two cliffs, with white sheets of water rushing off either side.

The Fold.

My heart clenched with panic. I kicked harder, fighting against the currents in any way I could, but they were strong, like an unrelenting wind. My jar of chilis tumbled out of my pocket, the extra dumplings I'd brought for Elang too. They were sucked into the Fold, where they vanished amid the torrents of water. Soon we'd be next.

"Shani!" I shouted, trying to stake my umbrella into the seabed for purchase. We were skidding for the edge of the cliff. "Shani, do something!"

It was the oddest comfort, seeing the demon's red eyes glimmer with annoyance. In a beat, she changed into a squid and clung to the rock bed with her tentacles.

"Any more good ideas?" she hissed. "We're stuck. If we

try to go back up, those cataracts will crash down on our heads. I'd survive, obviously, but you? Sea foam."

I pressed my face to her back, too winded for words. Beneath my feet, the sea poured down into an unfathomable abyss. What could we do?

Let's go down there, I thought. *Into the abyss.*

The demon didn't hear me, which was probably for the best.

It sounded mad, yet it made sense. There was no frost where we were, it wasn't cold enough. This wasn't where we were meant to be. But down there . . .

I craned my neck. I spotted a flash of green that had landed below—on what looked like a narrow ledge. I squinted. "Shani, do you see that? Could it be . . ." I gasped. "Mailoh."

Shani saw too, her body starting to shift back into its usual form. "Hold on."

Her winglike fins extended at either side as she dove into the Fold, spiraling through the walls of waters. It didn't take us long to reach Mailoh. The turtle lay supine, inside a cave carved within the cliff. Frost rimed her eyelids, and icicles laced her shell. I almost didn't see the long crack on her back.

She was unconscious.

"Can you lift her?" I asked Shani urgently.

She didn't get a chance to respond. The currents, raging only moments ago, went still.

It was a shock, how placid it had become. How *dark* it had become. The water turned black, and sulfurous fumes curled out from an unseen hollow, illuminated by the glow of Shani's red eyes.

The demon clamped her fin over my mouth and pushed me deep into the cave.

Nine Hells of Tamra, she seethed into my mind. *It's not a cave. It's a lair.*

Fear iced my blood. A lair—for what?

I soon had my answer.

Amid the interminable silence, I heard a clicking sound from deeper within the chasm, like crab legs skittering across rock. The sound echoed. It was getting louder.

Shani, I thought, gripping my umbrella and wishing it were a weapon. *What is that?*

Thadu. The demon's voice dropped an octave, turning gruff. *One of Nazayun's monsters.*

Nazayun's monsters. I'd read of three-headed giant crabs, tentacled snakes, but I'd thought they were all tales. It seemed I was wrong.

A pincer shot out of the dark, slicing through rock. I screamed.

He's here, Shani shouted.

Next came an eye, a fleshy sage-green orb. It pressed upon the opening in the cave, gaping at me.

So you're a rude monster, I thought through my fear. I hated when people stared. Through my irritation came an inkling of courage. I propped up my umbrella as if it were a spear—and gouged Thadu in the eye.

With a roar, he fell back. I caught flashes of metallic skin and a pink tongue clicking against pointed teeth. Then his pincer came clawing into the cave, finding Mailoh's shell.

"NO!" I shouted, shielding the turtle with my umbrella.

Shani shoved me aside. "Are you *trying* to get killed?"

She threw herself at Thadu, lashing out her tail and wrapping it around his pincer.

Thadu thrashed. As the spiked end of Shani's tail bit into his flesh, silvery strands peeled off his skin, like glass noodles. And then Shani's eyes glowed red. Ravenously red.

I'd never seen a demon devour a soul before. The edges of her form began to shimmer, and as she drank, the sound was a wet sizzle that brought bile to my throat.

His head rearing, Thadu retreated, snapping his claws as he dug out of the cave.

"Now you flee?" Shani shouted. She smacked her lips. "Coward. He wasn't even tasty—"

Click, click, click.

I clamped Shani's mouth shut. Thadu was just outside the cave, skittering across the rock. Was he retreating? My heart fluttering in my ears, I crawled forward to get a better look, and gasped.

He was a thing of nightmares—what I imagined the child of a centipede and crab might look like. Hairy white legs sprang along the length of his spine, and teethlike spikes covered his head, which was studded with ten unblinking eyes peering out from every direction.

Those eyes tracked me, holding me in their bulbous gaze. Thadu let out a hiss.

"Get back!" Shani yelled, blocking the mouth of the cave with her body. Hot, sulfurous spit sprayed out of Thadu's mouth, and Shani arched back, shuddering in pain.

Click, click, click. Thadu's laugh grated against my ears. His pincers scraped outside the cave, trying to pry Shani from the opening. Puffs of hot air stole in from the cracks around Shani's fins, clearly hurting her, but she didn't give in.

Thadu hissed again, his tongue clicking obscenely. Another spray, then he rammed his head against the mountain.

It was like being thunderstruck. The sound alone deafened me, and my entire body vibrated with the impact. As the walls fissured, debris spilling from every crack, I dropped onto my stomach and covered my head.

This was not looking good.

You can't hold the cave forever, I shouted into Shani's thoughts.

Do you have a better idea?

No, but I had *an* idea. I'd seen the way Thadu had squirmed while Shani had snacked on his soul. If only she could do it again, we might have a chance....

I'm going to jump onto your back, I said. *When he sees me close, he'll try to spit steam again. That's when we'll dive into his mouth.*

What? Are you—

Serious? Yes. And with that, I leapt.

At the sight of me, Thadu widened his jaws once more, about to launch another revolting projectile of spit. "Go, go, go!" I shouted as soon as I landed on Shani's back.

We barreled out of the cave and shot straight into his mouth. Heat scalded my skin, and demon turds, his breath was foul—like rotting death. As if that weren't bad enough, his tongue pushed against me, slimy and wet, and his teeth sawed back and forth in anticipation of crushing my bones.

A beat before Thadu's teeth came biting down, I stabbed upward. The monster snarled, his jaw convulsing. Silvery threads unraveled from every point of his body. Thinking fast, I jammed my umbrella between his tongue and the roof of his mouth like a stake.

He bucked. Steam hissed out of his palate, a fetid perfume of sulfur and iron and decay. I buried my face in my sleeve, trying not to breathe in while I held on to the umbrella. It had already proved to be astoundingly sturdy, but it wouldn't last long. "Shani, hurry up!"

This time, Shani didn't drink with relish. She flew out of Thadu's mouth, her expression solemn as she sipped. "Long you have suffered," she told him when the silver glow of his strands turned dull. "Be free, Thadu. In your next life, do well to avoid the wrath of dragons."

Thadu let out a groan. I could feel the heat of his breath turning cold, the fat capillaries in his head swelling as his ten eyes throbbed, almost spasming. Vertebra by vertebra, he began to fold over.

It was my sign to get out of there. His tongue was lolling from side to side, pushing me back. My robe snagged on a tooth, and I couldn't swim away fast enough.

The roof of his mouth came falling, and he plunged, taking me with him. Down we fell, into a darkness without end.

CHAPTER TWENTY-TWO

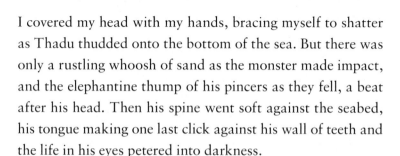

I covered my head with my hands, bracing myself to shatter as Thadu thudded onto the bottom of the sea. But there was only a rustling whoosh of sand as the monster made impact, and the elephantine thump of his pincers as they fell, a beat after his head. Then his spine went soft against the seabed, his tongue making one last click against his wall of teeth and the life in his eyes petered into darkness.

I sucked in a breath of relief. Using my umbrella, I pried his jaws open and crawled out. I stumbled into a puddle of glassy, bright blood. It was sticky, the globs clinging maliciously to my palms. Disgusting.

My dress was in tatters, and my hair was slick with monster saliva. With a sharp exhale, I waddled out of the mess and sprang to my feet. Slowly I took in my surroundings.

The Fold. It was the valley between the expanse of cliffs, a mysterious vacuum in the already desolate chart of Yonsar. The water was murky, but if I squinted, I could make out a dim silvery light fanning across the seabed. Under my feet was a field of sand, and veins of frost marbled the mountain face. I shivered, rubbing my hands together for warmth. The sea's cold bite was already seeping into the marrow of my bones. If I didn't get out of here soon, I'd freeze.

"Shani?" I called, tapping on the ring. *Shani, can you hear me?*

My voice echoed off the desolate cliffs. Shani wasn't here.

I gulped. On the bright side, that hopefully meant the demon was on her way back to the castle with Mailoh. On the not-so-bright side, it meant I was alone.

An icy knot hardened in my gut. Or maybe not as alone as I thought.

I trod along the sandy bottom, following the silver light. Swirls of thick fog laced the water, obscuring its source. But I had a feeling.

"Nazayun," I whispered.

His eyes blended well into the fog, yet nothing could mask the lightning crackling in his pupils. They glowed bright, watching me.

This was the moment I'd foreseen. A tremor came over me, and I clenched my teeth to keep from making any sound. I stumbled over the sand, crumpling the sketch of my vision in my pocket. No matter what, Nazayun couldn't know about my Sight.

"W-why do you lurk in the dark?" I said, hating how my voice quavered. "Are you afraid to show yourself?"

The words had an echo of what I'd once asked Elang. Except his grandfather chuckled, the same deep and cryptic laugh he had made when we'd first met.

"Such disrespect," he murmured. "Careful now, Thadu was punished for a lesser offense. He used to be quite handsome, if you can believe it."

"Are you going to punish me too?"

"Not yet."

That was when he burst out of the fog, shooting over me in a ghostly arc. I dropped the umbrella and fell flat, choking on sand.

To my disappointment, Nazayun was as I'd foreseen, a watery projection piercing out of the mountain walls. His head hung forth like a hulking lantern, while the rest of his body looped behind him, thick as a whale's.

The Dragon King peered down at me. "What odd and fragile creatures you humans are. Everything shows on your flesh. Your anger, your fear, your cold. What would Elangui say, I wonder, if his new bride froze to death under my watch?"

I didn't get up. I lay in the icy sand, pretending to be gripped by fear when, in fact, I was memorizing every detail of his face I could. His whiskers curled up, not down; there were three pinpricks of light in his left pupil, two in his right. His lower jaw had four incisors, all hooked like the ends of an anchor.

But then I got to the finer work. I counted his scales, I looked out for cracks in his nails, I studied the pebbly texture of his throat, and most of all, I studied the structure of his tail. It undulated behind him, long and serpentine, just like Shani had shown me.

I pulled myself to my knees, my teeth chattering.

"I've seen what I need to see," said Nazayun. "You are interesting, little bride, but you are not impressive. Still, if Elangui claims to love you, then so begins your trial."

If I hadn't been freezing, I would have put my hands on

my hips. I'd already married Elang—what was I supposed to do to save him? Kiss him? Fall in love with him?

My imagination had drifted to such possibilities several times, but none of them felt right. Nazayun wouldn't have made it so easy. So obvious.

Besides, Elang acted as though I repulsed him. He didn't even want his pearl back.

I know precisely where it is, he'd said.

That was when it struck me. "*You* have his pearl."

A laugh scraped out of Nazayun. "I took it, yes, but that was a long time ago." He tilted his massive head. "He hasn't told you much, has he, little bride? You have quite the task, then, before you break his curse."

I gritted my teeth. "Why are you doing this? He's your grandson, your blood."

"Elangui is a monster," Nazayun said sharply. "No different from the Thadu you just gored and killed."

"Except you can't seem to get him to die," I shot back. "Could it be, the God of the Four Supreme Seas is afraid?"

I was lifted up, as if an invisible hook were under my chin, bringing me eye to eye with the Dragon King.

"Who are you to speak of fear?" he growled. "I have ruled since before the sun and moon were born, long before your kind befouled the earth. This realm is *my* creation, my domain. Every being here is born with my permission, and allowed to live through my grace."

"Except Elang."

Steam puffed out from Nazayun's mouth; it took me a while to realize he was chuckling. "Strange as it may be, your husband and I have something in common. We put the future of Ai'long first, above all. Unfortunately, we have come to perceive each other as dangers to the realm, and therein lies the root of our discord."

"You're the one sending storms to Yonsar. You don't think you're a danger to this realm?" I retorted.

"You, like your husband, fail to understand that I *am* Ai'long. I know what is best for these seas, just as I know he would bring their destruction. I will not let that happen."

His conviction was impressive. I wondered if all gods had such a gift for self-delusion. "Why not make it easy for yourself, then, and crush Elang's pearl between your claws?"

"A dragon's pearl cannot be destroyed," Nazayun replied, "even when it belongs to an abomination like your husband. I didn't think he'd meet his match, but now that you're here, I am quite curious to see how this will all end."

I tensed. I didn't like the direction this was taking.

Nazayun's head, as large as a sailing barque, loomed above me. "I give you a chance, Bride of the Westerly Seas, to reconsider your allegiances. I've heard you have a father who passed into my realm. It would be tragic indeed if something were to happen to him."

Suddenly I couldn't breathe. My temples throbbed, pinched by an unrelenting pressure. My voice crawled out of my throat, a bare whisper: "Is he alive?"

"It depends on what you mean by alive."

"I want to see him."

"Then tell me why you are here. Tell me the truth, and father and daughter will have a reunion."

I swallowed hard, clenching at my skirt. "Is that a promise? Same as the promise you made not to kill me?"

Nazayun bared his teeth. "That promise only holds so long as you are his Heavenly Match. Better that you tell me the truth and leave Ai'long when you still can."

Immortals were bound to their promises, I remembered, and Nazayun was one of the oldest in the world. All I'd have to do would be to show him the crumpled vision in my skirt, and then I'd see Baba again. I'd bring him home to Mama and my sisters, and my family would be whole at last, the family we used to be. I wanted it. More than anything, I wanted it.

But then I thought of the turtles who'd perished in the storm, and of how tight Elang's voice had gone when he told me Baba had been found in Ai'long. If the Dragon King truly cared about his realm, as he said he did, he wouldn't let his subjects suffer. He wouldn't break families apart.

I'm sorry, Baba. Just a while longer. I promise, I'll bring you home.

"Isn't it obvious why I'm here?" I finally replied. "To break Elang's curse."

The Dragon King leaned forward, his pale blue eyes unblinking. I could feel them scrutinizing my every pore, every hair and fiber of silk on my body.

He whispered, "You lie."

A blast of lightning shot out of his eyes, missing me only by an arm. I staggered into a puddle of Thadu's blood.

"If you wish to see your father again, bring me the truth. I won't ask again." In a puff, Nazayun disappeared. And the water began to freeze.

It happened fast. The puddle hardened, thickening from slush to ice. I yanked my foot out of Thadu's blood an instant before it solidified. Even the bubbles of my breath turned to ice. As I shot up, my every movement made the water crackle.

"Move, Tru," I told myself. I grabbed the umbrella and started kicking. "Swim up."

I tried, but the temperature plummeted faster than I could rise. I could feel my lungs constricting, my breath congealing in my throat as my muscles choked, swiftly going numb.

My thoughts scattered with panic.

No! I refused to die here, in this forsaken pit of the sea. I needed to stay alive and save Baba. I needed to free him from the Dragon King.

I focused my thoughts on my father. On the hot sugar water with rice flour he'd make in the winter to keep us from getting sick. On the snake-eye chilis he'd toast in a pan, then crush in a mortar, until the entire kitchen was smoky with spice.

I thought of the fairy tale he used to tell, about the carp who swam upstream for weeks to reach the gates of Ai'long. Once she arrived, she failed to leap across, but she wouldn't give up.

Every time she fell, she picked herself up and tried again.

I clenched the umbrella. My knuckles had gone bone white, the rest of my skin so pale I could see the map of my veins, distressingly blue.

Chin up, not down, I told myself. *Stay defiant, Tru.*

I leapt, kicking as fiercely as I could. Every inch I gained was a little farther from the cold, I told myself. A little more. I had to persist.

Seconds or hours, I didn't know how long I swam. But eventually I could make out the faint gray light of Yonsar, blooming like one of Elang's flowers. I reached out for it with both hands, my fingers drooping as my eyelids turned heavy, my muscles rusted, and my pulse slowed to a glacial speed, the silence between beats becoming longer and longer.

Don't . . . give up, I thought as a white cloak fell over my head. Before I could look up, a dragon tail hooked around my waist, and we shot up out of the Fold.

It was Elang.

"Tru," he said, so close I could feel the heat of his lips against my cheek. "Tru, stay awake. Stay with me."

"You're late," I said, part delirious and part needing to have the last word.

Then I passed out.

CHAPTER TWENTY-THREE

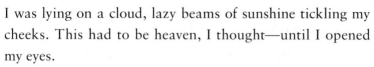

I was lying on a cloud, lazy beams of sunshine tickling my cheeks. This had to be heaven, I thought—until I opened my eyes.

Bubbles of air trailed out of my mouth as I jolted up. I was still in Ai'long, and sitting on a sponge-soft divan, long enough for an eel. Turquoise flames capered from a pot at my side, warmth that I hadn't felt in days, and a blanket had been folded over my legs and feet. Draped around my shoulders was a familiar white cloak, its hood tucked over my head.

Across from me, carrying a bucket and a scrubbing brush, was Elang. He wore spectacles, the same pair I'd noticed on his desk in Gangsun. They were brass and round and sat awkwardly on the ridge of his nose—slightly too big for his human eye and too small for the dragon one. I liked them.

"You really have a death wish, don't you?" he said, in lieu of a greeting. "Didn't I tell you to go back into the castle?"

I threw off my hood. "If I'd listened to you, Mailoh would've died."

"Mailoh was bait."

"That doesn't change the fact she was in trouble."

Elang bit back a retort and touched my forehead. His fingers were warm, chasing away the residual chill inside me. "You were in trouble too."

The words were chiding, and yet, from the stack of books at his side, the empty cups of tea lining the table, and the lines creasing his brow, I sensed he'd been waiting a long time for me to wake up. That he'd been . . . worried.

"Is she all right?" I asked.

"She's resting." Elang's voice lost some of its edge. "Her shell was cracked. It will need healing. But yes, she'll be all right."

I exhaled in relief. Slowly I sat up, tugging off my cloak, which Elang caught before it floated away. "Where's Shani?"

"In her ring," said Elang. His jaw tensed. "You encountered my grandfather in the Fold. What did he say to you?"

I sobered. "No surprise, he doesn't believe we're a blissfully wedded couple—he asked me why I'm here." I bit down on my lip as my chest pinched from remembering. "He offered me my father back . . . if I told him."

"You didn't," said Elang.

"Obviously not," I retorted. "You dragons don't exactly have a reputation for being honest and honorable. It's bad enough I made a deal with *you*. I'd be an idiot to trust the actual Dragon King. Besides . . ." I inhaled through my nose. "Besides, I got something out of him. Now I *know* that my father's here."

Elang said nothing and merely dipped his cloak in a bucket, which wasn't a surprise. He was heartless, after all.

I peeled off my blanket, rather pleased with myself when I didn't start floating off the divan. As I got my bearings,

I became aware of the bandages on my arms, the ointment soothing cuts I didn't even know I'd gotten. The bowls of soup gone cold at my side, the floating plate of steamed buns. Even my umbrella, which I'd dropped in the Fold, had been washed and was hooked against the arm of my chair.

"Thank you," I said then, quietly.

"I can't have you dying." Elang scrubbed at his cloak. "There's no time to find another human who can paint."

I stifled the urge to make a face. Every time I started to think he might not be so bad, he found a way to make me reconsider.

I stuffed a bun into my mouth, appeasing the grumble of my belly, then I observed my surroundings: a circular room with a pinched ceiling and honeycomb walls sparsely decked with books and scrolls. A litter of crumpled papers spontaneously drifted about, and a pair of towels hung from two of the floating sconces, dangling like flabby jowls.

"I didn't see this room on my tour," I remarked while I chewed. "A bit messy to be yours, isn't it?"

Elang set down his cloak. "This is the library."

"There aren't many books."

"The rest are in your room or still in Gangsun." His tone was curt. "You recall that I was in exile."

"You brought back your tea. Mailoh mentioned your secret stash."

"Tea is different. It needs to be consumed."

"So no art either?" I pressed. "You had quite the collection."

"I forgot how many questions you ask." He reached for

the pot simmering on the hearth. Before offering me a bowl, he presented a dreaded vial of sangi. "Drink this first."

I recoiled. "For someone with a dragon's nose, I don't see how you stand this smell."

"Humans smell worse."

"Even me?"

A flicker pleated Elang's brow; he clearly missed the hours I'd been unconscious. "Just drink."

"Humans aren't all that bad, you know," I said. "We invented noodles and silk and porcelain. And we discovered tea, your favorite."

"The *immortals* discovered tea."

"There's no proof of that."

"Don't debate history with a dragon, Lady Saigas. It is fact."

"Then why do you drink human tea?"

Elang turned back to his cloak. "Because I am not permitted to drink in the presence of the gods, let alone partake of their tea."

Oh. That silenced me, and out of penitence, I finished my sangi in one gulp.

"Now, this," said Elang.

A marble bowl floated my way, bubbling with a tawny orange liquid.

"Another potion?" I asked.

"I've wasted enough magic on you. What else is there to enchant?"

"It could be a love potion," I said archly. "Might make acting as your wife a bit easier."

Elang wasn't amused. "Drink. Be careful, it's still hot."

Hot was an understatement—it was practically boiling. Cautiously, I brought the bowl to my lips. Medicinal soups were bitter, so I grimaced in anticipation. But this was sweet. Almost pleasant.

"Ginger, codonopsis root, red dates," I murmured. All ingredients to help blood circulation and improve healing. I wondered—but I didn't dare ask—if he'd brewed such a soup especially for me. "And a dash of turmeric."

Elang looked vaguely impressed. "You have training as an herbalist."

"Hardly," I said. "My mother used to make me drink all sorts of concoctions to try turning my hair black again." I warmed my hands around the bowl. "Sometimes I'd get sick, and I'd have to drink a soup like this to feel better."

"What was wrong with leaving your hair blue?"

"I think she was worried. The neighborhood children would spit at me whenever I passed. One girl even tried to burn my hair off."

The hint of a frown clouded Elang's face. "Don't tell me you let them get away with it."

"I didn't." I hid a smile behind my spoon. "I punched that girl in the face. Quite sure I broke her nose. She left me alone after that."

"Do you still wish to change your hair?"

"I never did."

He turned back to his bucket and scrubbed at a particularly stubborn stain. "Good."

Good? What did he mean by that?

While I drank and pondered, Elang dipped the garment for one last rinse, then gave a satisfied grunt. It was a strange thing to witness, the half dragon laundering a cloak in the middle of his library, and the sight brought an unexpected warmth to my heart.

"You really care about that cloak," I remarked.

"I've had it a long time." Elang gave it a final wring. "Here, you wear it."

"Me?" I balked. "No . . . no. I'd get it dirty."

"Then I'd wash it again. Keep it, you need it more than I."

I accepted the cloak into my arms. The cloth was softer than it looked, and I resisted hugging it against my chest. "Aren't you worried I'll steal it?"

"You're a forger, not a thief."

"Some would argue those are one and the same."

"They're not to you," he said.

My pulse fluttered. It was simply his way of speaking, as though everything were fact, yet the certainty in his voice took me aback. It was true, they weren't. But how could Elang have known that?

I leaned against the wall, running my fingers down a long crack. "You know, sometimes I feel like I've met you before."

Elang pushed his spectacles up his nose. "That's not possible."

"Maybe not," I agreed. "But it's a little coincidental, isn't it? Me falling into your garden when you were looking for a painter with Sight?"

Elang retrieved the blankets I'd discarded, taking a sudden interest in folding them into a neat stack. "What are you saying?"

"I don't know." I found the red string around my wrist. I hadn't paid much attention to it at our wedding, but now I noticed a black thread braided into the center knot, as subtle as a strand of hair.

I tipped my head back against my divan. "Maybe instead of us pretending to like each other, we could try to be friends. It'd make all the smiling less agonizing. I've been told I grow on people—like moss." I hesitated. "Gaari made it up. The friend you helped me—"

"I remember. What did he say?"

I stared into my tea. The memory was over a year old, but still clear in my mind.

"Who would have thought a clumsy thief like you would grow on me, Saigas?" Gaari had said to me with a chuckle. "You're like moss, you know."

"You're likening me to a weed?"

I finished the rest of my tea in one gulp. "He said, 'Moss is better than a weed. It brightens up the world with its presence, and flourishes even when all is against it.'"

Elang considered this. "He must have thought highly of you."

"He was a good friend," I said softly.

There was no point in feeling sorry for what had happened to Gaari. He wouldn't want that. Still, it took effort for me to muster a smile. "How about it, Prince Elang? Friends, from now on?" I refilled my teacup and raised it to him. "You can even call me moss if you want."

He looked at me blankly.

"That endearment you asked for." I shrugged a shoulder, but I was smiling. "I still can't think of anything else."

"Moss," Elang repeated. The faintest smile lifted the corners of his lips. It was nothing short of enchantment, how such a simple shift changed his face entirely, taming away its beastliness. I didn't even realize I was staring.

He did. Suddenly my reflection blinked out of his eyes, and that hint of a smile vanished. He drew himself tall, as if recalling where he was, and with whom. "Make no mistake," he said, taking a colder tone than I'd heard in days. "I endure your company for the sake of Yonsar. Any notion of befriending a human is offensive to my senses."

I felt my cheeks flame with indignation. So much for the strongest bridge being made of truth. I retracted my hand. "Why even bother pretending if it's all a lie?" I said. "The soup, the dinners—"

"There will be no dinner until you resume your duties," he spoke over me. He sounded actually cross. "You forget, Lady Saigas, that you are only here because by some *forgery* of fate, you seem to be capable of the impossible." He drew out his words. "The fall of the Dragon King."

The water felt suddenly cold.

"In the future, should you choose to disregard my warnings and put our mission at risk, your family will pay the consequences." His gaze narrowed. "Now, I advise you get back to work."

Leaving me utterly speechless, he left the room.

CHAPTER TWENTY-FOUR

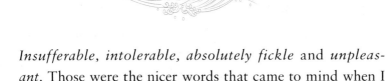

Insufferable, intolerable, absolutely fickle and *unpleasant*. Those were the nicer words that came to mind when I thought of Elang the abominable half dragon.

What had possessed me to court his friendship? To tell him my stupid little moss story? I should've poked him in the eyes with my brush. That smug yellow one first.

I snatched a sheaf of parchment from under one of Elang's stacks of books, recorded every detail I could remember of Nazayun, practically ruining the brush with my livid strokes. In my head, I was warring with myself, griping at how callously Elang had rebuffed me—at how embarrassingly close I'd come to thinking he was . . . he was . . .

Nothing, I snapped, shutting off the thought. There was no way I'd harbor even an *inkling* of feeling toward him.

Just why did he have to be such a convincing actor? That kiss he'd planted on my hand, that offhand *good* when I'd said I never wanted to change my hair.

I must be lonely, I thought. *If Nomi and Fal were here, I'd never fall for such a monster*—I caught myself—*a monster's* tricks.

When the door opened again, I shot to my feet, ready to tell him exactly what I thought of him.

Except it wasn't Elang.

"General Caisan," I said, my tone coming out flatter than I intended. "To what do I owe the honor?"

The turtle dipped his head so he could enter through the door, then straightened. "I had presumed you sought Lord Elang's affections for the sake of bettering your life of squalor, but now I see that you are too improvident to have such ambitions. My apologies."

I was taken aback. Honestly I didn't know whether I ought to laugh or be offended. Caisan was a soldier through and through, even in the way he fashioned greetings.

"I most begrudgingly accept your apology. Does that mean you no longer deem me a hoodlum?"

He grunted. If I'd wondered whether he might have a sense of humor, I had my answer: no.

"You shouldn't have gone into the Western Fold," he said, ignoring my question. "Even a hatchling would have sensed the ambush that the Dragon King had planned for you."

"A simple thank-you would suffice. I did save your sister."

"My scouts would have found her in time."

"Unlikely."

Caisan clenched his spear, the only visible sign he grew irritated. "I have not sought you out to argue."

"Then why have you come?"

Rather than respond, the general barged deeper into the room, settling beside the hearth where Elang had boiled my medicinal soup. The fire flared at his presence, green flames zapping to life.

"In light of your mistake, you will need additional

protection," Caisan said at last. "I offer myself as your personal guard."

Personal guard? I dropped my brush onto the table. "Why would you offer to protect me? You despise me."

General Caisan bored his round, unblinking eyes into mine. "When have I said I despise you? It is true, I distrust your kind—I find humans covetous and opportunistic." He pointed his spear at my opal ring. "But I distrust demons even more."

"I already have a guard," I replied.

"That demon will betray you."

I disagreed. "If not for Shani, I wouldn't have made it back from the Fold alive."

Caisan made a snorting sound. "Think carefully. How is it that she helped you vanquish Thadu, then conveniently disappeared right before King Nazayun found you?"

I couldn't believe what I was hearing. "We were separated."

"She was leaving you unprotected! She hasn't told you, has she, that she once belonged to Nazayun? For millennia, she served him."

The opal on my ring grew colder. Shani was stirring inside.

"You disbelieve me, but it's true. Ask the demon yourself—since the First Era, Shanizhun was King Nazayun's most loyal servant. Her cruelty is unthinkable. Her crimes, unspeakable. Entire cities have fallen because of her. Countless lives—*innocent* lives—gone. All to stoke her wicked hunger."

"It can't be," I said. "Elang would never trust someone who—"

"There are no other water demons in Ai'long," interrupted

Caisan. "Shanizhun is the last—because she betrayed her own kind."

At the accusation, Shani flew out of the ring. Caisan must have been expecting her reaction, for with a swing of his spear, he impaled her fin.

"Behold the last water demon," he said, swinging her over the blazing hearth. "There is only one thing that will quell her treachery, and that is fire."

"Stop!" I exclaimed, wrestling Caisan for his spear. "Let her go."

The general blocked me with his shell. "You did not think twice when you stabbed Thadu in the head. You thought him a monster, an unfeeling beast about to make soup out of my sister's blood. What if I were to tell you that the demon you harbor at your side is far, far worse?"

I lowered my gaze to Shani. She'd become a piteous sight, half-melted into a blob as she writhed above the green flames, steam hissing from the edges of her form.

"Elang trusts her," I said.

Caisan scoffed. "Do you know why your lord husband was banished from Ai'long? It is because of this demon. She painted herself a victim, a tortured captive—and deceived him into freeing her. Since then, the Dragon King has taken every opportunity to punish the Westerly Seas, and Yonsar has spiraled into the wretched wasteland that you see."

"If that is so," I said slowly, "then it is the Dragon King you should be blaming. Not Shani."

"You don't understand. We try to rebuild, and Nazayun sends a storm. We try to fight back, and he brings his sharks. Coincidence?" Caisan dropped the tip of his spear deeper into the fire. "I think not."

"Stop, you're hurting her!"

"Am I? Shanizhun is more powerful than I. She could easily free herself from my grasp, but she manipulates you—the way she did his lordship. It is what demons are good at."

It was true, Shani was suffering from the flames, but she didn't fight them. She was watching me. Testing me, I sensed.

"*I* trust her," I said in my steeliest voice. "Without Shani, I never could have rescued Mailoh. I would never have survived Thadu. If there is indeed a spy within the castle, it is not her. Release her—that is a command."

Caisan lifted his spear from the hearth. As she slid off the crystal shaft, I caught her in my arms. The demon's weight startled me. It was like cradling a cat, she'd become so light and so small. Her fins went flat against me, limp as sackcloth, and her eyes were two hollow eggshells. She was shaking from the heat.

"You've made a grave error today, Lady Saigas," he said. "I pray you will not regret it."

With a lurch, he swam away.

Once he was gone, Shani squirmed out of my arms. Life was returning to the demon, and a glower spread across her translucent face. Still, she was shaking, even though she tried to hide it.

"Are you hurt?" I asked worriedly.

"You think that overgrown croaker could injure me?"

"Why did you stay in that fire? Why let him hurt you in that way, when you could have fought back?"

"And what would that achieve?" she snapped. "His kind and yours are not so different. You'll seek any reason to vilify demons. If you provoke us and we attack, *we* are the ones called monsters. But we have something to lose, just like everyone else."

I was only beginning to see the demon for what she was, behind those flinty red eyes and the sharp bite of her words. "You're not a monster," I said. I nudged her with an affectionate poke. "No monster would blot out my bad paintings as cleanly as you do, and no monster would have helped me find Mailoh."

A harrumph. "You'd have gone off on your own and gotten yourself killed if I hadn't."

"Probably," I acknowledged. I gave her a small smile. "Then again, I swim slower than a seahorse, so maybe I wouldn't have gotten very far."

"At least you know it." Shani flexed her tail, sticking out her spikes. They'd regained their usual gleam. "You saw Nazayun in the pit. Was he as grand as you thought? Or was he a colossal eyesore?"

She was as petty as ever, and my smile widened. "A colossal eyesore. I'm going to be painting until my fingers fall off."

"You'd better get started, then, or Elang'anmi will have both our heads. The water tells me he's in a bad mood."

So he was, but I wouldn't disclose why. Instead, I changed the topic, asking something I'd been wondering for some time. "Why do you use the honorific *anmi*?" I asked. "I've never heard it before."

"It's a title demons use when they're bound."

"Bound," I repeated. "Like a contract?"

"It's not a contract," she said sharply. "It is a debt of honor, one that cannot be refused."

"Because he freed you from the Dragon King." I understood. "I didn't know demons had honor."

I hadn't meant it as an insult, but Shani's face contorted with displeasure. "There's a lot you don't know about demons."

Fair enough. "How will your debt be repaid?"

She leaned close, sending a chill deep into my bones. In her lowest voice, she whispered, "With vengeance."

Vengeance. I, too, was acquiring a taste for the word. It was bitter like poison, and I could taste it even in my dreams.

It was spring, and we were strolling through Gangsun's Central Gardens. The air smelled green and oily, and the wind scattered peach blossoms across the cobbled paths.

I walked, feeling the grass prick at my ankles and watching the butterflies dance from flower to flower. The gardens were never this empty in the spring. They were crowded and loud and full of pickpockets hiding in the peony bushes. But the air was fragrant, the sun doted on Baba's dark blue hair, and my skirt flared at my ankles as I walked, a happy bounce in each step. Just for a few minutes, I wanted to believe this was real.

"Your mother tells me you've been living in the dragon realm," Baba said at my side. "How long are you visiting home?"

"A week," I replied.

"A week with my daughter." He exhaled. "I've missed you." From his jacket, he drew out a cloth-wrapped figure. "I finished it, like you asked."

It was my wooden ship, completed. The mast was fresh and smelled of cedar, the sails fully battened with thick, woven linen. Its figurehead was a bird, its wings spread wide.

"Birds always know where home is," Baba said, repeating something he often used to say. "This one will find her way back to you."

It felt so real in my hands, the weight of it, the smooth wood, the creases in its sails. I fell deeper into the dream. "It's beautiful."

"You should see the ship they built from this model," said Baba, nodding when my eyes flew up to him. "It's real, my Tru. My next voyage is in a week. Come with me."

I set down the wooden ship. "No. I can't."

"Why not? Nomi and Fal are coming too."

"I can't. I have to go back." I touched the opal on my ring; it was warm. "To Ai'long."

"To Ai'long," repeated my father. "Let me guess, your mother put you up to it. I hope not for the money."

Baba was teasing, but still the words made my ears burn. "No," I said. "Not for the money. For you."

"Then you're in luck." Baba gave a hearty laugh. "Here I am."

His hand was extended to me, and my fingers twitched, longing for his warmth. But in a hundred dreams, I'd taken his hand. And a hundred times, I'd woken up alone.

"What's the matter, my Tru?"

"Tell me where you are," I whispered. "Tell me, and I will find you."

The smile on Baba's face faded. Tears carved tracks down his cheeks. "I'm sorry."

"Don't cry." I wiped his face with my sleeve, but the tears

came down faster. Everywhere they touched, his skin turned gray. Panic leapt into my heart. "Baba!"

The flowers under my feet withered, the gardens vanishing. The sky started to fall, devoured by the raging sea.

And there was Baba, standing on King Nazayun's palm, looking as small as the wooden figurines he used to whittle for me.

He'd been turned to stone.

Nazayun closed his fist around my father, his laugh echoing in my ears.

"*NO!*" My body convulsed, writhing itself into consciousness.

"You were screaming," said Shani, misting into view. Her fins enveloped my shoulders, holding me still. She let me go, but her voice was gentler than I'd ever heard it. "Bad dreams again?"

I bunched my blanket in one hand, haunted by what I'd seen. Baba turned into stone. Baba shattered into a thousand pieces.

For five years, my family and I had feared he was dead. This entire time, he'd been a prisoner in Ai'long. And for what?

Gods help me, I was going to find out. And I would make the Dragon King pay.

CHAPTER TWENTY-FIVE

In the days following the storm, everyone was devoted to the castle's repair. The storm had damaged our defenses, and the Dragon King was bound to strike again. We had to hurry, or we'd no longer be safe here.

I helped however I could, clearing debris and tending to the wounded, repairing cracks in the walls with Kunkoi and patching the crevices with moss and algae. Then, at night, I worked on my portrait of Nazayun.

On the third day, I was in the kitchen—sweeping chunks of broken marble while waiting for my noodles to boil—when Elang found me.

"There you are," he said. He had sand in his hair and silt on his cheek, and his tone was maddeningly offhand. "I need you to get changed. They'll be here in an hour."

I set aside my broom. "Who?"

"Queen Haidi's entourage," said Elang. He blew out the green flame on my stove, then gave my noodles a stir so they wouldn't cling to the bottom of the pot.

I'd never seen him in such a rush. "Queen Haidi . . ." I racked my memory for the name. "The ruler of the merfolk?"

"Kunkoi's secured us an invitation to her court—you'll need to be on your most charming behavior."

He was giving answers that only led to more questions. "What is our objective?"

Elang finally faced me. His expression was grim. "We are going to ask for help," he replied. "The damage to the castle remains beyond repair, and my magic is not enough to provide an adequate shield. It'll be a gamble going to Queen Haidi, but I will not allow Yonsar to suffer any more casualties."

Three days with hardly a word. Only Elang would have the gall to pretend like nothing had happened. Without a doubt, he was the most exasperating person I'd ever met.

"Why would asking for help be a gamble?"

"Because no one is permitted to come to my aid," replied Elang darkly. "Or they risk Nazayun's immense displeasure."

"He's found every way to be a turd, hasn't he?" I muttered.

"Yes." I could have sworn he almost smiled. "He'd turn you into one if he heard you just now."

"Then it's good he's not here." I reached for my ladle. "Let me eat, then I'll come. I'm far less charming when I'm hungry."

"Don't rush," said Elang. "Your noodles could use another minute."

I stole a glance at him. "I didn't know you cooked."

"I didn't always live in a castle." His eyes gravitated to the pot, avoiding mine. "My mother taught me when I was young."

His mother. I tried to cobble together a mental portrait, taking in Elang's freckled nose, his brooding eyes, his regal brow. *She must have been beautiful,* I thought before I could stop myself. I turned back to my pot, glad Elang couldn't read minds.

"Dragons truly are mercurial," I said dryly. "Last we met, you spurned my offer to be friends. Now here you are making sure my noodles aren't undercooked."

"I don't need you making a poor impression on the merfolk. You said it yourself—when your stomach is empty, you're at your most disagreeable."

I crossed my arms. "Maybe you should go alone, since my presence is so difficult to endure."

A muscle ticked in Elang's jaw. "Those words were uttered in poor taste," he replied at length. "Most humans are difficult to tolerate; I shouldn't have said the same about you."

"Because it isn't true or because it's rude?"

"Both."

Both. I tilted my head, mildly startled. Was that his way of apologizing?

I wouldn't be won over so easily. "You should know I haven't had a vision," I said, "if that's what you're here for."

"We'll discuss your visions later." He cleared his throat, pausing. "Will you come?"

I didn't reply. Night was falling upon the sea, casting an argent sheen. I could see the dark half-moon staining the area under Elang's human eye, accentuating new hollows in his cheeks. His scales were more gray than blue.

Word around the castle was he never took a rest. I wondered whether he was sleeping enough. Eating enough.

"I'll come," I decided.

He looked faintly relieved. "I've asked Mailoh to help you prepare for the journey. You'll need to leave Shani behind."

"She won't like that."

"It doesn't matter what she likes. Demons are not permitted in the realm of merfolk. Shani, least of all."

"Then who will be my guard?"

"Kunkoi will see to your safety." Another pause. "As will I."

He started to leave, but I raised a halting hand. "We're supposed to spend dinners together," I said, ladling noodles and soup into a fresh bowl. "You've missed three. Four will be bad luck for our marriage."

Elang arched an eyebrow. "I didn't take you to be superstitious."

"I'm a fortune teller's daughter, of course I'm superstitious. A little, anyway." I twisted my lips. "Mama always says bad tidings come in fours, and we could use all the luck we can get. So eat with me now—unless you truly dislike noodles."

"There were noodles at the wedding banquet, were there not?"

"You hardly touched yours."

Elang expelled a breath. "You don't miss anything."

"You did hire me for my Sight."

"So I did." He picked up his bowl with a claw and downed the noodles in a single gulp. "So I did."

Then, with a bow of his head, he left the kitchen.

Precisely an hour later, Elang knocked on my door.

It was a miracle I was ready. The instant I'd returned to my room, it'd been a whirlwind of Mailoh tearing apart my closet and making me try on every dress in sight. I voted for a dusky pink robe with emerald accents, which Mailoh thought was too plain. But she grudgingly accepted the choice, so long as I pinned up my hair and accented my gills with little pearls.

"Yonsar's fate rests upon the impression you make on Queen Haidi," Mailoh had said dramatically. "You must look regal, Lady Saigas. Not too magnificent, but not too humble either." She came forth with a plump sprig of greens. "How about this?"

"Is that moss?" I asked.

"It's one of the few plants that have survived the storms," she replied. "I know it's not beautiful, but I thought it'd be a sign of . . ."

"Resilience," I said, taking a sprig and setting it behind my ear. "I'll wear all of it."

Elang waited at my door, attired in a dark green robe with brocade fittings. He'd cleaned up nicely; his white hair was tied back, the dirt on his cheeks scrubbed away. Even his sickle-sharp nails had been trimmed.

I made a little twirl, holding up the ends of my skirt. "How do I look?" I asked him.

The question must have caught him off guard, for as his eyes swept over me, his lips parted. For an instant, he seemed to forget how to swim and actually floated up, just a little. Then he caught himself, straightening with a pained furrow in his brow.

"Is it that bad?" I asked. He seemed partially paralyzed, and I suddenly worried that the moss in my hair looked too silly to greet a merqueen. "Should I take out the—"

Elang found his voice, gruffer than usual. "It'll do."

He escorted me outside, where a clamshell carriage awaited,

drawn by two giant seahorses. Kunkoi hovered along one side, his purple hair coiffed high.

"Ready?" said the merman. "You look nervous."

"I've never met a queen before," I replied, untwisting my hands. "Of course I'm nervous."

"You've no need to be," Elang said. "Do not forget, you are a lady of the first rank among dragons. That makes you equal to any queen, if not greater."

Though his tone was austere, Elang seemed a little nervous himself. Every now and then, I caught him glancing sidelong at me. What was he looking at? The umbrella behind my shoulder, the moss in my hair? Or was it the white cloak he'd given me, which Mailoh had begged me not to wear because it ruined the elegance of my robes?

"Is it too long?" Elang asked, gesturing at how I'd bunched the cloak's fabric in my hand.

"It's too *ugly*," said Kunkoi before I could reply. "That cloak will show my queen what a wretched state we're in."

Before I could protest, Elang reached out, his fingertips landing gently on my arm.

Where he touched it, the cloak began to change. The plain white cloth melted into soft gold brocade with a viridescent trim that matched the moss in my hair, and tiny golden flowers embroidered the collar where a bronze clasp, of a phoenix, now held the cloak over my shoulders. It even had pockets!

I glanced up at Elang. In the reflection of his darker eye, I saw myself aglow.

"Better?" he asked, clearing his throat.

Honestly, I wanted to take it off and admire every thread, to spin it around and watch how its golden sheen caught the light. But Elang wasn't done. The umbrella at my side shrank into a pair of jade butterflies hanging on a dark red cord.

I touched the pendant. It was cool against my skin, the delicate wings a vibrant green, my favorite. I gave Elang a quizzical look.

"For luck," he said. "Besides, you don't need the umbrella's help anymore."

He said it matter-of-factly, not intended as a compliment. Still, something fluttered in my stomach. Jade *was* lucky, but butterflies . . . butterflies were symbols of love. Something Kunkoi must have silently observed as well, for his eyes twinkled with mischief.

If Elang noticed, he made no sign of it. He had turned away, looking out to the sea. "They're here."

As he spoke, the merfolk arrived. They slipped out of an invisible seam in the sea, their shimmering hair bejeweling the gray water. Nine had come, guarding their queen, a mermaid with the longest hair I'd ever seen. It brewed an inky tempest behind her back, the ends of each strand sparking with light as she swam. From afar, she looked like a shooting star.

Kunkoi approached her first, with a deep bow. "Your Majesty, the lord and lady of Yonsar are honored to welcome you to the Westerly Seas."

"It's been many years since I have come to these waters," said Haidi, surveying the state of the castle. Her face was plain, but her eyes were round and ancient like the moon. "Things have changed."

"I must apologize for this urgent appeal," said Elang. "We would not wish to involve you in the affairs of dragons, but—"

"But there was no choice. I understand." Haidi nodded. Her long fingers were webbed, and gossamer silk spun out of the rings on her fingers, arcing over her umber-gold fins. "In truth, I also wanted to meet your wife."

I became aware of the gentlest pressure from Elang's hand on the small of my back. When had he gotten so close?

"Your . . . Your Majesty," I stumbled. "You honor Yonsar with your presence. I am Truyan Saigas."

Queen Haidi touched my chin, lifting it. "The mortal who's captured Elangui's heartless heart," she murmured. "You're the talk of Ai'long, Lady Saigas. Come, I want to hear more about how you accomplished the impossible."

She turned, and her long tresses fluttered as if beckoning for us to follow. Elang saw me into the carriage, then took his seat at my side. Together, we trailed the queen and her guards past the castle grounds.

Once we entered the open seas, Haidi blew into the water. A low keen passed through her lips, and the sound drew a ring of ripples that crystallized into a flat and lucent pool.

"I will pass first," she spoke. "It goes against King Nazayun's decree to welcome you to my realm . . . but there's no rule that I cannot leave the gateway open."

With that, a wrinkle of silvery sea unfolded before us, and we followed her into its mysterious depths.

CHAPTER TWENTY-SIX

It was like stepping into a dream. The water was bluer than the richest indigo, and it was warm! I'd gotten so used to Yonsar's wintry bite that I'd forgotten what it was like to not be constantly shivering. Below the carriage, the gray rock beds had become plains of vibrant green algae, and shoals of little fish poked in and out, flurrying about in darts of color. This much was exciting enough, after so many long days shrouded in gloom. I'd forgotten Elang's presence next to me when he suddenly tugged on my sleeve, pointing.

"Look there, a pod of flash whales."

I glanced to the left just in time to see a pair of white-streaked whales gliding below us. They were enormous, as long as Dattu Street. Our clamshell carriage rumbled from the vibrations they made in the water, and I jutted my head out to keep watching them.

"They're incredible," I breathed. "Did you see how they swim? Like they're dancing."

Elang actually smiled. Then he faced forward again, assuming his usual solemnity. "We're nearly at Nanhira. It will be a more pleasant experience for you than Yonsar."

I heard the thickness in his tone. "Yonsar isn't so bad. It has its charms."

"But it's gray."

Like his eye, I thought. "Gray is the color of truth. The same in art as it is in life, nothing is ever as black and white as it looks."

Elang regarded me, taking a long moment before he responded, "Well said."

He inclined his chin, diverting my attention to the city ahead. "There it is, the Veiled Realm of the Merfolk."

Framed by a lush kelp forest, Nanhira was a colossus of crystal and marble. And the energy! Schools of fish fluttered, their fins dancing like dragonflies, and the sea anemones flowered their colorful tentacles when we passed. As the carriage picked up speed, I lost count of how many arched bridges we swooped over and under. Merfolk sped down the highways, riding dolphins and whales and turtles, many laughing and shouting out to greet their queen.

At the end of our journey was the palace. The walls shone a creamy pearl, and each door was inlaid with subtle jade carvings. It was plain, compared to the magnificent spiraling towers and shell-bricked villas outside, but upon entering, I felt more serene than I had in days.

Elang escorted me out of the carriage, and the guards led us to a receiving chamber. There we were seated at a wide coral table studded with colorful anemones, and I was offered Red Hearts tea, a specialty of the realm. According to Queen Haidi, its leaves grew at the bottom of a red canyon and could only be cut with magical scissors. I inhaled, savoring its rich aroma, until I glanced at Elang, who hadn't been offered a taste.

"You may drink without unease," Queen Haidi said, taking the seat across from us. "To mortals, Red Hearts tea is floral and light, whereas immortals find it earthy and aromatic. I would offer your husband a cup, but—"

"He is not permitted?" I guessed.

Haidi gave a guarded smile. "I am not a god, Lady Saigas. My tea is not restricted to divine palates. I merely withhold a cup because he's had a taste before and did not find it to his liking. A story I'd best leave to your Elangui."

My Elangui.

At the invitation, Elang leaned forward, wearing the charming facade I'd seen him put on for Governor Renhai and my family. "It was in this very room that I met Her Majesty," he recounted. "We sat at this same table." He folded his arms over the surface. "A rare and ancient coral, beautiful upon first glance—but be wary of its anemones. They'll sting if they don't like you."

"You sound like you have experience," I said mildly.

"I was a boy when I was first brought to Nanhira, and the anemones dislike being poked by curious dragon claws. They gave a few warning stings." The corner of his mouth made the barest lift. "Her Majesty kindly sent this tea by way of consolation."

"What did it taste like to you?"

"It was sweet. My predilection is for more bitter brews."

"He has the taste buds of a dragon," Queen Haidi commented. "Just like his father."

His father, whom he never mentioned. "He brought you here?" I dared ask Elang.

There came a wrinkle in my husband's charming facade. "Yes."

"Elangui doesn't like to speak of his parents," Haidi murmured. "We'd do well to change the—"

"There is no need," said Elang. "I've been waiting for an opportunity to tell Truyan what happened to my family; they are as much hers now as they are mine."

The ends of Haidi's hair swirled about her arms. She was observing us keenly. I only wished I knew what for.

"My mother was human," Elang began, "a sorceress of considerable talent. She protected me, taught me, and raised me on land—until my father interceded. Against her wishes, he brought us both to Yonsar. He thought that I'd be safer in Ai'long under his care, and that he might convince my grandfather to let me live. He was wrong.

"My mother died protecting me from the Dragon King's assassins. Soon after, my father brought me to Nanhira to seek sanctuary."

"I came close to taking him in," said Haidi. "Very close. But in the end, I refused."

Hearing Elang recount his past so calmly and without feeling, I could venture a guess why. "Because he has no heart?"

"That was the reason I gave Lord Ta'ginan. But truthfully, I refused because your husband asked me to. He came to me, disguised as one of my folk, and declared:

"'With due respect, Your Majesty, I cannot stay trapped in your realm. I am going to find my pearl, and when I do, I will become the greatest dragon Ai'long has ever seen. Greater, even, than the Dragon King.'"

I mustered a smile. I could envision this young Elang, full of pride and mettle—and desperately yearning to become a dragon. I wondered what had changed him.

"Grand words for a boy, no?" Haidi tickled one of the sea

anemones that had opened by her side. "I see that his quest is still ongoing."

"I've had setbacks," Elang said.

"Yes, banishment and a curse, so I've heard. And now your castle is falling apart." Haidi cocked her head. "To be frank, I used to think you *would* have fared better staying in my realm."

"But then, I wouldn't have met Lady Saigas."

"Indeed." The queen lowered her cool gaze to me. "Tell me, Elangui, if she breaks your curse, will you choose to rule the Westerly Seas as a dragon, or will you become a human and live out your mortal days with your wife?"

"You make the choices sound so disparate," Elang said.

"Don't evade the question."

"I will go wherever Truyan is."

"But what if she is not accepted by the Oath of Ai'long? What if she doesn't want to become immortal?"

"We have yet to cross that bridge. And when we do, I might have a better option."

"Oh?"

His lips lifted an infuriating fraction, almost a smile. "I will persuade her to become a whale with me."

"A whale?" I repeated, choking on my tea in surprise.

"They're fascinating creatures," he replied seriously. "They sing and play together, they grieve, they love." Was it my imagination, or did he linger on that last word? "It would be nice to be a whale."

Haidi's fins unfurled over the carpet, and her hair slowly sank below her shoulders. "You *have* changed."

"Then will you help us?" he asked.

For the first time, she laughed. A short laugh, but I sensed

Elang had eased some of her doubts. "Ever the businessman. I suppose *some* things do not change. Unfortunately, if it is safe haven in Nanhira that you seek, you know I cannot grant it."

"I am not asking for sanctuary. My request is to borrow magic, enough to repair my castle and protect it against my grandfather's future attacks. We will only need enough to last through the Resonant Tide."

"Is that when your curse comes to an end?"

"It is when many things must come to an end." Elang gave me a meaningful look, and my stomach made the smallest flip. Come the Resonant Tide, our arrangement together would draw to a close. I thought I'd been looking forward to it, but now I wasn't so certain.

"In exchange, Your Majesty, I will give you the secret to sangi."

Haidi arched an elegant eyebrow. "Your most prized secret in exchange for a few weeks' protection?" She was considering. "I am no stranger to the kindnesses you have granted the merfolk of Yonsar, but if I help you, Nazayun will surely retaliate."

"And if you don't, the consequences of inaction could be far graver. You are mistaken if you think you can prevent Nanhira from suffering the same fate as Yonsar."

"Truth," Queen Haidi allowed. "You've gotten better at negotiating, Elangui. I will take that risk, then, but I will need assurance from your end."

"How can we prove ourselves?" I asked.

With a flick of her hair, Haidi sent her guards and servants away. "Do you know how Nanhira protects itself from the Dragon King?"

I shook my head.

"Look around you. You will find that my realm is shielded

by a cloak of silk. Enchanted silk spun by my ancestor Liayin, long ago, when the merfolk and dragons were at war. She was the most gifted weaver in all the realms. But despite the admiration that Liayin's talent brought her, she wished only for one thing."

I seemed to be the only one who didn't know the story.

"Love," said Haidi softly. "You see, she'd wed a human, to her family's great distress. It wasn't even a prince or a king, but a young shepherd who played the flute. To be together, they were forced to endure many trials. Like you and Elangui, Lady Saigas."

I gave a tense nod, sensing these parallels might lead to an unsavory end.

Haidi rose from her bench, her hair billowing behind her. "In honor of the lady Liayin, I have invited you to my court, because I am sympathetic to plights of the heart. I know, Elangui, that you are without one, but I see the changes in you that Lady Saigas has wrought. And so, my request is simple: Show me that there is love between you. Real, genuine love that might break the curse upon Elang. In return, I will give you my aid."

Show me that there is love between you.

Never had my mind gone so blank so quickly.

How did two people show that they were in love?

They make excuses to be near each other, Fal would say, quoting one of her romance novels. *They look at each other as if there's no one else in the world.*

Until a few days ago, I could hardly look at Elang without recoiling. I *still* thought him beastly. This was not going to work in our favor.

Elang apparently had the same reaction. "There is no

need for such a trial," he was saying. "I value Truyan's life more than my own. Any spell will prove this as truth."

"I do not question your devotion, Elangui," replied Haidi. Her gaze gravitated to the red strings around our wrists. "I have seen that your marriage bonds are made of merfolk silk. No thread in this world is stronger. Some say it's strong enough to unite lovers from one life to the next. But only when that love is earnest and true. Show me that your love is indeed deserving."

At my side, Elang had gone rigid. I couldn't blame him. How embarrassing this was, for both of us. But what choice did we have?

I turned to him, venturing close enough that our elbows touched. His nostrils flared, and as I laid my hand on his sleeve, his muscles went taut, cording up his arms.

He pressed his palms to mine. We faced each other the way we had during our wedding, and the red strings tied around our wrists touched, ever so briefly. Elang parted his lips.

"Truyan," he started. "I love—"

I don't know what struck me. The acute realization that he was about to lie to the merfolk queen—or how much I didn't want to hear that particular lie. But my every instinct told me I needed to silence him.

I grabbed him by the neck.

I'd never seen his eyes so wide. WHAT ARE YOU DOING?

I'm going to kiss you, I rushed out silently, a beat before I crushed my mouth against his.

It was strange at first, kissing a mouth with two sides. The dragon half was covered in scales that were smooth and cool to the touch, while his lips—his *human* lips—were warm.

Softer than they looked. And it sounded crazy in my head, but I found I didn't mind it.

With my free hand, I entwined my fingers with his. It was meant to look romantic, but I did it mostly so he couldn't push me away.

He didn't push me away. In fact, at first he seemed frozen, every muscle so stiff I wondered if I'd shocked the life out of him. Then the hard brackets around his mouth soothed away, and he took me by the waist, pressing me to him as he kissed me back, his lips molding to mine, surprisingly urgent in a way that I didn't expect.

Heat pooled in my stomach, and damn my heart for the way it started to race. This was an act to convince the queen; I wasn't supposed to *feel* anything or *be* anything other than curious about what it'd be like to kiss a dragon. My plan was to count to ten, then let go, but I'd long since lost track of the numbers, and instead of shunting him aside, I was pulling him closer.

I became aware of our hands. His were pressed firmly against the valley of my spine, and I could feel them caressing the ends of my hair as he tilted my head back. And mine? One had climbed up to the crook of his elbow, and the other was on his face, my fingers dancing along the hard scales on his cheek. The tips of our tongues were touching, just beginning to explore one another, and as I let out a soft sigh, I gathered the courage to move my hand up his arm to his chest. And there, for the most fleeting of moments, I was sure I felt the ghost of a heartbeat drumming inside.

Elang's eyes went wide. With a jolt, he stepped back.

His hair had turned black, and his face was pale, contorted

like he was trying hard not to retch. I reached out to him, thinking it was his curse making him ill.

Then I realized it was me.

With a pang, the heat in my stomach vanished, and my face burned with humiliation. Sometime during our kiss, we had begun floating, and now I let myself sink, curling my toes into the orange sea flowers carpeting the ground.

Elang wouldn't look at me. He remained at my side, intent on pretending I didn't exist.

I wanted to kick him. After all this effort, the least he could do was go on with the act instead of showing Queen Haidi how much I repulsed him. Now there was no chance she would believe us.

Under the folds of my sleeve, I clenched at my skirt. Pride be damned, I would beg her if I had to. "Your Majesty—"

"Are you convinced?" Elang interrupted. "Your Majesty."

Queen Haidi leaned back. She wore an inscrutable expression.

"It is late," she said, after what felt an eternity. "Rest with us until morning. I will need the night to prepare some silk."

I was stunned. "Does that mean . . . ?"

"You may keep the protections until the Resonant Tide," she confirmed. "The merfolk hold a tenuous peace with the dragons. This is all I dare give."

"Thank you," I breathed. "You don't know what this means to us."

I was so happy that I backed up into Elang, forgetting he was behind me. As my head tipped against him, I listened again for that faint pulse in his chest.

There was only silence.

CHAPTER TWENTY-SEVEN

We had supper with Haidi and her court, where a generous helping of every dish found its way into my bowl, leaving me fit to burst. The goblets were carved of aquamarine, the wine was briny and smooth. Braids of lotus dangled from the walls. After the meal, musicians sang and played lutes made out of shells, a concert of plaintive melodies that I sorely wished I could memorize as well as I learned faces. Then there was dancing. I'd never been gifted with rhythm or grace, but a mermaid thrust a ribboned fan in my hand, and soon I found myself somersaulting up to the ceilings, heady with laughter.

Every time I looked down, Kunkoi was flirting with someone new, and Elang . . . Elang sat in a corner the whole time, spectacles on, reading a book. He was the subject of many stares, and I was equally worried that someone might throw a knife at him as ask him to dance. Weeks with him now, and I still couldn't guess which would invite the worse reaction.

Once or twice, I caught him watching me, lips twisted in a grimace. He'd look away immediately, but it was obvious he was annoyed. I wasn't looking forward to when we'd have to be alone.

At last the merfolk tired of revelry, and it was time for rest. Elang and I were shown down a long and winding hall, to *our* room. My stomach twisted the entire way. After what'd happened during our trial earlier, I pictured we'd be given the traditional newlyweds' chamber, an intimate space dressed in matrimonial red, with scrolls of romantic poetry hanging on every wall, and so many flowers that I'd sneeze. The very thought of Elang and me locked in such a place for the night made my cheeks burn.

Thank Amana our room was enormous. At least three times the size of my cave in Yonsar, with no canopy over the bed, no poetry on the walls, and only a simple bouquet of water lilies on the tables. I thanked our guide excessively before he swam away, thinking I'd had too much to drink.

Then Elang and I were alone.

"I hope that kiss didn't catch you off guard," I blurted, unable to help myself. "I would have asked first. I *should* have asked first."

Elang took off his spectacles. He looked tired. "Don't ask."

I blinked. "What?"

"A wife wouldn't ask her husband if she could kiss him. She'd simply do it."

How did he do that—pretend like nothing had happened?

It was an act, I reminded myself. Elang knew that as well as I did. Yet try as I might, I couldn't forget the sharp flutter in my stomach. That undertone of desperation and urgency when our lips had met, as though he'd wanted the kiss as much as I had. And then there was that ghost of a pulse I'd felt in his chest. . . .

"Oh," I said belatedly. Now I was embarrassed I'd been embarrassed.

Silence stretched between us, heavy and awkward. Was he staying here tonight? Neither of us dared broach the topic of sleeping arrangements, and as I unhooked my cloak, Elang observed outside the window. "Look outside. Nanhira occupies higher waters than Yonsar; you can see the moon from here."

The moon. Once I found it, I couldn't stop staring. Round and full, its appearance was magnified by the lens of the sea. "It's like a pearl," I murmured.

"I used to think it was mine, when I was a boy. I'd climb every dune and rock I could and try to reach it."

It wasn't often that he spoke about his past. I lowered my guard, just a little. "The Sages say when the moon is brightest, so is your longing for home," I said. "I finally understand what they meant."

"Your heart is your home," we spoke, almost at the same time.

I looked at him in surprise, but he'd turned off to the side. He changed the topic. "Shanizhun tells me you've been staying up late every night to paint."

I tilted my head. "What else does she tell you?"

"That you've gotten better at painting dragons. That Kunkoi's been flirting with you."

"Are you jealous?"

"If I were jealous, he wouldn't be snoring like thunder across the hall. He'd be shark bait."

I laughed. Elang could be funny, maybe even charming, when he wanted to.

"I should check on Kunkoi," he said. "He has a weakness

for wine, and he surely imbibed in excess tonight. I might need to stay with him until morning."

It was an excuse to let me have the room alone, and I appreciated it. But as he turned to leave, my hand went up to my butterfly pendant. "Will you tell me the story of Lady Liayin and the shepherd before you go?"

Elang twisted back, uncertainty furrowing his brow. "Now?"

"I won't be able to sleep if I don't know what happens to them," I confessed.

"I'm not good at telling stories."

"Try your best."

To my surprise, he sat on the chair opposite the bed. "It's a famous story in Ai'long, the tale of Liayin," he began. "She spun silk unlike any other. A gown woven when she was happy would bring its wearer great luck. A sash spun when she was angry might become a ward against demons. There was a war between the merfolk and dragons back then, and as Liayin's reputation spread, her parents sought to marry her off to a heavenly prince in exchange for aid from the gods."

Elang's words settled into a steady cadence. "She became betrothed to the Crown Prince himself—a high honor. But Liayin did not wish to wed a stranger. And so, night after night, she rose to the surface, where she could weep alone and unseen. Her tears became pearls, and as they washed away with the tides, she had an idea. Rather than let them go to waste, she gathered the pearls in a kelp net and ferried them to shore, where a young shepherd later chanced upon them. He shared the pearls with his village, but he would not say where he had found them. Instead, he waited patiently on the shore until Liayin at last returned, weeping as before.

"When he worked up the courage to approach her, she leapt back into the sea. But he played his flute, so sweetly that she couldn't help but listen. She returned, and slowly the two became friends. They fell in love."

I leaned forward. I'd always loved a good love story.

"Months passed, and as Liayin's marriage to the Crown Prince approached, she and the shepherd decided to run away together. One night she cut her hair so that no one from home might find or follow her. With the last of her magic, she transformed her tail into legs.

"She married the shepherd and lived happily among humans for many years. But one day, her children found the silk robes she had woven. They were too radiant for the mortal world, and when her daughter brought them out of Liayin's hiding place, a crab on the beach spied them. The next day, when Liayin went to the river to gather water, the merfolk dragged her back into Ai'long."

I drew in a thin breath when Elang paused. "Don't tease me like that. That can't be the end."

He almost smiled, stretching his arms behind his head. "Her husband and her children searched for her for years. Finally they came to a temple dedicated to worshipping the sea, where her children prayed for their mother to return. While they prayed, luminous pearls showered upon their heads. They were Liayin's tears, aglow with her love.

"The king and queen of Nanhira took pity on her and said that if she could weave a cloth that would surround and protect the merfolk realm, then they would allow her to be with her mortal husband and children again. It took her many years, but the strength of her love endured. Liayin wove the Cloak of Nanhira, which still protects the merfolk realm today, impenetrable even for the Dragon King."

"Was she reunited with her family in the end?"

That was what mattered most to me, and I was relieved when Elang nodded. "She returned to the mortal realm, where they lived happily for the rest of their days."

"I like that story," I murmured. "I'll tell it to my sisters when I go home."

"There's a little more. At the end of the war, the merfolk sent Liayin's tears to light Ai'long's waters—as a gesture of peace. It is a tradition that has continued."

"The Luminous Hour," I remembered. Mailoh had mentioned it on my first tour. "It's a few days before the Resonant Tide, isn't it? That's soon. Will it come to Yonsar?"

"I expect so." His gaze shifted downward. "I should like you to have one fond memory of your time here, before you go."

What a strange thing for him to say.

"My time here hasn't been all bad," I allowed. I tickled the moss in my hair. "Some things are growing on me. The garden, the clothes, Shani, even."

One sprig came undone and started to float away, but Elang caught it. "Moss isn't your favorite flower, is it?"

"Moss isn't a flower. You should know that."

"What about chrysanthemums, then? Lilies? Orchids?"

"Waterbells," I replied.

"The New Year flowers?" His brow pinched. "Because the bells look like gold ingots?"

I laughed. That was why A'landans bought them during New Year's, to welcome prosperity into their homes. "I find them interesting because they're born in the dark, yet only bloom in the light. Seeing them reassures me that better times are ahead. Besides, they're never anyone's favorite."

"Not like peonies."

Everyone always says their favorite flowers are peonies, I'd told my sisters on the day I'd left for Ai'long. I'd been certain Elang had been eavesdropping, and he had.

I hid my amusement. "When I was little, I used to think their bells made music, and if you rang them, golden coins would come sprinkling out of the petals. I even tried to grow a garden of them because I thought I'd make my family rich. But we Saigas sisters all have the killing touch when it comes to plants."

Elang was quiet for a moment. "It helps to talk to them," he said. "The flowers."

"Is that your secret to growing sanheia?" I teased. "What do you talk to them about?"

The faintest smile bloomed across his lips. Then he said, "It's late. Even half dragons have to sleep."

He didn't look tired. His yellow eye burned like a torch, and moonlight caught in the other, turning its gray into silver. There was something familiar about that one. Usually it was dark, resembling smoke from a flame blown out. But under the glaze of the evening tides, it was different. Paler. I couldn't shake the sense that I'd seen it somewhere before— a specter of the past.

Impossible, I told myself, pushing the thought away. Yet still it preyed on me, a small annoyance—like a pebble in my shoe.

"Good night, Tru," he said, oblivious to my thoughts. He placed the moss in my palm. "Don't stay up too late watching the moon."

When I opened my hand, the sprig of moss had turned

into a single waterbell, blue petals abloom. I set it beside my bed with a smile. "Good night."

In the morning, we returned to Yonsar, accompanied by Queen Haidi.

I hadn't expected a welcome party. But it never crossed my mind that we'd face an ambush.

Sharks were everywhere, barring entry to the castle. There were hundreds of them, sectioned into groups. Swarms, I assumed, until I realized that they were divided into formations, tactically positioned for attack.

"Shells out!" Caisan hollered at his soldiers. "Spears forward!"

Kunkoi immediately leapt forward to marshal the soldiers, followed by the merfolk who had accompanied us from Nanhira. I started too, until Elang took my arm.

"Stay with Her Majesty," he said, tucking a strand of my hair behind my ear. "Please."

I regarded him, my heart skipping a beat.

"Don't look so disappointed, Lady Saigas," said Queen Haidi, smiling at us. "Your husband can fend for himself. Come with me."

I followed her, but I kept looking worriedly over my shoulder. The sharks had pinpointed Yonsar's every weakness, from the cracks that had yet to be repaired to the injured turtles stacked on the Gate of a Thousand Shells. From the looks of it, they'd begun their offense while we were away. Again and again, they rammed the gate, each time ripping just a little deeper past Yonsar's defenses.

"Let the soldiers do the fighting," said Haidi. "You have your own task."

I turned to her, confused. "What am I to do?"

"Ah, I take it Elangui didn't explain. He requested that you be the one to speak to the seas."

"Speak to the seas?" I repeated stupidly. "Are they . . . alive?"

"Not quite." She took my arm and drew me into higher waters, farther from the fray. "As you know, the waters of Ai'long are enchanted. But the magic has no mind of its own, it takes no sides; it is simply here, as universal as air on land. Yet it is powerful magic—older than the gods themselves—magic that gave the Dragon King his pearl. And you, as the lady of the Westerly Seas, are connected to it."

"Forgive me if I don't understand," I said. "What does that mean?"

"It means the seas will listen to you when you speak to them," Haidi explained. "They may not heed you, but they will hear you. Sometimes, that is all you need to change the tides."

She passed me a swath of iridescent cloth, exquisite as a fragment of rainbow. "I have woven this ward to protect Yonsar from the Dragon King's wrath."

I stared. The cloth was barely wide enough to cover my shoulders.

Haidi acknowledged my disbelief with a nod. "Yes, it may not look like much, but the threads are strong. Therein comes your part. You must appeal to the waters and ask them to disperse it across Yonsar."

Appeal to the waters, she said, as though it were as easy as planting a seed.

"And if they don't?" I asked. "Help, I mean."

Haidi's calm was unflappable. "Then today will be Yonsar's last."

I was starting to wish I'd eaten a second bowl of breakfast. At least then my stomach wouldn't be churning the way it was, with immense anxiety.

"What do I do?" I asked.

"Swim as high as you can," said Haidi. "Then plead your case to the seas."

All right, it was a start. After taking a deep breath, I jetted up high above the seafloor until I overlooked the castle. A battle raged below, lashes of kelp whips and clangs of spears and swords disrupting the peace of Yonsar's waters. Each second I hesitated, the sharks advanced deeper. I needed to hurry.

I had no idea how to speak to the seas or even make myself heard, so I simply swam upward, the silken ward shimmering in my arms. I was nearly high enough to see the streaks of crimson in the tides, the mysterious auroras of light like an underwater sun. Here, I slowed. I listened. The calamity of the battle below had grown distant, replaced by a low and constant hum.

It was gentle, yet persistent enough that it made my skin buzz. I had never heard it before; then again, I'd never tried to listen.

Could this be the magic of Ai'long?

It was worth a try. "Reverent waters," I murmured, "I beseech you for aid. Yonsar is in danger, we are in need. Her Majesty Queen Haidi has woven this ward of merfolk silk to protect us. Please, accept it. Help us."

I held out the bundle in my arms, as if I expected someone

to come and take it from me. But there was no response. The sea was as still as it had been before I'd spoken, and the hum went on, unbroken.

The disappointment stung, and I hugged the silk to my chest. Here I was, floating in the middle of the sea without a clue what to do next. Below, I picked out Elang fighting among the sharks. He ought to be the one appealing to the seas, not me. I wasn't raised here, I had no connection to Yonsar. Or to Ai'long.

That's not true, I thought. *I have Baba. He's here, waiting to be found. He needs me, just as Yonsar does.*

Elang had once said that the strongest bridge was made of truth. Perhaps this was my chance to build that bridge—with Ai'long.

Reverent waters, I tried again. This time, in my thoughts, I spoke plainly: *You probably know already that I'm not truly Elang's Heavenly Match—the only reason I'm pretending to be is because the Dragon King stole my father away, years ago when I was a little girl. It's been so long I can't even remember the sound of his voice.* A lump hardened in my throat. *Now that I'm here, I see that I'm not the only one who's suffered. Yonsar is everything to Elang, and it's come to mean something to me too. I'm not asking you to take a side against the Dragon King, because I know that you cannot. But if you can, please help us protect the Westerly Seas.*

For a second time, I held out the merfolk silk, but I didn't wait for the water to respond. I let the silk drop from my arms, releasing it as though it were an offering.

Down it fluttered, graceful as a crane's flight. Beams of iridescent light appeared then, carried by a rippling wave, and they ferried the silk down, draping its gossamer threads upon the castle and the nearby mountains. Suddenly I felt a heaviness in my body, making me sink back to where I'd started, at Haidi's side.

My offering had been accepted, but the queen's work had just begun. The long ends of her hair fanned out, conducting the silken ribbons across Yonsar, twisting and spinning to guide them into place. Then came the most splendorous magic.

The silk spun off into glittering ribbons, knitting itself through the castle's stone walls, up and down, left and right. No corner was forgotten, no window or eave neglected. And its effect took place immediately.

Invisible barriers prevented the sharks from advancing. The ones that were already past the gates were suddenly sent reeling back, stung by the power of the woven ward. The turtles and merfolk chased them into the backwaters, and I let out a cheer.

"We did it," I cried.

Merfolk surrounded the castle. Echoing their queen, they touched their hair to the walls, and strands of shimmering magic traveled across the stone and marble, filling the cracks made by the storms. Before long, the castle exuded a soft sheen of enchantment, and the turtles raised their spears in triumph. They honked in celebration as the castle became whole once again, its crumbled walls at last repaired.

When the magic was complete, Haidi's hair settled into a river behind her back. Her body sagged from the effort, and I caught her arm, holding her upright before she lost her balance.

Queen Haidi cast me a startled frown, and I let go.

"I'm sorry—"

"No." She smiled. A true smile of warmth—and friendship. "Thank you."

"I—I should be thanking *you*," I stammered. "We're grateful . . . for everything that you've done."

"You should be protected from future storms," Haidi said. "But be mindful, it will only last through the Resonant Tide. After that you will be at Nazayun's mercy."

"I understand," I replied quietly.

Haidi and I had settled in front of the castle, and while I observed Yonsar's forces gathering home, the queen observed me. Her brow furrowed. "Something is troubling you."

"The Dragon King can make monsters out of squids and eels," I said slowly. "Why should he care so much about a mere half dragon like Elang?"

"A mere half dragon?" A tendril of Haidi's hair brushed across her lips, lingering there as if it were passing a secret. "Elang is more than that. He is a symbol of defiance, a creature who should never have been born."

I didn't understand.

"Dragons do not multiply easily; this is why they sometimes seek mates outside their kind. Merfolk, usually—and on rare occasions, humans. The late lord Ta'ginan did not follow the proper rites when he met Elang's mother, and so your husband was born in secret, without King Nazayun's blessing."

"And because Elang didn't have this blessing, Nazayun hates him?"

"That is part of it." Haidi paused. "Have you heard of the Eight and a Half Immortals?"

"I know of the Eight Immortals," I replied. "Not Eight and a Half."

"There's a legend—forgotten by most, immortals and mortals alike—that when a god is no longer deserving of their divinity, eight and a half immortals will come together, bringing forth nine celestial treasures. A hammer that strikes thunder, a mirror that casts lightning, a drum that summons rain, and so on. Together they will create a weapon so formidable that it will vanquish the unworthy god and strip away his power." Haidi folded her hands. "Nazayun believes that he is a target."

"With good reason," I muttered. Then it occurred to me: "He thinks the half immortal is Elang."

"Correct." Haidi lowered her voice. "Nazayun has been trying to kill Elang ever since he was born, but each attempt has been unsuccessful. He believes Elang is protected by the Eight Immortals. The mere possibility of a threat is unacceptable; that is why he cursed him."

"Nazayun fears him."

A nod. "A fact that he tries to hide, lest it bring him loss of face in the dragon court. Even still, no one dares help Elang."

"*You dared,*" I said softly.

Haidi made the barest nod. "Ever vigilant, ever alone. That is what we used to say about the young lord of the Westerly Seas." She touched my shoulder. "I am glad he is not alone anymore, Lady Saigas."

I couldn't help the flush that warmed my cheeks. I didn't know what to say, so I simply nodded.

She lingered one last moment. "You've spoken to the sea, now listen to it," she said. "This is the lesson my mother gave when I was chosen to rule. The waters will never lie to you."

Haidi drew a deep breath, then let out a low keening

sound, calling her people together. The shimmering pool appeared once more, and the merfolk slipped inside, leaving as quietly as they had come.

I waited with the turtles until the merfolk departed and the seam between their world and ours knitted closed. The fog in the waters was clearing, and in the distance, beyond the farthest corners of Yonsar, I could see the Floating Mountains for the first time.

Truly they were beautiful, like mountains spun straight out of a dream, suspended by enchanted threads.

Yet the most warming sight was Yonsar. After my journey to Nanhira, I'd gained a new fondness for this solitary kingdom. Yes, it was gray, its land barren and desolate, but what great painting did not begin on an empty page? Even the most splendid of gardens arose from a hollow field. I had faith Elang would see Yonsar bloom.

I slipped past the gates into the castle, the faintest premonition tingling down my fingertips. Things had to get better from here, I was sure of it.

CHAPTER TWENTY-EIGHT

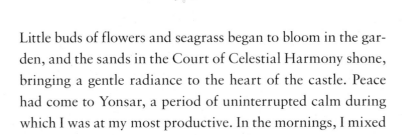

Little buds of flowers and seagrass began to bloom in the garden, and the sands in the Court of Celestial Harmony shone, bringing a gentle radiance to the heart of the castle. Peace had come to Yonsar, a period of uninterrupted calm during which I was at my most productive. In the mornings, I mixed colors and painted, then for lunch, I joined Kunkoi in the kitchen and made noodles by hand—a routine I began as a respite from my grueling lessons with Shani.

The demon was impossible to please, but I'd finally graduated to drawing Nazayun's full body. I did my most fastidious work, spending hours on the light that reflected off his scales. Still, I couldn't shake the feeling that something was lacking. When I'd painted my vision of Elang, he had practically flown off the page, so real I could hear the whir of his tail before it splashed into the sea. I didn't feel the same way about Nazayun.

"It's his scales," Shani pointed out. "The color is off."

"I know," I said. All week I'd been mixing paints, trying to re-create the proper shade—but none came close to capturing the brilliance of Nazayun's tyrannical hide.

"A god can't be painted with ordinary colors. It has to be something special." She flicked a fin in the direction of my hair. "You could use these blue ragweeds on top of your head."

"You mean my hair?"

"You're not a mermaid, it wouldn't be a sacrifice for you to go bald."

I glared. "Even if I could make a dye out of my hair, I don't have enough."

"Alas." The demon dangled her tail off my back, swinging it left and right. "Then ask Elang'anmi."

Ask Elang? I hesitated a beat too long.

"What's the matter?" Shani leaned forward with a whiff of conspiracy. "Your pulse just sped up three beats. Have you got a crush?"

I shoved her off my shoulder. "No!"

"Good." Shani floated, her tone thick with warning. "Because I wouldn't fall in love with Elang'anmi if I were you. You'll only be disappointed."

"I know that," I said. I stuffed a brush into my sleeve, purposefully snubbing the pocket Elang had conjured.

Since coming back from Nanhira, he had become even colder than before; he barely acknowledged me during our dinners together. Every time I so much as sat next to him, he'd pull away to the seat across. I learned to bring a book, but behind its pages I'd secretly study him.

There was more to this surly half dragon than I'd realized. I was used to attributing his hot and cold behavior to the act we had to put on, though lately it had become hazy what was for show and what was not.

I found Elang in his library, delivering a lecture about thorns and pruning-knife technique. His only disciple was Kunkoi, who sat before a jug of dark, bubbling sangi, stifling a yawn.

As I entered, the merman's head bobbed up. "Lady Saigas is here," he announced, taking my presence as an excuse to rise. He scooped up a small jar of green peppers from the table. "Look what was found this morning."

"My snake eyes!" I cried. "I thought I lost them in the Fold."

"They washed into the dunes," explained Kunkoi. "I was trying to convince His Lord Highness to grow them in the garden so I could distill their poison into a weapon against intruders. Unfortunately, he didn't approve of the idea."

Elang cleared his throat.

"Rightly so," I said, ignoring Elang. "They're peppers—they're not poisonous."

"Not poisonous? I ate one and nearly died."

"You mean, you saw a glimpse of heaven," I teased. "Trust me, it's not so bad. I'll make you noodles with chili sauce for lunch. That'll change your mind—"

"That's enough," Elang interrupted with a growl. He hurled a bundle of thorned sanheia into Kunkoi's arms. "Bring these to the storeroom."

The merman blinked, looking rather hopeful. "Does that mean the lesson is over?"

"Go. Now."

Faster than a sailfish, Kunkoi somersaulted off. Once Elang and I were alone, the half dragon became preoccupied with washing an assortment of vials and flasks. I swam up to help.

"Don't touch anything," he said, pushing the bowls away from my reach. "Some of the ingredients are still active. You might contaminate the potion."

"Sorry." I pursed my lips. "Were you teaching Kunkoi how to make sangi?"

"Attempting to teach."

I sent Elang a curious look. "First Queen Haidi, now Kunkoi? Soon it won't be your precious secret anymore."

"It was never meant to be a secret. I only kept it one to protect Ai'long. But soon I'll need others to carry it on."

"In case you decide to become a whale?" I joked.

He didn't smile. "Yes, well . . . half dragons don't live forever."

My humor faded. Elang had turned his back to me and was corking the flask of bubbling sangi to cool. "I'm busy, as you can see. What brings you here? Have you had a vision?"

"I've had a tingle."

"And?"

"I need paint," I said, steering the conversation away from my Sight. "I've been working on sketches for Nazayun's portrait, and the blue's not right."

"You cannot start the portrait without a vision," said Elang crisply.

"Why not? Have you *seen* your grandfather? It'll take weeks to paint him, and I'm halfway through my time here. I need to get started."

As usual, Elang wasn't going to provide a useful explanation. "If you haven't had a premonition, then your presence here is unnecessary. Dinner isn't for several hours."

My husband, ever the pleasant conversationalist. I gritted my teeth, striving to be patient.

"I need more paint," I tried again. "Look."

From inside my sleeve, I pulled out my latest sketch of Nazayun and unrolled the parchment. "I've tried everything, but I can't mix the right shade of blue for his scales. Maybe if you've got some pea flower tea in that treasury of yours, I could try it."

"What treasury?"

"That secret room where you keep your teas and maps and demons know what else."

"You went through my crates? There's a reason that gallery is hidden."

I crossed my arms, vexed by *his* vexed tone. "Do I look like I've had time to hunt through your tea tins? I probably should have, given how difficult you're making this."

"Let me see that." With a grunt, Elang took my sketch. He adjusted his spectacles and studied it silently. "The color's too dull," he said at last.

"That's what I was trying to tell you."

Elang wouldn't let go of the sketch. "What is he looking at?" he asked, pointing at Nazayun's head. "His eyes are cast skyward."

Were they? I'd painted Nazayun perched upon a cliff, claws digging into the rock, his tail lolling behind him in a series of bounding hills. I'd shaped him like the mountains themselves, so that from a distance, you had to look twice to see that he was a dragon.

"I pictured this as the moment he finds out that he's been defeated," I replied. "So he's looking up at—"

"The moon," Elang and I said at the same time.

We were side by side, our elbows almost touching, and he hadn't moved away.

"I see you made the composition of his body like a landscape," he murmured. "It almost feels like a deception."

"I've always liked hiding secret meanings in my art."

"Clever. You've improved."

"Thank you," I replied over the skip in my heart. It was rare to get a compliment from Elang, even one as grudging as this.

He straightened, returning the sketch to me in one terse gesture. "I'll source the paint for you by the end of this week."

"I'll need at least a cask-full."

"Let that be my concern, not yours."

His tone had become thick, making it clear I was dismissed. Just to irk him, I stayed on.

"There's sand on your shoulder," I said, dusting it off. It was black, rocky sand, not the star-shaped stuff found in the Court of Celestial Harmony. "Did you venture into the Fold this morning?"

"Only to hunt for spies." He paused for a fraction of a second. "Your chilis were found along the journey."

I twisted open the jar. "You say that with such disdain. Is there no hope of a pepper garden in the castle?"

Elang's eyes narrowed. "Do you know how the character for spice is built?"

"No."

Using his finger, he wrote the character on his palm. "A bouquet of suffering. I think Yonsar has suffered quite enough."

He said it deadpan, but still I gave a snort. "That only means you haven't had the proper experience. I'll show you."

I picked a few peppers from the jar. "Snake eyes are so

fragrant that you can rub their husks on your palm and smell it on the back of your hand." I demonstrated and inhaled, taking in every note: the toasty husks, the crisp tang of citrus, the woody undertone that rushed up the back of my nose. "Try."

Elang humored me by rubbing a chili on his palm. He sniffed, carefully.

He seemed to be at a loss for words.

"Isn't it amazing?"

"*Amazing* is not the word I'd choose. I think my nose has gone numb."

It was true; both sides of his nose had turned red. My hand jumped to my mouth. "I should've warned you it might tingle. It'll sting less once you build up a tolerance. Try again."

"I think you've discovered a new form of torture," he said, but he rolled the pepper across his palm a second time, more slowly and intently than before. "I thought you were from the South. Where do you get this love of spice?"

My breath caught in my throat. The question brought about a rush of melancholy—and déjà vu—that I couldn't quite place. "My father," I replied belatedly. "Snake-eye peppers were his favorite—he used to pick them fresh off the trees when he was a boy in Balar."

"They're not A'landan?"

"A'landans would tell you they are, but they stole the seeds from Balar and started trading them for profit on the Spice Road. They'd pay people like my father to shuttle them across the continent." I rolled the chilis on my palm. "Sometimes Baba would sneak a handful to bring home. We'd eat them with dinner, then he'd crush any leftovers into paint." I smashed a chili between my nails and showed Elang the powdery smear on my finger. "He'd say this made for the exact green of the mountains in his hometown."

It was a memory I'd never shared before, and a lump rose to my throat. "He promised to take me one day."

Elang said nothing, but he brought the pepper to his nose once more. He inhaled, deeper than before, and closed his eyes. "Maybe you could put it in my soup," he said slowly, "a pinch at a time. I think then, over a period, I might grow accustomed to it."

Scourge of Saino, what was it about Elang that made me want to slap him one minute, then kiss him the next? He was growing on me.

He saw my smile. "I'm going to regret this, aren't I?"

"Most definitely. But it's too late, the seas heard you agree."

"So they did." He started to laugh, then his eyes snapped up, his wide brow furrowing. "Do you hear that? A wrinkle in the current . . ."

I felt it as soon as he mentioned it. Instinct had me grab Elang by the arm, pulling him behind a pillar—an instant before a jellyfish exploded into the library, barbs shooting out of its tentacles.

They fired fast as raindrops, piercing into the thick folds of my cloak. With a whip of his tail, Elang seized the creature. Fresh barbs shot out, ripping past his arms as he clawed through the jellyfish, restraining its head in his fist.

"Who let you through the wards?" he demanded.

Light pulsed through the jellyfish's head, accelerating until there was a brilliant flash. I shielded my eyes with my sleeve. When I looked again, the creature had gone limp. It was dead.

"What did it say?" I asked shakily.

"Nothing." Elang pulled out a barb from his torso with a grunt.

Kunkoi found us rushing into the hall, Mailoh at his side. He spoke rapidly, and I only caught the words *sanheia* and *Caisan* before Elang's spine went rigid and I heard him curse for the first time.

His rage manifested in the water, which roiled under my feet, so fierce I worried he might knock down a wall. As soon as he noticed, he closed his fists and drew himself tall. The waves receded.

"Where is Caisan?" he asked in a low growl.

"In your personal quarters," replied Mailoh, nervously gesturing down to where the hall tapered off. "Shanizhun's subdued him."

"You may go. I'll take care of it from here."

I felt sorry for the turtles who paddled out of our way as if their lives depended on it. Elang hurried to his quarters, and I followed.

Inside was General Caisan. Unconscious.

Shani hovered above him, invoking a shimmering mantle of floating beads. Within each one was a memory, and Shani's eyes shone like I'd never seen before, a deep, hypnotic red. "Here's your spy." She called forth a bead. "He let the jellyfish into the castle while you were brewing sangi."

I felt myself pale. Elang had trusted Caisan to monitor Yonsar's wards. Why betray that trust? It didn't make sense.

"Why did they come?" I said. "The jellyfish—were they trying to kill Elang?"

"They were looking for something," replied Elang, whose

eyes didn't leave Caisan. "Something I've kept hidden for a long time."

His voice was low, but if the betrayal still aggrieved him, he did not show it. "Return the memories to the general."

Shani protested, "What—"

"Do as I say."

The demon muttered under her breath, but she obeyed. She swam around Caisan, flinging the beads of his memories back into his mind.

"Take General Caisan to the keep," Elang ordered her. "I'll deal with him later."

While Shani took Caisan away, I surveyed Elang's chambers. Weeks into our "marriage," I'd still never been invited here. It felt more like a vagabond's quarters than a prince's. Only one bookshelf, a wide bed with a blue quilt, an empty vase that looked rather forlorn. I rifled through a chest, looking for a spare cloth.

"What are you doing?" he demanded. "Did I give you permission to go through my—"

"You're bleeding. You need a bandage."

"That isn't urgent right now." Elang pulled me up, lifting me above a mess of ripped scrolls and overturned chests. Sanheia flowers floated everywhere. Their stems were snapped, the petals shriveled up like flakes of black snow.

I almost didn't dare to ask: "The sangi, is it—"

"Destroyed." Elang held up a single rose. "This is all that's left. Barely enough to make a day's supply." He crumbled the petals in his hand, trying to hold in his anger. "The dose you took this morning was the last I'd prepared."

Its bitterness still lingered on my lips. "Why would Caisan let in the patrols?"

"I've told you before, not everyone in this castle can be trusted."

"Surely, he had a reason." I frowned. Caisan was far from my favorite creature in Yonsar, but I'd thought him loyal.

As if he could read my thoughts, Elang said, "I never said anyone in this castle was disloyal. A spy can be bribed, they can be coerced." His jaw drew tight. "Sometimes they act because they have no choice."

"You think he was threatened?"

"I don't know." His expression was grim, and he reached into a chest for a satchel, then swung it over his head. "I'll question him when I return."

"Return?" My eyes widened with realization. "You're leaving!"

"I've no choice but to go to Gangsun. You need sangi."

"Then I'm coming too."

"You will stay." He was firm. "This is what Nazayun wants—for you to abandon the safety of the castle."

"But my family—"

"Will only be endangered by your presence. You have to focus on our mission."

My heart clenched. I hated that he was right. I missed Mama and my sisters so much.

"What about you?" I took his arm. "You . . . you're hurt."

As I spoke, I saw just *how* hurt. I gently rotated his arm, not letting go when he twisted away. I could see the angry red cuts the barbs had left. Worse yet, across his back was a gruesome network of scars. Lacerations and slash marks, like one got from a fight, and deeper, shorter cuts . . . as though someone had tried to gouge out his scales.

Most of the scars looked old, faded over years—except for

a wound below his left shoulder. It was still pink, still deep and malicious. Almost certainly from being recently stabbed.

"Who did this to you?" I asked.

"Various assassins" was his brusque reply. "They're nothing."

"The barbs—"

"Forgive me, Tru." He shook my hand off his arm. "But every second I linger here is valuable time onshore. Keep close to Shani and don't leave the castle."

He touched his spectacles, and a mask materialized in their place. He pressed it to his face.

I hadn't seen him wear the mask in weeks. It seemed to sever the fragile friendship we had built together, leaving us strangers once more.

"I'll tell your family you said hello," he said.

And without another word, he was gone.

CHAPTER TWENTY-NINE

The castle was in turmoil, turtles combing every nook and cranny for intruders. I'd gotten used to the muffled rumbles from outside—of the patrols trying to wear down the castle wards. But now each sound jolted me.

"No need to look so worried," said Shani. "The waters will tell you if Elang'anmi dies."

I scowled. I'd forgotten about her. "It's rude reading people's thoughts."

"Then you shouldn't make them so interesting," she replied, licking her lips. "I taste gossip, and it's sweet."

"Get out of my head."

"What happened in Nanhira between you and Elang'anmi? The merman cook won't tell me. Isn't like him to withhold anything."

Sometimes it stunned me, how callous Shani could be. Then again, she was a demon.

I ignored her the rest of the way, not stopping until I found Mailoh. As I feared, she was being detained for questioning.

"Let her go," I ordered the guards.

"But, Lady Saigas, Mailoh is the general's sister. She could have been an accomplice."

"Let her go," I said again. "I won't repeat myself."

Reluctantly the guards released Mailoh. The turtle was visibly shaken, her bright eyes dulled into a dry and weary green. Still, as much the backbone of Yonsar Castle as the Spine itself, she gathered her poise and made a deep bow.

"I plead on my brother's behalf, Lady Saigas," she said. "I cannot speak to what made him act against Lord Elang, but I assure you Caisan has been loyal to Yonsar his entire life."

I wanted to believe her. "Will you come with me to see him?"

Mailoh drew a sharp breath, then nodded somberly. "Follow me."

The keep was on the lowermost level of the castle, beneath the barracks. It was a dungeon in all but name. A single lantern floated across the sunken ceiling, and the metal bars cast shadowed stripes over the general's supine form.

Caisan was burrowed into the sand, and he made no move to rise when he heard our approach.

"This certainly isn't the time to hide in your shell," Mailoh huffed. "The lady of the castle has come to speak with you."

"Leave me be," Caisan grunted. "I have nothing to say to her."

"Do not shame me, Caisan. Traitor or not, you owe Lady Saigas respect."

She knew just how to goad him. He jutted out his head, sand spilling down the slopes of his face. "I am not a traitor."

"Then you are a coward," said Mailoh. "Which do you prefer? If you will not face her, she will have to assume one or the other is true."

Caisan rose. His enormous feet made indents in the bedrock as he pounded forward to the bars. "Why have you come?" he grumbled at me.

"For the truth."

"The truth, you say." The general scoffed. "Yet you bring the demon."

"Caisan," Mailoh warned.

"I told you before what she was." He stared mistrustfully at Shani, who floated behind me. "Think. There's only one creature in this castle with the ability to possess a mind. Who else would know how to destroy Lord Elang's sangi? Who else could allow Nazayun's patrol to enter the castle unseen?"

At the accusation, Shani's watery countenance darkened. She raised her tail, and frost crackled across the sand in Caisan's cell, traveling swiftly up the walls. The entire keep turned cold.

"Turtle is most delectable when chilled," she murmured, before her tone took on an edge. "Question my loyalty again, and you won't even have bones left for mourning."

"That's enough." I grabbed the demon by the tail. "And you, General—you should know that Shanizhun is honor bound to Lord Elang."

The general lowered his head. "You think demons have honor?"

"I'll show you honor!" Shani pulled herself up to her full height and breadth—and kept growing—her red eyes dilating as she loomed over the cell.

"Enough," I warned her. "That's a command, Shani."

With a hiss, she spiraled back into my ring.

Mailoh sent her brother a scathing look, then faced me. "Hear me, Lady Saigas, please. General Caisan is loyal. He has served Yonsar for—"

"Three centuries!" Caisan boomed. "Centuries, while that demon has been at Lord Elang's side only a few years. I tell you, she is Nazayun's servant still!"

"Will you desist with this malice toward Shanizhun?" Mailoh cried. "It is *your* honor that is in question."

I was silent, withholding judgment. I used to think I was good at reading faces, but lies were not always easy to unearth. I could tell Caisan genuinely believed in his own innocence. That counted for something. "I will consider your warning, General," I said at last. "That will be all."

The floating lantern followed Mailoh and me back to the barracks. I touched my opal ring as I ascended the stairs.

Shani, I thought, *when will you learn to control that temper?*

I sighed when she didn't respond. There was a traitor somewhere in Yonsar. In my gut, I didn't think it was Caisan, nor did I think it was Shani. So who was it?

I didn't know, but I was going to find out.

My fingertips burned with a vision, and I sat at my desk, brush trembling. I had a feeling I wouldn't like the future I was about to paint.

I balled my fists, digging my nails into my palms as I tried to hold it in. Night after night, I'd been dreaming of Baba turning into stone. *Is he alive?* I'd asked Nazayun.

It depends on what you mean by alive.

There came a tap on my door, and I shot up with a jump. "Kunkoi."

"Hungry?" he greeted me. "Even the kitchen's been cordoned off for the investigation, but I remembered our lovely Lady Saigas would need lunch."

"Is it that late already?" I set down my brush. "I'd forgotten."

Kunkoi set two canisters on my desk. "My special soup noodles. I've been wanting to make this for you, but I had to wait until Lord Elang was away."

I arched an eyebrow. "He doesn't like them?"

"Not anymore." Kunkoi shrugged.

I started clearing my desk. In Ai'long, Elang had been gone mere hours. It'd have been over a day on land. "Will he be safe?"

"He'll probably encounter a few assassins, but he hasn't survived so long for no reason."

My chest went tight. "A few assassins?"

"Nothing to worry about." Kunkoi eyed me. "I heard *you* visited General Caisan in the keep. *That'll* worry Lord Elang."

"He insists he's innocent."

"I'd be surprised if he weren't. Caisan's too dense for treachery. All turtles are."

"So who do you think the traitor is? It can't be Shani. She hates Nazayun."

"I don't know," the merman replied. "What I do know is this isn't something you solve on an empty stomach."

He opened the two copper canisters, stacked one atop the other. "Try this before it gets cold. It's one of my specialties."

The tingle in my fingers ebbed as I opened the lid. The first canister contained a thick, still-simmering broth, with mustard greens and carrots and tiny clams floating inside. The second, a generous portion of wavy egg noodles, which I combined with the soup.

Praise the Sages, it was delicious. I licked my lips, my eyes slowly widening as the aftertaste matured on my tongue, releasing a familiar punch of savory deliciousness. "This soup . . . it's . . ."

"Incredible?" The ends of Kunkoi's hair curled with pride. "I know."

The soup *was* delicious, but that wasn't what I'd meant to say. I dipped my spoon, chasing a morsel of steamed fish under glistening beads of oil. "What's in it?" I asked.

"Anyone else, I'd tell them my finest scallops and abalone, a sprinkling of my noblest spices, and five cordyceps petals." He leaned close. "But for you, Lady Saigas, I'll share the true secret: the broth is kelp based. Simple as that. You boil it for a night, then after that, you can put whatever you want inside."

Kelp based. Gaari had told me that once, about the soup we'd adored at Luk's. I swirled the broth in my mouth, reveling in the salt and fat as my tongue unwove new flavors, from the thickness of the spring onions to the springiness of the noodles. A familiar taste from a lifetime ago. Could it be . . .

My breath grew shallow, my pulse faster with each beat. I stared at Kunkoi, mentally superimposing Gaari's face over him. No, it wasn't him. The merman hadn't left Yonsar in years.

Then?

In my mind, I already knew the answer, but I refused to consider it. It was impossible. *Impossible.*

Still, I had to ask. "Kunkoi," I started, each syllable scraping out of my throat like rock against rock. "Where did you learn to make this soup?"

"A cousin taught it to me," replied the merman faintly. He was counting the chilis I'd added to the broth, and he wasn't very attentive once peppers were involved. "I forget which one—I have far too many cousins, but he was sent to land years ago. Said he'd start a restaurant there. Farsighted of him. Elang tried to send me to the shop, but I stayed here."

"The shop. In Gangsun?"

"I don't know the mortal realm well enough to say, but Lord Elang would know—he used to frequent the place every other week." Kunkoi noticed the intensity in my voice. "Is something the matter?"

My head was growing lighter with each passing moment, and I started floating off my chair, forgetting how to keep myself anchored.

The noodles, which I couldn't stop eating only an instant before, now tasted like sand.

I set aside my bowl, suddenly feeling unwell.

"Lady Saigas, are you all right? You've gone pale. Is it the food?"

My heart was hammering. "Will you send for Mailoh?"

Kunkoi lurched for the door. "At once."

With bated breath, I waited until the door closed fully, then I shot up. I had to be quick.

With only a twinge of guilt, I twisted off my opal ring and dropped it into a teapot.

"Sorry, Shani," I muttered, shutting the lid. Then, feeling like an interloper in my own castle, I sprang out of my room.

I knew exactly where I was going.

CHAPTER THIRTY

The secret room smelled of tea. The malty, nutty black tea that Elang was always drinking.

There were at least a hundred crates in the room, a few floating along the ceiling. So this was Elang's treasury.

It's where Lord Elang keeps the valuables he acquires from his trips to land, Mailoh had informed me before that first tour. *Tea is his main conquest. Last I checked there were also a few old maps.*

Every crate I opened confirmed her words. I encountered countless tea tins, a few carefully rolled maps of western Lor'yan, then an arsenal of books, enough to fill a library. After a while, I gave up on the crates and started knocking against every surface I could find, hunting for a hidden compartment. With a frustrated grunt, I sank to the ground, sitting beside a pile of books that had fallen out of their crate. What was I looking for, anyway?

A few of the books started to float, and I caught them with a frown. Elang had told me that the rest of his books were still in Gangsun. But here were boxes upon boxes of books. Surely a good part of his collection.

I sprang up, letting myself hover above the crates.

"Reveal yourself to me," I spoke aloud. My words were shaky and vibrated against the walls. I gathered myself, speaking more forcefully: "Reveal yourself to me. Nothing shall be hidden from the lady of the Westerly Seas."

It took a moment for the sea to comply, but Queen Haidi had been right—the waters did *not* lie. Before my eyes, the books in the crate flickered, then reappeared in their true form. Almost as if a mask had been peeled away.

They were not books at all, but scrolls upon scrolls of . . . art. Paintings, sketches, even drawings on scraps of crude rice paper.

Suddenly I couldn't breathe. I recognized these works.

How could this be? Here, deep in the legendary realm of dragons, in a secret vault in a derelict castle, was every painting I had ever sold through Gaari. From the sketch of the prefect I'd drawn when we'd first met and the portraits that I had forged and sold at auction, to the dragon Elang had snatched from me in his garden.

Every single one of my works—even the practice drawings I'd discarded because they weren't good enough—were here, carefully stored.

My hands shaking, I held up one of my earliest pieces.

"*I want you to paint something with only one color,*" Gaari had instructed. "*Let's try your favorite. Let me guess, blue?*"

I skipped past the pot of blue he offered and went straight for green.

"*Green,*" *I said.* "*The color of the most expensive jade. The color of pine and moss and the first chilis I ever ate.*"

"*The color of life,*" *Gaari mused.*

I dipped my brush and drew a stalk of bamboo. "My father used to say, 'Green is from blue, and is better than blue.'"

"What does that mean?"

I gave Gaari my cheekiest smile. "It means you learn to surpass your teachers."

How he'd laughed. I shoved the painting back into the crate.

It couldn't be, I told myself. Gaari was dead.

But there was no other explanation. There was no doubt.

I closed the crate lid, confusion and anger rattling inside me. Three years, I'd known the old man. I'd always questioned who he was. Part of me had guessed he wore a disguise, and more than once I'd teased him about that long white beard of his. It couldn't be real, I'd said. And I'd been right.

How had I not seen it? The adulation for good food, the meticulousness, the stormy gray eye and disdainful glowers.

The gardening!

I mined my memory for every encounter, every word I'd exchanged with Gaari. Gaari had been garrulous and fun, charming—and a friend. If not for him, my family would have starved. I'd have ended up in the governor's prison.

Gaari always had a big heart.

Whereas Elang . . . Elang had no heart. He was cold and distant, calculating and . . .

Gave your family a place to stay. A treacherous voice stole into my thoughts. *Took a barb in the chest for you.*

"Only because he needs me," I snapped aloud, waving the thoughts away.

I dug into my pocket for the waterbell he'd given me in

Nanhira. It sat on my hand, petals unfolding gently, as fresh and blue as the day he conjured it.

Now it served as a painful reminder of how close I'd come to trusting him. This entire time, he'd been lying.

"That stupid merman," purred a voice. Shani misted into being, uncrossing her long fins over my neck. "I had a feeling he'd give it all away."

"So it's true." The words clung to my throat like the bitterest pill. "Elang is . . . Gaari."

I needed to say it aloud, more for myself than for Shani.

"Congratulations," said the demon. "Turns out you didn't marry a stranger after all."

"This entire time, you *knew*."

"Of course I knew. You think Elang'anmi could've survived so many years in exile without my help?" A scoff. "The longest five years of my life, living on that hellhole you humans call land. And more than half of it was wasted on pursuing the likes of you."

"I knew it couldn't have been a coincidence," I said. "Me falling into his garden. Him needing a painter."

"You should've listened to your instincts." Shani twirled the opal ring around her tail. "I knew all that gold would muddy your senses."

"Did he plan this?"

"There are few things that Elang'anmi does not plan."

I felt sick inside as the confusion evaporated out of me, leaving a flare of anger in its wake. "Did he plant Yargui's men too?" I demanded. "The attack on the noodle house? His *death*?"

"Maybe he did, maybe he didn't. What does it matter? In a few weeks, you'll never see each other again."

"Of course it matters. He's—"

"Your husband?" Shani managed to pluck the last words I was going to use. "Be upset all you want, but I wouldn't waste my breath if I were you." She smirked. "Don't forget, you're short on sangi."

She dissolved back into mist before I could reply.

I crumpled the waterbell, loosening my fist just before the petals broke. Yes, I was angry with him. When I went too long without blinking, I could see little white stars floating in the sea, specters of my fury. But beneath the anger was a knot of emotion far sharper, far more difficult to untangle. . . . The feeling that I'd lost something dear.

Was it because I'd finally begun to like Elang, even think of him as a friend?

My chest tightened. Or was it because we *had* been friends all along—and I'd never known it?

Shani was right; it didn't matter. Soon enough our link would be severed, and we'd go our separate ways. Me, home to my family. To live and grow old and tell tales about my time among the dragons until the memories faded and even Elang's face became a blur of the past.

There was only one problem, I thought, as I blew the waterbell off my hand, letting it float free.

I never forgot a face.

CHAPTER THIRTY-ONE

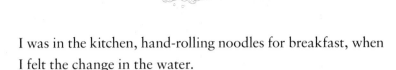

I was in the kitchen, hand-rolling noodles for breakfast, when I felt the change in the water.

A rumble came from outside, followed by the sounds of a skirmish. Shouts. Spears clanking. It didn't last long. Soon afterward was joyous celebration and an extra shimmer of warmth riding in the currents.

Elang was back.

I heard Mailoh fuss over him, her voice jumping an octave. Meanwhile I slapped my raw noodles against the table, cutting them thin as ribbons. My soup was near boiling.

That was how he found me, cooking with my back to the door.

"A little early for noodles, isn't it?" he said when I didn't turn around.

Gaari had adored noodles for breakfast, a memory that only fueled my anger. I bunched the dough together and made a sharp slice across. "I couldn't sleep."

Elang drew closer behind me. "I have the sanheia," he said, sounding worried. "Give me a moment to prepare it."

I clanged the lid back onto my pot and turned to regard

him. He looked tired. His eyes were duller, his scales less vibrant. Any other day, I would have asked whether he was hurt, but I was in an arch mood.

I inclined my head to the bundle under his arm, wrapped in cheerful red paper.

"That doesn't look like sanheia," I remarked.

"I brought gifts from your family. I told your sisters how much you hate taking sangi, so they sent something to sweeten the ordeal."

He unwrapped a box of fresh dragonbeard candy—a dozen frothy white cocoons of sugar and peanuts, neatly packed. One piece was missing.

"Nomi offered me some," he explained. He must have been drunk on air, for he actually smiled. "I was curious because of the name. It's a horrible name for a candy."

Did you like it? I almost asked, but I bit my tongue just in time. Elang didn't like sweets.

Also in the bundle was a tin of dried peppercorns, three knotty bulbs of ginger, and other food items from Mama, who clearly worried I wasn't eating enough.

I folded the gifts back into the paper, my heartstrings growing tight. I could practically smell home: the sandalwood from the incense Fal liked to burn, the first frost on the larch trees, the oil from Mama's cooking.

"How are they?"

"Your family is well," said Elang. "But I suspect they're growing bored. Your mother tried to get me to play tiles with her."

"Did you?"

Elang was still smiling. He was in an oddly cheerful mood.

Playing tiles with my mother? Did he think we were actually married?

He probably cheats, I thought, simmering alongside my pot.

"Did you have noodles when you were back?" I asked crisply. "You were away nearly a week in the mortal realm, and there are *exceptional* noodles in Gangsun."

"I only ate at home," he replied. "Your sisters were full of news I'm to relay to you."

My breath hitched. "Did they write?"

"They wanted to, but I couldn't risk the patrols finding any letters. I'll share their stories at dinner."

Dinner. Never before had he anticipated eating together except to inquire about my visions. Why was he different today? Were I a bit more delusional, I might have thought he'd missed me.

I seized a long coil of kelp, dropping it purposefully into my broth.

"You should rest," he said obliviously. A basket of roses had arrived in the kitchen, and he unloaded them onto a table. "Don't be alarmed if your gills start feeling tight—we still have a little while. I'll have the sangi brought to you as soon as it's ready—"

"When were you going to tell me that you were Gaari?" I interrupted.

I relished the way his back went rigid. The way his two faces folded, the cautious joy of his mood vanquished.

He said, quietly, "You found the paintings."

"I found everything."

He inhaled through his nose. I'd pictured his reaction a hundred different ways. Him locking me in the dungeon with

Caisan, ordering Shani to erase my memories, even shifting into Gaari and laughing in my face. But I did not picture him looking relieved.

"I'm glad," he said.

"You're glad?" I repeated, my voice rising. "Is that all you can say? You made me think he was dead! You made me think Puhkan sank a knife into his chest."

"He did," Elang said, picking up a rose and nicking off its thorns. "I have the scar to show for it."

I remembered that odious scar. When I'd first seen it, I couldn't imagine what might pierce a dragon's scales. But if Elang had been human, and disguised as an old man when he was wounded . . . so many things now made sense.

"I took a carriage home," he went on. "Narrowly beat you to Oyang Street before you fell into my garden. I wore black so you wouldn't see the blood."

He'd been swathed in black, I remembered now, roaring and growling like a beast. What pain he must've been suffering! That umbrella he'd leaned on had been a cane, the pallor of his skin from blood loss.

Revelation made my throat burn, and the gills on my neck constricted. It hurt to breathe, it hurt to even think. I thought of all the times Gaari had come to me with a new job, right when I needed money the most. The way he could read my moods and know how to make me laugh. He had been my mentor, my friend. Now my every memory of him was tainted with Elang's betrayal.

"Why?" I asked. It was the only word I could muster.

Elang didn't turn around. He shredded a handful of rose petals with his claws. "I have to finish preparing your sangi. I must ask that we continue this discussion—"

"Damn the sangi." I grabbed his arm. "Why the ruse, why waste three years pretending to be my friend when all you were going to do was just . . ." The words dried up inside me, heat swelling up to the backs of my eyes. Damn it, I would not cry in front of Elang.

He touched a button on his cloak, transforming it into the drawing I'd made on the day Baba left home. His voice was soft. "This is why."

I looked down, facing the dragon I'd drawn so many years ago. He looked far too familiar. Crescent horns jutted out of his temples, and his scales were silvery blue, each a shining teardrop. But most damning were his eyes: one was yellow and the other smeared with dark ink—like day and night.

"No," I said hoarsely. "I painted this when I was a child. It can't be—"

"It is," Elang said. "You painted me."

I shook my head, refusing to believe it.

"It was the beginning of your Sight manifesting. Shanizhun is the one who found your drawing in Nazayun's palace. She gave it to me after I freed her—about five years ago, not long after your father's ship sank. I left immediately for Gangsun to find you, but Nazayun's assassins followed me. I was afraid they'd find you too, so I hid. I had Shanizhun watch you, help you when she could. When I was ready, I came to you."

"As Gaari," I said flatly.

His lips thinned. "There were others before Gaari. You wouldn't remember."

"What do you mean, I wouldn't remember?"

His silence only fed the anger gathering under my skin. He could have been any person on the street, and I wouldn't have known. The boy who sold the cabbage dumplings I hated so much, the palanquin carrier shouting that he could bear two grown men on his back, the old beggar sleeping on the corner of Rolan Street with one missing shoe.

"Was it fun?" I seethed. "You and Shani spying on me, throwing me pity coins when you worried I might starve. You could at least pretend to be sorry."

"Would that make you feel better?"

Yes, I thought petulantly, but I knew it wasn't true. We were long past the point of apologies.

"I don't enjoy lying, Tru," said Elang tiredly. "That's part of the reason I let Gaari die."

"Then why come as him at all? Why the disguises and the lies when you could have come to me as yourself?"

"Like this?" Elang faced me fully.

His fangs were bared, his golden horns fully extended so they gleamed in the kitchen fires.

I'd known him for weeks now—was *married* to him—and still the sight of his two-sided face made my breath hitch. As a stranger, I would have quailed. But would I have run?

Elang took my reticence as a yes.

"It took years to find a potion that made me look human," he said through his teeth. "Even then, I could only erase *this*"—he touched the dragon part of his face—"for minutes at best. Over time, I learned that the less I looked like myself, the longer I could keep it up. That's why I made the old man."

"You *made* him," I repeated. "People aren't wooden figurines that you carve and chuck away when they no longer suit you."

Elang bowed his head low. "He was a character I played to earn your trust. I'm not proud of it, but I did what I had to.

I needed you to develop your skills as a painter, and believe in your art."

"For your mission." It was always about the damned mission.

"Yes."

Behind me, my broth had reached a boiling point and was on the verge of spilling out of the pot. I ignored it. All I could think of was the way Gaari's cheek used to twitch. His sudden excuses to leave. The days and weeks I'd go without hearing from him. One time we had gone out for dinner and his beard had flickered like lightning, then he'd bowled over in pain. When I'd asked if he was all right, he'd said, *I must have had a bad prawn. Excuse me, Saigas. I'll find you when I'm better.*

Bad prawn, my foot! It was magic taking its toll on Elang. Making him pay for his lies.

"How much of it was even real?" I whispered. My voice had gone tremulous, every word a vehement stab. It was becoming harder to breathe. "The cons we went on together, the stories you told, the auctions! You have all the paintings from my auctions!"

I couldn't stop the tears anymore. They welled up in a rush, trembling on my lids. I wiped them on my sleeve, hating that Elang could rouse this storm of emotions inside me while he stood like a pillar, unfeeling and unmoving.

"Tru," he said, "your sangi—"

"You really are a monster," I interrupted. I tugged on my collar. My gills were needling my skin like fiery pinpricks, making it hurt to breathe. But I ignored the pain. The ache in my heart was sharper.

"All these years, you played me for a fool," I said. "You lied to me, you made me trust you, then you manipulated me into leaving my family and coming here—on this *sham* marriage. The worst of it is, I could have forgiven you all that. But you know what I can never forgive?" I clenched my fists, drawing a ragged breath. "I thought you were my friend."

The words landed hard, and Elang's face drew long. He looked at me, his lips parted. I waited for him to defend himself, to apologize and explain, but he returned to his sangi preparation. With his back to me, he said, "That was your mistake."

I'd had enough. The broth spilled, sizzling over the stove. As the flames sparked and danced, I spun for the door.

"Tru, wait—"

I could feel Elang reach out, so I swam faster, until the rippling waves drowned out his calls. I'd made it as far as the Halls of Longevity when my lungs went suddenly tight, the gills in my neck stiffening. The rest happened quickly. The weight of the sea came crushing down, pressure making my head go light and heavy at once. The water turned thick. I couldn't breathe. I couldn't see either. My eyes burned.

Strong arms caught me from behind. I couldn't see his face, but I felt the ends of his long white hair brushing against my cheek.

I turned to find Elang, half-transformed into a dragon so he could catch up to me. His bones were still rearranging themselves, and he was breathing hard. The glow in his yellow eye dimmed as he held me. He pressed a kiss to the side of my lips. At least I thought it was a kiss, until he blew into my mouth. Softly, gently, as if I were a flute.

Air swept into my lungs, and I became aware of his

fingers on my chin, the edges of his claws gently trying to part my lips.

"Drink," he whispered.

Sangi trickled down my throat. The burning made me wheeze, and I grabbed Elang's collar to steady myself. It was then, in that instant, that my fingertips sensed the faintest thump coming from his chest.

He arched away from me, as stricken as I was.

When I blinked, he was gone.

CHAPTER THIRTY-TWO

The next day and the next, no one sought me out, not even Shani. I stayed in my room, eating Nomi's candies and trying not to think about Elang's betrayal.

By now it'd be midwinter in Gangsun. I imagined the snow dusting the top of my hat, and Mama lowering the scarf wrapped high over my neck so it didn't obscure the lucky mole on my cheek. I'd be haggling at the market over yams to boil for our stews, then listening to Fal complain my soup was too spicy, then reading with Nomi by the window, our stomachs warm and full.

A pang rose to my heart. It hurt, how much I missed my family.

Don't hold back your visions, Mama had told me before I left for Ai'long. *Let them bring you home faster.*

The last few days, my fingers had itched with premonition, but I'd shied away, afraid that I might see something terrible about Baba. No longer.

The sooner I learned to master my Sight, the sooner I'd find Baba—and bring him home.

I sat at my desk, steadying my breath. Maybe I couldn't

control what I foresaw, but I could at least practice letting myself fall into a vision. With my brush in my hand, I let my eyes roll back, and muscle by muscle, I uncurled my fingers. The tingles rushed across my fingertips, hot like fire. And once I let go, it was the fastest I had ever entered a trance.

The first thing I painted was the water. As my fingers reached for the familiar gray of Yonsar's depths, I pinned my concentration on Baba.

Show me my father.

My brush then sought a brighter blue. The water in my vision turned crisp and luminous, and my hand moved in furious motion, sweeping the parchment with a series of curved lines. Within a few strokes, I had the beginnings of a face. This was far more intention than I'd ever been able to achieve during a vision.

Baba?

When the mouth formed, I knew it wasn't my father. It was small and boat shaped. My father had thick lips. Then came long ears, and two deep-set eyes like bulbs that had never seen the sun.

It was a woman, vaguely familiar. Yet something was different, something was off.

My brush kept moving. Under its fibers, the woman turned monstrous. Her long black hair formed a swirling mass that writhed like eels, the ends crowned by barbed and gleaming hooks. Then her two arms became eight, her teeth grew serrated edges, and in her fathomless eyes, I saw my own reflection.

That was when the brush clattered from my hand. My heart roared in my ears, and I couldn't stop shaking.

"Nine Hells of Tamra," I whispered.

It was Queen Haidi.

"Show me how we'll overthrow Nazayun," I said, barging into Elang's chambers. "Tonight. There isn't time to lose."

If Elang was surprised to see me at his door, he hid it well. He set down the sanheia flowers he'd been carefully dethorning. "You had a vision?"

"See for yourself."

I had no name for the creature Queen Haidi had become. I couldn't even look at her without my blood going cold. "He's going to punish her for helping us."

Elang was studying the painting. His lips drew thin. "I need to know, do you always encounter the subject of your visions afterward?"

"Always. Why? What does that have to do with Queen Haidi?"

"I'll explain later. For now we cannot warn her, or we risk word of your Sight reaching the Dragon King."

"Can it be undone?" My heart was still pounding. "Tell me she won't be like this forever."

"It will depend."

"On what?"

Elang set aside my painting. "Listen closely," he said, sounding graver than before. "I'm going to tell you a secret."

I leaned forward. I was ready.

"There is an ancient scroll that even the gods fear. No book records its presence, and for a time, anyone who uttered its name was struck down.

"The scroll was made from eversnow bark, its fibers soaked for nine hundred years in tears of lingering sorrow, dried by the hellfires of the Demons' Cradle, then woven in secret by the Mother Goddess herself. It is called the Scroll of Oblivion, for whatever is painted on its page will vanish from this earth."

Understanding dawned. "This is the weapon of the Eight and a Half Immortals."

"You know the story?"

"Haidi told me. Nazayun thinks you are the half immortal. . . . It's why he wants you dead."

"It's why he's wanted all half dragons dead," said Elang grimly. "I am the last."

"Who are the other immortals?"

"Deities across the realms," he answered. "Each of us plays a specific role in Nazayun's downfall." His gaze met mine, dark with stories untold. "My role was to find a mortal with enough skill to harness the Scroll. The Painter."

I kept my expression stony, but an ache rose to my throat nonetheless. That was why he'd come to me as Gaari.

"My grandfather wasn't always the vengeful creature you see today," Elang went on. "Long ago he was a beloved king, who built Ai'long in the splendor he wished all realms to enjoy. His greatest pride was Ai'long, and I truly believe a part of him still believes that his every action is for the good of the dragons."

"He lost his way." I understood.

Elang nodded. "To be immortal does not mean to be constant. He's watched the merfolk flourish and humanity grow in number and strength. He became fearful of the other realms, convinced they sought to undermine the dragons' power.

"This fear was a poison; it changed him, and over time, he became cruel. He ravaged land and sea alike with storms, he turned his own servants into stone, he made monsters out of anyone who dared defy him."

"What could he be afraid of?" I asked. "He's a god. He cannot die."

"He cannot," agreed Elang, "but he *can* be made weak. He *can* be made irrelevant."

I drew in a deep breath. "With this scroll."

"Any subject painted on the Scroll is sent to Oblivion. But it must be rendered exactly, so perfect that every hair is in place, every muscle and ridge and scale."

It was brilliant. Outrageous, but brilliant. And humbling. I was no fool. I knew the limits of my skill.

"The Scroll is what the patrols were searching for," I realized. "Where is it? I want to see it."

"It's been with you all this time."

A beat, to process my astonishment. Then I knew.

I looked down to my wrist. I'd noticed the single black thread knotted into my red string, so slender and ordinary it was hardly visible. It felt like a mistake, or a carefully braided trick. Knowing Elang as I did now, it was obviously the latter.

"Here," I said, raising my arm.

The light fell over Elang's face, turning his dragon eye lambent. "Well done."

In a rush of magic, the black thread unraveled from my red string, materializing into a thick wooden rod. From it distended a wide sheet—a roll of parchment long enough to wrap across the walls of this chambers multiple times.

The Scroll of Oblivion.

It didn't look or feel any different than regular paper. Slightly thicker, maybe, grainier. It gave off no sparks of enchantment when my fingertips grazed its surface; it did smell nice, though. Like almonds and damp wood.

I could feel the weight of Elang's gaze, but I didn't meet

it. We hadn't spoken in days, and I wasn't oblivious to his cautiousness around me, or the cold formality of our conversation. Circumstances were forcing us to work together; that didn't mean I had to forgive him.

"May I test it?" I asked, gesturing at the Scroll.

"You may," said Elang. "However, be mindful of what you paint. The Scroll cannot be destroyed, and once an object is set upon its page, the course to Oblivion cannot be reversed."

"Understood. I'll choose something small that won't be missed."

Aware that he was watching, I picked up the teacup on his desk, running my thumb across the tiny grooves and indents along its clay surface, the white chip along its lip.

"This will do," I said. I turned to Elang. "With your permission."

He gave a nod, and I positioned the cup in front of me, then picked up my brush. Never had I been so nervous to set ink upon paper. Carefully I copied the cup, each stroke checked twice in my mind before I committed it to paper. It was painstaking work: emulating every line, the way the light fell on the lip, and the gradations of color on the two lotus blossoms rimming its bottom.

Meanwhile Elang brought out a set of inks, mixing a precise palette of gray, blue, and white. Normally I preferred to do it myself, but he anticipated exactly what I needed. If my paint became charry, he'd bring me a pan of water; if I was about to start coloring, he'd bring just the goat-hair brush I needed. He was quiet when I needed him to be, and murmured short observations when I overlooked something. The way we worked together reminded me that it wasn't our first collaboration. As Gaari, he'd often helped me with my art.

Leave it in the past, I reminded myself.

My lips pressed tight in concentration, I dabbed one last white coat over my cup and made a few fine strokes on the lotus blossoms. There, I was finished.

Elang set the teacup and my painting side by side. "You've captured the shine in the porcelain," he started. "The stain of tea on the inside of the cup too. I tried for ages to wash it off." A small smile took over his face. "Well done, Saigas. It's impossible to tell which is which."

Saigas. Gaari's old nickname for me. I didn't smile back. "Nothing's happening."

"There's one last step," replied Elang. "To cast the enchantment, the Painter must touch the object that shall be sent into Oblivion." He regarded me. "Whenever you're ready."

It sounded too easy. I lifted one finger, and slowly, ever so slowly, I tapped the teacup. Immediately the porcelain went soft as clay, puckering slightly where I'd touched it. Then the entire cup flickered and vanished from the table.

I was spooked. "It's gone."

"Trapped in the parchment," he confirmed.

Goose bumps rose on my skin. "Forever?"

"Forever."

The paint on the Scroll was fast fading, and soon it was empty once more.

Elang tapped on the Scroll's rod. In a spark of magic, it swooshed into a single thread, sweeping back into the string around my wrist and knotting itself in place.

For the first time, I could understand why Nazayun feared Elang. As one of the greatest, oldest gods, it was unfathomable that Nazayun had a weakness. Yet here, in my mortal possession, was the sole weapon that could vanquish him.

"That was easier than you expected, wasn't it?" said Elang. He'd read my mind. "Too easy."

"That's because an object like the porcelain cup doesn't move, so capturing it is a simple matter. The task is more challenging when it comes to living, breathing subjects."

Like the Dragon King. "What will I have to do?"

"The rule of the Scroll is that you must only paint the truth. Art must mirror life, always, but therein lies the difficulty." He inhaled, his dragon nostril twitching. "Life is always moving, always changing. Thus, to capture someone alive—like my grandfather—you must paint him in the final moment before he is sent to Oblivion."

I frowned. "How would I know his final moment?"

"You won't," Elang allowed. "Any premonition you have of him will simply be a chance. But that is already far more than any other painter can give." He regarded me. "I have confidence in you, Tru."

I wished I could say the same. Now I understood why he'd asked if I always met the subject of my visions: I'd need to physically touch Nazayun for him to disappear.

I held in a sigh. Elang had certainly thought this through. Now I needed to, as well.

"What will happen to Ai'long if Nazayun disappears?" I asked. "Is there a plan, or will the entire realm be thrown into chaos?"

"My cousin Seryu'ginan will take the throne."

I'd read about Prince Seryu in one of Elang's tomes. He was the Dragon King's heir, his favorite—though it was hard to picture Nazayun showing affection. "You would trust someone who has your grandfather's favor?"

"Seryu would rather race whales and dally with humans

than embroil himself in plots for power. Nazayun appreciates that. I do too."

Interesting. It was rare that Elang and Nazayun agreed on anything. "Where is he now?"

"I wouldn't know. He avoids Ai'long as much as he can. Likely wandering the Forgotten Valleys of Heaven and cavorting with fairies." Elang twisted his lips. "We haven't spoken in years."

I waited for more, but he didn't elaborate. It sounded like the cousins had been friends, long ago. "Will he be a good ruler?"

Elang cast his gaze downward and wiped an ink stain from the table. "Becoming king is the last thing Seryu will want. He'll abhor the responsibility and will try every which way to foist the role upon someone else. But once he accepts it—yes, he'll be a good ruler. He has a heart, a bigger one than most."

He has a heart. High praise coming from Elang, though I couldn't miss the heaviness in his voice.

I still had one last question. "If I do this," I said softly, "if I succeed in painting Nazayun, and sending him to Oblivion, will Haidi . . . ?"

"Yes," replied Elang, just as softly. "She'll be freed of him. Your father too, if he is still alive."

The hope that pinched my chest was sharp. I drew a measured breath, wondering, *What about you, Elang? Will you also be free?*

I didn't ask. I was still angry with him. What did I care what happened after my job was done?

"When will we leave for Jinsang?" I asked, getting to business.

"Once you've gained some control over your Sight."

"No. We'll leave sooner."

Elang tilted his head, a question perched on his brow.

"You need me to copy a vision of your grandfather onto the Scroll," I replied. "The problem is, whatever I foresee won't be detailed enough to produce a giant, true-to-life portrait."

"That's why you've been studying with Shani."

"Yes," I said dryly, "and I'll continue memorizing how many scales are on his left ear and the exact shape of his toenails, but it won't be enough. I thought it was only the right blue that was missing from my sketch. It's more. Back in Gangsun, the artists in the shophouses were always critiquing the energy of a painting, the flow of it."

"*Spirit*," Elang remembered.

Yes, *spirit*. It was the most difficult element to achieve. A painter could produce the most meticulous brushstrokes, plan the most perfect composition, and apply just the right colors and layers—but if there was no spirit, then the result would be like a dragon with no eyes. Lifeless.

"I couldn't have painted the teacup into Oblivion without seeing it, being in its presence." I was adamant. "I need to see Nazayun. Not just some ghostly projection. I need to see the real Dragon King."

Elang was quiet awhile. "Then I'll take you. After the Luminous Hour."

I hadn't expected him to agree so quickly, and I had to deflect my surprise. "Is it soon?"

"The pearls are expected within the week. It would raise suspicions if we didn't celebrate their arrival, but we can leave that evening and follow them into Jinsang."

He made it sound so simple, when I knew it would be

anything but. "All I need is a glimpse of him," I said. "I don't even need to be close."

"Good, because that's all I can offer. There's a ceremony where Grandfather will receive the pearls into Jinsang. I'll prepare a disguise so we can watch, but we'll have minutes at best."

"That'll be enough." I gave a firm nod. "I won't fail."

"I know." He resumed nicking thorns off the sanheia. It was far too many flowers just for me, but I didn't ask what they were for. I had my task. The less time I spent with Elang, the better.

I left without looking back.

CHAPTER THIRTY-THREE

I didn't hear the knock on my door.

I was caught in a rhythm, oblivious to everything except my work. A practice scroll filled my entire room, and even then I barely had enough space to render Nazayun's tail.

It'd taken me four days alone to sketch his body, and now I was starting on his scales. From afar they all looked about the same, smooth and glossy, no more different from each other than grains of rice in a sack. But I knew that capturing the slightest variation in size and sheen was critical.

With the sketch complete, I labored over the texture of Nazayun's scales.

"Looks like lychees," I mused aloud.

During my first year with Gaari, he'd made me paint fruits and flowers to "master the basic techniques" before I could go back to producing portraits. Painting lychees had been my least favorite lesson, and the most difficult, thanks to the tiny hexagonal bumps on the fruit. Gaari wouldn't let me progress to a new subject until I'd mastered them. Back then I'd thought he was trying to torture me with the task. Now I knew better.

I clenched my jaw. Even then he'd been preparing me to paint Nazayun.

My brush moved deftly from scale to scale, outlining the bumps in dark green, then varnishing each plate with a preliminary coat of azure. The work was tedious, but I didn't dare paint loosely. One mistake could cost everything.

Another knock. Louder this time.

"Lady Saigas!" Mailoh was crying from outside my door. "I have something for you. May I come in?"

No, she could not. My room was a catastrophe.

Hastily I set my brushes aside, wiped my desk clean, and raked my fingers through a clump of paint in my hair. It wasn't only art I'd been practicing; I'd been trying to exercise my visions too, to summon them at will and focus my intent when I encountered the future. Progress was slow; most tries, I accomplished nothing. But I could feel my heart growing steady, my fears easing into a calm and purpose I never had before.

I rolled up my practice scroll and counted to seven, rubbing my hands until the chill in my blood dissolved, then I went to the door.

Outside, Mailoh awaited with a basket of familiar blue flowers. Each had five points, like a star, with a yellow bell in the center.

"Where'd you get waterbells?" I asked.

"Lord Elang grew them. He said you needed them for your art. Look."

From her pouch, she proudly revealed a fat bottle of paint. The pigment was that of crushed blue sapphires—a shade deeper than the waterbell petals, and richer than the indigo dyes Baba used to trade across Lor'yan.

I stared, taking the bottle into my hand. The color matched

Nazayun's scales exactly. "Elang extracted this from the waterbells?"

"Indeed." Mailoh beamed. "You are pleased?"

I plucked a flower from the basket, twirling it by the stem in my fingers. "How many did he grow?"

"These, he planted by the Court of Celestial Harmony, but I'll expect the rest to bloom under the light of the Luminous Hour. Which is quite apt, I'd say."

"Apt? What do you mean?"

"It's merfolk tradition to plant flowers for someone you love. They say if you present them during the Luminous Hour, your love is sure to be returned."

It sounded like a scam my mother would've run in her old fortune house. "How romantic."

"I think so too." Mailoh shrewdly inserted a waterbell into one of my braids. "How apt, too, that Lord Elang should grow you an entire field of flowers."

My eyes went wide. An entire field?

"He grew them all on his own," Mailoh went on. "Last night, I might add. He wouldn't let anyone help. Never have I seen a man more devoted."

I must have looked stricken, for she chuckled. "No need to be so shy, Lady Saigas. I can see how the curse burdens you both." She made a subtle nod in the direction of Elang's separate chambers. "Once you break it, you can finally be together without hardship."

A bloom of heat prickled my cheeks, which only served to encourage Mailoh. "Trust me, a love like yours is meant to last from one life to the next."

I bit back a protest. It would have done no good anyway; Mailoh had a belief and she wasn't going to change it.

Still, I thought as I twirled one of the waterbells from the basket, *he could have chosen a different flower.*

It was true, Elang really *had* planted an entire field of waterbells.

I surveyed them from the Court of Celestial Harmony, hovering just above the rooftop. Tiny blue buds covered the grounds, cascading down beyond the rubble from the last storm to the edge of the gate.

The sight was breathtaking. I was starting to reach into my pocket for my brush when I felt another shadow touch mine.

"Just wait until you see it under the light of the pearls."

That was how Elang found me, precariously floating above the roof, my paintbrush slipping out of my sleeve. I didn't see him and windmilled after it, expecting to float but quickly sinking instead. His arm wrapped around my wrist as he brought me safely onto the roof.

I whirled on him. "I wasn't going to fall."

"I wasn't going to take the chance."

My mouth went dry. Ever since I'd found out the truth about Gaari, Elang had abandoned some of his cold facade. It frustrated me, how difficult he was making it to dislike him. How much I'd missed my old friend.

He let me go, handing me back my brush as I shuffled to the side.

He was dressed finely tonight, silver platelets braided across his wide shoulders. His robes were white and black, with a rich purple lining that, to my embarrassment, matched the gown Mailoh had selected for me.

"I had a feeling I'd find you here," he said. "You always knew how to find the best seats in the house, Saigas."

"That was Gaari, not me." I crossed my arms. "I just wanted to be alone."

He settled at my side, landing soundlessly. "That's why I used to come here too. I would watch the dawns every morning and wish I were on the other side of those crimson lights."

"I thought you hated the human world."

"I didn't hate the sky or the stars, or the way the sun illuminates the secrets of the world after a dark and ruthless night. Or the noodles."

I rolled my eyes. Intolerable dragon.

Elang caught my sleeve before I could leave. "Look," he said, pointing. "It's beginning."

Light tiptoed past the dark cliffs, sweeping the mountainside in shimmering white pinpricks. The shimmer came from the pearls. They traveled in a gentle flurry, as graceful as drops of moonlight. Little by little, they warmed the sea. They swelled past the dunes and gray plains, crowning the jagged horizon until everything glowed: the seams between my fingers, the tiny sand crabs crawling across the roof tiles, even the field of young waterbells.

I'd always thought waterbells special because they budded in the dark but bloomed in the light. Yet never had I witnessed this actually come true—until now.

Under the glow of the pearls, my favorite flowers came alive. Their stems stretched out of the earth, and their blue petals unfolded like the soft kiss of a butterfly's wings. As the flowers opened, there came a gentle current, tickling the petals so they seemed to vibrate.

"They look like stars," I breathed. I reached for my brush.

"Wait," said Elang softly. "It's not over."

The pearls were descending upon the castle. As they neared, I saw that each one was ringed by a shining aurora, bright and silvery like the sun and moon at once.

The pearls dipped into the Court of Celestial Harmony, and the sand spun up in little plumes, like ribbons of gold dust lifted by the wind. In gilded streams, the pearls swirled around us. I reached out to touch one. Its light exuded a wondrous warmth that tickled my fingers.

The pearls didn't linger. Once their light had touched every corner and crevice, they moved on. I knelt on the roof, utterly enchanted.

"The Luminous Hour is special to Ai'long," Elang murmured, crouching beside me. "I'm glad you were able to experience it."

I said nothing. His hair was over his eyes, in dire need of trimming, and he was wearing those brass-rimmed spectacles again. They were still crooked on his nose. I closed my hands, forbidding myself from reaching over to straighten them. Was it another power of his, turning my anger into some slippery thing like the sand beneath us, impossible to grasp?

Countless ruses we had plotted together, only for the greatest trick to be played on me. I had every reason to hate him. So why, when I sat at his side, when I remembered we'd never been strangers at all—but friends for years, *partners* for years—was there a warm and prickly feeling buzzing in my stomach? To my mortification, it wasn't entirely unpleasant.

It felt a long while that we stayed on the roof, content in each other's silence, before cheers from the garden moved time forward again.

Below, Kunkoi was passing out flower-molded sponge

cakes and skewered fish balls, and the turtles were chasing watery illusions of seahorses and cuttlefish. It reminded me of a festival back home. Even Shani had joined the fun, popping bubbles with her nails.

"The race is starting soon," noted Elang. "It's a game children often play in Ai'long. Everyone chooses an animal, and whichever completes a lap around the garden without dissolving wins."

Soon after he spoke, the turtles gathered in a line. Even Mailoh had conjured a contestant, choosing a frilled octopus that glided gracefully about. Kunkoi, inexplicably, had chosen a giant lobster.

"I'll show you how to play," Elang said. He wheeled his hands, molding a watery whale. It was a simple creation, but its form was well thought out. "When you finish, give it a breath for life." He blew, and away the whale swam, down into the garden to join the races below. "Do you want to try?"

A group of young turtles were giggling at Elang and me, and I waved. It would be all right, I thought, to put up with the act a little longer. To have some fun tonight, then resume being angry tomorrow.

"Do you always choose a whale?"

He shrugged. "I like whales."

I didn't know why my shoulders went soft, or why that warm buzz in my stomach turned even warmer. "So I recall."

I drew my finger along the water, outlining a book-sized fish with dangling fins. I took my time. The water scintillated with magic, and all I had to do was trace the creature I wanted. Soon my fish was formed, and I added three careful spots to her head.

"A carp?" said Elang.

"They're good luck." I noted his blank look. "There's a legend of a carp who found the gates of Ai'long. There she encountered a tremendous waterfall, impossible to leap over. But she hadn't come so far to give up. She jumped again and again, until she vaulted across the gate. As a reward for her courage and effort, she became a dragon."

"Is that really a reward?" asked Elang wryly.

It was my turn to shrug. "It's Nomi's favorite story. She always loved dragons. And I've always liked the lesson it teaches."

"What is that?"

"Fortune finds those who leap."

I blew after the carp, and off she swam, catching up to Elang's whale. I found myself glued to the race, laughing and cheering when both our whale and carp zipped around the garden, dissolving instants after finishing their lap.

"Yes!" I exclaimed. I caught myself before I grinned at Elang. He was at my side, doing his best to hide a smile. If I hadn't known better, I would have thought he was watching me instead of the race.

"You had fun," he observed.

I did. "Now I see the appeal of those cricket races you used to watch."

"You wish you'd joined me?"

"Definitely not. It's gambling."

"Many things are. How bleak life would be, if we left nothing to chance."

"Ironic, coming from you," I spoke. "Was our meeting even chance?"

He merely smiled, a small, sad smile that did not reach

his eyes. "Mailoh told me you were pleased with the paint she brought today. I take that to mean the color is suitable?"

Of course he would change the subject. "It's perfect," I had to admit. "I can't believe you grew this entire field of waterbells. You could've asked me to help."

"I seem to recall, the Saigas sisters have the killing touch when it comes to plants. I couldn't chance it."

Turds of Tamra, I couldn't help it, I laughed. "I should've known from all the gardening you were Gaari. Where did you pick it up?"

"From my mother." It was the subtlest thing, how every muscle in Elang's face softened. "We spent one spring in the hinterlands of A'landi. She kept a garden there."

"What was she like?"

The ghost of a smile touched his mouth. "Her name was Lanwah. She smelled of sun and camphor, and she always kept a bag of preserved plums in her pocket—for my bones to grow hardy, she'd say. She hoarded luck in little charms and trinkets and prayed to the gods every night. It wasn't easy for her, raising a half-dragon boy alone. I spent my childhood on the run."

"From your grandfather?"

"From humans too," Elang said darkly. He knelt on the roof. "I had a fever one day, and while my mother was out to buy medicine, bandits broke into our home and assaulted me. They wanted to skin me and sell my scales. When my mother came home and found them . . ." Elang didn't need to finish—I'd seen his scars. "She spent all her magic saving me. It nearly killed her."

I sat beside him, my heart wrenching inside. I could see how hard it had been for him.

"That was the first time that I remember *feeling*," he said. "Fear for my mother, along with wrath. Hate."

"How'd you escape?"

"She changed the bandits into goats. Her spells didn't last long, and I wanted to kill them before they turned human again. My mother stopped me. It took a long time before I realized that she was more afraid of me than of the bandits. Afraid that my heartlessness would turn me into a . . ."

"Monster?" I said gently.

"Yes." He paused. "That spring, she brought me to A'landi. It was dangerous for us, being closer to the sea, but she thought it an important lesson to grow a garden together. She taught me to care for the flowers and nurture them, from seedlings to withered husks." He looked to the field of waterbells. "At first I didn't have the patience. But my mother was persistent. She believed, one day, I would break my curse."

"You already have," I said. "You're not as heartless as you think."

He made a soft, soft laugh. Then his eyes fell on the pendant hanging from my neck. "Do you know why butterflies fly in pairs, Tru?" he asked. "When I was in my mother's garden, I used to think it was because they were afraid of me. But I was wrong. They fly in pairs because . . ." He hesitated. "Because they're in love."

Under the heat of his gaze, my cheeks burned. "You should take this back," I said, starting to unclasp the butterflies. "I shouldn't—"

"Keep it," said Elang. "Dragons give each other a piece

of their hearts when they marry. This is the closest I can offer to mine."

My lips parted. I didn't know what to say. "Watch your tells, Demon Prince. I might start to think you actually like me."

It was a joke, yet Elang didn't laugh. "I always liked you, Saigas."

I meant to scoff, but my heart rattled in my chest, every beat a roaring peal. He was close enough that I was worried he'd take it as an invitation to kiss me. Blast my treacherous heart, I hoped he would.

It was a war I waged against myself, the way I forced my body to draw back. "Then why didn't you tell me the truth from the start? Why act like a stranger, why act like you wanted nothing to do with me?"

Elang was quiet. "Do you recall Gaari's third rule?"

"How could I forget? You drilled those silly rules into me for an entire month. No details. Business is business."

"Very good," he said. "I stand by the third rule."

I wanted to smack him on both sides of his blasted face. "You're impossible."

"Wait, Tru." Elang caught my sleeve before I turned away. He hadn't meant to sour the mood. I could tell by the twist of his lips that he wished he could take back his words. Gaari had been the same.

"You asked if any of it was real. My name was real."

"Your name?"

"My human name—the name I was born with—was Gaarin, but my mother called me Gaari." A deep breath. "When I met you, I chose it so it'd feel less like a lie. I know it won't make up for what I did, but I would have told you everything from the start, if I could have."

"You made up the third rule so I wouldn't ask questions."

"I made it up so we couldn't become too close."

"Because of your curse." I understood. "You don't want me to break it. Why?"

He shook his head. He wouldn't tell me. He couldn't.

"Damn it, Elang," I said, throwing up my hands. I rose and twisted away to leave, but blast my foolish tongue. "Are you in love with me?"

That question changed the air between us. The line of his mouth went taut, and the beleaguered look in his eyes washed away, his dragon nature taking primacy as he let out a low, vexed growl. "Do you remember the promise I made you on the day we were married?"

My thoughts drifted back to that summer day in Gangsun, to the rain and the hanging red lanterns. It felt so far away, yet I could practically smell the smoke from the firecrackers, the horses outside Elang's carriage, when I was about to receive his brusque instruction:

"'If I show you kindness or favor,'" I said, "'it means nothing. If I give you a gift, or bestow upon you praise, it means nothing. Everything is for appearances only, and should you occupy a place in my thoughts, it is only to facilitate the mission we have agreed upon.'"

"And there you have your answer," Elang said. The light in his eyes was gone. "This Luminous Hour is over."

He was right. The pearls were sweeping away, and the golden cast that had illuminated the sea faded. I let myself sink, feeling as hollow and gray as the waters around me.

"Make your preparations," he said, putting distance between us. "We depart for Jinsang at darkest tide."

He spun back for the castle, leaving me behind.

Once he was out of sight, I yanked the waterbell out of my hair. So much for fates bound across lifetimes.

Yet as the flower sat on my palm, petals falling one by one, I thought of the other promise he had made on our wedding day: *I bind you to me, Tru Saigas. Until the end of our days upon this earth, under this heaven, and across the seas, our fates are one, our destinies entangled. Whatever course you may wend, I will follow.*

Too late, I wondered if he'd remembered the same.

CHAPTER THIRTY-FOUR

That night, Elang and I left the Westerly Seas. We told no one of our departure, and only Shani joined us, adopting her stingray shape and soaring through the water. I rode on her back as we quietly pierced the castle wards and trailed the pearls toward Jinsang.

The seas grew rougher the farther we traveled, and more than once, we encountered Nazayun's patrols. Elang had prepared a drowsing potion, and whenever he could, he fired little darts at the sharks so they would sleep instead of pursuing us. Half the time, it worked. The other half made for a long night.

At dawn I saw the Floating Mountains. They levitated in the sea, tall and rounded like a series of camel humps. It mystified me, how there was nothing underneath them. No roots, no base. Only vast and empty sea.

Jinsang was on the other side of the mountains. Patches of verdant seagrass started appearing among the rocks, hatting the bald mounds, and the water turned bluer by the second.

Elang took my arm as we ascended to the upper seas. All night he had been quiet, only speaking to warn of nearby patrols or update me on our progress. His jaw was set, and his lips were pale. I wondered what was on his mind.

"We've arrived," he said softly, once we could see an emerald green valley beyond the gray plains. "Welcome to Jinsang."

I smelled the sea flowers first. They turned the water sweet, and I moistened my lips as I lifted my gaze. I'd expected the heart of Ai'long to be dazzling, even in comparison to Nanhira. Even then, I wasn't prepared. I gasped.

The royal city arched over a teeming garden, lush with vibrant coral reefs and a kaleidoscope of sea flora. In place of roads there were floating highways alit by coruscating nautili, and even their traffic was beautiful: luminous carriages and pods of spotted whales, young merfolk cartwheeling through mantles of hanging algae. Buildings sprouted seamlessly amid the plant life, marble houses with prismatic crystal roofs that gleamed different colors from every angle.

Most magnificent of all was the Dragon King's palace. It hovered above the city, floating high as the mountains behind it. No matter how I craned my neck, I couldn't get a good view. The palace was fortressed by enchanted white waterfalls and a forbidding stone gate. Not to mention, it appeared that every citizen of Jinsang had amassed at the entrance, many of them dragons. For all my time in Ai'long, I'd only met Elang and his grandfather. To see hundreds of dragons at once! I couldn't stop staring.

"Let's stop here," said Elang. In his hand was a slender white vial. "Drink this. It'll give you a tail like the merfolk, and alter your appearance so you won't be recognized."

There was only one vial. "Aren't you coming?"

"I can't." He hesitated. "No potion in existence could make me fit in here."

"But—"

"You'll blend into the crowds easier without me. I won't be far." Elang touched my cloak, turning it plain black. "Don't get too close to the dragons. They'll smell that you're—"

"*Krill?*" I suggested.

It wasn't quite a smile, that twitch in his lips. But it was close enough. "I'll take care of the patrols." A pause. "Good luck, Tru."

"We'll need it," said Shani, scooping me onto her back.

She swam low, diving into a field of seagrass as we approached Jinsang. I swallowed Elang's potion in one gulp. The sour taste brought a pucker to my lips, but it didn't burn like sangi.

The change was swift. A shot of cold bristled across my legs, and I kicked my heels together, feeling the sudden urge to wriggle my toes. When I looked down, I had a pale green tail and matching fins. My hair was the color of cabbage, my skin like jade.

Put me next to a stalk of seaweed, and few would be able to tell us apart. Perfect.

After my transformation, Shani shrank into a seahorse and hid in my hair. It felt like the old days in Gangsun, getting ready for the next con. Back then I'd been afraid of prefects and gangsters. In hindsight, I much preferred them to gods and dragons.

I slipped into the crowd, making my way through the droves of fish, turtles, merfolk, and dragons, all seated in hierarchal order.

Such solemn faces, I observed. *Are they nervous Nazayun might have a fit and turn them all into stone?*

He wouldn't risk such a display in public, replied Shani.

What do you mean?

Dragons are supposed to be creatures of wisdom and protection, not rampant destruction. That goes against their nature; makes them lose control. Shani sounded smug. *Nazayun hates losing control. His eyes turn white, and* ...

And what?

And sometimes, said the demon very softly, *though it's unthinkable: he makes a mistake.*

The last word she whispered, so low that it vibrated in my blood. I nearly jumped when crystal bells suddenly pealed from above, loud and resounding.

The assembly was beginning. The cloudlike formation of pearls had gathered behind the palace. There, before a cascading waterfall straight out of Baba's stories, was the Dragon King, in his full and immortal glory.

He dominated the space between two pillars, lording over the audience that had gathered. Even the pearls slowed their course in his presence, bathing Nazayun in their light.

"Faithful subjects of the Four Supreme Seas," he declared, "beloved brothers and sisters of our great Kingdom of Dragons, today we rejoice in another season of peace. Today the miracle of Liayin's tears returns to grace our magnificent realm. Behold, the Luminous Hour!"

Cheers clamored from every direction. The seabed shook, and puffs of sand shot up, inciting further excitement. It was all very dramatic, especially as the pearls swept in, a cluster of them even orbiting the Dragon King's body.

Yet through the chants, the murmurs of approval, and

praises of Nazayun's might, I sensed a different sentiment vibrating through the Dragon King's subjects. I scanned across the fields of seagrass, to where the dragons had congregated. Here were the greatest, most magnificent creatures in all the immortal realms, and each had their head bowed against their chest, their tails folded into what seemed a deliberately painful position. The merfolk were the same, bent in a deep kowtow, and so were the whales, the mollusks, every other creature I could see. It set a chilling reminder of Nazayun's might, and his absolute rule.

I reached for the ink and paintbrush in my pocket. A few mermaids eyed me curiously, so I set aside my sketchbook. Instead I rolled up my sleeve and drew surreptitiously on my arm under the folds of my cloak.

Frantically I took notes. I sketched the green undertones of Nazayun's belly, the steely blue in his eyes. I captured the angle at which his whiskers wilted, and how his throat bobbed while he spoke. Faster than I'd ever worked, I was recording every feature I could, not daring to blink. While it was true that I didn't forget a face, I wouldn't chance losing a single detail.

Shani nudged me in the ribs. *We have to go.*
I'm almost done. Just one more—
We have to go. Now.

"This Luminous Hour is a special one," Nazayun was saying, "for we have a visitor."

I grew very still. Did he mean Elang—or me? I didn't dare turn to look.

My answer came soon enough.

A cage misted out of the waterfalls. It was sculpted like a bell, bronze and heavy, and if I squinted, I could perceive the outline of a woman inside. Her hair, long and flat as a sheet, obscured her face. A dull brown tail languished behind her.

Queen Haidi!

Shani covered my mouth with her fin, stifling my gasp. *Don't. Tread backward. Slowly.*

The demon had shifted into her stingray form, and I let her drag me through the tall grasses. We couldn't go far. Patrols had appeared, cordoning off the area.

Shani cursed. *We'll have to go another way. Come on.*

As I followed her, Nazayun continued speaking: "Many of you will remember Ai'long's darkest era, when merfolk and dragons were at war. A deadly period in our history, ignited by festering resentments and broken promises. I have sworn to you, it shall never again be repeated. There will be peace in Ai'long." His whiskers turned wiry. "And any threat to that peace, I will *burn.*"

My hackles rose. I knew where this was going.

Nazayun raised a claw. "Today I bring forth Her Majesty, Queen Haidi of Nanhira, beloved ruler of the merfolk. She has always been a loyal subject, a voice I've admired and respected. An old friend, or so I thought. . . ." He made a gravid pause. "It's come to my attention that Queen Haidi has secretly harbored and abetted the renegade Lord of the Westerly Seas against me. This act of perfidy, I cannot forgive."

The cheers died, replaced by a brittle silence. No one dared move. Even the radiance of Liayin's tears was muted, the pearls slowly receding from Nazayun to circle Queen Haidi.

Don't just stand there. Shani bit me in the wrist. *Move!*

Obediently I glided backward, keeping my gaze on Haidi.

She stood before the crowd with all the pride befitting a queen of her kind, but only a fraction of the strength. What had Nazayun done to her, to reduce her to *this*?

Fight him, I mouthed silently, as though she could hear.

Shani, I whispered in my mind. *Isn't there something we can—*

No. The water demon wrapped her tail around my wrists so I wouldn't swim off and ruin everything. *The best way you can help is by not dying. Now, keep moving.*

Nazayun was still speaking. I watched the dragons in the crowd relax, their fear easing as they realized they were not the target. Some looked amused by this turn of events. The wiser ones, however, remained stolid. They knew Nazayun's mood might change at any moment; he'd turn the entire city into stone if it pleased him.

"She must pay the price," one of the dragons in the front said. "It is the law."

"Yes! She must pay!"

"You know me to be a merciful god," Nazayun went on. "A generous king. For centuries I have kept us free from the strife that plagues the mortal world and the discord that corrodes the harmony of the heavens. And so I ask you, what have I done to deserve such treachery?"

"Nothing," Nazayun answered himself with a growl. His whiskers tilted upward, and the outline of a pearl bulged within his chest. Rimmed with gold, it glowed like a moon, and the silhouette of Ai'long could be seen within.

At the sight of it, the crowds grew restless, fervid support for their king mounting.

"Thus, I am left with no choice," he went on. "As punishment, Her Majesty the Queen of Nanhira has seen her last light of Liayin." With a sweep of his tail, he banished Liayin's tears into the distance. "From this hour forth, she shall be reborn."

It was a sound I'd never forget, the quick slash that Nazayun made across the queen's long hair.

Haidi's mouth rounded with pain. Tears welled in her eyes, crystallizing into tiny white pearls as the dark strands of her hair fell about her in lifeless whorls. The merfolk stiffened in horror. Their hair was a life force to them, the way blood was to humans. And they knew, as I did, that it was only the beginning.

Her neck was the first to change. It stretched grotesquely, growing until her head was like a kite, her neck its string. Next was her skin, which melted from her body, the flesh beneath it gray as ash. She bucked, writhing in pain as her arms split into two, then four, so there were eight in total.

Bile rose to my throat. I didn't want to watch anymore, but I couldn't look away. Around me, the merfolk paled. Those closest were trembling.

The screaming stopped. It was eerie, how abruptly it halted, like a music box clamped shut.

Haidi wasn't moving. She'd gone as limp as the severed locks of hair still floating around her.

"Is she dead?" The dragons speculated among themselves. Their laughs receded. So did the claps.

It was no fun if Haidi was dead, came the murmurs. They hadn't even gotten to see what she could do.

I couldn't listen anymore. I dragged my gaze back to Nazayun, every part of my body vibrating with hate. His brow was lifted, his nostrils flared. He was waiting.

Then from the silence came a wretched sob, faint and melancholy as a song.

Haidi peeled out of her stupor, her many arms hanging lank at her sides. Her eyes were changed, charred and hollow. The eely mass of her hair was barbed with harpoons. I'd seen fishermen hunt whales and sharks with such weapons. I had a bad feeling that Haidi's was meant for hunting dragons.

With no further warning, she launched out of her cage into the crowd. Everyone scattered, sending up thick clouds of sand from the seabed. Under their cover, Shani and I raced into the grass, attempting to retreat. We weren't fast enough.

What sorcery led Haidi straight to us, I didn't know, but she trounced Shani from behind. Both the demon and I fell back, and Haidi rolled me onto my back, the ends of her barbed hair pressing against my cheek. At her touch, my disguise dissolved. My hair turned blue once more, and my fish tail split into two knobby legs.

"It's me," I strained. "It's me, Truyan. Please, Haidi. Stop this."

Her black eyes flickered, swirling brown for the briefest of instances, and I thought *maybe,* just maybe, she recognized me. Maybe she wasn't a monster.

But no.

She picked me up. Her fingers were long and stiff, wrapping twice around my neck, and I heard the crunch of my muscles constricting. Into my ear, she whispered, "I smell a traitor."

Her hair braided itself into one thick rope, blades pointed down at my throat. I didn't need prescience to know what was about to happen. Haidi's blades dug in deeper, piercing through the collar of Elang's cloak. Then—

All I saw was a silvery whir, fast as a comet. With a wet and trenchant hiss, it arced across Haidi's back, drawing dark blue blood. She dropped me and snarled.

Elang stood in the distance, catching his short blade as it flew back into his grasp. My pulse spiked—what was he doing here?

"Let her go," he warned. His yellow eye burned. "I won't ask again."

"There, there, Elangui," said Nazayun. "Haidi was only testing your wife's mettle."

The sea's turmoil abruptly subsided, the currents going still.

"Our fortunes are doubled today," the Dragon King declared. "Long have I wished to welcome my grandson and his bride to Jinsang." The palace gates rumbled. "Subjects of Ai'long, this Luminous Hour is over. Begone."

Coming out of nowhere, a raging current swept me off my feet, carrying me into the Dragon King's palace. Before I could catch my breath, it deposited me into a wide chamber with black marble walls. A hundred shipwrecks floated above me, trophies of Nazayun's conquests upon the seas and oceans in my world hanging to create an unsettling gallery.

Nazayun was waiting, his body unfurled across the empty room and his head high enough that his movements caused the dangling ships to sway.

"Welcome at last, Bride of the Westerly Seas."

I hated how small I felt, how I instinctively shouted in order to be heard. "Where's Elang?"

"Not to fear, Haidi will bring him to us. You will be reunited in time." Nazayun gestured at Shani's fallen form, floating at his side. "As for the demon . . ."

"Don't touch her. If you hurt her, I'll—"

"Hurt her?" The Dragon King chuffed. "I would never hurt the last water demon of Ai'long. She is my honored guest."

I had to be delirious. Did he just say that Shani was his honored guest?

"That's correct," Nazayun said, reading my disbelief. "Shanizhun is my guest, and she tells me you have brought a gift."

"I bring you no gift," I spat.

That was when Shani herself came to. She wasn't hurt at all. In fact, as she swam up, she made a show of somersaulting up to Nazayun's shoulder, perching precisely where I'd seen her perch at Elang's side many times. As if she knew it would sting.

"Truyan Saigas has a talent for lying, Your Eternal Majesty," said Shanizhun. "Fortunately, I've gotten to know her well."

Shani's gaze bore into me. "I know her secrets, and all you need to do is ask."

CHAPTER THIRTY-FIVE

I couldn't speak. My lips wouldn't part, and my tongue was heavy as stone. My entire body had gone numb.

Shani. I sought the demon through our thoughts. What are you doing?

She ignored me. Her mind had become a closed door, and I wasn't allowed inside.

"She's a painter," Shani reported. "An art forger who Elangui found on land. Their marriage is a sham; he hired her to paint your likeness—on the Scroll of Oblivion."

Nazayun's eyes were electric. "She has the Scroll?"

"She carries it in that string around her wrist."

My fingers leapt to my hand, but it was too late. Shani threw me against the wall, trapping my arms with her tail, then pinning her weight against me so I couldn't move. The Scroll unraveled from my red string and flew straight into King Nazayun's grasp.

"You traitor," I seethed. "Elang trusted you."

"That was his mistake. Also his mistake, letting you come here alone with a demon."

I thrashed against her. "It was you all along. *You* led Haidi's monster to us. *You* let the patrol into the castle—"

"And destroyed your precious sangi," Shani finished for me. "Don't look so dejected, krill, you're still alive. Though the next time I see that blockheaded general . . ." She made a slurping sound.

Gods, we'd locked Caisan up for Shani's crimes. "What happened to your vengeance? What happened to being honor bound?"

Shani's eyes blazed a dangerous shade of red. "Demons have no honor."

She grabbed my hand, and the opal ring slid off my finger. It clattered to the floor, and with a whip of her tail, she smashed it. Broken white bits flew, narrowly missing my eyes.

She spun, her tail still raised. I was next.

"That's enough," said Nazayun. "I'd like Lady Saigas to be conscious for her reunion."

The fight in me went out like a flame. *My reunion?*

"You seem to have forgotten," he intoned. "I promised you a reunion with your father."

I looked up at the shipwrecks dangling from the ceiling like lanterns, and scanned the torn sails and smashed hulls for any trace of the trading ships Baba used to charter. One of these vessels had to be his.

"Where is he?" I asked.

"Your father isn't up there," responded Nazayun. "He's *here*."

A swell of water carried a wooden toy boat right into my hands.

Shaking, I clasped it. It was smaller than I remembered,

its length fitting neatly across my two palms. Then again, the last time I'd seen it, I had been a child. Now I was grown, a woman.

Its wood had darkened with age, and barnacles grew along the corners. The details were as I remembered: the clean-cut sails, the beginnings of a bird along the figurehead, the gently curved crescent shape of the hull. But one thing was different.

On the deck, standing behind the coarsely chiseled rails, was a detail I didn't remember. A painted man, so lifelike he looked alive. Stubble dotted his cheeks, but that couldn't hide the slant of his lips, the dimpled chin I used to pinch when I was a child.

Heat rushed to my face, smoldering the backs of my eyes. So many years, I'd wondered what had happened to Baba. Now, finally, I had the answer.

"This is him," I whispered, touching the painted man. "He's trapped inside this ship."

"An Oblivion of his own, I like to think." The water around Nazayun's face bubbled with amusement. "At the time, I didn't even know his daughter would be the Painter, but the fates are masterful poets indeed. Your reunion could not be more fitting."

I wasn't listening. My heart was thundering inside me, and my thoughts flew back in time, to Baba on the last night of his life. I pictured the waves thrashing against his ship, the rain pounding. Baba, choosing to save the lives of his sailors even if it meant he'd never see his family again.

Five years of thinking he was dead. Five years of counting every copper and thanking the gods every night I kept my family off the streets, five years of holding myself together by the barest thread. All because Nazayun wanted to have a little fun.

Hate came rushing in. The pillar behind my back began to vibrate with my anger. More than anything, I wanted to make the Dragon King pay. I wanted to obliterate that godly smirk from his face and erase him from all existence. The worst of it was that I could do nothing—for now—except buy time.

Smothering my emotions, I lowered myself until I was genuflecting. "Please." I didn't need to put on an act to sound small, broken. "Let him go."

"How quickly the flame goes out," murmured Nazayun. "Now you see, Bride of the Westerly Seas. You are mine."

The words turned my blood cold. I knelt lower, mutinously tracking the Dragon King as he loomed across the chamber, his spine curved against the ceiling. In my head, I listed all the adjustments and revisions I'd make to his portrait. First chance I got, I'd destroy him.

Until then, I wanted answers.

"Why him?" I asked. "Hundreds of sailors have been lost to the Taijin Sea, and you pay them no heed. Why spare my father?"

"Arban Saigas." The name rolled on Nazayun's tongue. "A hapless merchant, barely able to feed his family. Forgettable in every way. But fate is unpredictable, Lady Saigas." Nazayun's eyes sizzled with smug satisfaction. "Your father made a trade of transporting worthless trinkets across the seas, useless baubles that only your fatuous kind might covet. He was of no interest to me—until his last voyage. Can you guess why?"

A treasure's been found in the North, Baba had told us, *and I'm to transport it to the capital.*

For years Mama and I had tried to find out what exactly that treasure had been, but every one of our investigations had led to a dead end.

"You don't know?" Nazayun gave a taunting laugh. "Then I'll tell you. On your father's ship was a dragon scale. A great and priceless treasure in your realm, I gather."

I sucked in a breath. A dragon scale? How was that possible? A single scale alone would have been worth thousands of gold jens. A fortune beyond my family's wildest dreams.

"Normally I would have sunk his ship for such an offense, and squeezed out the souls of every sailor down the middle of the Straits of the Lost. Then I discovered just whose scale it was."

"Elang's," I whispered, with a sting of realization. He'd told me the story only yesterday. "From the bandits who tried to kill him."

"Yes. And thus, our story becomes far more interesting."

"My father didn't know anything! You could have let him go."

"I could have," he agreed. "As I said, Arban Saigas was no one special. But I've lived long enough to mistrust coincidence and recognize the strands of fate at work, even in something as abhorrent as Elangui's scale. So I kept your father as an investment. I had a feeling he'd be valuable in the future." Nazayun dipped his head, the tips of his whiskers grazing the marble walls as he moved. "And lo, look at where we are today. You wouldn't be here if not for his poor choices."

I was still on my knees. "Let him go," I said again. Every word cost me dearly in swallowed pride. "Please."

Nazayun ignored my plea. "The fates are indulgent," he said. "Even I wouldn't have guessed that the Painter and

Elangui's Heavenly Match would be the same, but now that I see it . . . there is no solution more elegant, more profane." His blue eyes danced to me. "Lady Saigas—if you wish to free your father, you shall do something for me."

I lifted my head, temples pounding, dread corroding my courage. He knew, just as I did, that for Baba, I'd do anything.

"What do you want?"

"For you to paint," replied the Dragon King, as if it were the simplest request in the world.

The Scroll of Oblivion unspooled from Nazayun's fingertips, winding across the vast chamber. It tumbled along the marble walls, unfurling white and wide like a bubbling brook.

I braced myself. Minutes ago, I'd witnessed him deliver brutal retribution to Queen Haidi for aiding Yonsar against his storms. What would he do to me for daring to wield the one weapon prophesized to end him? My imagination flashed forward to the cruelest possibilities, but in the end, Nazayun did the one thing that chilled me most.

He smiled.

"Beginning now, you'll start anew on a fresh subject," he said. Lightning flashed in his eye. "One you know dearly."

Yes, I knew. I whispered, "You want me to send Elang into Oblivion."

"Ever vigilant, ever alone." Nazayun's tone made a mockery of kindness. "Oblivion might be just the home he's been looking for."

I felt sick. It took all my restraint to hold my tongue, to keep from slinging my foulest curses at him. But that wasn't how the game was played. I needed to get the Scroll back. In order to do that, I had to put on an act. And gods, I knew how to put on an act.

"If I do this," I said, finding my voice, "you will free my father?"

"You have my word."

Immortals were sworn to their promises, Elang had told me, and the power of Nazayun's word jolted the sea like an electric charge. I looked up, finding my reflection in his eyes, mirror sharp.

"Then you leave me no choice," I said. "I will paint."

"We are agreed, then."

"We are agreed."

The water beneath my feet howled, currents gathering into a whirlpool. Before I could register what was happening, I was pulled into its swirling depths.

The fall was short, barely longer than a breath. I landed on a marble stool, facing my new prison: a catacomb with a line of grim-looking statues guarding the walls and a squat table in the center. On it were brushes of every hair and size, water bowls, and ink that had been mixed precisely to match Elang's coloring. How thoughtful.

"You will not leave until your work is done," boomed Nazayun from above. His voice resounded against the walls, making my ears hurt. "Any tricks, and your father dies. Do you understand?"

I didn't reply. I was listening to the sea, and I could feel Elang's presence. Not far, somewhere in this palace, he was a prisoner like me. *Because* of me.

"I'll need to see Elang," I spoke, "if I am to paint him."

"You should have memorized your husband's face by now," said Nazayun. His eyes glowed. "You and Elangui may say your farewells once you are finished. You have until the morning, Bride of the Westerly Seas."

With that he vanished from the chamber, leaving me alone with my impossible task.

I was defiant at first. I paced the room, circling the Scroll of Oblivion. It lay in a grainy river, its folds collecting sand.

"I see you've chosen to be stupid," remarked Shani, misting into the room. She'd turned shapeless, her presence marked by the iridescent outline of her form. "It isn't often that the Dragon King offers an exchange. If you want to save your father, I wouldn't infuriate our king by dawdling."

I couldn't believe her audacity. Giving me advice?

"I'm thinking," I snapped.

"You should know Elang's face by now."

It wasn't lost on me, how she no longer used the honorific *'anmi*.

"It's no coincidence His Eternal Majesty selected this room for you," Shani said. "Shall I introduce you to your company?" Shifting back into a stingray, she curled around the closest statue, of an elegant mermaid with sorrowful eyes. "That was Nahma, former high lady of the Southerly Seas. She was turned into stone for sympathizing with your husband when he was banished. Next is Nazayun's own daughter, the mother of Seryu'ginan, the heir—"

"That's enough," I interrupted.

My shoulders fell, and with them went my anger. "Why betray us?" I asked her quietly. "We had the weapon to destroy him. I have it now. Right here."

Her face went amorphous. "Nazayun offered me a deal

once, not too different from yours," she said thinly. "Serve him and live. Refuse and die. What do you think I picked?"

"But we were so close," I appealed. "I know you're afraid. I know you think you don't have a choice, but—"

"But nothing," she barked. "You understand nothing."

"You have honor, Shanizhun," I persevered. "I've seen it."

Her tail came winging from behind, delivering a stinging slap. My neck jerked back, more out of surprise than pain. I touched my cheek, staring at the demon in disbelief.

"Haven't you wondered how Elang's mother really died?" she hissed. "*I* stole her supply of sangi, same as yours. Except he didn't make it back in time for *her*."

"Shani, no," I whispered in horror. "Nazayun made you do it."

"Never seek redemption for a demon. You'll be disappointed." Contempt spilled across her face. "Now paint, or I'll *make* you."

My cheek still smarting, I sank onto the stool. When the demon wasn't looking, I folded my sleeve down, covering the precious notes I'd taken of the Dragon King.

I painted slowly at first. Every stroke was reluctant, for I knew there was no way I could save Elang. In exchange for Baba's life, I'd doomed my husband's.

But what could I do? I felt like the miller's daughter in the story Baba used to tell. It was rumored that the girl could turn straw into gold, so a prince locked her away to create mountains of gold for him, just as I was forced to paint for Nazayun.

"*And do you know what her reward was?*" Nomi had asked, making a face. "She had to *marry the prince. Can you imagine anything so vile? I would have turned the prince's* entire castle into gold. That way, it would have collapsed under its own weight and crushed him to death."

"So violent, Nomi!" Fal exclaimed.

Nomi shrugged. "It's what he deserved. Clever women get revenge."

In my head, an idea was starting to form. It was only a sprout, nurtured by desperation. Even in my thoughts, it sounded ludicrous. But if it worked . . .

My fingertips tingled. To send someone into Oblivion, I would have to capture them in their final moments. Not an easy task, but not impossible—especially if I could manipulate my Sight.

For years, I'd wavered between dreading my visions and desiring them—in the fervent hope that they could change the future. When a vision did come, trying to control it was like steering a skiff against a fearsome wind; I only ended up awash.

Today I would open up my sails. I would ride the storm.

Letting my eyes roll back, I set my palm upon the Scroll, and slowly, I began to draw Elang's face.

I painted the smooth contour of his human cheek, the pebbly texture of his dragon one. The trickiest part was capturing the split in his features, where he changed from human to dragon. The part in his lips, the uneven nostrils, the break between his thick brows.

I had to paint carefully. If my idea was going to work, the deception would have to be nearly imperceptible, even to the Scroll itself.

Luckily, I knew Elang. I'd known him for years.

I would not fail.

"I'm finished," I announced loudly, moments before the first tides of dawn appeared.

Shani materialized, looking skeptical. "You're done early."

"*Serve him and live. Refuse and die.*" I quoted her flatly. "What do you think I picked?"

"We shall see."

While the demon surveyed the Scroll, I hung back, clasping my hands to keep my fingers from twitching. Would Shani notice the trick I'd concealed in the painting?

"It seems you're as much a traitor as I am," murmured Shani at last. "But you've forgotten the eyes."

I'd purposefully left them white, hoping that the stark emptiness of Elang's eyes would be a distraction, and no one would notice the unusual composition of my painting. I replied, "A dragon's pearl is its power; a dragon's eyes are its spirit. An artist always paints the eyes last."

Shani gave me a pointed look. "You're not an artist, you're a forger. And you're up to something."

"I'm a mere mortal," I said innocently. "Do you think I'd dare deceive the Dragon King?"

The water demon lashed her tail out, pressing its serrated tip to my chin. "If you dare, you'll fail. Consider yourself warned."

I bowed my head, catching the vial of sangi she flung my way. Ironic that Shani herself had taught me how to paint a dragon. It was thanks to her that I'd mastered the form—enough that I could hide a secret inside.

A forgery of fate, as Elang would call it.

I only hoped it was enough to save us.

CHAPTER THIRTY-SIX

My father had told me once that anyone visiting A'landi's Summer Palace had to climb ninety-nine steps before reaching the entrance. The first emperor had designed it that way to ensure that every visitor would arrive out of breath and fall into a bow upon greeting him. I used to think the story utterly absurd. But now I understood where he'd gotten his inspiration.

The Dragon King's throne room was a nine-tiered tower with sloping roofs on each level. The walls were studded with jade and opal, and the gables were plated with the purest gold. Instead of stairs, there were colossal sheets of tumbling water, impossible to cross without Shani's help. Even then, I was panting by the time I reached the top.

There, lounging upon a cloud of sea foam, was the Dragon King. And by his side, sitting cross-legged on a slab of speckled crystal, was Elang.

I'd always thought him tall, but next to his grandfather, he looked small. Insignificant. I couldn't tell whether he was hurt. His eyes were bloodshot, his shoulders tense, and yet the instant I entered, something in him lifted.

I looked away, schooling my face into a stony expression.

Never play games with a dragon, the old saying went. Against all sense, I was throwing all my tiles in against the king. I prayed I wouldn't lose.

"Your Eternal Majesty," I said with a deep bow. "I have done as you asked. Behold."

With a flick of my wrist, I sent the Scroll unraveling. In a long white ream, it fell, and there, for all to see, was my portrait of Elang. A careful congress of water and ink, every existing detail was finely rendered, as true to life as I could have drawn.

Elang didn't even glance at it.

Stop looking at me, I wanted to shout at him. *Look at the painting.*

For three years, I'd known him as Gaari. He knew my art better than anyone, but it was the greatest gamble of my life—whether he'd see through the ruse I'd woven into his portrait.

I bit my bottom lip. During our cons, that had always been my tell. I hoped he'd remember it.

Meanwhile, the Dragon King surveyed my work. Several of his attendants gathered around the Scroll, comparing it to Elang himself, who still sat on a crystal slab. I straightened. It was clear for all to see, my work was as accurate as life itself.

"You've done well," Nazayun allowed. "But where are Elangui's eyes?"

I'd been waiting for this. "I will paint them after you release my father."

Displeasure rumbled in the Dragon King's throat. "You are in no position to bargain. Complete the portrait. Now."

The sea boiled with his rancor, making me stagger back

several paces. I steeled myself. "It is not a bargain; it is part of your promise."

"Bring the girl's father back to life," Elang spoke up. His voice, hoarse yet commanding, startled everyone in the chamber to attention. "Bring him to life but keep him in Ai'long. Show her what she will lose if she defies the Dragon King."

Nine Hells of Tamra, whose side was Elang on? This wasn't part of my plan at all.

Nazayun seemed to like this idea. He considered it, then in a blink, it was done.

Baba's toy ship reappeared, close enough for me to see each individual strand of my father's hair.

"Awaken, Arban Saigas," said Nazayun.

The ship began to glow. The painting of Baba peeled off the wood, and a tempest of water and ink surrounded him. Within, I could make out the growing silhouette of a hand, the ends of a green scarf I'd all but forgotten.

"Baba!" I whispered. The tempest was growing, and so, too, was Baba's silhouette inside. He was as tall as I'd remembered, and I waded closer, reaching for him. "Baba, I'm here!"

My fingers clasped a sleeve, then an arm still becoming whole. I held on. I felt his bones stretch into place, his muscles and veins cord around his arm. When I could count five hard knuckles on the back of his hand, I knew it was really him.

The tempest receded, and there was my father.

He lay in the water, floating supine. At first I thought he was dead; his skin was gray, and he wasn't moving or breathing. Behind me, Elang drew out a vial of sangi and poured it between Baba's lips.

Baba's face contorted, his muscles jerking before they calmed. His eyelids twitched, struggling to open, but one of his brows shot up. Then he breathed, his first breath in five years.

"Truyan?" Baba whispered.

Joy clotted my throat. I rushed forward, forgetting completely where I was. My only thought was for Baba, wanting to embrace him, touch him, be with him.

Then ice frosted Baba's lips and eyelids. He shivered violently, eyes closing once more.

"Finish the portrait," Nazayun snarled. "Now."

I clenched the brush, my entire body glittering with hate. He wanted me to paint? By gods, then I would paint.

With great flourish, I outlined the shape of Elang's eyes and painted the first one yellow. Then I turned to the other.

I used to think his yellow eye upstaged the gray, but now I found myself contemplating the many shades within that gray. Ashen when he was angry, pewter speckled when amused, and charcoal dark when he was in pain. The shade I mixed for this portrait was achingly deep.

I leaned forward to dot his pupils. One last stroke, to capture the light, and I'd be finished. I braced myself, about to mark it upon the Scroll—when Elang spoke.

"Wait," he said, shattering the chamber's brittle silence. "A last request, if you may. Before I am sent to Oblivion, I should like one kiss from my wife."

I nearly dropped my brush.

"A kiss, Elangui?" The Dragon King's laugh made the walls shudder. "Look at your bride, ready to betray you for all eternity. No kiss will make her return your love."

Love?

"Didn't Shani tell you it was all a sham?" I blurted. "Elang doesn't love me."

The moment I spoke, the water in the room went utterly still. The Dragon King dipped his head, coming close enough that I could feel the electricity sparking from his whiskers. His eyes beheld me, just as mirror sharp as I'd remembered.

"Elangui doesn't love you?" he repeated. "Surely, Bride of the Westerly Seas, you cannot believe that. If it were true, my patrols would have slew you as soon as you entered my realm. But they did not."

He was lying, wasn't he? I blinked, thinking back to the day I'd arrived in Ai'long. The jellyfish had wrapped their tentacles around Elang, testing him for any traces of deception. I'd been so preoccupied with getting them away from me, I hadn't been paying attention to what they had done to him. Only that he had passed the test, because . . . because . . .

"They heard Elangui's heart," Nazayun answered for me.

His heart, I thought, over the pounding of my own. "But . . . how? I thought he had none."

"He doesn't. Unless he's with his Heavenly Match."

It was like I'd been struck. My head jerked up, eyes flying to Elang, certain he would deny such a ludicrous claim—the way he had when we'd first made our bargain.

Don't be dense, krill, he had said, the tips of his ears burning red. *Don't imagine I would choose to take someone like you as a bride. It would be for appearances only. Until our business is complete.*

But he was silent. His eyes were unwavering, not even daring to blink. His gaze, stuck on me.

And suddenly I knew.

"It is simple," Nazayun explained. "When he is in your presence, his heart returns. Away from you, it vanishes. Too long apart from his love, and Elang suffers, he grows weak.

The curse resembles an affliction common among mortals—what is it called? Ah yes, a broken heart." He leaned forward, his voice falling to a soft purr. "I'm told it can be deadly."

My brush snapped under my thumb. I was vibrating with anger, and it took my greatest self-control to bury it and speak, in my iciest tone. "Like the demon told you, our marriage isn't real. Why should I care if he dies?"

Nazayun impaled me with his gaze. "You *sound* as though you care, Bride of the Westerly Seas."

"She does not," said Elang.

"I didn't ask you." Lightning fired out of Nazayun's eyes, striking Elang in the chest. "I asked the girl."

Elang jerked back. Smoke sizzled where he'd been hit. It was the hardest thing, masking my horror and feigning cold aloofness. But I stayed rooted in place, silently choking on my fury. No matter what, I would not give up the game.

Nazayun peered at me. "Do you love Elang?"

I parted my lips, an answer on the precipice of my tongue. In the past, I would have barked a refusal without hesitation. Now the words wavered unsteadily.

This much I knew: Elang wanted me to hate him. From the start, that had been his plan. Why, I still didn't understand, but it had to do with his curse. Which explained why Nazayun was so fixated on my love for him.

But I didn't have time to ponder that question.

I mustered a scoff. "Elang is a monster. He forced me into a false marriage, trapped me in the realm of dragons, and endangered my entire family. All I want is for things to go back to the way they were. *Before* I met him."

To punctuate my point, I made my final stroke on the Scroll, angrily stabbing a bead of ink into Elang's pupil. Dear

Amana, I prayed that Nazayun had never bothered studying art or painting technique. I prayed he was paying more attention to his grandson's missing pupils than to the actual shape and composition of the painting. . . .

"It's done," I declared. "The portrait is finished."

"But here I remain," spoke Elang. His voice startled me. It'd become even more hoarse, and there was a hitch in his words. "The Painter must send her subject off to Oblivion with the Touch of Entrapment. I ask once more, let it be a kiss from my wife."

It was a good thing I'd completed the portrait. At his confession, my entire world went out of focus. I could barely hold myself upright, let alone breathe. *Elang . . .*

"Go on," allowed the Dragon King. "Bid your husband farewell."

I swam to Elang's side. The sea was heavy, causing me to sink with each stroke. Yet my heart felt heaviest of all.

"Why so sad, Saigas?" Elang said softly. "Dare I hope you'll miss me?"

His eyes were too sincere, too tender.

"Yes," I whispered. For the first time, I realized it was true.

"It'll be all right." He touched his forehead to mine. His voice fell to a whisper. "The shrimps are secured."

Shrimps. That was our old code word for the money. But there was no money here. I looked up at him in confusion—

And that was when his lips found mine.

It was a better kiss than the one we'd shared in Nanhira. Maybe that was because it wasn't an act anymore. Gone were the pretenses; the lies were exposed and deceptions unearthed. And still I found I wanted him.

He pulled me to him by the waist, and I tasted his lips, taking my time. The black was seeping into his hair, and the cold scales of his dragon face turned warm, almost hot. And when I heard his heart, beating wildly against mine, I held him close, desperately worried that if I let go, he might disappear from the fabric of the universe forever.

Don't go, I thought, a feverish heat swelling in my chest. *Don't go.*

He was the one who let go, and in that moment, I swore all of Ai'long went still.

I waited with bated breath, half convinced that he might vanish any second.

He didn't. A grin slowly spread across his face. "Clever, Saigas," he murmured. "Ever so clever."

And that was when Nazayun realized that he'd been deceived.

We didn't wait for the consequences. We wouldn't have survived them.

I threw myself onto Elang's back. Grabbed him by the horns. A beat later, the ceiling shattered.

In a blitz of golden debris, General Caisan and a brigade of turtles had arrived.

The seas rocked. Lightning dazzled out of Nazayun's eyes, and entire walls and columns were turned to stone, barely missing Caisan's forces. The turtles were fast, and their shells were strong. The first thing they did was cluster together to form a shield, swooping down as one to rescue Baba. It was a small miracle I'd remember forever, the sight of General Caisan with my father astride his shell.

I clung tighter to Elang, straddling his back as he swerved

toward his grandfather. Water roared, gathering into a vicious force. We only went faster. Elang was an arrow primed to his target. Nothing could stop him, not even Shani.

Thanks to his years acting as Gaari, he knew my art better than anyone. He knew my lines and strokes, the way I composed my subjects and chose my colors, but most of all, he knew how much I liked to bury little deceptions in my work. Deceptions, like the fact that I hadn't painted Elang at all. I had painted his reflection—inside the pale blue orb of Nazayun's *eye*.

Reaching that eye was like scaling a cliff in a storm. Lightning ripped after us, and Elang narrowly scraped past each blast. The heat was blistering. Even my tears burned.

"Hold on, Tru," Elang whispered. "We're almost there."

Yes, we were close. I could almost look up and see Elang's reflection in Nazayun's pupil. Any moment now.

To send someone into Oblivion, I had to paint their final moment. And this was what I'd foreseen: Elang, invading the Dragon King's line of sight, his gray and yellow eyes ablaze. My body trembled as it came true.

Now I only had my part to play.

For Ai'long, I thought, letting go of Elang's horns. *For Baba*.

Throwing myself as far as I could, I leapt for the Dragon King. I kicked furiously, aiming for the highest whisker on his cheek, tilted just above his brow.

With a silent prayer to the gods, I oustretched my hand. Down I tumbled, past the storm of his white hair. My fingertips grazed down the rough hood of his lid, peeling past his lashes—for the fathomless black pupil below.

I wished I'd had enough time to paint the damned entirety of the Dragon King into Oblivion, but for now this would do. A touch was all it took. The Touch of Entrapment.

His eye vanished, as if it had never existed. And Nazayun let out an anguished cry.

I didn't wait for the aftermath. As fast as I could, I grabbed the Scroll and I hooked Elang by the arm. "Go."

CHAPTER THIRTY-SEVEN

We fled the palace.

It was the most tumultuous, dizzying ride of my life. The halls flashed by in a wash of color. Spears sang past our ears as we left our enemies behind.

Past the gate, we sped through the seagrass. Queen Haidi was hunting us. Her barbs tore through the field, skinning past rocks and reefs alike.

Elang pulled me into a narrow cave, the ridges on his back tensing as Haidi combed the area for us. At his touch, my clothes matched the algae-covered rock. So, too, did his scales and long tail.

I reached for his hand, held it tight. The minutes crawled by, and instinctively we breathed at the same time so we wouldn't make any extra sound. I watched as the magic took its toll on Elang. His yellow eye twitched, its vibrance turning dull and cloudy. The warmth was bleeding from his scales. I pressed my ear to his chest and listened for his heart. Faint and unsteady it beat. My own pulse spiked with worry.

"I think she's gone," Elang finally whispered. He rolled to his side so we faced each other. "Are you hurt?"

Was *I* hurt?

One of Haidi's harpoons had found the sinewy human flesh between his scales, just above his chest. He was trying to hide it, but there was too much blood. It pooled between the seams of his fingers, drenching his white cloak.

I heal faster than full-blooded humans, Elang had told me, *but I bleed like you, and I hurt like you.*

Do you die like us too? I wished I'd asked. From the looks of it, the answer was yes. His scales were losing their luster, and even with the cloak on, he wasn't getting much better.

"It's nothing—"

"Stop talking." I swept aside his healing cloak and gripped the bottom of the harpoon shaft, my knuckles turning red with Elang's blood.

"One," I said aloud. "Two."

Three. With all my strength, I yanked out the harpoon. There came a grisly crunch that made my insides clench, and Elang's chest heaved. I folded his cloak over him, rolling him onto his back. I swallowed hard. "Does it hurt very much?"

Elang attempted a grin. "Less, now that you're here."

Liar, I almost said, before I realized he wasn't lying at all. "You never were good at flirting."

"I never had a chance to practice. As Gaari, I thought it would make you uncomfortable. And after that, we were already married so it didn't seem necessary."

Again, that urge to slap him as much as kiss him. I settled for kissing him, twice.

The sea had gone still, allowing us a moment of precious repose. Together we lay in our grassy cove, cheeks pressed together, savoring one another's warmth. We didn't have long, and I roamed my fingers into his hair, twirling the tufts behind his ears. A bloom of color crept back to his scales wherever I touched.

Elang lifted his head, ears pointed. "Caisan will be here any moment," he said. "He'll take you to shore."

"You're not coming with me?"

"I heal faster in the water," he said gently, "and you'll be safer on your own. Once my grandfather recovers, he'll come looking for me. Best we're not together."

"You won't make it back to Yonsar like this," I pointed out. "You'll be captured."

"Better me than you," he replied. "My part in this mission is done. Yours is not. You'll have more time on land."

A sharp tingle prickled my fingertips where I'd touched Nazayun's eye. I closed my fist. I knew Elang was right; a day in Ai'long meant almost a week back home. But still . . .

"Nazayun told me what will happen to you if . . . if we spend too long apart," I said. "If I don't break your curse."

You'll die, I thought, but I couldn't say the words.

He raised my hand to his cheek. "One day you'll understand everything. But until then, I'm sorry. For deceiving you and lying to you—most of all, for hurting you."

In my heart, I'd already forgiven him, but I liked the beseeching look in his eyes and the way he was holding my hand, as though Lord Tamra himself would have to strike him down before he let it go. "I know."

"Don't forgive me yet," he said softly. "I have one last confession to make."

"Another one?"

He regarded me, looking more nervous than guilty. "I lied to you twice. Once as the old man Gaari, then there was another time."

He looked down at our hands, fingers interlocked. "On our wedding day, I told you that everything I said and did would mean nothing." He drew a deep breath. "When in fact every word we exchanged, every glance, and every moment where I didn't have to pretend . . . it meant everything—to me."

Gods. It was good I wasn't on land, for my knees would have buckled beneath me. I thought back to our wedding, to the smile he'd worn after lifting my veil, that intent gaze he'd given me when he'd uttered his vow, even the firm grasp of his hand next to mine as we'd borne our umbrella against the rain. I swayed, and Elang wrapped his arm around me, letting me land against him.

"When I was Gaari, I'd come up with lesson plans or excursions—for you to practice, but also as excuses for me to see you. You made me laugh. The disguises you would wear, with your hair piled up like knots of bread, the way you'd argue with me over art."

"I should've argued more. You weren't even a real dealer!"

"I spent two good years studying for the role," said Elang, sounding mildly defensive. "But you were right more than I let on."

"You bought my paintings at auction," I remembered. "Were they so bad that no one else wanted them?"

"There were other bidders," he confessed quietly. "I just wanted to have them."

"Why?"

He lowered his head. "In case you never looked at me the way you are now."

My heart skipped a beat. "You wastrel."

He leaned closer, a devious one-sided smile flitting across his lips. I would miss this smile, I realized too late. I would miss the sound of his voice, the range of it from cold and stern to tender. I'd miss how he said my name.

Funny, how his face had grown on me too. I didn't find it so monstrous anymore.

I opened my mouth, about to say so, but that was when he kissed me.

No one was watching us, we had nothing to prove. And that made it all the more true. Below the seagrass, our legs entwined. Our fingers laced together as our backs sank against the ocean floor. I didn't know that even the gentlest of kisses could be full of longing. That a touch of skin against skin could turn my body into fire, and that time could become my cruelest enemy.

All too soon, it was over.

Elang's lips slid from my mouth to my ear, his cheek nestled in the bed of my hair. "Caisan is here," he whispered gently. "You need to go."

My thoughts were languid and soft. I longed to stay. I was so warm.

Elang kissed my throat, my neck, then my hand. Slowly, together, we emerged above the grass.

"Be safe," he said, "and don't leave the protection of the manor."

"I won't."

Feeling a ripple in the waters, I turned around. Caisan was here, Baba secured to his wide back.

My father didn't stir even when I held his hand, but I could feel a pulse. For now, that was enough.

"He is recovering," said Elang, at my side. He tore off his cloak and folded it over Baba. "You needn't worry about the sangi I gave him. So long as his first breath was underwater, he'll be fine on land."

My voice quavered with emotion. "Thank you."

"Your Highnesses," spoke Caisan gruffly. "The Dragon King's forces are preparing for attack. We must hurry."

There came a pinch in my chest. I wasn't ready to leave.

Elang set me on Caisan's back, behind Baba. "Tru," he spoke. His two faces strained from warring with one another. "If at any time you change your mind about completing the portrait, give the Scroll to Caisan. He will see it returned to me."

"After all the work I've put in?" I shook my head. "Don't you insult me like that. I'm not going to change my mind."

"You have lost years with your family already. No more. I release you from your contract. Be with your parents and your sisters, live a long and happy life with them."

"Are you trying to get rid of me?"

That made him laugh softly. "Never would I dare," he said. "My heart, my home—they are yours. They always have been." He touched my hair, both his eyes sad and solemn. "I only want you to have the choice—to forget me, if you will."

I didn't get the chance to argue—or even say goodbye.

Elang withdrew from my arms, and Caisan took off like an arrow. Up we soared, rushing through the violet light to escape the realm of dragons. And my journey ended the same way it began—with all I had come to know being washed away.

CHAPTER THIRTY-EIGHT

It was morning when I returned to the world above the sea. The sun was young, magpies sang in the larch trees, and the garden was white with winter.

As Caisan floated across the pond, I held out my hands, catching snowflakes as they fell.

"Are you cold, Lady Saigas?" asked the general.

"No." The air was brisk. My breath came out in swirls of steam when I exhaled, but I wasn't cold. Not after my time in Yonsar.

I glanced down at Baba, who lay on the general's back. He had slept the entire journey, and a soft wheeze passed through his nostrils.

I raised Elang's cloak to cover his shoulders. How many times had I prayed to the gods, begging for Baba to come home? How many nights had I dreamed of seeing him again, only to wake up to the vicious reality that he was gone?

No more. My heart ached with joy. I couldn't wait until Mama and my sisters saw him.

"Mama!" I shouted. "Fal! Nomi!"

I started to slide off Caisan's shell so I could wade closer to the house. "Mama!" I shouted again.

That was when a warm hand clasped my own.

"Truyan?" came Baba's hoarse whisper. "Is it really you?"

Tears welled in my eyes. I couldn't speak, so I held his hand, bringing it to my chest. He was still cold, warmth shivering back to his skin gradually with every second. But his smile was real. *He* was real.

"It's me." The words scraped out of my throat. "It's me."

I'd never seen Baba cry before. His eyes filled as he steadied himself with my arm, his gaze sweeping over my face. "My little girl, you've grown up." He inhaled. "How long . . . how long was I away?"

"Five years."

I could hear the breath go out of him.

"Five years," he murmured. "The last thing I remember was a storm, my ship sinking. The realization that I'd never get to see my girls grow up."

My throat closed, a lump swelling painfully inside. "We can talk later. We need to get you inside, get you some warm food and tea. Mama should be awake by now."

At the mention of Mama, a thousand questions burned in his eyes. He didn't recognize the mansion in front of us, and I could see his astonishment when he realized we were floating on the back of a giant turtle.

"Is this your home?" he asked in disbelief. "Your mother, she didn't remarry. Did she?"

I had to laugh. "She didn't." A blush rose high on my cheeks as I realized I'd have to tell Baba *I* was the one who'd married. That could wait.

"Let's see who's awake." I cupped my hands around my mouth. "Mama!" I shouted. "Fal, Nomi! We're home!"

A door slid open, and Nomi came rushing out. "Tru!" she yelled. Then her eyes bulged.

There was a book in her hand, and my ever-sensible sister tossed it into a bush before she not-so-sensibly rushed into the pond. It was freezing, thin ice crackling from where I stood.

"Don't rush in!" I warned.

I dove forward, catching her before she skidded across the ice. I held her close. "I've got you."

Nomi threw her arms around me, hugging me so fiercely I could hardly breathe. "You're back. You're finally back." Her loose hair was crimped from yesterday's braids, the collar on her tunic adorably misbuttoned as always. I rested my chin on top of her head, finding she was taller than I remembered.

Five months, I'd been away. For Baba, it'd been five years.

"Don't I get an embrace too?" he said gently.

Nomi turned to him, eyes shining with tears she didn't dare let fall. "Are you real?" she whispered. "Or are you a dream? I warn you that no matter what you are, I won't let you go."

"I'm real." Baba opened his arms, hugging us both. "I promise I'm real."

That was when Falina came running out the door, her jacket unbuttoned and her slippers falling off. Her teeth chattered as she shouted, "Nomi, get out of the pond! You'll catch sick—"

She stopped short, her words freezing into a gasp. "*Baba?*"

Her mouth still hanging, she leapt into the pond right behind Nomi, chattering teeth and all. "Baba!"

Baba grabbed her by the arm. I took her other hand. "My pine, my plum, my bamboo," he murmured, words I'd forgotten how much I missed. Tears glistened under his eyes, freezing before they could fall, and his voice grew hoarse. "You've grown so strong, so beautiful."

That was all he could manage before my sisters and I hugged him. We were like fools, laughing and crying and clinging to each other as we splashed toward the bank. In the end, it was Caisan who ferried us out into the garden. Aiding him were two merfolk, who threw blankets over our backs and ushered us toward the house, shaking their heads at us while they enchanted our clothes dry again.

The gods could've thrown a blizzard at me and I wouldn't have noticed. With my sisters at my side, I held him by the arm and brought him inside.

Mama was in the kitchen, cooking. She hadn't heard the commotion in the garden, so when our footsteps came pattering in, she said, "Falina and Nomi Saigas, didn't I tell you two to wash the rice. . . ."

The words died on her lips.

"Devils of Tamra," she whispered, stunned. She spun to my sisters, raising a rice paddle at them. "What manner of illusion is this?" she demanded. "Are the merfolk at their jokes again? This isn't funny, Falina—"

"It's really them," Nomi spoke over her. "Baba and Tru—they're home."

Mama lowered the paddle, her face paling. She stared at Baba. "Arban?"

"It's me," he said softly. He bowed. "I'm sorry I kept you waiting."

The paddle dropped from Mama's hand, and Baba caught her in his arms as she fell back.

"Weina," he started.

"Look at you." She tapped his cheeks, pinching his earlobes. "You haven't aged at all." Her voice hitched. "You should've given some warning you were coming back. I would've braided my hair, put on some powder." She sniffled, wriggling out of Baba's arms onto her feet. "Gods, what must you think seeing me like this? These gray hairs and wrinkles under my eyes—all from worrying about you!"

There came a wheezy laugh under Baba's breath. "You haven't changed. Still exaggerating like you used to."

"Exaggerating!"

He swept a loose hair from Mama's temple. "You know what I think? I think today is my most joyous day. My children have bloomed into young women, and my wife has never looked more beautiful."

It was true, I thought. I'd half expected to find Mama dressed in silken finery, enjoying all the luxuries Elang's manor had to offer. But she wore simple twill robes and an apron, and the only jewelry was the same jade bangle she'd worn for years. The one Baba had given her as a wedding gift.

Mama crossed her arms, but a flush reddened her cheeks. "You and your silver tongue. All these years, and not a single letter? You'd better have a good reason for it."

"Mama...," I started, but Baba silenced me with a touch.

He reached into his pocket, handing Mama the wooden toy boat he'd once carved for me. "I was captured by the Dragon King."

Mama's arms fell to her sides. Her lower lip trembled. "What?"

"This is the boat I carved for the girls," Baba said, trying to keep his tone light, despite the shadows that had fallen over his face. "I was trapped inside for years. It wasn't so bad. I didn't feel any pain—or anything, really. The next thing I knew, Tru was there to save me."

"Tru saved you?" Mama turned to me then, pinching my cheek. "Thank Amana. I always knew that mole of yours was lucky."

There was a crack in her voice, and she sniffed, trying to hide it. "You must be hungry, the both of you. Breakfast is nearly ready. This weather makes me famished. It's the coldest winter we've had since I was a girl, and all this ice came about last night. Will you look outside—my persimmon trees are doomed!"

"You've been gardening?" I asked, surprised. I noted the oil stains on her apron. "And cooking?"

"Every day," chirped Nomi. "Miracles do happen."

Mama glowered at her youngest, then she began scooping congee into an assortment of wooden bowls. I hadn't seen her so busy in years. Here was a glimmer of her old self, strong and boisterous and always moving. It warmed me to see.

"The clapping magic got tiresome after a while," she said. "The congee was always too salty." Her eyes were bleary, her voice cracking as she spoke, but she was doing her best to hide it. "Anyhow, there's nothing else to do around here. So I cook, Fal makes clothes, Nomi tinkers with ways to destroy the manor."

She set three bowls on a tray. "Your contract is done, I take it. Where is Lord Elang? He said he'd bring you back, but he's nowhere to be seen. A good son-in-law should keep his word."

"Son-in-law?" Baba repeated. "Does that mean . . . Tru?"

"She hasn't told you?" Fal asked slyly. "That'd be the Demon Prince. Oh, don't worry, he's not an actual demon, he's just—"

"My husband," I said thickly. I touched my chest, remembering the butterflies that sat over my heart. "We married right before I left for Ai'long."

"You should have seen the wedding," gushed Mama, who seemed to have forgotten her disdain for the event. "It was a grand affair. Even the governor came! And I combed Tru's hair the night before like how your mother combed mine. She was so beautiful."

Mama dabbed her eyes with her sleeves. "Oh, damn these onions. They're hurting my eyes." She blinked, and I noticed that there were no onions in the kitchen, only watercress, carrots, and snow peas.

Baba saw right through Mama's ruse. He touched her arm. "I'll stay and help you. Let the children eat first."

My sisters and I quickly excused ourselves. We shuffled down the long hallway, carrying bowls of congee and huddling together as though we were children again, picking up from that last morning Baba was home. A painting of the Eight Immortals hung on the wall, and as I passed it, my chest tightened.

Falina linked arms with me, oblivious to my thoughts. "He's really back," she breathed. "And you, Tru. Just in time for the New Year."

"It's perfect timing." Nomi clapped. "I've been making my own fireworks, but Mama thinks they're too dangerous to test in the garden." She plopped onto a chair in the dining chamber. "Now that you're back, we can finally go out again, right? I can smell the festival food from Bading Street."

My smile wavered. How did I tell her I couldn't leave the manor?

"Let's wait awhile," I said, dipping my spoon into my congee. "Baba's just returned. He'll need his rest."

"And Mama will want news," added Fal. "We've wondered what you've been doing in Ai'long."

"Yes." Nomi leaned forward, wearing a devious arch in her brow. "Especially whether you're going to stay married to that dragon prince."

Nearly six months away from home, and I could no longer read the inflections behind my sister's words. "Why *would* I stay married to Elang?" I asked, hoping I sounded indifferent. "I thought we all hated him."

Fal and Nomi exchanged looks.

"I don't hate him," Nomi started. "I mean, I *did*, but then he gave me the key to his library with all the potion recipes. He's quite clever, for a fake demon prince."

"Potions! I thought you were studying for the National Exam?"

Nomi shrugged, stirring peanuts into her congee. "Who would turn down magic lessons from a dragon?"

"I don't hate him either," Falina said. "He showed me the flowers in his garden and asked the merfolk to teach me how to weave silk. And from the way he was talking about you when he visited, I assumed that he . . ." She let her voice trail.

"He what?"

"That he loves you," Nomi said softly.

The pinch in my heart vanished, and suddenly my pulse was thudding in my chest.

I value Truyan's life more than my own, Elang had told Queen Haidi. *Any spell will prove this as truth.*

Had everyone known—my sisters, Queen Haidi, even the Dragon King himself—Elang's true feelings? Was I the only one who hadn't seen?

Until it was too late, I thought miserably.

Nomi touched my shoulder. "You've gone pale, Tru. Did we say something wrong?"

"I've got a headache," I said.

More like a heartache, but Nomi didn't get the chance to correct me.

Mama and Baba entered the room, shoulders touching. "Who's got a headache?" Mama asked.

"Tru," supplied Nomi. "We were talking about Elang, and the medicines he taught me how to brew. Remember how he cured your cough, Mama?"

"Yes." A faint smile touched Mama's lips. "At first I was upset Truyan hadn't come too, but . . . we got along very well, the dragon and I. He was much more charming than the first time, but not so good at tiles. It's a good thing we weren't gambling." She chuckled to herself. "We took our meals together, pruned the sanheia from the gardens, exchanged stories about Tru. I almost forgot they weren't really married."

Heat rushed up to my eyes. I remembered what an oddly good mood Elang had been in when he'd returned to Yonsar. "You sound as if you like him."

Mama spooned a heap of congee into her mouth. "You know, I've two minds about the Demon Prince," she said, chewing. "Part of me thinks he might actually be a good son-in-law. But you can never trust these dragon sorts; I warned him he'd better bring you home safe, or I'd skewer his eyeballs and flay his scales into a new coat."

Only Mama would dare heckle a dragon. "What did he say?"

"He said you'd be safe, and if there was even the barest scratch on your skin, *he'd* cut his scales out for me, so I wouldn't have to dirty my hands." Mama pinched my sleeve, admiring the crystal beads inlaid into the silk. "And he kept his promise, didn't he?"

"He did," I said solemnly.

"Trust me, Tru, when you come across a man like that, half dragon or not, you keep him. Especially if he has a house such as this." Mama tapped the table. "What a good day this has been. My husband is back from a shipwreck, and our daughter is married to a prince. Didn't I tell you fortune would turn in our favor?" Though Mama's voice was high, her eyes were still moist. She cleared her throat. "Now, who wants crullers?"

Baba laughed, and my sisters hid smiles behind their spoons. I was happy for them, but under the table, I worried the red string around my wrist.

I only want you to have the choice, Elang had said, *to forget me, if you will.*

At first I'd been confused, indignant even. How could he suggest such a thing, as if the last month—the last *three years*—had meant nothing. Yet now that I was home, slowly putting the broken pieces of my family back together again, I understood.

It would be so easy to end things, to divorce myself of Elang and his war with the Dragon King, and mark this as the beginning of the rest of my life.

The only problem? I was starting to realize I loved him back.

CHAPTER THIRTY-NINE

Night fell, and while my mother, father, and sisters reveled in their reunion, laughing over memories and stories retold, it began to rain. After dinner I slipped outside. My fingers had been tingling ever since I touched Nazayun's eye, stiffening my muscles with the burden of a premonition. Soon it would come.

I walked through Elang's manor, past the whale sculptures and the paintings of the Eight Immortals. Everything in his home held a new meaning, even the domed pavilion overlooking his garden. I stood by the window, watching the pitter-patter of heaven's tears against the roof.

Although I'd returned to land, a part of me was still wed to the sea. It was an extra awareness against my skin, how I could feel the winds churning against the garden pond or the frozen rain riming the windows. Even this storm carried a trace of the sea, and I reached my hand out to touch it, as if I were reaching out to Elang.

I drew my hand back. The rain was falling harder. Elang's manor was high in the hills, safe from any flooding, but outside the coating of ice had washed away, and the pond overflowed its banks.

"Lady Saigas, you should return inside."

General Caisan drew out of the shadows, his head stooped so it didn't touch the ceiling. For such a massive creature, he moved quietly.

With a nod, I let Caisan escort me back to my room.

"I thought you would wish to know," he said, "His Highness has returned safely to Yonsar."

My eyes flew up to the turtle. "Is the castle safe?"

"For now." As he spoke, lightning whipped the sky, thunder booming not far away. "The storms will grow worse as the Dragon King recovers. So long as you possess the Scroll of Oblivion, he will be searching for you."

I could read the warning between his words. "I'm not returning it."

Caisan's expressions were few, generally limited to disdain and displeasure. But he lifted his head out of his shell, a faint hint of approval curving on his mouth. "Then I will make sure he does not find you." A pause. "It will be harder for him anyway, with only one eye."

A smile spread across my face. He really was Mailoh's brother. He had a good nature, it was just concealed beneath a thicker shell. "I misjudged you, General," I said. "I am sorry for it."

"You were deceived. There is no need to apologize."

"You warned me about Shani. If I'd listened to you, if I'd believed you when you insisted that she was Yonsar's traitor, then—"

"Then I would not have been alerted to the several cracks

in our dungeon walls," Caisan interrupted. "And perhaps a more nefarious villain than myself might have escaped."

"Like me?" I teased.

Was that a smile from Caisan? I couldn't tell.

He walked me back inside my room. "Do not blame yourself for what has happened," he said. "The demon Shanizhun has only survived on account of her treachery. There used to be hundreds like her, but the Dragon King had them slain. She survived only by becoming his servant."

"Do you mean, she had no choice?"

"Don't sympathize with her. Look what good that did Lord Elang. You'd do best to remember that demons are not like us."

He was right, much as I wished it weren't so.

Caisan padded toward my door. "You've had a long journey, Lady Saigas. Rest now—the merfolk will guard the manor. Lord Elang has sent his best to protect you."

"I know," I said, acknowledging him. With a nod, I returned to my room. But I had no plans to rest.

I knelt before my desk, rolling back my sleeves carefully, then taking out a piece of paper. One week until the New Year. Painting the Dragon King in that limited time would be no easy feat.

On my left arm, the notes and drawings I'd sketched of Nazayun were smeared, barely readable. But all wasn't lost.

When I closed my eyes, I could still see him. I could envision the light of his pearl radiating from sapphire scales, how the tips of his whiskers were like rat tails, slightly thicker than the other dragons'. I imagined how I could paint the space between his scales the way I did bamboo nodes: a flick of the wrist to the left, then slide my brush back to the right.

Mama had told me that my grandmother learned to see years beyond her time—she could even glimpse multiple variations of the future. I was beginning to understand her secret: it began with the heart.

"For Baba," I murmured, picking up my brush and pressing its hairs to the parchment. My voice was thick. "For Elang, and Shani, and the folk of Yonsar. For Ai'long."

As I spoke, I saw washes of color and textures in my mind, moving and swirling. The future in motion. And so I began.

Stroke by stroke, I painted the Dragon King arching over a murky sea. His claws were brandished, his tail bounding over the water as the waves came crashing and rafts of smoke obscured the sky. Most troubling was the streak of red in his lone eye, bright as a smear of blood. A reflection of the sun, I decided. I didn't want to think too hard about what else it might be.

I worked all night, burning through my store of candles. The roof shook, thunder and lightning battered the sky—neither could rattle me out of my trance.

Only when I could feel the sleep spirits hovering over me, turning my strokes languid, did I set down my brush. My candle had long since guttered out.

As rain drummed against the roof, I let myself drift into slumber. For the first time, I dreamed of Elang.

I found him in the garden, sitting inside the blue-roofed pavilion. He was leaning against a wooden post, his back to the sun as the morning light washed out the sky. When he heard me approach, his horns receded into his temples.

He turned to face me. In his hands, he clasped a golden pearl. It was the size of a small melon, its surface smooth as fresh snow. Even from across the pavilion, I felt its warmth.

"Your curse is broken," I breathed. "You have your pearl."

For someone who'd at last found his prize, Elang didn't look contented. His dragon jaw was tense, his brow thick with anguish. "Will you help me choose?"

"How?"

"Paint me."

I found a brush in my pocket, and paper materialized in my hand. I pressed it against the wall, until Elang shook his head.

"Not a portrait." *He rose, erasing the distance between us.* "Paint *me.*"

He reached for the other end of my brush, pressing its hairs upon his cheek. "Human, and I stay with you. Dragon, and we go our separate ways. Which will I be?"

My fingers shaking, I pried the brush from his grip. I knew my answer.

But in this dream, my brush had a mind of its own. As I swept it across his skin, it blotted out the freckles on his nose like a god erasing the stars, and it covered his cheek with scales that hardened into the real thing. It painted away every semblance of his human self, even the smile I'd come to cherish on his mouth. Soon he was no longer the Elang I had known.

"Wait," *I choked out.* "I—I made a mistake."

Elang pressed my fingertips to his lips. "You made the right choice."

Still holding my hand, he pressed the pearl against his chest.

The change was immediate. Luster spread across his

silver-blue scales, casting a luminous sheen over his skin. His horns pierced through his temples, and his muscles swelled, black robes ripping as his bones stretched and his body grew. Last was his gray eye. It shone, spangled with gold. Then he blinked, and it was no longer gray, but a pool of sunlight like the other.

A fully formed dragon emerged. When he stood, I no longer came up to his chin. He dwarfed me, his horned head towering above the pines. In his chest glowed his pearl.

The brighter it shone, the more my own heart hurt. The pain had edges like a knife, and as it grew, I feared that it would cut me out of my own dream.

Just before it became too much to bear, the red string around my wrist snapped, the threads spinning away in the wind.

"Wait!" I shouted. "Elang!"

It was no use. His fingers tore away from mine, and a great wave surged forward. It devoured him, claimed him back into its depths. When the water receded, he was gone.

Too late, I realized he had taken my heart with him.

CHAPTER FORTY

"There's something I need to tell you," I said to my family the next morning.

Over breakfast, I recounted the truth behind my arrangement with Elang. I told them about his plan to overthrow the Dragon King, how we'd sought help from the merfolk, and confronted him at Jinsang Palace. Nomi and Fal listened intently, and Baba asked many questions. Mama, however, only showed interest in the Scroll of Oblivion.

"This is the vision I had last night," I said, unrolling my sketch of Nazayun. "I'm going to copy it onto the Scroll. It should take me about a week if everything goes well."

"If everything goes well," Mama echoed, finally speaking. All this time, she'd been quiet, not interrupting even once with a question. In fact, she'd started trimming snap peas in the middle of my story. The sharp snips of her scissors made me nervous.

"The Dragon King doesn't look like he's about to be defeated," she said of the vision I'd painted. "He looks like me when I'm about to win a game of tiles. Are you sure you've captured the right moment?" She didn't wait for me to answer.

"And the waters, they're so dark. Are you going back to Ai'long?"

"No." Baba traced the lines of the sea to a pier. "See there, that quay by the harbor, those fishing boats behind the fog. This is Gangsun."

"So Nazayun will bring the darker waters here?" Falina asked.

"I don't know," I admitted.

"Seems like there's still much you haven't planned," said Mama, setting aside the snap peas. "Truyan, dear, is the Scroll of Oblivion really inside that bracelet of yours? That must be magic, can I see?"

I was far too gullible when it came to my mother. I raised my wrist. "The Scroll's in the center black threa—"

Mama grabbed me, clipping at the red string with her scissors.

"Ma!" I jerked away before she could cut it. "What are you doing?"

"Saving your life," she snapped. "I knew this was all too good to be true! Give me the bracelet, Truyan. I'm ending your contract."

"You can't." I pulled down my sleeve. Thank goodness for the strength of merfolk silk. "Going up against Nazayun is a choice I've made on my own."

"As your mother, I forbid it. Humans don't take revenge against gods, it never ends well for us. Oh, don't make that face at me. Your husband is half dragon, he can take care of himself. If he dies, we'll build an altar in his honor." Mama's voice fell to a grave whisper, and her shoulders folded in. "But if *you* die . . ." She swallowed. "After all we endured with your father, I *will* not go through that again. I *cannot*."

I let go of my balled fists, and my shoulders fell.

"You wouldn't have left Baba in Ai'long," I reasoned. "You would have seized the first chance to save him, no matter the danger."

"Your father is our family," said Mama.

"And Elang is mine."

She stared at me, drawing a sharp breath. "Nine Hells, Truyan. I told you to seduce the dragon. I didn't tell you to fall in love with him."

"It's too late for that," I replied quietly.

Baba turned to Mama. "A son-in-law *is* family," he reminded her. "Yesterday you said you liked the man."

"Half man," said Mama peevishly. "And I changed my mind. Why should Tru risk her life for him? It's entirely possible that he's bespelled her with a potion—"

"Mama." I gave her a firm shake of my head.

"It's inauspicious," said Mama, who had to have the last word.

Baba took her hands. "Need I tell you a little tale, about two strangers who pretended to be married?"

"I don't think the children need to hear this."

"It was during a storm just like this, and they were next to one another, trying to board the last ship out of Jappor to Port Lumsan—in search of rumored gold along the coast. There was but one cabin left, and they were ready to throw punches at each other over it, until they came up with a better idea."

Nomi's eyes widened. "Is that how the two of you met?"

"And fell in love," confirmed Baba.

"It was different back then," Mama mumbled. "Besides,

your father was an ordinary sailor. There was no dragon king set on obliterating him from this earth."

"That dragon king took Baba from us for five years," I said through my teeth. "And we're lucky compared to most. It's only because of Elang that I found him."

I could see my mother wavering, and I clasped my hands around hers. "I've got to try. I won't—I can't lose Elang."

"I can't lose *you*."

"You won't," I promised.

Mama held my chin, her eyes scanning my face as though she were reading me. Then she let out a sigh. "I knew the typhoon was an omen. Such weather at this time of year! It's because of you, isn't it, Tru? Stirring up trouble in Ai'long."

Without waiting for an answer, she rose. "Nomi, Falina, gather the merfolk. We have work to do."

"Where are you going?" I asked.

"You're not underwater anymore, you can't just swim around, painting. You'll need ladders, and a frame to hold the Scroll in place."

I couldn't help smiling. This was the Mama I'd missed. She was back, just like Baba.

"I'll have your father design one for you," she was saying, "and Tangyor will start with the construction."

Tangyor? I recognized the name of the man who'd once pushed me out a window, but didn't expect to hear it here. Then again, any associate of Gaari's was also an associate of Elang's. I laughed to myself. First chance I got, I'd seek him out for a reunion.

By mid-morning, everyone in the manor was involved. Caisan and his turtles discussed the vision I'd painted, deliberating over every daub and mark as they devised a battle plan. The merfolk scouted the mansion for the longest wall, then cleared it as a space for me to paint. Mama gave strict orders that I wasn't to be disturbed.

And so my work began.

I gained a newfound appreciation for my lessons with Shani. In the hours it'd taken to paint my premonition of the Dragon King, I had captured him perfectly: his scales and horns and whiskers and the breadth of his movement. But on a canvas such as the Scroll of Oblivion, which had expanded to accommodate the Dragon King's physical size, my work would require far more detail. Detail, like the jagged curves of his nails, the tiered layering of his scales, the inflections of silver in his horns—which would separate a portrait from a true rendering indistinguishable from life itself.

I only hoped a week would be enough.

Late one night, Nomi came to find me while I was painting. She relit the candles that had blown out and observed the shadowy dragon taking shape upon the Scroll. There was no book under her arm, so I knew something was on her mind. Something serious.

"Tru," she started, "have you kissed Elang?"

I startled, feeling a flush come over my cheeks. Kissing Elang was not something I wanted to discuss with my youngest sister. "Once or twice," I admitted. "Why?"

Nomi frowned. "I suppose it wouldn't be that simple."

"What?"

"Let's say you're able to paint the Dragon King into Oblivion. That still leaves you with Elang's curse. I've gone through all the books in the library, but I can't find anything on how to break it."

"I don't think the Dragon King is the sort to leave hints."

"But Elang is," insisted Nomi.

I squeezed the water out of my brush, then set it down. Truth be told, his curse preoccupied my thoughts more than anything else. It was the reason I had trouble sleeping.

"He wanted me to despise him from the start," I said slowly, voicing the few hints that I'd gathered. "I think that's the real reason he came to me in disguise. As Gaari, he could act more like himself, yet it'd be safe because I'd only ever view him as a friend."

"Why wouldn't it be safe for you to like him?"

"I don't know," I said with a shiver. "It must have to do with the curse."

My sister bit down on her lip, hating that, for all her brilliance and learning, she, too, had no idea how to save Elang. But Nomi was practical, if nothing else.

She took off her shawl and draped it over my shoulders. "It's cold, and too dark in here for you to paint," she said softly. "I'll bring more candles."

A few hours later, I had a visitor.

I felt the demon's icy presence right away, crawling through the window and slipping into my workroom. I thought about calling for Caisan, but I pretended to continue painting. Shani had taken the form of a small sparrow. I waited until she fluttered behind my back, one claw reaching for the wooden handle of my Scroll, before I grabbed her.

I held her by the wings over my candle. "What are you doing here?"

Shani blew out the flame, looking unimpressed. "Is that how you greet a friend?"

"You're no friend," I hissed. I pointed my brush to the Scroll. "Try anything and I'll paint *you* into Oblivion. I know your watery hide well enough to do it in three strokes."

Shani scoffed, but the twitch of her beak suggested that she believed me. "If the Dragon King wanted to abduct you, he wouldn't need the likes of me. It'd be as easy as drowning you in your sleep."

"Lies. He sent you because you're the only one of his minions who can enter this manor. That changes tonight." My voice rang with authority. "Now, what do you want?"

The demon melted into water, slipping out of my grip. She shifted into her phoenix form in midair, coming to perch on one of my paint pots. "His Eternal Majesty sends his regards. He demands that you return the Scroll of Oblivion."

"No."

"In exchange, he will—"

"What?" I snapped. "He won't murder my family? I've heard all this before; my answer is no."

"Don't interrupt," Shani trilled. "It's rude." The demon cleared her throat. "In exchange, the Great and Eternal One shall lift the curse that afflicts Lord Elangui of the Westerly Seas and return his pearl to him."

Thunder cracked the sky, but the clamor of my pounding heart drowned it out. "He can do that?"

"Gods do as they like." Shani folded her wings. "There are terms, naturally. You and Elang must take the Oath of Ai'long and swear your allegiance to the Dragon King."

"Then what? All will be forgotten, and he'll give up trying

to kill Elang?" I pounded my desk in frustration. "Really, Shani? You of all demons believe that?"

She shot me a warning look. "Never has the Eternal One extended such magnanimity. I would advise you to gratefully accept."

"Never has the Eternal One extended such magnanimity," I repeated, "because never has he been so close to losing. He's afraid."

Shani's feathers froze into icicles, chilling the air. "If you do not accept, the Dragon King will smite you with his wrath. You will die, as will everyone and everything you love."

"I'll die? If I recall, Nazayun swore not to kill me."

"There won't be a curse to break if Elang is dead," said Shani flatly. "His promise will be nullified."

Just like that, the fire went out of me, leaving me cold, beaten.

Shani sneered. "If you want to save him, you will accept."

I searched her red eyes, certain I'd find some sign of my friend within. *And what about you?* I thought. *Can I save you?*

There was a part of me that still hoped, that still *believed* she would stay true to us in the end.

"You can tell the Great and Eternal One that I refuse his most generous offer."

Shani sniffed. "Stupid krill. Very well, then, I'll see you at the Resonant Tide." She spread her wings. "You'll have until sundown to save Elang's heart—and yours."

Petty as ever, she iced the paints in my pots before she evaporated into the air.

I picked up my frozen paints, placing them near the brazier to thaw.

"*You'll have until sundown to save Elang's heart,*" I repeated slowly, "*. . . and yours.*"

It was a taunt, obviously. But what did *my* heart have to do with it?

Suddenly, realization hit—so hard I nearly toppled off my chair. A shiver raced down my spine.

I knew how to break his curse.

CHAPTER FORTY-ONE

It was the last day of the dragon year. The rain had finally stopped, and lanterns bobbed from the roofs all across Gangsun. Branches laden with plum blossoms arced over the streets, and pots of waterbells dotted every garden, the fresh scent of spring rising from the frost. All auspicious signs for the new year to come, but if you looked closely at the harbor, the water had turned a dark and foreboding gray.

Back at the manor, my family surrounded me. No one dared make a sound as I bent forward to make my final brushstroke—the mysterious red light gleaming in Nazayun's eye.

Holding my breath, I swept my brush upward with a small flick of the wrist. *There.*

"It's finished," I said, hardly able to believe it.

I stepped back.

In my painting, King Nazayun loomed tall, his claws extended and lightning flashing from his horns and whiskers. His tail lashed out behind him, light and shadows dancing off each scale of his body. He looked so real that part of me expected him to leap off the Scroll, to whisk me away into the sea. But he remained unmoving on the parchment, his merciless smirk making me shudder.

After giving the Scroll a moment to dry, I gave its black handle a tap. It never ceased to amaze me how the reams of paper rolled themselves, whooshing back into the threads around my wrist and leaving no trace of the priceless relic Elang had entrusted to me.

Once the Scroll was back in its place, though, that wonder was gone. My hands trembled. Not because I'd been painting for days and barely sleeping. I was on edge. Morning had passed, and the day was aging fast. Too soon I would face the Dragon King. There was no guarantee that I'd come back alive.

The last thing I did was wash the paint from my hands and tuck a tiny vial of sangi into my shoe—a dose good for a few minutes. I hoped I wouldn't need it.

"Can't we come with you?" Falina asked as I mounted the horse Tangyor had prepared. "We can help."

"Stay in the manor," I told my sisters. "You'll be safe here."

"But—"

"I need to go alone," I said, cutting off their protests. After hours of strategizing with Caisan, we had agreed this was the best course. There was no guarantee of success, but we could at least minimize the risk of failure.

"Take this," said Nomi, passing me what looked like a thin firecracker. Seeing my skepticism, she added, "It's small but mighty. Trust me. You don't even need a flame, just pull the string." She winked. "Just be careful not to get too close."

"Thank you." I pocketed it, then I kissed Nomi and Falina on their cheeks and nodded to Mama and Baba. "I'll see you tonight."

I urged my horse into motion. The sun was high, yet below the hills, the harbor was black as ink. Nazayun couldn't be far.

I was almost at the bottom of the hill when the birds stopped chirping and the wind stopped teasing the loose pebbles across the road. My horse skittered, his forelegs bracing with apprehension.

"Steady," I murmured. I tightened the reins, compelling him to keep going. "Steady."

Tangyor had promised that my horse was the manor's most intrepid. He could ride through storm and blaze, unafraid of tigers and snakes and sword-wielding assassins.

But most valuable of all, he had a unique ability to sense—

"Demon," I cried, a beat before Shani flew out of the trees, her talons arcing forward like scythes. With a rattling snort, my horse reared.

I jumped off his back. "Get," I shouted, sending my horse back up Oyang Street.

There was no running from Shani. From behind, she tackled me to the ground and tore Elang's cloak off my neck.

"Where is the Scroll?" she bellowed, finding only the string of fate around my wrist.

Inside I was trembling, but I gave the demon my most brazen smile.

"You really want to die, don't you?" Shani snarled. "As you wish."

Down came her talons, clawing at my head. As she looped her tail around my waist, the last thing I saw were red eyes burning away the edges of the world.

CHAPTER FORTY-TWO

It was just before sundown when I awoke.

I'd lost the afternoon. Wind stung my eyes, and my head throbbed where Shani had struck it. But most disorienting of all was that every direction I looked, there was the sea. The blackened sea, gilded by one lone band of rusty sunlight.

Shani had dropped me on a ship. It wasn't one of the shrimping boats or fishing dinghies that lined Gangsun's ports—but a gleaming crystal ship. The dread creeping up my stomach calcified into horror as I recognized the sapphire-blue light emanating from every plank, the mast carved into the body of a dragon. There was no captain, no crew, only—

I whirled, finding King Nazayun at the prow.

He'd come as a man, white of beard and hair but neither old nor young, in plain blue robes that trailed in a silken river behind him. Were he a passerby in the city, he would have commanded little attention. But I could feel how the wind choked in his presence, how the moisture in the air stood still.

"It has been many long years since I've walked the mortal realm," Nazayun mused, batting himself with a fan. "Your buildings are taller, and your roads longer. Yet the stench remains."

I could feel the blood draining from my face. I couldn't send him into Oblivion like this. This was not the dragon form I'd painted onto the Scroll.

"Will you not bow before the god of dragons?"

My knees weakened against my will. I fell to the ground, frost crackling under my knuckles as I bent.

"That's better." A breeze lifted Nazayun's hair from his face, exposing his missing eye. In its place was a cluster of blue-green dragon scales, with a silvery bead lodged in the center.

"You are more cunning than I gave you credit for, Lady Saigas," he said. "Your little trick caught me by surprise. But that's all it was, a trick."

"Bold words," I replied. "If you're not afraid, why conceal your true self in the lowly form of a human?"

"Oh, I *am* afraid," Nazayun confessed. "Indeed, it is my fear that guides me. And that is why you'll not win today."

Cold wind bit the nape of my neck. "You can hide as a human all you like, but it'll do you no good. I've seen what is to come."

"Have you?" said the Dragon King. "Your Sight is powerful, but as you've shown, the future it reveals can be rather . . . misleading." He smiled darkly, the tips of his incisors grazing his lower lip. "I have a feeling it's not *my* end you've foreseen—but your own."

Don't let him rattle you, I thought, digging in my pocket for Nomi's firecracker.

But it was gone. Taken. All I had was my tiny vial of sangi, hidden inside my shoe.

I gulped. "Gloating is poor form, Your Majesty."

"So speaks the girl who didn't even bring the Scroll with her." Nazayun's shoulders shook with mirth. "That's what I love about you humans, you're deluded with hope. You haven't even asked how Yonsar fares. Whether my grandson still lives."

It hurt, how hard my chest clenched. "He isn't dead. I would know if he were."

"As we speak, Queen Haidi launches her final assault. Yonsar is fallen. Along with it, your dear Elangui."

"You lie," I whispered.

"It would be a kindness to lie, and I am not kind." Nazayun's face was placid, his pale eye gripping. His pupil carried no trace of the red gleam I'd seen in my vision. "The luck of the dragons is with you, Bride of the Westerly Seas. Now my attention turns to this foul city. Your home."

Lightning forked out from the ship's mast—spinning in fiery pathways across to a faraway shore. The first sparks landed upon the boats dotting the harbor and the piers along the coast. Small fires blossomed like a thousand stars speckled across the dark sky, growing brighter and brighter as their flames spread toward the city.

"Stop!" I yelled. I threw myself at the Dragon King. "STOP—"

He grabbed me, spinning me to face the horizon. The skyline was turning orange, as I'd foreseen. But I had assumed the light came from sundown—not from Gangsun in flames.

No, no. My thoughts floundered with panic. *Had* I misinterpreted the vision?

"Beautiful, isn't it?" Nazayun murmured, reveling in my distress. "The embers ensnared in the billowing smoke, the ravenous fire burning brighter the more she consumes." He inhaled with relish. "*This* is art. What a perfect night to culminate my perfect curse."

I had to stop him, but I had no weapons. No sword, no club or whip. Not even a jar of peppers.

So I did the first thing that came to mind. The first reckless, suicidal thing.

I punched him.

Turds of Tamra, I was aiming for his remaining eye but hit the missing one instead. The dragon scales around it were steel tough, and I withdrew my fist, biting back a cry of pain.

I might as well have punched a mountain. Not a muscle on the Dragon King's face moved; he didn't even blink in surprise. Yet as I cradled my fist, blood humming with dread, his human face shimmered for the briefest instant, revealing the dragon beneath. Then it was gone.

"I admire your viciousness, Bride of the Westerly Seas," he said with a sardonic clap. "Your talents are wasted on a human."

"Turn me into one of your monsters, then. You'll see how vicious I can be."

"In your next life, perhaps." He closed his fan with a snap, lightning brewing in his eye. "This one ends tonight."

I pivoted, my heart cannoning in my ears as I ran for the rails. I clenched the crystal beam, looking down. It'd be madness to jump. The water was dark, impenetrable. It was impossible to confirm any presence, friendly or not, beneath the surface. Yet I felt something. *Someone.*

Nazayun fired, a flare of sizzling white light.

To the Hells with it all. I swigged my sangi and threw myself overboard, entrusting my fate to the sea.

CHAPTER FORTY-THREE

Of course there were sharks.

I could barely see them—couldn't even see my own arms flailing against the waves—but I could feel the vibrations they made, tiny currents pulsing against my skin in sharp zings.

Even dosed with sangi, trying to outswim a school of sharks was a fool's errand. Ironically, the darkness helped. I wasn't keen on knowing how many sharks pursued me, or how close they were to gnashing my flesh into bloody ribbons.

As fast as I could, I kicked toward the stripe of sunlight glittering at the surface. The light seeping into the bay was faint, fading, as the sun sank lower.

The sharks circled closer. Light fanned over their mirrored eyes and white mouths, and my stomach churned with fear. They looked very hungry.

"Help!" I cried. "Someone, help!"

In the terror of the ensuing silence, the sharks charged.

Their maws were wide and gaping, coming toward me. I could count three rows of pointed teeth and glimpse the fleshy tunnel of a gullet. Punching would do me no good, but still I curled my fists, ready to fight to the end. Suddenly there came a cold and slippery lash against my ankle.

With a yank, my world went spinning. Next I knew, I landed on a hard tortoise shell.

"You have a harrowing sense of timing, General," I rasped, catching my breath.

"It could not be helped, Lady Saigas," Caisan replied, wrapping his kelp whip back around his spear. "Your Scroll appears to attract all manner of ruffians."

The Scroll of Oblivion was tied in a careful knot around his neck. I took it from him, took one of the small knives strapped to his back too. I wasn't going back to Nazayun without something sharp.

"Now hold on."

He rocketed upward, nearly to the surface, when a sudden quake rattled the seas. The force of it pushed Caisan's head back into his shell. He twisted to protect me from the brunt of the waves.

The sharks took advantage. They came rushing from all sides, intent on murder. Caisan shouted, "Jump, Lady Saigas!"

I let go of his back.

It was as though I'd been pulled into a rip tide. I flew back, caught in the waves dragging me down. The harder I kicked, the faster I sank. Down, down, away from the light.

I thought it was a shark at first, that vibration in the water. But it was warm, and familiar.

A faint yellow glow lit the water, and a dragon's arms locked around my waist, gliding me out of the current. He had claws, curled with pointed tips, but they were tender with me and took care not to pierce my skin. I leaned against his chest and slid my fingers across cool, pebbled skin, making out the shapes of teardrops.

"Elang," I whispered, twisting to face him. "You're alive!"

His yellow eye burned. New shadows traced his cheeks. Whatever battles he'd fought in Yonsar had weathered him, but gods, he looked pleased to see me. With no greeting at all, he swept me into an embrace and kissed me.

His lips took in my own, gentle yet demanding, as if I were air and he hadn't breathed in days. I felt the same. I wrapped my arms around his neck, observing, with a secret thrill, that his eyes became brighter, his scales warmed to my touch. When I leaned my head against his shoulder, I could hear his heart, racing as mine was.

"Foolish, foolish girl," he murmured, his lips still on mine. "I told you not to come back."

"And miss out on the three chests of jewels?" I said. "You fiend, my mother would never have it. Besides"—I inhaled—"I have a curse to break."

Elang drew back, his voice thickening. "Tru, if I don't get a chance to tell you later—"

"Hush." I pressed my finger to his lips. "You can't talk like that. I forbid it."

Though he gave a nod, I could see how his face closed. He was thinking about his curse, and for the first time, I understood why that would trouble him, why the set of his mouth would go suddenly tense.

I brought his chin up level to mine. Playfully, I covered his yellow eye with my hand and held a lock of his white hair up to his chin.

"What are you doing?"

I tilted my head, pretending to study him. "Seeing how much you look like Gaari."

"That old man?" Elang pretended to look offended. "And, do I?"

"White hair," I started, "thick neck, inflated sense of self . . ." I laughed as he made a face. "Not at all," I admitted. "Except for here." I thumbed the scales beneath his gray eye. "They always say a dragon's spirit is in their eyes."

The corners of Elang's mouth played into a smile. Under the glow of his yellow eye, his horns grew long, and a sinuous tail swelled beneath his robes. He held me tight, and we surged upward for the surface.

It was the final hour of the dragon.

CHAPTER FORTY-FOUR

The sea had become a stage for this last act of Nazayun's curse. Thunder pounded. Cords of lightning stung the sky. The tides rolled like drums, and as the new moon rose, the sun knelt before heaven. No time could be riper for a god to fall.

The Dragon King was no longer alone on his gleaming crystal ship. Shani had returned, perched in the rigging with her wings spread wide, feathers crackling.

It was almost an affront, how gracefully Elang landed us on the deck. As if to show his grandfather, *Once more, you have failed to end me.*

Despite it all, Elang bowed in the god's presence. He would not dishonor his grandfather.

I couldn't say the same. Now that our act was done, I could be myself. A piddling con artist from the slums of Gangsun. Rather than bow, I made a point of standing tall and raising my Scroll so Nazayun could see it. "Shall we try one last time, Your Majesty," I proffered, "to kill each other?"

The Dragon King's gaze narrowed. All he said was "Shanizhun."

The demon dove, icy wings cutting the air with a wet

hiss. Just before she hit the deck, she slid into the form of a watery tiger and rebounded into an ambush on Elang.

A sword materialized in Elang's hand. Shani's momentum made him stagger, but he wrestled her, dragon against tiger. Dragon won. She flew back, charged again. He swung, hard. The demon splashed to the deck before the blade struck. She knew how he moved. Knew how he thought. She angled her teeth into his claws. Her fangs were dagger-sharp icicles, the hairs on her head a thousand frozen needles. As she jammed her head against his, blood trickled down Elang's face, catching along the rims of his scales.

I was used to seeing Shani on Elang's shoulder, two unlikely friends, both the last of their kind. She must have been there when he was Gaari. Invisible at his side, making dry quips and unwelcome commentary about his life choices. There was something heartbreaking about seeing these two as enemies. I wondered if Elang felt it too. If that was why he withheld the full power of his strikes, and wrestled her with the flat of his blade instead of its edge.

Or maybe the demon was simply too strong.

Half of the sun remained. Night was falling fast, and every minute we wasted fighting tilted the battle in the Dragon King's favor. Of course Nazayun understood this. He remained at the prow, unmoved by the violent winds and thrashing waves. Smiling as more blood was spilled.

Little by little, I stole toward him, holding on to Caisan's short knife.

The Dragon King looked different than he had just minutes before. Underneath his storm of white hair, the number of scales around his missing eye had visibly increased. The wiry hairs of that side's brow had also grown thicker, curling up at the ends like they did when he was a dragon.

I clenched my knife. Could this be a rip in the cloak of magic that gave him human form? Could it be torn further?

If I needed confirmation that I'd discovered something, it came from Queen Haidi's arrival. From across the deck, she sprang toward me, the spikes of her hair launching over the ship's rail like deadly grappling hooks.

It was inhumanly fast, how Elang knocked Shani to the side, then spun to parry the barbs. They were faster than arrows, tipped with fiery white magic. One shot sniped past his blade, poised to strike him in the chest. I didn't think twice. I released the Scroll of Oblivion.

The barb ricocheted off the parchment, which was still tumbling free of its bindings. Elang sent me an astounded look.

I shrugged. "You told me the Scroll can't be destroyed."

"So I did, Saigas." His mouth split into a grin. "But I don't think anyone's tested it that way before."

I pushed him back to attention. "On your left!"

A new volley of barbs fired our way. I raised the Scroll again, while Elang lunged to engage Shani. With a snarl, she came charging at Elang. She feinted a blow at his face before vaulting high. In midair, she morphed back into a phoenix. Down she swooped, but Elang was no longer her target. Her claws came slashing at *my* throat, the rush of air from her wings scalding my cheeks.

I rocked back on my heels. The Scroll went careening, and I barely hung on, sending it back into my red string—just before Shani crashed into me.

"Tru!" Elang shouted.

I couldn't move. My blood had turned to ice, my thoughts numbed. Was this what it was like to have my soul devoured by a demon?

Your soul would be too disgusting for me to devour, Shani retorted. She wrangled me still. *Now watch. This is how it all ends.*

On the deck, Elang barreled past Haidi's barbs, not even bothering to shield himself.

The merqueen changed tactics. She clubbed at him with her tail, with her tentacle arms and her spiked hair. Her blows were hard and ruthless.

She clipped him in the shoulder, tearing a hole in Elang's black robe. He wore the color often enough, usually as a belt or an inner robe or even as armor paddings. The only other time I'd seen him clad entirely in black was when I'd met him as the Demon Prince. *So you wouldn't see the blood,* he'd told me.

Oh gods.

Now I saw clearly. He fought differently than he had against Shani. He was favoring one side, blocking and dodging more than hitting. Haidi was ferocious, yes, and no mortal would stand a chance against her. But Elang was half dragon, and he had a dragon's strength. That he didn't use it against her meant he couldn't . . . because . . .

Haidi flew at him with her tail raised. A feint. Her hair came swinging instead, slamming down from above. Her spikes hooked into his chest precisely where, mere days ago, I'd wrenched her harpoon out with my bare hands. It ripped through his flesh with a whipping sound I knew I'd never forget.

I was the one who crumbled. *ELANG,* I tried to yell, but Shani tightened her grip around my throat.

Elang crushed his jaws and fell on one knee, growling against the pain.

"Well done, My Queen. Well done." Nazayun clapped, his pleasure amplified by thunder. "Now kill him."

"No!" This time my voice boiled out of my throat. I twisted free of the demon, claiming my body as my own. Caisan's knife was still in my hand. I threw.

The blade went soaring. High and true, it arced squarely for the place where the Dragon King's empty eye socket had once been. I'd never know whether it was fated to hit him, though, for Shani snagged the knife out of midair.

Faster than I could get to my feet, she pinned me back down. She trapped my arms and dug her talons into the small of my back.

"Let me go, Elang—"

"Shut up," she barked. She dangled Nomi's firecracker over my head, and I stopped, my breath cut short by the acrid fumes of sulfur. "It's time to finish this."

"Don't," I cried. "Shani, listen to me. You could have killed me many times over by now, but you didn't. You left the sangi for me. You held back fighting E—"

"I said shut up." Shani struck the back of my head, sending me face-first into the ground.

I bit my tongue as I fell, and the metallic tang of blood filled my mouth. Still I didn't give up. I turned to our thoughts. *If you have any honor left in you at all, help Elang. Please.*

Against my ear, the demon pulled the firecracker string. The explosive sizzled. *My vow was never to help Elang'anmi.*

Taking the cracker with her, she evaporated into a cloud of mist. *It was to kill the Dragon King.*

Just as Haidi was about to deliver her final blow, Nomi's

firecracker fell from the sky. My sister was right, it was no ordinary New Year's popper. *Boom!* In a white and blazing blast, the merqueen was thrown from the deck, shreds of red paper fluttering past her.

Amid the ensuing smoke and disarray, Shani stole into Nazayun's missing eye socket and vanished with a snap.

The change in him was immediate. A violent shudder rolled over his body, as though he had swallowed the wind itself. He tore at his face, trying to pluck the demon out, but it was too late.

As if he were being painted by a divine brush, sapphire-blue scales plated his human flesh, and his white beard billowed into a cloudy mane about his head. Silvery horns stabbed out above his eyes, and his neck stretched long and thick until it became part of his body, serpentine and winding.

I stumbled toward Elang. Nazayun's head was already looming by the mast, his body uncurling like a snake's. It wouldn't be long before the ship sank under his weight. We had to get out of here.

"Get on my back," Elang said.

Together we sprang, diving underwater a moment before Nazayun's head came smashing against the deck, his horns rending the ship in half. Crystal shards caught the gleam of the sun as the great ship sank.

From a safe distance, Elang and I broke the surface. The Dragon King was once more in the sea, his fingernails curled into talons, his whiskers piercing out of his cheeks. His tail grew out from under the hem of his silk robes; the threads hardened into ridges, and its lustrous sheen became the glow of a celestial hide.

When he opened his remaining eye, it was red.

Like Shani's.

The demon had done it. Nazayun was returned to his dragon form, and the sky, the sea, the storm—everything was just as I had painted. The portrait of a god's fall.

It was time to send him into Oblivion. I started to let go of Elang's horns, but he caught my hand. In a tone that would brook no argument, he said, "I'll take you."

We leapt into the air, swooping over the mountainous waves that rose from the sea.

We had to be swift. Nazayun was stronger as a dragon. Already his powers were multiplying, and the color of his eye flickered unsteadily, red to blue, blue to red. Shani was struggling.

Blue again. With a blink, Caisan and the merfolk were turned to stone.

I let out a furious cry.

Just bear it a little longer, Shani said weakly, her thoughts straining to make contact with mine. *He's almost there.*

Almost where? Then I remembered: *Dragons are supposed to be creatures of wisdom and protection, not rampant destruction. That goes against their nature; makes them lose control.*

Red, barely.

Blue.

Bluer.

Then finally—

Elang and I were gaining ground, only a leap away, when I saw the change. Nazayun's eye, whiter than the moon! His whiskers flashed, his hair began to hiss, and in a tumultuous burst, lightning crackled up his spine, sparks spitting from his scales.

His body came ablaze, turning the sea silver. There was no way I could get near him. I couldn't even look at him without my eyes watering.

Crafty tyrant, I thought. So much for this being his moment of weakness. If I so much as touched him, I would die.

Then again, that was what he wanted, wasn't it? For me to die. Nazayun had been so focused on my being the Painter, had he forgotten I was also destined to break Elang's curse? My heart pounding, I glanced at the horizon. Only a quarter of the sun remained; there were minutes left until dusk.

"When an immortal breaks their promise"—I nudged Elang—"what did you say they suffer?"

"Divine consequence," he replied. "Why?"

A smile took over my face. "I'm going to jump."

"Wait," said Elang. I was worried he'd protest, but from his sleeve, he gave me a slender paintbrush. "I'll bring you closer."

He rode the waves to the highest crest, bringing me level with the Dragon King's brow. The wind was fierce, and Shani's red glow grew dimmer with every second.

"Go now, my love," Elang said before kissing me on the cheek. "And—may you have the luck of the dragons."

I fell for the sea, the wind hollering in my ears. As loud as I could, I let out a cry: "NAZAYUN!"

Just as I'd predicted, just as I'd *hoped,* Nazayun turned.

Through the blur of the sea's icy spray, I saw him rise before me, taunting me with how close I'd come. His very presence was enough to singe my hair, scald my bare skin, and strangle my breath. But I was undaunted.

Gripping my paintbrush, I summoned the Scroll of Oblivion from around my wrist. With a hiss, the great dragon I'd painted unraveled across the sky and beat against the wind.

It was like putting the Dragon King to a mirror. What I had painted was equal to him in every measure, and as I fell onto the Scroll, landing between a pleat of blue-painted scales, it was as though King Nazayun himself had caught me.

"Impressive, isn't it?" I shouted. "It looks just like you."

I raised my brush, as if to make one last stroke.

A killing blast brewed in the real Nazayun's eye. I felt its heat before it came hurtling at my heart, lashing out in a whip of fiery steel. I had the Scroll, I could have raised it to save myself. But that wasn't my plan.

Through Elang's curse, Nazayun had sworn not to kill me. Breaking that oath would bring divine consequence upon him, but nothing had been said about *protecting* me. It was a gamble, putting myself directly in the line of certain death.

Thunderbolts of Saino, I prayed, *grant me courage*. This was my only chance to get close enough to Nazayun to effect the Touch of Entrapment. I had to take it.

The light was dazzling. It turned my world white, so bright I had to shield my eyes. I waited for the blast to strike, for all of me to explode into a firework of flashing embers.

That end never came.

The blast entered my brush with a shudder. Its hairs came aglow, charged by the lightning of Nazayun's wrath.

The Dragon King let out a roar of disbelief. His eye flickered red one last time, and in a cloud of smoke, the fire blazing from his scales went out. With one divine sweep, the sea turned dark once more.

"An immortal is bound to their promises," I strained through my teeth, "and you have broken yours not to kill me. Truyan Saigas, the Heavenly Match."

I leapt onto his head, wrapping my long sleeves around one of his horns. My whole body was shaking, I couldn't tell whether from the cold of the sea or from the gravity of the fate I was about to deliver. It didn't matter. Pushing back my sleeve, I leaned down to whisper in his ear, "Rest well, Your Majesty, in Oblivion."

Then, with one bare and unflinching hand, I pressed my fingers upon his brow.

From the Scroll came a great wind, surrounding the Dragon King. It howled, or perhaps that was the sound of Nazayun himself, I couldn't tell. The world was swaying, every second thundering forward, the past and future colliding as a violent tremor came over me.

I slid down his horn onto his brow, clutching his mane. He was writhing, his claws thrashing against the sky and sea. Little good it did him. Stroke by stroke, my portrait of him was fading from the Scroll, and he, too, began to vanish. A whirlpool formed at Nazayun's belly, swirling with ink as it wrenched him from this world—into Oblivion.

If I didn't get out of here, it would consume me too.

"Jump, Tru!" Elang cried over the clash of sea and wind. "Jump, I'll catch you."

I lurched toward him—until I saw Shani. The demon clung to the Dragon King by her stingray fins, hanging just under his eye like a teardrop.

I couldn't leave her. "Shani," I shouted. "Take my hand."

She was too weak. *You fool*, she whispered. *Save yourself.*

Not a chance. I climbed down Nazayun's temple, using the ridges in his scales as holds. Wind hammered at me from every direction, threatening to knock me into Oblivion too.

I stretched my arm, scrabbling for the end of Shani's tail. One good yank, and the demon flew up into my grasp, her wings nearly throwing me off balance. But I had her.

Slinging her over my shoulder, I spun toward Elang. He'd followed as closely as he could, but he still couldn't reach us through the battering winds.

Fortune finds those who leap, I thought as I took the biggest jump of my life. Straight into his arms.

Against the hollering wind, the Dragon King let out one last cry. He was fading fast, drowning in the vast tides of Oblivion. The last thing I saw was the pale light of his eye going dark, before the Scroll snapped to a final close.

And the God of the Seas, and ruler of the dragons, was no more.

CHAPTER FORTY-FIVE

The winds receded, and the sky cleared. A gentle rain loosened from the clouds, washing out the flames of Gangsun.

Darkness ebbed away from the seas, and not far away, Caisan and the merfolk gasped to life, no longer stone. Queen Haidi, too, was changing. She staggered onto a rock, where, under the crimson glaze of dusk, her monstrous form melted away and she became a mermaid once more.

One by one, the Dragon King's enchantments were coming undone.

All but Elang's.

He was weaker than he'd let on. The light of his yellow eye was dim, and his tail had reverted to two human legs. It was his dragon side that healed faster, but he seemed unable to channel that strength to help the other.

He landed us on a fishing boat, a lone vessel plying its way through the rough currents. As we fell in a pile of tangled nets, a voice I'd recognize anywhere shouted:

"Truyan!"

I squinted. *Mama?*

Sure enough, it was Mama at the rudder navigating, Baba

at her side holding a lantern. My sisters were there too, tending the wounds of merfolk who'd fought beside us.

Staggering to my feet, I helped Elang stand. His hand was cold, his pulse throbbing in his neck. Halfway up, he stopped. The color drained suddenly from his face, and his mouth rounded into the shape of my name, *Tru*—

I caught him in my arms just before he collapsed.

My family rushed to my side, helping me lay him on his back.

Nomi handed me Elang's cloak. Her face was long. "Is he . . . dying?"

"Nomi," said Mama, shaking her head. My mother, a busybody by nature, somehow understood better than anyone that Elang and I needed to be alone. She shooed my sisters to the other side of the boat, then set a lantern at my side. Wordlessly, she touched my cheek, then she left too.

I knelt beside Elang. He was breathing hard, but as I draped the cloak over him, a faint grin lifted the corners of his lips. "I think your mother likes me."

"Only because you're rich."

"Not because of my good looks?" When he saw that I wasn't smiling, the humor fled his face. He looked down at our hands. "It pleases me to see your family together again, Tru. Should they ever need anything, what is mine is yours. I leave the manor to you, and—"

"Stop it," I interrupted. "I don't want your manor, I don't care about your three chests of jewels. Tell me what I need to do—to give you my heart."

His eyes flew up to me.

"Don't you look at me like that," I said. "You told me once that I knew you better than anyone. Of course I figured out how to break your curse."

"Tru." The word was short, but Elang held it long on his lips. "You have a family that loves you, a father who has only just been returned to you."

"You have a kingdom," I countered. "An entire realm that relies on you and needs you. I'll explain it to Mama and Baba and my sisters. They'll—"

"Understand?" Elang let out a throaty laugh.

I gritted my teeth. Only Elang, while mortally wounded, could find a way to vex me like this. "Stop being dramatic. It's my choice."

"It's a poor choice. If it's Yonsar that concerns you, General Caisan will safeguard it when I'm gone. The Dragon King's heir will honor this—"

I clamped my hand over his mouth. "You talk too much. Now hush." My tone was fierce. "I give you my heart, Elang. I end your curse by giving you my heart."

It was magic, what those words unlocked. They thundered inside me, releasing a fierce heat that I had never felt before. Light poured forth from my chest, spinning into the shape of a glittering white pearl. The same that I'd seen in my dream.

I cupped my hands, bringing the pearl into my palms. Its light was connected to my heart by one bright thread, not unlike the one I wore around my wrist. All I had to do was sever that thread, and Elang would live.

"Stop." Elang caught my hand. "Don't you dare. I don't want it."

"Damn it, Elang. Don't fight me. It's your pearl."

"Not at this cost. It's not a fight, Saigas. It's a choice, and I made mine long ago. You cannot change it."

Everything was clear. Why Elang had never wanted to

break his curse, why he'd gotten incensed every time I tried. Why he'd kept me at a distance and refused to show he cared.

From the beginning, he'd been trying to protect me. From the beginning, he'd known where Nazayun had hidden his pearl: inside the heart of his true love. *My* heart.

Only one of us could live. That was the Dragon King's curse. And Elang had decided that would be me.

The way my words were magic, so, too, were his. The pearl spun out of my hands, unraveling into an interminable strand of light that came rushing back into my chest, gathering there in a glittering pool.

"Stubborn dragon," I whispered. I reached into my sleeve for my brush. "If you won't take my heart, then I will make you a new one."

"Tru, what are you—"

I silenced him by unbuttoning his collar, pushing aside the layers of his robes until I found the bare skin of his chest. I pressed my hand to where his pulse beat. The closer I leaned, the stronger it beat. But it was faint. Fainter than ever before.

My fingertips tingled. "Here," I whispered, "is where your new heart will go."

I bent to press a kiss on his skin, and Elang's eyes went wide.

"Stop," he whispered, clasping a halting hand over mine. "Don't you think I've tried? You cannot change this."

"I'm not giving up on you," I said, my chin lifting from his chest. "Now, hold still."

I dipped my brush into the pearlescent light. Miraculously it clung to my brush, like the glitter of morning dew. It was my heart, after all, and every color of every memory was available to me.

I held Elang still, my brush poised. Then I rolled back my eyes and started to paint.

It was just a story Baba used to tell, a game he made up for my sisters and me to play, of a magic paintbrush. With it, anything the artist drew would come to life.

The best games have no winners or losers, he'd said.

Obviously, Nazayun had disagreed. The curse had been a game to him, one Elang and I couldn't win without losing each other. But we simply had to find a different way of playing.

I moved my brush in a gentle circle across Elang's skin, over the corrugated ridges of his scales and across his softer human flesh. The light from my heart became my ink; its brilliance made my eyes water, and its heat seared my fingertips.

With his hand over mine, I outlined a dragon's pearl on his chest. It was bright and beaming, silvery like the moon rising above us.

Just let him live, I thought. *Let us be together.*

A thousand possibilities flashed before me, glimpses of different futures that could come to pass, but I only needed one. Inside Elang's pearl, I painted a girl and a boy holding a green lantern. Snow dusted their heads, and a constellation of lights floated behind them. I painted flowers in the girl's hair and round brass spectacles on the boy's nose, but their faces were blank, unfinished.

Every detail mattered, so I doubled my speed, the tiny muscles in my fingers burning as my brush swooped in every direction, taking no rest between strokes. In a rush of light and color, I painted my face upon the girl, Elang's upon the boy. But before I could finish our eyes, the last of the sun vanished below the horizon—and the light in my heart went out.

No! I panicked. The pearl I'd painted on Elang's chest began to disappear, and I traced it desperately, as if it were an invisible ember I could spark back to life.

Then it, too, was gone.

Elang and I were left cradling each other in the corner of our boat. The tingle in my fingers fled, and my hand lay flat against his heart. His heart, which grew weaker with each beat.

He thumbed the tears from my cheeks. "Don't cry," he said. "Did you know, they say that when a dragon dies, he gets to choose his next life. Maybe we can get noodles together soon enough."

I choked back a sob, wishing I could go back in time to our old life in Gangsun, when we were just Gaari and Tru. "Every time you lie, you find a way to bring up noodles," I whispered. "I know your tells, *young* man."

Elang laughed, a soft, low laugh that I felt vibrate across his body. "Well, it was worth a try." He gave a rueful smile. "Would you really have been a whale with me, Saigas?"

He was trying to divert me, and I knew I shouldn't let him. Yet I couldn't help it. "Even a cockroach."

"A cockroach? Now who's the liar?"

"I would do it."

"I can see it." He half closed his eyes. "Skittering about with your blue antennae. The only adorable cockroach I'd know."

"Elang . . ."

"Or butterflies," he said, his voice growing faint. "We made a good team, you and I. We'd have flown well together."

Tears brimmed in my eyes. "Stop it."

He caressed his fingers through my hair. "I wish we'd had

a chance together," he said softly. "Friends from the start, with no secrets or lies hanging between us. I wish that we might have fallen in love the ordinary way, holding hands and stealing kisses under the trees." A smile touched his face, boyish and simple. "Watching the seasons change, and growing old together . . . in this life, in every life."

His smile turned sad. "Do you know how deeply you've grown on me? From the day I met you, I knew I'd never be free of you." His fingertips were growing cold. They slid from my cheek as he whispered, "I wish I could've shown you . . . I love you."

It was too sudden, how his warmth fled.

"Wait," I choked. A sob racked my throat. "Wait!"

It was like clinging to ice. His touch melted between my fingers, and his skin shimmered like rain. Before my eyes, he became the water itself, the caress of his lips but a brush of mist. Then nothing.

All that was left was his red string.

It sat on my lap, as forlorn and slender as a slip of twine. Before I could pick it up, a gust of wind swooped in and lifted it high. I shot to my feet and ran, reaching. The string danced between my fingers, always a beat ahead. But Saino help me, I would follow it to the bottom of the sea if I had to.

I stretched over the rails, closing my hand as I grasped one frayed end.

"Tru," cried Falina and Nomi, rushing to my side before I fell.

I was crying, and I wrapped Elang's string around my wrist before I crumpled into my sisters' arms. I'd seen the future so vividly; I was so sure I could save him. But I had lost.

I had lost.

CHAPTER FORTY-SIX

I didn't remember the journey home. Didn't remember getting in a carriage and falling asleep in Mama's arms, didn't remember who carried me up to my room or how Baba's jacket ended up over my shoulders. What I did remember was the fireworks at midnight. They startled me awake, shooting up to the sky in a burst of boisterous joy. There, before the heavens, they bloomed like fire flowers, in dazzling scarlets and golds to welcome the New Year. Their smoke clouded the sky, and I couldn't see the stars.

Go back to sleep, murmured a voice in my head.

I tried to sit up. "Shani?"

It was the gentlest I'd ever seen her, the way she stroked my hair as she floated over my bed, her ruby eyes blinking in the shadows.

Sleep, she said again. *We'll speak tomorrow.*

She swept her feathers over my face, and her watery softness was an unexpected balm to my grief. My eyelids grew heavy. The last thing I saw was the moon, shining high like a dragon's pearl.

In the morning, there came a knock at my door. "Go away," I mumbled, but my throat was swollen from crying and I had no voice. My visitor entered.

Mailoh had come with a tray. "Don't be alarmed, it's only tea, not sangi."

I sat up slowly on my bed, rasping, "I'm . . . I'm not—"

"Lord Elang gave very clear instructions," the turtle interrupted. "If you don't drink it, I'm to wait until you finish the cup."

I started to protest, but she wasn't done.

"He left something for you," Mailoh said.

She drew a long envelope from the pouch over her shoulder and placed it on the tray before she left.

Inside was the drawing I'd sketched before Baba's last voyage. I traced the clumsy lines I'd made to illustrate my three sisters, Mama holding hands with Baba in front of his ship.

It was the very drawing Elang had promised to return when our contract was completed. I set it on my lap, remembering how much I'd loathed him then—for forcing me to marry him, for withholding information about Baba.

He had promised that our marriage would be dissolved once I finished painting the Dragon King. Never did I think to ask how.

We'll go our separate ways, he'd said. *You'll never see me again.*

I'd thought that it'd be as easy as cutting the red string around our wrists—I'd never thought that Elang would die.

But that had always been his plan. From the beginning, he'd known.

The tears welled again.

"Look at you, eyes and face all bloodshot and puffy," said Shani, who appeared in a swirl of mist.

She crawled out onto my arm. Her movements were slow, as if she hadn't recovered from her fight against Nazayun. She settled on the nook of my elbow, letting her wings fall on either side of my arm.

"Shani," I said hoarsely, "everything you did. Was it all arranged—"

"I didn't come to chat," she said crisply. "I'm here to give you something."

What, I meant to ask, but it hurt too much to speak.

"Memories. Some, I stole from you. Some, I stole from him." Shani sniffed. "I've kept them all these years." She sent me a pointed look. "They're good ones, some might even make you smile."

"I can't smile right now."

"We'll see." With that, Shani touched my forehead.

The water demon landed on the roof of the black palanquin with a thump.

She was new to land—unaccustomed to flying. Only yesterday she'd discarded her fins for wings. The new form wasn't all bad: a phoenix with crystalline wings and a long gossamer tail. Her every feather contained the energy of a cascading waterfall, and her red eyes were brighter than rubies. A pity no one could see her.

"There she is," she said to the young half dragon inside the carriage. She extended a wing toward a girl traversing the market street. "The Painter, who also happens to be your Heavenly Match."

Elang held his breath and pinched the curtains to the side, glancing out the window. The stench of Gangsun assaulted his nostrils. There were few things he'd appreciated about living in Ai'long; not having to be around humans was one of them.

He looked to where Shani pointed, finding a young girl self-consciously holding a straw hat over her head. From his investigations, he knew her to be Truyan Saigas.

She was tall and reedy, with dull eyes and a round mole by her mouth. She looked unexceptional in every way.

"She's a mercenary," he said, closing the curtain. "Her intent is to make money, not cultivate her art."

"What is your point?"

His expression hardened. "She won't do."

"The fates are already against you. Nazayun has her father, and she *has the Sight.*"

"I'll deal with her." Elang's tone was cold. "There are other Painters."

"You think it'll be that easy to kill her?"

"She's been doomed ever since Grandfather hid my pearl in her heart."

"That's not what I meant," said the demon. Her smirk grew when Elang raised an eyebrow. "Go ahead, then, and try. I'll be watching."

He decided on poison. It wasn't easy preparing one that'd kill instantly and with minimal pain—but the girl was innocent. At the very least, he owed her the extra effort.

A few weeks later, he was ready. He put on a mask, donned the robes of a fourth-rank magistrate, and set out into the heart of Gangsun.

"Your Heavenly Match is on Dattu Street," reported Shani, sitting invisibly on his shoulder. "She just left the bakery. She should be heading home, but it looks like she's got an entourage."

That wouldn't do. He needed to catch her alone.

Wordlessly he followed her as she made a sharp turn down an alley.

Shani was right, Truyan wasn't alone. Five young women had indeed followed her, but from the stench radiating off of their spirits, he could tell they were up to no good. They surrounded her, tittering in high-pitched laughs that made his ears ring.

"What's the rush?" said a girl who smelled like rotten lilies. She knocked the hat off Truyan's head so her hair came loose, blue and bright for all to see. "Just as I thought. Balardan filth."

Truyan ignored her and continued forward. The end of the alley was steps away.

Run, *he thought, even though she couldn't hear.* Don't keep walking.

From behind, the girls yanked on Truyan's tunic, hard. She fell, and they grabbed the basket out of her arms. "The bandit's got stolen bread!"

A slew of steamed buns tumbled to the ground. Unfazed, Truyan began picking them up.

Her composure rattled the girls, who made a game of kicking the buns toward the nearby canal. "Hungry?" *they taunted.* "Blue-haired scum. Go back where you came from."

"*This* is where I came from." Truyan rose to her feet, her eyes shining with irritation. "I was born here, idiots."

"Idiots?" Rotten Lily sneered. "Girls, hold her down."

Her friends restrained Truyan's arms, and Lily struck a match, intent on setting her hair on fire.

Looks like the dirty work is being done for you, *Shani remarked to Elang.* Shall we leave, or should we make sure she dies?

There was an odd and unfamiliar pressure in Elang's chest. "She needs help."

He reached into his pocket, skipping over the vial of poison for a changing potion. He drank it quickly, gritting his teeth as his face spasmed, dragon half contorting to match the human one. At the last minute, he turned his mask into a pair of spectacles.

He stole out of his hiding place, only to witness firsthand Truyan's ferocity. She butted her head into Lily's and slammed her hip into another girl, effectively shoving her into the canal. Then, as she wrested a hand free, she punched Lily in the nose.

Shani watched, amused. *I like her more when she's angry.*

Elang wasn't listening. Truyan's actions were only making the bullies angrier. They surrounded her again, this time with rocks in their fists.

He stepped into the alleyway, wearing his harshest, most authoritative scowl. "What goes on here?" he demanded.

"A magistrate!" cried the girls when an errant rock flew at his face. With startled shrieks, they fled.

Truyan ought to have fled too, but she remained. As if he didn't exist, she stooped to pick up the steamed buns, counting them under her breath. When he approached, she barely spared him a glance. "Your spectacles are broken," she merely said. "I hope you're not expecting me to pay for them."

This disarmed Elang, if only momentarily. "Is that how you speak to a magistrate of this county?"

"I know the face of every lizard around here," she replied matter-of-factly. She blew at her bangs. "You're not one."

"Lizard?"

"Magistrate, I mean. They're all the same. Beady eyes, lumpy skin, mouths pressed tight like it costs them coin to smile. Lizards."

"I see." Elang's lips twitched with amusement as he helped her pick up a steamed bun. He wondered what she'd think of his real face. "Are you hurt?"

"No." She took the bun from him, wiping dirt off its surface with her sleeve. "Just a bunch of girls who don't like my hair. It happens."

Her face was swollen in spots, and bruises were already blooming on her arms where the stones had hit her. Yet she acted as if the greater crime was that her lunch had gotten spoiled.

"I know what it's like," Elang started. "My face—my real face—has earned me many enemies."

"Your real face?" She looked up at him, eyes bright with curiosity. "What are you, a demon?"

"No—" He started to laugh, but Shani, who had turned invisible, flitted to his side.

This would be a good time to kill her, *the demon reminded him.*

Not yet. He wouldn't admit it, but now that he'd met his match, he was curious about her. She wasn't anything like what he'd expected.

You only have a minute left until your potion wears out.

Still he hesitated. Truyan was eyeing his silence. He could tell her the truth, let her see his face. But then what? She'd run in terror. She'd never want to speak to him again.

There came a twinge in his chest that he'd never felt before. The stirrings of a pulse.

He clutched at it, letting out a gasp.

Your heart is your home, his mother used to say. Until you understand that, you belong nowhere.

Finally, after all these years, he knew where he belonged.

Truyan had observed how pale he'd gone. "Are you all right?" she asked.

He inhaled a deep breath, noticing for the first time that unlike other humans, her presence didn't make the air reek. She brought a freshness to the air, like a garden in spring.

"I have to go," he said. For the first time he could remember, a smile slid onto his lips. "Try not to forget my face."

But I *had* forgotten his face. Shani'd made sure of that, at least until today.

Scene after scene from my own past—and Elang's—flashed by. I saw him during the ensuing months, finding excuses to meet me. Never as the same person. Sometimes he was a peddler on the street who gave me an extra-large bowl of the noodles I liked so much; others he was a street musician or a government prefect. Often he sent Shani to leave gifts for me and my family. Silver coins that my sisters might find on the street, a pair of winter boots along the gutters of their room, a box of oranges under our blankets. As the memories continued to unspool, one in particular snagged at my heart:

"It's been a year," said Shani one day, confronting Elang in his garden. "I take it you've decided to let the krill live."

He sliced off a sanheia thorn with his nail. "I won't kill her."

"So you'll let Nazayun win?"

"He won't." Elang took another flower. "Her art is improving, and she's been learning to trust her visions. I have faith that she'll be ready for the Scroll soon."

"I'm not talking about the Scroll," said the demon tartly. "You seem to forget that if the curse isn't broken—"

"I don't care about the curse anymore."

"Because you care for *her*."

"Yes." He resented the stumble in his breath. "Something she must never know."

For her sake, it was best if Truyan didn't even like him. Better, if she despised him. He'd make sure of that when she met him as his true self.

Shani hopped onto his arm, curling her talons against the trim on his robes. "You surprise me, Your Highness. I never would have taken you to be a romantic."

Ordinarily Elang would have chided her for her insolence, but today he was quiet. "Can I count on you when the time comes, to do what must be done?"

"You mean, can you count on me to carry on with the mission if you falter?" Shani didn't bother mincing her words. "What? Look at how you've lapsed already, whenever you're with that blue-haired thief. Grinning and telling jokes and acting like a madcap fool. It's not a blight on you, Elang'anmi. You're half-human, after all."

"Can I count on you?" he repeated.

Shani folded her wings. "You have my demon's honor. I will not fail."

Elang expelled a breath. "Then we can begin with the plan."

Shani lifted her wing from my forehead.

I was crying. Fresh tears brimmed in my eyes, and every new breath I drew was sodden. But she was right, the memories did make me smile.

"I always wondered when we first met," I said. "Thank you for showing me."

"I warned you not to fall in love with him," Shani said quietly. She tucked her wings to her sides. "The last thing Elang'anmi told me was to take care of myself. Now I say it to you, take care of *yourself*. If . . . *if* there is still a chance for him, you will be the torch that brings him out of the darkness."

I touched her wing, unable to speak.

To my surprise, she swept a gentle wing across my cheek, drying my tears. "I'll only say this once—you grew on me too."

No words from the demon could have moved me more. I raised my hand to hold her wing against my cheek, but she dissolved into the air. Without a word of farewell, she slipped through the cracks in the window, disappearing beyond the trees.

When I closed my eyes, I could feel her dipping into the ocean, on her way to where she belonged.

I reached for my tea, taking a long and bittersweet sip.

May the tides bring you home, I thought. *May the sea watch over you, until we meet again.*

CHAPTER FORTY-SEVEN

In the weeks that followed, I tried to keep busy. It wasn't as difficult as I'd imagined, with new bodies bobbing to the surface of the pond every other day.

The first time it happened, Mama let out a scream that shook the entire manor. But it turned out most of the bodies were human—and alive.

They were the Dragon King's former prisoners; some had been held captive for a few years, others for decades. They stumbled out of the pond, braids of kelp tangled in their hair, always with the same dazed look.

"What year is it?" they would ask. "Who is the emperor?"

Now I understood why Elang had grown so much sanheia: in the expectation that one day, the humans trapped in the dragon realm would be rescued, and they'd need sangi to return to land.

And so I took in Ai'long's refugees. Patiently I answered their questions and listened to their tales. Many of them had lost everyone they'd known while they'd been in the dragon realm, and I comforted them, I cried with them. If they wished, I sent them home. Mama organized each journey.

She chartered ships and served as navigator, with Baba as captain and Tangyor as steersman. My sisters took turns going, one always staying behind to be with me at the manor.

In this way, weeks passed, then months. Gradually, life found a rhythm again.

Then one spring afternoon, something in the water changed.

It was like a soft breeze tickling the nape of my neck, a chorus of whispers brushing against the tiny hairs on my arms. Even the pond had gone divinely still, not a ripple in sight—the way it did in the presence of . . . a dragon.

"Truyan."

Queen Haidi sounded different on land, her voice high and airy. Her brown eyes were rich with flecks of starry gold, and her hair had begun growing back, curling past her elbows. I waited on the footbridge while she emerged from the pond. I searched the water hopelessly for a glimpse of Elang. But she had brought no familiar faces with her, no entourage at all, in fact—except for a surly young man wearing white.

He was leaning against one of the longan trees, his arms crossed. He had silvery horns and long green hair, half plaited over his head and tamed by a crystal headpiece, half wild and unkempt. Though we'd never met, I knew exactly who he was.

I bowed, low and reverent. "Your Eternal Majesty."

Seryu'ginan uncrossed his arms. "Sons of the Wind," he muttered. "Call me that again, and I'll call *you* Bride of the Westerly Seas."

I rose. "How shall I address you, then?"

"Seryu will do. All things considered, we're family." He stepped onto the paved path. "Is his altar in the manor?"

His, meaning Elang's. I stiffened. "I didn't prepare one."

"Because you still think he's alive."

"Your Majesty." Queen Haidi's hair flicked up in mild admonishment. She turned to me. "Lady Saigas, we apologize for intruding while you are still in mourning. King Seryu was crowned only yesterday, and he—"

"I wanted to see who was to blame for overthrowing Grandfather and shackling me to the throne," interrupted Seryu, tugging at his pearled collar. He straightened, and as his red eyes found mine, his tone lost its edge. "I also wanted to pay my respects to you, Cousin Tru."

The young dragon king regarded me. "You know, *I* brought a human to Yonsar once, and Elang made such a fuss about her being a blight upon the universe. . . ." He made a quiet scoff. "You must have been very special to change his mind." A pause. "Or deluded."

I understood now why Elang had been fond of his cousin. "I get the sense you were friends."

"Elang didn't have many in Ai'long," Seryu allowed. He plucked a longan from the nearest tree and popped the entire fruit into his mouth without peeling off the shell. "We used to chase whales and spar against the turtles together. Then Grandfather became obsessed with having him killed, and I became the royal favorite."

"He did that to drive a wedge between you two."

"Something I wish I'd realized sooner." Seryu plucked half a dozen longans with his claw and pocketed them in his sleeve. "Grandfather deserved Oblivion."

"Let us not speak ill of our ancestors, Your Majesty." Queen Haidi cleared her throat, adding quietly, "There's another reason for our visit."

"You've come for the Scroll," I said. I'd foreseen this visit weeks ago. "I thought it couldn't be destroyed."

"It cannot, except by those who created it."

"Are *you* one of the Eight?"

"Am I?" Haidi mused. "Perhaps the next time you visit Nanhira, I'll tell you a story."

I nodded, but I made no promise. I wasn't ready to return to Ai'long anytime soon.

Slowly I rolled up my sleeve. One last time, I brought forth the Scroll of Oblivion and sent it materializing into Haidi's awaiting hands. The queen slipped it into her hair for safekeeping, then bowed her head.

"You did well, Truyan," she said to me. "You did the best you could."

We both knew she wasn't talking only about the Scroll. My voice broke when I replied, "I know."

The wind had grown still, the only sound in the garden a series of plops in the pond. They came from Seryu, who was skipping stones by the handful.

"You ought to come with us," he said, dusting his hands when I joined him beside the water. "The waters of Yonsar grow warmer with each day. The kingdom is rebuilding; would you like to see it?

"Bring your family, if you'd like," he said softly when I didn't respond. "The years pass more swiftly in the dragon realm; the food isn't as good, but . . . the waiting will be easier."

I observed the moss creeping across the pebbled path, the footbridges, the latticed frame within the pavilion's windows. It was the one thing that had thrived in the garden since Elang had left.

"If he comes back," I said, "he won't be a dragon."

Seryu raised a feathery white eyebrow. "He told you this?"

"In a way." I reached to my neck, holding the jade pendant that hung from the remains of Elang's red string. "Butterflies fly in pairs."

Something in his red eyes warmed. "If you change your mind, my offer will always stand. I hope you won't have to wait too many lifetimes, Cousin Tru."

He walked me back to where Queen Haidi was waiting. Then, with a clap of his hands, his human form washed away, and I caught a glimpse of his true magnificence. He leapt into the pond, and Queen Haidi disappeared after him.

Alone once more, I stood on the arched footbridge, watching the ripples in the pond recede. Soon the carp returned to nibble on the floating lotus blossoms, and frogs jumped across the lily pads.

I crouched to dip my fingers in the pond, drawing a tiny whale in the water. I released it with a flick, and it swam to the other side of the footbridge, where a carp chased it until it dissolved.

Seeing them race, the heaviness in my heart lifted, and the barest smile touched my lips.

I went back into the house to help my sisters prepare the table for lunch.

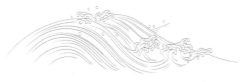

EPILOGUE

Three Years Later

It was the fifteenth day of the monkey, the last day of the New Year's festivities. Much had changed in Gangsun: Governor Renhai was ousted for corruption, new laws were made, and Madam Yargui was never heard from again. The manor became quiet as most of the merfolk returned to Yonsar. Even quieter when Nomi was accepted into the National Academy. Mama started reading fortunes again (though only for entertainment), and she and Baba began charting a pleasure trip they would take across the Taijin Sea once the weather warmed.

Falina opened a shop on Dattu Street selling embroidered boots and slippers with the upturned toe caps she loved so much, and coaxed me into becoming her business partner. She sewed, I painted designs for her to embroider. Slowly but surely, I gained a reputation for my dragons. By the end of our first year, we had so many orders she had to hire two extra seamstresses to help.

"My fingers are going to fall off if I sew another stitch," Falina announced on the last day of New Year's. She tossed me a pair of boots. "Put these on. I know you're itching to go out. Everyone's at the Lantern Festival, and—is it snowing outside?" My sister clapped with glee. "This is the perfect opportunity to show off our boots and drum up some business."

"Don't you already have more orders than you can handle?"

Falina clucked her tongue like Mama. "What is it the Sages say? Dig the well before you get thirsty." She stepped out the door. "Hurry, Mama and Baba are coming too!"

It was early afternoon, and the streets teemed with festivalgoers: children juggling tangerines and slurping warm bowls of glutinous rice balls in syrup, market vendors shouting, "Steamed chestnuts, firecrackers!" Glowing paper lanterns hung from every eave.

Winter had been fierce this year, and thanks to a stalwart frost, even the plum blossoms were slow to bloom. Normally there would be carts all over the city selling waterbells, but I didn't spy a single one.

Falina dusted snow from my shoulders, then touched my cheek. The New Year was still difficult for me, and she could read what was on my mind. "Look!" Trying to distract me, she pointed at the large crowd before one of the shops. "They've started on riddles already."

It was a popular game during the festival: You would buy a paper lantern, decorate it, and compose a riddle on one of its sides, hiding the answer on the inside. The shopkeeper then hung the lanterns for all to see. Whoever solved the riddle first could claim the lantern as their own. My sisters and I couldn't afford to buy our own lanterns when we were younger, so we'd loved competing over who could solve the most riddles. Now that Nomi was away at school, we couldn't bring ourselves to play without her.

"Let's paint one," Falina exclaimed, purchasing a lantern.

Mama and Baba were already at the shop, and Mama beamed at the fellow customers. "My daughter's a famous artist. She's going to paint the most beautiful lantern of the festival, just you wait. No one's ever solved her riddle." She elbowed me. "Tru!"

I'd already started. In my neatest calligraphy, I wrote:

I have wings that cannot fly,
a mouth that cannot speak.
Born in the dark, I rise in light—
A star lost from the sky.

Every festival, I wrote the same riddle, and after three years, no one had solved it. I exhaled warm air into my hands, rubbing them before I began on the art.

I painted a girl and a boy holding a lantern, while hundreds of others floated off into the sky. It was the vision I'd once drawn on Elang's heart, but with each passing year, I added more details. A pair of butterflies behind them, the girl's blue hair, the boy's gray eye. A garland of vibrant belled flowers—and moss, which gave the lantern a wash of green.

Had it really been a vision of the future, or merely a wishful fantasy? I still didn't know.

The shopkeeper, Aunt Vosan, recognized me. "You'll need a new riddle this year, Truyan," she said cheerily.

I looked up. "What?"

"Yours was solved this morning. Your lantern from last year, that is. I kept it on display since it was so pretty."

Air rushed out of my lungs. I was too stunned to speak.

Luckily, Mama was there. "Who solved it?" she asked.

"It's a shame, you just missed him. He was here an hour

ago—a handsome young man. He was quiet but very polite." Aunt Vosan whirled. "Which reminds me, he left this for the artist."

She handed me a single waterbell, its petals still moist with dew.

"A waterbell!" Falina exclaimed. "We haven't seen one all winter. It must be a sign spring is on its way."

Fingers trembling, I cradled the flower on my palm. My knees had gone numb, and Baba steadied me by the arm before I lost my balance.

"Where did he go—the young man who solved the riddle?"

"I didn't ask," replied Aunt Vosan. "It's been busy. Everyone is trying to get a lantern for the lighting tonight."

It couldn't be Elang, could it? After three years, I was no stranger to disappointment, and despite what people kept saying, the pain didn't get easier. I only got better at hiding it.

Falina tucked the waterbell above my ear and folded my scarf around my neck. "Go find him. You'll cry off the disappointment if it's not him. But there's a chance that it is . . . and you'll regret forever if you don't find out."

"When did you become so wise?"

"I learned from you, sister. All those years Baba was missing, you never lost hope."

Oh, Fal, I wanted to say. The truth was, the years that Baba was missing, I did lose hope. Many times. I was familiar with how cruel hope could be, a knife to the heart, paring it away slowly, one cut at a time.

But, as I'd learned from Elang, I had a rather big heart.

I shouldered my way through the teeming crowds, not even daring to blink lest I miss him. There had to be thousands of people in the streets today—the odds of finding him were scarce.

I'd take the chance.

I trained my eyes for a green lantern, but each time I found one, it wasn't mine. An hour slipped away, then two. Soon it was nearly dusk, and I'd walked so far I could feel the sinews in my knees twinge with each new step. My belly, too, chastised me. I hadn't eaten since morning.

Ahead, by the canal, children were selling sweets. Fried dough stuffed with peanuts, candied berries on sticks, sugar-blown animals to celebrate the New Year. I looked around for something spicy, but the line for noodles went around the corner. Pickled vegetables it was, then.

I counted my coins and went up to the stall. That was when I saw my lantern.

It hung from the crossbar of a wooden cart, tucked beside a quiet bridge over the canal. The cart was full of wildflowers. A wide hat obscured the profile of the young man tending them, but I recognized those shoulders—straighter than the horizon. That rigid spine, that audaciously set mouth.

I ventured toward him. *Elang*, I was about to cry—when my stomach growled. Loudly.

I heard a chuckle. "If you're looking for Tama's fishball stall, they've already closed for the night."

That voice. It was warmer than I remembered, the dragon's growl sanded away. Though I had no ear for music, I'd have known the sound of it anywhere.

Elang turned to face me. From under his hat, I saw his eyes. Both were gray, and framed by brass-rimmed spectacles that sat on the bridge of his nose, a little crooked, as always.

Joy bubbled to my throat. "I wasn't looking for Tama's," I said softly. "I was looking for you."

"Me?" It was no act, the surprise that flitted across his brow. "Can I help you, miss?"

Miss. That one word was a lance into my joy, turning my muscles cold. I searched his face, certain he was teasing. But there was no recognition in his eyes. His expression was blank, as though he'd never met me before. As though I were a stranger.

"It's me," I said.

Tru. Saigas. Your moss. Your wife.

He took me in, his eyes falling to the waterbell in my hair. The pleats in his brow unfolded, and a flicker of recognition brightened his face, just a touch.

"Sons of the Wind," he said. "You're the artist. The girl with the blue hair!"

I took a step back, my world swaying. Was it possible to be so deliriously happy and devastated at the same time? Never, in the thousand dreams I'd dreamed of Elang, had I imagined he might forget me.

"Yes," I said, swallowing hard. "You solved my riddle. No one's solved it in three years."

"It was a tricky one. But it helps that I work with flowers."

"Did you grow this waterbell?" I asked, touching the one in my hair.

"I grew enough to fill the entire canal," he replied, eyes twinkling. "Would you like to see?"

Behind the cart, he had an entire boat brimming with waterbells. Hundreds of them, all on the brink of blooming. An impossible feat in this weather, but here they were, made even more beautiful by the fresh coat of snow dusting their petals. I was awed.

"Do you want to know the secret?"

He'd told me once before. "You talk to them?"

I'd forgotten how beautiful he was when he smiled. "I do. But that's only half of it."

He took off his gloves. His fingers were long and human now, no more claws or sharp nails. Carefully he lifted a box from the stern of the boat. Inside was a planting bed teeming with spongy green mounds.

"Moss!" I recognized.

He looked pleased that I knew. "They're a vital part of every forest and every garden. Waterbells especially take to them. They thrive together even under the harshest of conditions. Even during winter."

So he hadn't forgotten everything. Me, yes. But not everything.

I wanted to know his name—whether he was Gaari or Gaarin or someone else entirely. I wanted to know what he'd been doing these last three years, how his wounds had healed, and if he still had a connection to the sea as I did. If he still chased after whales and ate noodles at Luk's.

But I had to be patient. One question at a time. "What do you talk to the flowers about?"

From the way he hesitated, I could tell no one had asked him this before.

"There's a dream I've had many a time," he confessed, "of waterbells floating under the moonlight, and in spite of the cold, it warms me to dream it. Like I've found home." He forced a chuckle. "I suppose that's why I was drawn to your lantern. Why I keep planting the same flowers year after year."

I couldn't hold it back any longer. I burst, "Elang, don't

you remember me?" I pointed to the lantern, to its river of waterbells, the starry night, the girl and the boy. "This is us."

Whatever rapport we'd built in these few moments of conversation, I'd ruined it. He took a step back, his gray eyes turning cloudy, and there was a beautiful sadness to the way he shook his head.

"It's getting late," he said softly. "They'll soon be lighting the lanterns and sending them off. You shouldn't miss it."

It was a polite dismissal.

Tears prickled the corners of my eyes. From under my scarf, I lifted the cord around my neck, my fingers lingering on the jade butterflies. Two flying in a close pair, never to be parted.

"This is your red thread," I said, my voice shaking. "Your promise to me, a lifetime ago." I pushed it into his hand. "Maybe it'll help you remember."

He caught the cord by its pendant, clasping the butterflies before they fell onto the ground. Something in his eyes flickered then, as he held them, like a pinch of light sieving through the clouds.

A trick of the sun, I thought, turning before I suffered another disappointment.

I fled back into the crowds, losing myself among the sea of endless faces. The only direction that mattered was the one farthest from Elang's cart. I forced myself to keep going and not look back. I knew I'd crumble if I did.

It'd gotten colder, and an icy rain glazed the air. I folded my hood over my head, ignoring the calls from the food vendors as they appealed to the dull pangs in my stomach.

I was crying, and it hurt to breathe. He was alive, I told myself. *That* was what mattered. Not the fact that he didn't remember me, that he had looked at me with those cloudy gray eyes like he'd never seen me in his life. If he was under another curse, I'd break it. If he'd simply forgotten me, then I'd try again tomorrow, and every day after until that changed.

But not today. Today the hurt was too much.

I picked up my pace. Lanterns were floating into the sky, speckling the night with a constellation of paper stars. A magnificent sight, but I didn't enjoy it. I couldn't.

Soon I was halfway through the market, rushing past Luk's Noodle Shop for the street where I'd left my family. Mama and Baba were shopping for tea, and I slowed before the store to unwrap my scarf.

"Wait!" Someone was shouting from behind. "Wait, Tru!"

I walked inside. My pulse still throbbed in my ears, and under my hood I couldn't hear that I was being followed. Until, three steps in, I felt the change in the water.

It called to me—from the tea being poured, the frost coating the rooftops, the steam of my breath. It was a tickle of snow, like a gentle kiss upon the back of my neck. Slowly, I turned.

There he was. The red string was wrapped twice around his wrist, jade butterflies dangling, and he was carrying my lantern. Its light bathed his face, making his gray eyes shine. As he beheld me, there was a spark of recognition in them, growing brighter with each second.

Tru, he'd called me. I'd never given him my name.

My parents exchanged sly smiles, and Baba tossed my scarf back over my neck.

"Don't stay out too late," he said. Then Mama pushed me out the door.

I stumbled over an icy step. I wasn't about to fall, but a firm hand caught me anyway, the ends of our red strings entwining as he laced his fingers with mine.

I looked up at Elang, daring to hope, not daring to speak. Around us, everywhere I looked, waterbells began floating down the moonlit canals, heads bobbing. The petals unfolded as they floated, and under the light of the floating lanterns, they glowed. Just like I had painted. Just like I'd foreseen.

I reached out to hold the other side of the lantern, a tingle glittering down my spine.

"Took you long enough," I whispered.

He drew me close, his heart pounding against my ear, steady and strong—and a little too fast. I took his face in my hands, studying the side of him that used to be dragon. I traced his hairline and ran my fingers across his cheek, down the slope of his nose, ruddy from the cold, with freckles on both sides as if they'd always been there. Lastly, I landed on the firm bow of his lips. A masterpiece, this face. Every line on it was perfect. Except one thing. I straightened his spectacles.

"What are you thinking?" he asked, sounding genuinely nervous.

"I'm thinking I miss the dragon, just a little." I patted his cheek. "But this is a good face too. My mother will be pleased that your ears are even thinner than they were before. A good trait for a potential husband."

"Potential?"

"Our marriage wasn't real. You'll have to woo me again."

"It *was* real." The spark in his eyes grew brighter than even my lanternlight, almost golden, and a corner of his mouth played into a smile. "But I'm willing to start over, if that's what you desire."

"I'm not going to make it easy for you."

"I know." His eyes shone rich and clear, two raw coals drinking me in as though I were fire. He bent down, and I lifted in expectation of a kiss, but he merely tucked my arm through his. To my indignation, his smile widened. "We'll have to hurry if we want to beat the crowds."

"Where are we going?"

As soon as I asked, I knew.

"Tru," he said, tipping my chin toward his. "My love. Tell me . . . do you fancy noodles?"

I grinned like a fool, unable to help myself. "Just kiss me, you fiend." I took him by the collar, drawing his lips to mine. "I always fancy noodles."

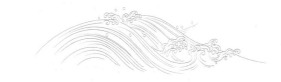

ACKNOWLEDGMENTS

Thank you to my agent, Gina, who knew Tru was the one from the beginning. Thank you to my editor, Katherine, for your rigorous edits and all the brilliant ways you've made this book shine inside and out. To Lili, Josh, and Cynthia, my publicists, as well as to Gianna, Sarah, Ray, Stephania, Kelly, Michelle, Elizabeth, Dominique, Alison, Lisa, Judy, Kerianne, Melinda, Barbara, and the fantastic team at Knopf Books for Young Readers. I am ever thankful for all the effort and care that you've contributed to bring *A Forgery of Fate* into the world.

To Tran, for your talent and hard work in bringing Tru to life in as perfect a way as I could have imagined. To Virginia, for yet another gorgeously detailed map. I am an eternal fan of you both.

To my team in the UK: Molly, Sophie, Natasha, Kate, and Lydia, thank you again for your heartfelt dedication to my books and for bringing *A Forgery of Fate* across the world. And to Dong Qiu, for a breathtaking and colorful cover that captures Tru's world so elegantly.

To Anissa, for being a staunch supporter of my stories

as well as a good friend. To my beta readers: Alena, Amaris, Doug, Eva, and Leslie, for your treasured friendship and honest critiques.

To my parents and my sister, for your love and encouragement, and for the help with babysitting! To Adrian, for your love and great editing prowess. I'm filled with wonder and joy that I get to spend life with you. To my daughters, I say this each time, but it's always true: these stories are for you.

Lastly, to all the librarians, teachers, bloggers, reviewers, students, and readers who have picked up this book—and any of my other works: thank you.